Also by Dora Jane Hamblin

POTS AND ROBBERS
BURIED CITIES AND ANCIENT TREASURES
THE FIRST CITIES
THE APPIAN WAY, A JOURNEY
with Mary Jane Grunsfeld
THE ETRUSCANS

That Was the

That Was the

BY

Dora Jane Hamblin

W · W · Norton & Company · Inc ·

New York

Published simultaneously in Canada by George J. McLeod Limited, Toronto. Printed in the United States of America.

First Edition

Library of Congress Cataloging in Publication Data

Hamblin, Dora Jane, 1920–
That was the Life.

Includes index.
1. Life. I. Title.
AP2.L5473H35 1977 051 76–30804
ISBN 0–393–08764–6

1 2 3 4 5 6 7 8 9 0

To

Everyone who ever worked there

Contents

Preface

I like to think of this book as one volume in what I hope will become a five-foot shelf on the subject of a great magazine, *Life*.

This is not an authorized book. On the other hand it is not *un*authorized. I never sought permission from Time Incorporated, the parent organization, to write a book about *Life*, and Time Incorporated never sought control over what I wrote. We have been much aware of each other throughout, but we have treated one another precisely as we did at *Life*—with trust, generosity, and humor.

Everyone from Time Incorporated Editor in Chief Hedley Donovan to the newest employee in the library has responded quickly and helpfully to my occasional cries for aid, and many of my former colleagues have taken precious time to recount to me their favorite stories or to confirm versions of episodes we all remember in our own ways. I will not list their names because they would read like the masthead itself, and because they know who they are and what they contributed.

I do wish to thank particularly Joann McQuiston, for all the hours of interviews she conducted on my behalf; Barbara Brewster, whose expertise was crucial in the selection and procurement of photographs for the book; and Mary Jane McGonegal of Time Incorporated who enthusiastically helped clear rights and permissions for use of materials owned by the company.

I have benefited from patient and helpful editors at W. W. Norton, Edwin Barber and Michelle Cliff, and from a former *Life* managing editor, Edward K. Thompson, who read the manuscript at my request. He did not suggest one single episode or item of what follows, nor was he asked to. With a temerity I wouldn't have dared twenty years ago, I asked him to be a "checker." That's what he did. Nobody who helped me is in any way guilty of any errors which may have crept in; they are mine alone.

To all the others, those whom I consulted and those whom I did not, I apologize if I have omitted from this brief account their favorite stories or exploits. I also apologize to those colleagues whose names have been omitted. A former editor said to me early in this project, "Remember that you can't tell it all." Quite true. To him, to everyone, all I can say is that I can't wait to read *your* book.

To the non-*Life* reader, I beg pardon for some confusion I may have created in the titles and positions of persons in the pages to come. *Life* was a very mobile magazine and people changed function frequently. I have here identified them by the positions they held during each specific episode.

I have also not indicated in the text which of the *dramatis personae* are no longer living. We were a big magazine, part of a big corporate entity, but in the end it all came down to people. This book is about those people, how they worked, what the office was like, how we got the story. Like the weekly magazine itself, those who are no longer with us are very much alive in the things they did and in the vivid memories of the staff of *Life*.

Acknowledgments

Grateful acknowledgment is made to Time Incorporated for permission to use the name and logotype of *Life* magazine on the cover and dust jacket of this book. The name and logotype are trademarks which are owned by Time Incorporated.

Similar acknowledgment, with thanks, to Time Incorporated for generous provision of photographs owned by the corporation, for permission to excerpt from editors' notes in *Life* magazine, from the company in-house publication *f.y.i.*, from promotion materials relating to specific stories published in the magazine, and to Ralph Graves, corporate editor of Time Incorporated, for permission to print the words he spoke on the morning of December 8, 1972.

That Was the

1

A High-Flying Magazine

Shortly before midnight on January 29, 1965, a charter bus from Manhattan scrunched through light frozen snow to the dim environs of hangar 3 on the outer fringes of John F. Kennedy International Airport. There it disgorged thirty-four very noisy passengers who struggled out clutching armloads of books, briefcases, file folders, and some suspicious-looking brown paper bags.

Nobody had any real luggage, and there was no chatter about "where are you going to stay in Paris?"

At 1:03 A.M., January 30, aircraft No. N 801SW revved up for take-off. The thirty-four bus passengers were the only ones aboard the yawning DC-8 except the crew, but the moment the "NO SMOKING" sign went off they managed to fill the entire plane. One group rushed forward to a flying darkroom just behind the command cabin and began uncrating developing tanks and chemicals. Behind them another group connected light-tables and arranged boxes of paper layout pads, pencils, cutters, glue, and type samples.

Four young women and a man slid reference books into temporary shelves installed above long work-tables: *Debrett's Peerage,* Shakespeare's *Henry V,* a concise history of World War II, the collected works of Sir Winston Churchill.

Others sat down to typewriters on stands bolted to the floor and pecked away tentatively.

At the rear of the plane a row of hostesses arranged trays, bottles, glasses, plates, and smiles for the onslaught. At the sight of the bottles some of the passengers surreptitiously slipped the brown paper sacks into their briefcases.

Within minutes the housekeeping was done and the party was on. No two eyes met any other two on the plane without a gleam of near-conspiratorial pleasure.

We were off to do a dazzler, to be first, best, and most flamboyant magazine on earth—*Life*. This time it was a high-wire act, touch and go at 33,000 feet, a race against time and distance. Our mission was to get to London just after the funeral of Sir Winston Churchill, pick up the film our photographers had shot that day, then turn tail and chase the setting sun across the Atlantic to the printing plant in Chicago. En route we would develop the color film, make the layouts, write the captions and text, submit to checking changes, make the pesky headlines fit. We would, in brief, "put the magazine to bed" as we raced through the sky at 600 miles per hour.

There was never a doubt in our minds that we could do it. It was in the proud tradition of the magazine, and it was our kind of story: from its very first issue, November 23, 1936, *Life* had been fascinated by spectacle. State funerals like John F. Kennedy's or Sir Winston's, Rose Bowl parades, debutante balls, floods, Hollywood extravaganzas, all were the stuff of great visual impact.

On the cover of the first issue was the massive Fort Peck Dam being built in Montana by the WPA. Inside was an aerial view of Fort Knox, the first aerial ever published of that repository of the nation's gold, and another spectacular on the brand-new Bay Bridge in San Francisco. But there also were some intimate scenes of Fort Peck Dam builders whooping it up on a Saturday night in the sleazy beer joints and shanty towns where they lived. And there was a startling full-page picture of an obstetrician holding up a newborn baby by its heels, with a coy headline "LIFE BEGINS."

It is difficult to explain, to those too young to remember the first issue, the stunning impact of its size alone. Opened out flat, the magazine measured 13½ by 21 inches, a display space larger than many of today's television screens and in pretelevision 1936 a revelation. Furthermore its images held still, fixed forever for perusal and study.

What ensued when *Life* hit newsstands and mailboxes that first week was near-riot. News dealers across the nation telephoned and

CREDIT: MARGARET BOURKE-WHITE © TIME INC.

Life's *first cover was a gee-whiz spectacle shot of the towering Fort Peck Dam on the Missouri River in northeastern Montana. Begun in 1933, the dam was finished in 1940: 250 feet high, four miles long.*

telegraphed for more copies. Presses creaked, groaned, and broke down trying to keep up with the demand. Reserve paper stocks dwindled and ran out, occasioning frantic telephone calls for "more paper, find more paper." All other activity stopped in high school study halls as kids devoured the first issue of the first big picture magazine they had ever seen.

For those who obtained most of their sex education from the *National Geographic* (I, personally, was long under the impression that only African women had breasts), the baby picture was utterly fascinating.

Housewives decided their laundry could wait a minute; tired businessmen switched their trade to well-lighted bars so they could read *Life* after work; all wrote in droves, either lyric with praise or livid with shock. It quickly developed that Americans, bereft of king or emperor, pope or potentate, loved looking at those colorful creatures from afar. Those too poor to travel in Depression days found the world in their mailboxes in the pages of *Life*. As for intimacy, the magazine skirted the fringes of public sensibility so often that to the staff it seemed there were literally thousands of people whose pleasure in loudly cancelling their subscriptions was surpassed only by the avidity with which they studied the offending photographs before cancelling.

By 1965 the stunning effect of the first years had long since worn off, and *Life* was as familiar and as casually accepted a part of American life as baseball and the jukebox. Yet the basic pattern had never changed, and Sir Winston Churchill's funeral was a natural—full of pomp and ceremony, emotion, great London scenes, and the bittersweet sense of an era ending.

What *had* changed was technique—and television. Most of the civilized world would see the funeral on TV, and even though millions would want *Life* to hold in their hands, to study the great moments all over again, the impact would be lost if we were too late. The impetus for the whole gaudy enterprise—chartered aircraft, flying darkroom—was to save time. *Life* in 1965 went to press on Wednesday night to be on the newsstands Monday. Sir Winston died on Sunday, which under normal circumstances would have given us plenty of time. But his funeral was decreed to be a state occasion with the participation of kings, presidents, prime ministers. These dignitaries needed time to get their medals polished, their ribbons and sashes pressed, their state occasion clothes and airline tickets together in order to get to London. So the funeral was set for the following Saturday, January 30. Had the magazine kept its customary closing schedule we couldn't have pictures on the presses until the following

Wednesday, and the issue which contained them would be in readers' hands at least ten days after the event and after the live TV.

"Hold the presses" sounds wonderful in old movies. In real life it is incredibly expensive and, beyond a certain point, impossible. Despite sophisticated techniques, overtime, and superhuman effort it still takes *x* number of hours to print *x* number of pages. *Life*'s press run in 1965 was over seven million copies a week and the decision to "hold" for twenty pages of color from Wednesday until Saturday night would make us late by sixty to seventy hours. But it was the best we could do.

A previous plan involved chartering a plane in London to collect the precious funeral film and streak for Chicago. That would be good, but we would lose the eight hours of flying time itself, between London and Chicago, and it would take another three hours in Chicago to process the film. It would be much better to convert a U.S.-based aircraft into a flying office, take it to London, turn right around and begin work, thus using—and saving—eleven hours of flying-and-processing time.

Wheels turned on both sides of the Atlantic. In New York nets were cast for a charter line which would accept the challenge; into the net swam Seaboard World Airlines. Nothing fazed them. Darkroom? Light-tables? Typewriter tables? No sweat. On the Tuesday after Churchill died, men from Seaboard and men from *Life* met in hangar 3 and spent the entire day crawling around on the floor making a chalk diagram of the interior of a DC-8. Grunting, swearing, calculating, they drew and erased, drew again. Finally the plan was done: a ten-by-fifteen-foot darkroom could be installed behind the captain's cabin where there should be the least motion to slop the developer or rattle the equipment. Light-tables, typewriter stands, all could go behind if they took out some seats.

There were a few mechanical problems. The aircraft's electrical system operated on 400 cycles per second, but lab equipment and electric typewriters use 60-cycle current. Seaboard found a converter to correct the discrepancy. Water was more difficult. The plane could carry only 100 onboard gallons instead of the 300 normally required for processing the amount of film the *Life* men estimated they would have. The darkroom crew agreed to make do with only 100 gallons. Then there was the film itself. Eastman, queried by a worried *Life* color expert, said it couldn't guarantee that color film developed at the unusual height of 33,000 feet would maintain its integrity. But they said they hoped it would, and they would be delighted to find out.

While all this was going on in New York, London dealt with its share of the problem. "Please, God, don't let him die on my time," has been the not-very-secret prayer of every journalist everywhere hoping not to be saddled with coverage of the death of a towering public figure. These occasions always involve endless days and sleepless nights, unseemly battles with bureaucracy and with other journalists, acerbic cables from the home office, and explosions of temperament among the staff.

London was ready, however. Sir Winston's biographical material and photographs had long since been collected and filed. The staff had detailed plans of funeral arrangements. Sixteen *Life* photographers were on hand, drawn from the London staff, from Paris, from the U.S., each man with an assigned spot along the funeral procession route or inside St. Paul's where the service was held.

When word of the flying editorial office reached London, British staffer Dorothy Bacon was dispatched to reserve twenty-five rooms in an airport hotel, rent twenty-five typewriters and have them delivered to those rooms, arrange for the delivery of all major London newspapers to each room. She spent two days organizing all this and spent the night of January 29 at the airport to be on call for emergencies.

While she was checking rooms and typewriters, Seaboard's jet arrived at hangar 3 in New York. There were only six hours until takeoff, and all the special equipment still had to be put aboard. Boxes, crates, and a forklift truck were lined up and waiting when the plane landed and crews got into action in near-zero temperature. The forklift hoisted the heavy material, men inside set it in place.

About the time Bacon settled down to a predinner drink in London, the plane took off from New York. As we buzzed dreamily through the night associate publisher Arthur Keylor whiled away the hours playing gin rummy with deputy editor Roy Rowan. Picture editor Dick Billings smooched in the darkened rear seats with administrative assistant Priscilla Work. Copy editor Joseph Kastner passed among his writers suggesting that a sleeping pill might be more efficacious than Scotch as a soporific. He didn't get many takers.

About 3:30 A.M. light broke in mid-Atlantic and the darkroom crew discovered pinhole leaks in the fuselage of the flying darkroom. Photo lab chief George Karas scrambled to cover them with masking tape. The engines droned on and suddenly there was a burst of winter dawn for us—almost high noon in England. The pilot dipped his wings to show us a view of Windsor Castle. It was a magnificent sight, the only true look at England we would have on our wild dash.

Then we were on the ground at Heathrow, hustled through customs, hustled into a hotel. It wasn't, unfortunately, the one Bacon had organized. Through some inexplicable mix-up we were sent to a different hostelry. I recall being ushered into a room which contained two rumpled beds, two half-unpacked suitcases, and a very lived-in air.

"Here?" I asked the clerk.

"Here, madame," he replied firmly. "Have a shower, have lunch. The guests resident will not return until evening."

Lucky "guests resident." Probably they were watching the funeral procession somewhere. Maybe they were even at St. Paul's. That was more than we could do. We were summoned for a quick lunch, allowed to view a few scenes on British television—mostly the barge bearing Sir Winston's casket on its way down the Thames to the family burial plot. Then back to the plane.

Departure time was dramatic. First three helicopters flapped out from central London, landed near our plane, and unloaded envelopes full of film, late editions of the papers, official lists of dignitaries in the procession and at St. Paul's. Next came a bunch of wild-haired motorcyclists called the Rockers. In the mid-sixties London was plagued by combative juvenile gangs who called themselves Mods and Rockers and who made the streets notably unsafe for each other and for innocent passers-by. Somebody at *Life* had decided to hire a group of Rockers as couriers, and these scruffy perils of the road performed heroically. They picked up the very last of the film and steered their roaring vehicles through alleys and turnings, mews and maws, to screech to the airport. Some of them carried, as a bonus, the Reuters news-service ticker tape, snatched from a receiver inside the London office and carried like pennants trailing behind. Each Rocker arrived exhaust-smeared and panting, with film and ticker tape intact, on time for the plane.

Just as the steps were about to be wheeled away so the plane could take off, correspondent Bacon arrived with a tall, handsome soldier whom she introduced as Major Peter Thwaites. Major Thwaites had functioned that day as official escort for Lady Churchill inside St. Paul's. He had also been on the committee which drew up military preparations for honor guards and ceremonials. He knew not only the order of events but also all of the important people. He had even, Bacon confided, played polo with Prince Philip.

Bacon had snagged him by chance. In her efforts to make all possible preparations for funeral coverage, she approached the Ministry of Defence and said she might need an expert. The ministry suggested that she approach Major Thwaites because he was "a literary gentleman," having once written a play which was performed in Edinburgh. In vain Bacon explained she needed not "a literary gentleman" but instead someone who could identify VIPs in photographs.

The ministry still failed to comprehend precisely what was involved and so, it turned out, did Major Thwaites. He boarded the plane late and out of breath, having been constrained to dash to his country home to pick up his passport, implore the American Embassy to give him a visa on a Saturday, escort Lady Churchill, then rush to the airport. He boarded with heady expectations of watching a high-powered American publishing team at work, of being pressed into instant and demanding service.

"They were all very cordial," he remarked later, "but then everybody went to sleep."

Not quite everybody. The darkroom men shut themselves in and began developing seventy rolls of color film. Head copy typist Bebe Cruikshank tried to test her typewriter and discovered that the electrical current on board was not sufficient to supply both the photo lab's needs and her machine at the same time.

A little knot of London lovers gathered toward the rear and talked quietly of old days when they had worked in the London office, of the times they had seen Sir Winston, or talked with him. He had been the subject of many a news story in *Life* before, during, and after World War II. But the relationship was more than that of public figure and journalist, because of his long friendship with the man most *Life* people called "the proprietor," Henry R. Luce.

Luce, the father of *Life,* had used his friendship with Churchill to help secure for the magazine the right to print excerpts from Churchill's war memoirs, published intermittently in the magazine from 1948 to 1953, and excerpts from his *A History of the English Speaking Peoples* from 1956 to 1958. Luce had alternately berated and beguiled Sir Winston into giving him one of the paintings the statesman had turned out during his "Sunday painter" period, and had won permission to reproduce some examples of the painter's art in the magazine.

Neither Luce nor Churchill was known for sentimentality, but on the night of the Churchill funeral flight their very special relationship was the subject of long and occasionally sentimental discussion.

□ □ □

It had taken considerable courage to start *Life* in the middle of a depression. But Luce, cofounder of *Time* magazine (with Briton Hadden) and founder of *Fortune,* had convinced himself that a popular picture magazine would reach a wider audience than his existing publications. He had become fascinated by photographs. There was some resistance to the idea in his staff, but he had a staunch ally in his wife, Clare Boothe, who had suggested just such a publication to her own employers, Condé Nast publishers, long before she married Luce. Condé Nast turned down the idea, and Luce steadfastly refused to let his wife interfere in his new publication, but at least she got to name it. "*Life*" was the name she had suggested to Nast and *Life* it became—after a struggle.

TAKEN BY MRS. HENRY R. LUCE

"The proprietor," Henry R. Luce, left, *with Alfred Eisenstaedt on a road overlooking Majorca harbor, in 1952.*

At first Luce wanted to call the magazine *Dime,* to emphasize that it would be sold cheaply to aim at an enormous audience. While his advertising and promotion men, advisors and subscription clerks tore their hair at the thought of the confusion implicit in magazines called *Time* and *Dime,* the provisional staff for the new magazine persuaded the boss to use *Showbook of the World* as a working title. The actual names used on two experimental prepublication issues were *Dummy* and *Rehearsal.* Some skeptics called it less complimentary things. The urge to be rude to unborn magazines seems endemic: in the early fifties when the magazine which was to become *Sports Illustrated* was in the planning and prototype stage, *Life* people asked to help on it referred to it as *Armpit, Muscles,* and *Jockstrap.*

Stopping his ears to the irreverence around him, Luce pressed on. It was he who insisted upon the unusually large page size, he who demanded use of an expensive and rare "coated" paper because he had been told it would reproduce pictures with startling clarity.

He got his way, and his way turned out to be right. He probably didn't visualize color in 1936, but color came, and by 1965 his magazine had developed the techniques to make color, too, print quickly with fidelity on the big page with the expensive paper. For Churchill's funeral, the coverage would all be in color.

□ □ □

To Major Thwaites's considerable relief, about three hours after take-off from London, everybody woke up. The color transparencies at last were rolling out of the lab. There had been one crisis most of the passengers didn't even know about, when the pilot detected rough weather ahead and abruptly changed his flight plan to turn north, fly almost over the pole, and avoid the kind of turbulence which would have sloshed developer fluid all over the airplane.

As the pictures came out, managing editor George Hunt, tieless and coatless as always when he worked, hunched over a light-table and squinted through a small enlarging glass which all but vanished in his big hand. Art director Bernard Quint, shoving his thick glasses up on his nose, crouched over one shoulder, Roy Rowan over the other. Quickly they voted "yes" and "no," quickly they made piles of "rejects" or "possibles" on corners of the light-table.

Only five hours remained before touchdown in Chicago. In this time a cover and thirteen pages had to be selected, laid out, written, checked. Banter stopped and in the silence we could pick out each other's breathing. We had heard Hunt breathe before, and Quint, and Kastner, when things were tense.

As each layout emerged up front, a writer was assigned and a reporter hurried back carrying a hastily sketched layout, photo identifications, newspaper clippings, and any source books the writer might need. The clatter of nonelectric typewriters, some muttered mild curses, filled the plane. Early on came a shriek from writer Keith Wheeler. Copy chief Kastner pounded down the aisle white-faced. Wheeler was one of his best, was he having a heart attack? Almost. Through some error the typewriter assigned to him was the sort political speech writers or TV prompters occasionally use, a machine with letters three or four times the average size. Seeing this incredible type appear before his eyes gave Wheeler a turn.

''This machine,'' he spluttered, ''is SHOUTING at me.''

The offending machine was removed, another one produced, Wheeler calmed. Pages began to fall into place. About every three minutes Major Thwaites and Bacon were summoned for help. The major was made to bend his considerable height to the level of a small eye-piece over a low light-table, and asked, ''Who's this? This one right here.''

''That would be,'' the major replied, squinting and fidgeting with concentration, ''Princess Alexandra. That's her husband, there, Angus Ogilvy, and next to him . . . no, behind them . . .''

''I know,'' said Hunt. ''That's King Baudouin of Belgium.'' Hunt was proud of his French pronunciation and loved saying names like Baudouin.

There was another expert on the plane—a London policeman who had been recruited days before as an identifier of people. It turned out however that he was an expert only on members of Parliament. Because there weren't many MPs in the layouts, the bobby had nothing to do but drink. He didn't seem to mind. He spent the flight buttonholing researchers and hostesses and proclaiming, with proper professional gusto, ''I'm going to Chicago, the city of crime.''

Back in London, writing the major piece for the magazine, were Australian journalist and author Alan Moorehead, who was doing a running account of the entire day's proceedings; columnist Loudon Wainwright, who had finished and sent a ''View from Here'' column about the strange hush of a nation waiting in anguish for a great man to die; and correspondent Lee Hall, who was writing a report on small-town British tributes and last honors to Churchill. All the five onboard writers had to do was grind out headlines, captions, and small blocks of text to accompany the pictures. But they had to do it quickly.

Everybody from the writers to the managing editor kept shouting for Bacon, who was the overriding expert on the precise location in which pictures had been taken. When she was summoned to the command table and asked, "Where is that?" she always asked in return, "Who took the picture?"

If the answer was "Pierre Boulat," she said firmly, "Fleet Street." Always she took a quick look through the magnifying glass to confirm her opinion, but that was mainly for form. She knew precisely where each of the sixteen *Life* photographers had been stationed, and what view each would have.

Only once was her aplomb shaken. There was a photograph of Churchill lying in state, with honor guards in scarlet coats standing at each corner of the casket. Somebody wanted to know the precise identity of the guards.

"They're Welsh Guards," she said. She had been there when the picture was taken, and she had double-checked with the men themselves. The information was in both her head and her notebook. But the head researcher on the flight, Jozefa Stuart, was not satisfied. Something of a London expert herself, Stuart was included in the crew not only for her skill but also because her daughter was living in London at the time and everybody at *Life* thought it would be nice if they could have a quick airport lunch together. Such sentimentality aside, Stuart knew the system.

She summoned the major, made him bend once more over the light-table, and asked sternly, "Who are they?"

"Welsh Guards," he said.

Several minutes later Bacon came upon Stuart busily thumbing through a thick volume which illustrated the uniforms and insignia of all British guards units.

"But I told you," ventured Bacon, "and Major Thwaites confirmed . . ."

Stuart threw her a dazzling but distracted smile. "I know," she said, "and I believe you. But this is our system. Check every source you have."

While this meticulous procedure was running its course in mid-aircraft, up front Hunt and Quint began making spreads (a layout of two pages, across the centerfold of the magazine), six, then eight, then ten. Early layouts were revised, tossed out, reinstated. All five writers turned out new headlines to fit new layouts, lengthened or shortened captions and textblocks as versions changed. The aisle began to fill slowly with crumpled pieces of copy paper ripped out of machines and tossed aside. The hostesses passed among us exhorting everybody to please be careful with their cigarettes. They also quickly picked up the lingo of the customers, and some strict orders from Kastner. One thirsty writer who trudged to the rear in search of

Scotch was asked by a hostess, in a distinctly schoolmistress-y voice, "Have you finished your textblock?"

Before the five hours expired, more than sixty pages had been laid out and written, in one version or another, to achieve the twenty-one pages and cover which appeared in the magazine. The initial plan had been to do only thirteen pages, but midway in the flight Hunt decided that the funeral pictures were so good we should scrap seven pages of earlier Churchill material which had been closed and were waiting in Chicago and use seven more pages of funeral coverage. Uncharacteristically, there were few arguments over photo choice, words, or emphasis. There wasn't time.

When at last the lab men and the layout men finished and could sit down with a drink, writers and checkers labored on and Hunt vanished to the rear of the plane to peck out his weekly editors' note. He began it with a sense of excitement:

> We are now 33,000 feet up in the sky, traveling at 600 mph. Below lies the Atlantic Ocean under a cotton matting of clouds. Behind us sprawls the old city of London, where today Churchill was honored in one of the most inspiring ceremonies of all time . . .

Ironically, our particular can of people, busily preparing to tell the readers all about it, contained some of the few in the Western world who had not seen it all on television. Yet we were all convinced, from the color transparencies and the newsclips, that it had indeed been "one of the most inspiring ceremonies of all time."

Like most good *Life* people, Hunt never lost his sense of wonder at the world, of wonder at what he and his staff could do to present the world to its inhabitants. He, all of us, rather regarded the world and the magazine as respectful and awe-struck equals.

□ □ □

Even with the Arctic Circle detour, flight No. 4204 of Seaborad World touched down in Chicago within a minute of the estimated flying time from London, eight hours and fifteen minutes. Just as the wheels touched the runway the overworked electrical system failed at last and plunged the plane into darkness. Still a cheer went up from all hands. We had made it.

Art director Quint, glaring at customs and immigration officials, bolted through the terminal like a halfback, clutching layouts and transparencies tightly to his chest. Outside there was a chauffeured car, provided by the Chicago bureau, and a police escort to lead it on

CREDIT: DOMINIQUE BERRETTY © TIME INC.

This cover was chosen because of the expressions of grief, strain, and rigid respect on the faces of young guardsmen who bore the weight of Sir Winston Churchill's casket.

a noisy dash to the lakeside sprawl of R. R. Donnelley, the U.S.'s biggest printing plant.

While Donnelley's experts rushed to make the plates for their presses, to run color corrections tests, to begin the whole laborious process of translating a picture to a page, the Seaboard maintenance crew ruefully surveyed the ravaged interior of their airplane, knee-deep in paper. Hunt, Kastner, and the rest of the flying blitz put the final touches on copy. The plane was scheduled to return immediately to New York and everybody not needed in Chicago was encouraged to fly home again. Nobody really wanted to go.

The Churchill funeral flight was typical of the magazine at its best—journalistic enterprise imaginatively conceived, carefully planned, flamboyantly executed, highly successful, thoroughly enjoyed by all its exhausted, unshaven, bleary-eyed participants.

On the following Monday morning *Life*'s advertising men, restraining their hyperbole, noted that "on the newsstands just two days after Winston Churchill's funeral, this week's *Life* carries 21 full-color pages of the event—a permanent memorial to the most memorable man of our age." Promotion men noted that ". . . at 3:45 P.M. Monday, February 1, a gentleman named Harry stepped up to a newsstand in the *Time* and *Life* building in New York and purchased the first copy of an issue of *Life* . . . which hadn't been photographed on Saturday morning."

Harry may have liked it, but he couldn't possibly have regarded it with the proprietary love of the forty people who had labored in London, the thirty-four on the airplane, even the forty or so who had spent the crucial flying hours back at home base in New York, laying out and writing alternate pages on Churchill in case something horrible happened to the airborne office. With the magazine on the stands and in our hands, somebody thought to ask this back-up crew what they had planned as a cover in case we didn't make it.

"Well, actually," they deadpanned, "we had engraved a color cover of managing editor Hunt."

□ □ □

There were almost twice as many people on the Churchill flight than there had been on the entire staff of *Life* when it began, and there were four times as many photographers working in London than there had been on the original masthead.

The *Life* staff on publication day in 1936 included nineteen persons and three offices—New York, London, and Paris. From the beginning Luce, who knew little about photography except that he liked pictures, pinned his faith on photographers and established them as the keystone of the new publication. The first four on the masthead were Margaret Bourke-White, Alfred Eisenstaedt, Thomas McAvoy, and Peter Stackpole. Luce once remarked, only half in jest, that his greatest ally in founding the new magazine was Adolf Hitler. Germany had developed the art of photojournalism to a degree unknown in the U.S., but so many of its talented practitioners were Jews that all Luce had to do was "sit in New York and wait for them to land."

Among the first was Eisenstaedt, a diminutive bundle of raw nerves and raw energy who had fled his native Germany and gone to work for the New York photo agency Pix. *Life* made a contract with Pix for his services. Before a single copy of the new magazine had been published, Luce sent the five-foot-three cameraman to take pictures of sharecroppers in Mississippi. Eisenstaedt went off with his trusty Leica and came back with a set of pictures which Luce often referred to as the first true example of U.S. photojournalism: i.e., not just single good pictures but pictures which became a sequence, built images in depth, told a consecutive and cohesive story.

Eisenstaedt's first days as a refugee in New York were spent on Ellis Island, an experience he never forgot. Reporter Helen Fennell remembers going back there with him to do a story in October 1950, when the regulations of Senator Pat McCarran's "Internal Security Act" were being rigidly enforced and any alien suspected of membership in fascist or Nazi organizations, however minor, were being detained. Amid the tears, confusion, outrage, and discomfort, "Eisie" got more and more nervous and kept asking, "Helen, are you sure we can get off the island and back to the city?"

One of my vivid recollections of him was the day in the late forties when we were assigned to cover the first shipload of displaced persons to arrive in the U.S. Eisie and I had arranged to get on the tender which took a harbor pilot out to meet the ship and guide it to port. As the tender drew alongside we could see frightened Estonians, Latvians, Lithuanians, hanging out of portholes and over railings, almost into the lifeboats, waving and laughing and crying. It looked like a wonderful picture, but when I turned toward Eisenstaedt he wasn't there. Eventually I found him, hunched and wiping his eyes, behind some cork liferafts. He had seen the picture long before I did and he had taken it. Then the memories became too strong.

Humanity shone across the pages of *Life* through the eyes of men like Eisenstaedt.

So, all too often, did scenes of inhumanity. The magazine published what has become a famous picture by Robert Capa of a man being killed in the Spanish Civil War. Readers protested.

CREDIT: GEORGE STROCK © TIME INC.

World War II came from Buna, New Guinea, to Mainstreet, U.S.A., in pictures like this notable one. Some readers found the war coverage "too brutal."

In World War II scores of photographers, correspondents, war artists, commissioned by *Life* sent back heart-clutching scenes from all the fronts. One ubiquitous image was of a small baby, crying, sitting in the wreckage of a city, the remains of a home, on blown-up railroad tracks. After World War II, Korea, Vietnam, many a *Life* staffer began to suspect that the photographers were carrying the same baby around, from war to war—or at least carrying the same suit, made of camouflage parachute material—to produce over and over again what became known in the office as "that heart-rendering [sic] baby."

Such cynicism apart, the images of World War II came home to America primarily because of *Life*. One of the single most dramatic photos ever published was taken by George Strock in 1943 at Maggot Beach near Buna, New Guinea. The picture, held up for days awaiting official clearance from the Defense Department in Washington, showed in the foreground a dead American soldier face down in the sand and behind him another on his back, arms outstretched. Neither faces nor wounds were visible but the soldiers looked so young, so vulnerable, their equipment and their uniforms so new.

Again there were reader protests, but veteran staffers recalled some firm words attributed to John Shaw Billings, managing editor during the Spanish Civil War: "If free men refuse to look at dead bodies then brave men will have died in vain."

Most Americans seemed to agree with him. *Life*'s circulation went up and up during World War II and kept on rising at its end. By 1956 the magazine had 251 editorial staffers, twenty-eight bureaus around the world, 317 "stringers" or part-time correspondents, and three editions: the weekly *Life, Life en Español,* itself the biggest picture magazine in Latin America, and *Life International.* At its peak, it sold eight million copies a week in the U.S. and Canada, almost another million abroad.

Each copy, market experts estimated, was read by five persons, not counting those who picked up the dog-eared issues lying about in doctors' and dentists' waiting rooms, public library reading rooms, and commuters who glanced at their neighbors' copies.

For many a year *Life* could proudly and accurately claim to be the biggest magazine in the world.

2

Overkill

Success went, with a rush of enthusiasm and waves of money, to occasional excess. *Life* often indulged in what can only be called journalistic overkill, absolutely smothering a story with troops of photographers and reporters.

A case in point occurred in Mexico, Missouri, pop. 11,000, on an otherwise peaceful Sunday morning, January 8, 1950. World War II was over and Korea not yet begun. The GIs were home, the long-feared postwar depression hadn't happened, and God was in his heaven. *Life* loved to show the big picture through the little picture, and what would be better than showing a small town, middle-American Sunday, loaded with local charm and the clear pure light of peace shining on mothers, fathers, happy children, and stray dogs?

To accomplish this a force of ten photographers and nine reporters was dispatched to Mexico, Mo. They arrived a day early, interviewed every parson in the place, and then arose at dawn Sunday to spend the entire day photographing goings on in each of the town's nineteen churches. Dutifully they noted that the day's activities included fifty church and Sunday School services, ten meetings of youth and study groups, nineteen baptisms, and two funerals. In the beginning there was a hymn service in the local jail at dawn and at the end a popcorn feast at the Congregational minister's home at midnight.

The story ran for ten pages in the magazine dated January 23, 1950, and no doubt it pleased small-city folk across the nation and brought a mist to the eyes of country people transplanted to big cities. Certainly it did no harm but it didn't prove much, either. Reporter Charles Champlin, now entertainment editor of the *Los Angeles Times,* recalls it with a mixture of pleasure and rue, and cannot forget that the magazine had more people covering that Sunday in Mexico than it had assigned to the invasion of France almost six years before.

"I was a junior hand on his first outing with the varsity," Champlin recalls, "and I thoroughly enjoyed the camaraderie of the weekend. It was life with *Life* at its gee-whizziest but there was a calculated folksiness about that Sunday. It was a flexing of journalistic muscles more than a genuine piece of reportage."

So was a typical *Life* exploit more than eight years later, when twelve photograpers were used to chronicle "the short happy life of a TV joke." A TV joke is a slender reed upon which to hang the talents of twelve men, and it wasn't even a very funny joke, but it did make a pretty gee-whiz story. The joke was on Ed Sullivan's show of November 30, 1958. He had a ventriloquist named Rickie Layne with a wooden puppet called Velvel. They were discussing football, and Velvel remarked that "I also played for Notre Dame."

"Were you a student?" deadpanned Sullivan.

"No, a goalpost," riposted Velvel.

Life, estimating that forty million Americans laughed (an outrageously optimistic estimate, in my view) at the same moment, published a story showing the inside of the studio at the moment the puppet splintered the airwaves—and then solemnly showed guests at a Brooklyn hotel swimming pool laughing at the same image on their TV sets; employees of Calumet Farms stable watching inside the horse barns at the Hialeah race track; the living room of a Chicago family vacationing in Palm Springs, Calif.; a Japanese wrestler named Tokyo Joe and his wife managing to suppress their giggles in a hotel in Delaware; traction patients in a new Detroit hospital ward; a tenant farmer and his family in North Carolina; a trailer-dwelling couple in Sarasota, Florida; a pair of state police radio men inside a cabin on a Colorado peak; the lobby of the Mark Hopkins Hotel in San Francisco; fifteen girls gathered around a TV set in Rosemary Hall in Greenwich, Conn.; and even inside the atomic-powered submarine *Nautilus* tied up in New London, Conn.

□ □ □

PHOTOGRAPH COURTESY OF CORNELL CAPA © TIME INC.

Mexico, Missouri, drowsed, but not nineteen Life *photographers and reporters.*

CREDIT: LISA LARSEN © TIME INC.

Sunday in Mexico, Missouri, with the George Rosenthal family trooping off to the Baptist church at 9:30 A.M.

That same year, little more than a month earlier, *Life* had swarmed all over a more worthy story, the death of Pope Pius XII. Known as "*Life*'s first pope" because his reign had spanned most of the years of the magazine, Pius's death afforded the first opportunity to go all out on the Vatican. New York sent troops from everywhere: photographer Mark Kauffman and correspondent Robert Morse from London; photographer Loomis Dean and correspondent Will Lang from Paris; photographer Jim Whitmore and correspondent Don Burke from Athens; photographer Dmitri Kessel from New York.

From a bureau of one—me—*Life* Rome became almost overnight a bureau of ten, including Rome contract photographers David Lees and Carlo Bavagnoli. Everybody was eager to produce something notable for the magazine. Only one of the New York–sent reinforcements, Whitmore, could speak Italian, and only one, Burke, was even distantly Catholic. Under the circumstances it seemed expedient to provide interpreters for some, drivers for others, and turn everyone loose to make his own way.

Thus it developed that on a chill and dreary morning in October 1958, I picked up Loomis Dean at his hotel and we proceeded to a prearranged appointment with a bribable Vatican policeman. Our mission was to get a picture of Pope Pius in state inside St. Peter's before the tourists and the official photographers turned up for the day.

It was just past dawn when, escorted by our guard, we tiptoed into the vast basilica. The first person we encountered was Dmitri Kessel, strolling about casually with an assistant, a step-ladder, and another Vatican guard. We avoided each other's eyes. High over our heads, cat-footing along a three-foot ledge, was Jim Whitmore, looking for the right spot from which to take one of the great *Life* photographs, an overall of St. Peter's "shot from heaven" as someone said later.

Loomis and I loomed beside the bier at last, only to hear a voice hiss, "Get out of my picture." There, tripod and camera and black cloth in place, stood David Lees.

Four *Life* photographers, at dawn, after the same picture. No wonder in many a published photograph of a great event staffers could pick out their colleagues—never identified in the magazine—in the background. They kept meeting each other lens to lens.

For years there was a rumor that Clare Boothe Luce's conversion to the Roman Catholic faith had given a pro-Rome tilt to *Life*'s coverage. This was not true. Mrs. Luce had nothing to do with *Life* except an occasional commissioned article—and her husband's pro-Presbyterian tilt far more than compensated for her Roman leanings. *Life* loved the Roman church for itself, for its spectacle: all those candles,

CREDIT: JAMES WHITMORE © TIME INC.

Pope Pius XII lying in state in St. Peter's. The photograph, "shot from heaven," ran in the issue of October 27, 1958.

processions, uniforms, nuns, piazzas, ceremonies. They made great pictures.

Similarly the magazine was not attempting to rejoin the British Empire, but the British throne is as pictorial as the Roman one and *Life* always went all out. Eight photographers covered the funeral of King George VI in February 1952, and preparation for the coronation of Queen Elizabeth II, though it was sixteen months away, began almost the next day.

By June 1, 1953, the London *Life* bureau had swollen to thirteen photographers and eleven reporters, all rehearsed, primed with passes and ready to go. Most of the photographers had "fixed positions," that is, assigned vantage points from which they could not move. Photographers hated fixed positions because they ruled out the kind of free-wheeling coverage all cameramen prefer, but on most state occasions they were necessary and unavoidable.

On Monday night, June 1, twenty-eight people slept on cots or in sleeping bags inside the London headquarters. At roughly midnight all were rudely awakened by jubilant British staffers who had just learned that "two of our boys," New Zealander Edmund P. Hillary and Sherpa guide Tenzing Norkey had climbed Mount Everest. Ordinarily that would have called for an all-night celebration but breakfast was served in the *Time-Life* building at 2:30 A.M. so reporters and photographers could get to their posts before crowds of spectators or police patrols closed all the access routes to the venue of the coronation procession. Photographer Carl Mydans and correspondent Joann McQuiston went to the Victoria Embankment at ten o'clock on the morning before the coronation, to photograph school children arriving by boat. In turned out to be such a good spot that they decided to stay there—for thirty hours. It was the most fixed of all fixed positions, a vantage point for the great procession to come but also a bit of very hard curbing on which crowds of would-be spectators kept converging, shoving the Mydans-McQuiston team into fewer and fewer inches of space. When one member of the team had to be excused briefly to use the toilet facilities in a nearby subway, the other had to fight to hold the vacated space. Runners from the London office scrupulously delivered umbrellas, blankets against the chill, thermoses of coffee and sandwiches to the stake-out.

Most of us had a less dramatic wait than did Mydans and McQuiston, but for all it was a long, long time in cold and rain before the first prancing horse, red-coated guard, or bedecked carriage passed in review to be photographed.

□ □ □

While some of us were overkilling London, others were taking on Chicago and the "I like Ike" convention of 1952. Their effort made ours look paltry. Forty people from *Life* went to Chicago, including fourteen photographers. Technicians from the magazine installed a ton and a half of stroboscopic flash equipment inside the International Ampitheater ceiling so Gjon Mili could photograph the delegates and the proceedings "candid," as the expression was then.

Life laid on radio-equipped taxis to transport staffers scattered in eight different hotels to the 1,500 square feet of space inside the lower exhibition hall of the Conrad Hilton Hotel, Republican convention headquarters. There was also a jeep for heavy photographic equipment, and a pair of motorcycles for rapid transport across Chicago.

Managing editor Edward K. Thompson surveyed his massed forces on the eve of the convention, put his tongue firmly in his cheek and said, "Don't let's overshoot." He eventually received 35,000 negatives shot by his fourteen men, had 2,000 of them printed, used 56 in the magazine. The story ran for a cover and fourteen pages in the issue of July 21, 1952.

To be sure they'd be ready with the winner, *Life* had prudently engraved in advance color photographs of Eisenhower, Taft, and Warren for the cover, then locked the Eisenhower plates on the presses the moment he was nominated. (In 1940, when the Roosevelt–Wendell Willkie race looked so close that the decision might have gone to the House of Representatives, *Life* had engraved covers of each of the contenders and also an obscure Hollywood starlet. Just in case. In the end Roosevelt both won and ran, and an appalled West Coast photographer shouted by long-distance telephone that "I told that girl she was on the cover!")

On the night Ike was nominated, staffers in a very depleted New York office watched the proceedings on television and expressed dissent to the Republican slant of the magazine by wearing campaign buttons which dated back to Warren G. Harding and forward to "I go Pogo." The *Life* letters department brooded over what to do with two giant "I like Ike" hubcaps which some antic reader had sent through the mail.

Overkill on things like the coronation and the convention not only accomplished its purpose in achieving spectacular pictures, but it also was rewarding to the participants. In retrospect it is clear that each participant could recognize his or her own contribution to the magazine. Small perhaps, but there. Almost always each photographer got at least one picture credit, and chortling reporters went around brandishing copies of the issue and bragging to each other, "See that comma, right there? *I* wrote that."

□ □ □

One of the most effective uses of overkill was the coverage of the sinking of the *Andrea Doria,* in 1956. The pride of the Italian line collided with the Swedish *Stockholm* on a steamy July night just outside the port of New York, and news of the sinking caught the late news programs on both radio and TV. When reporter Clara Nicolai heard it in her apartment in upper Manhattan she went straight to the telephone to call Irene Saint, head of the domestic news bureau. Irene's phone was busy because Boston bureau chief Bill Johnson had heard the late news too and had rung Irene. At almost the same time, photographer Jerry Cooke, in Stratford, Conn., was calling picture editor Ray Mackland.

It was the sort of convulsion to which staffers were accustomed: telephone calls in the middle of the night, hasty plans, a mass rush to the scene of the action.

Reporter Nicolai went back to bed and slept well. She had done her duty and she worked for the foreign news department. Because the shipwreck was just off the U.S. coast, it was a domestic story. But when Nicolai got to work the next morning she found everything changed. Teams were being dispatched from everywhere up and down the East Coast. Nicolai, of Italian descent, could speak the language. She was sent off with few preliminaries to get to the piers, with photographer Paul Schutzer, and try to photograph and interview survivors.

Meanwhile on the *Ile de France,* which had just sailed from New York, vacationing *Life* publisher Andrew Heiskell at 1:30 A.M. banged on the door of photographer Loomis Dean, en route to his new assignment in Paris.

"Loomis," said Heiskell, "there's some kind of shipwreck out here. I thought you might like to take some pictures."

Dean grabbed his cameras, went to work.

Photographer Yale Joel climbed aboard a chartered plane and photographed the battered *Stockholm.* Photographer Cornell Capa got aboard a Coast Guard cutter en route to the *Ile de France,* which was picking up survivors. Photographer George Silk and reporter Lee Hall somehow boondoggled rights to an admiral's barge from the Brooklyn Navy Yard, and later made use of a Moran tug, from which Hall, precariously balanced on a rope ladder, tried to interview survivors.

On the pier where exhausted *Andrea Doria* passengers were being unloaded, Nicolai and Schutzer cornered a Red Cross official and asked him to lend them a couple of armbands. If they had identification as Red Cross, they could go below to emergency wards where victims were being treated by medical teams. The Red Cross made

CREDIT: GEORGE SILK © TIME INC.

Reporter Lee Hall interviews survivors of the Andrea Doria.

them swear never to reveal where they got the armbands, then handed them over. Reporter Nicolai was so busy helping translate, down below, that she got few interviews, but Schutzer got dramatic photos.

In an eighteen-hour marathon, eight photographers and twenty-four reporters worked on the story in New York, the latter category including Dick Coffey, general promotion manager of *Life,* who had spent years perfecting an entirely fake Italo-American patois so convincing that he was pressed into service that fateful day as an interviewer-interpreter.

From Rome, departing bureau chief Milton Orshefsky rushed off to Genoa, home base of the *Doria* and her captain, Pietro Calamai, in an effort to obtain an architectural plan of the beautiful ship, her cabin layout, the passenger list, the safety equipment. I, Orshefsky's brand-new replacement in Rome, was sent to Italcable, the Italian cable and wirephoto center, to await delivery of the ship's plans and supervise their transmission to New York.

My arrival sent the Italcable men into shock. It being a typically sweltering July day, they were wandering about clad only in undershorts, and my presence set off a scramble for shirts and trousers. I attempted to apologize, in my four words of Italian. The men were gracious. To help while away hours of waiting for the diagram, waiting for a direct line to New York, I studied my Italian grammar book, *Prima Lezione*. The men gathered around to help. I learned a great many useful words and finally, about 2:00 A.M., I was able to perform my function: speaking English to the New York operator to inform the Associated Press that a wirephoto of the plan of the *Andrea Doria* would now be transmitted from Rome for *Life*. Elapsed time at Italcable, eight hours.

That diagram never appeared in the magazine. Nor did many of the photographs. The photo lab processed 120 rolls of color, made at least 750 prints. What readers got, in the issue of August 6, 1956, was a black and white cover converted into semicolor by a two-tone printing process, and fifteen pages of dramatic black and white inside.

Far from discouraging participants, this particular overkill set up a furious interior competition. Everybody wanted to be in on the act. Among the few who weren't were the gentlemen of the sports department, reporters Jack Newcombe, Jack McDermott, and Richard Anthony.

"We were stuck on one of those dreary pennant race stories which might have closed as the lead if the *Andrea Doria* didn't make it," McDermott recalls. "And we were plenty ticked-off when everybody else was sent to cover the shipwreck. Heroes were being made by the hour, and we were stuck in the office."

To console themselves they decided to do an "instant replay" of the accident. Newcombe and Bill Gallagher, a production manager in the layout room, conducted elaborate rehearsals with filing cabinet drawers, slamming them separately and in unison until they had achieved the proper shattering, shuddering crash of metal hitting metal in the night. They also rehearsed foghorn noises and the bong of bell buoys at sea.

When all was ready, McDermott and Anthony played the Swedish and Italian captains. The foghorns blew, the buoys bonged, the file cabinets slammed one final time, and Anthony began to shout, "Eh! Whattsamatta you bumpa my boat? You crazy?"

McDermott, equally outraged, demanded, "Deeden you 'ear my yingle yingle?"

This stirring drama was played out in the layout room, audible to most of Rockefeller Center, and intolerable to the temporary managing editor, Robert Elson. Elson was a nervous man that night because he was filling in for Thompson and he knew that he understood words much better than he did pictures. (He is the author of a distinguished two-volume history of Time Incorporated.) He stormed out of his office, admonished the jokers that they hadn't accumulated enough seniority or profit sharing to indulge in stupid jokes, and then advised them to go home and get a good night's sleep.

Not knowing for sure whether or not they had been fired, the actors retreated to their offices.

Anthony later got in on some of the coverage, and McDermott had the satisfaction of helping to cover, months later, an attempt by divers to salvage bits of the stricken *Doria*. He also recalls, in a delicious echo of overkill, the day a man sat before him in the office and asked for an advance of $1,500 for magazine rights to photo coverage of the raising of the *Doria*.

When McDermott expressed some doubt that anything could refloat the ship, the man leaned across his desk and whispered in a conspiratorial voice, "Mr. McDermott, even as you and I are sitting here, my partners are manufacturing thousands of ping pong balls, in a warehouse in Maryland . . ."

□ □ □

Sometimes overkill came not in the form of swarms of photographers and reporters, but in the quiet, earnest, maddeningly persistent efforts of well-meaning people to achieve the heart of the matter.

A landmark of this form was accomplished by the husband-and-wife team of photographer Grey Villet and reporter Barbara Cummiskey. It all started with a big *Life* party at which Mr. Luce made a speech in which he said something like "You're all going on Christmas vacation soon and while you're away I would like you to think about what is most important to you in the whole world."

Editor Ralph Graves went home and decided that what was most important to him was the family. When everybody got back to work he set reporter Jan Mason to researching families which might provide an in-depth essay for *Life*. When Mason turned in her research, Graves turned it over to the Villets.

The Villets, a highly introspective pair, didn't like any of Jan Mason's families and set themselves to writing a memo to the entire staff explaining what they did want. To the best of everybody's recollection, they needed a family which lived between Boston and Richmond, Virginia, certainly not farther west than the Appalachians; a family with residual wealth, near-landed-gentry types; a family in depth, three generations at least. On and on went the memo, and various members of the staff took umbrage.

"That memo was not only ridiculous, it was offensive," one contemporary still fumes.

From it came one of the longest-running and most popular of all *Life* in-house jokes, the outlandish and totally imaginary Van Phinque family. In the West and South, where the German influence is more pervasive, it was rendered as Von Phinque. The blaze of humorous rebellion seems to have ignited first in the entertainment department, in which theater editor Tom Prideaux was dubbed Rufus D. Van Phinque, known as Poppa, and movie editor Mary Leatherbee became Felicia Van Phinque, twice widowed, "Aunt Fizzy" for short, a jet-set traveler.

Over a winey lunch the members of the department all selected names and characters for themselves, and elaborated on their relationship to the rest of the family. Writer Richard Oulahan became the Rev. Horace Van Phinque, single, Episcopalian. Writer Dave Martin chose to be R. Dangerfield Van Phinque, married to Melanie, who was reporter Judy Fayard, but deep in a passionate affair with a black woman.

Reporter Gail Cameron was Amber Van Phinque, five-times divorced, and the plot foresaw that photographer Villet would fall in love with her midway through the photographic story.

Clyde Van Phinque, the Solid Bore, interested only in double-entry bookkeeping, was reporter Chris Welles; Vadna was reporter Ann Guerin, the horsey one who lived in the stables and drank only vodka; reporter Laura Bell decided to call herself Laura the Latent Lesbian, Van Phinque.

Within days the joke spread and was picked up in all quarters. Editor Ed Thompson sent a postcard from Mexico, where he was on vacation with his wife Lee Eitingon, to report that he had located El Stinko Von Phinque, named after the cigar manufactured by his cousin Eduardo on his mother's side. Reporter Helen Fennell wrote from the south of France, also on holiday, hoping to reestablish her kin, the de la Ffinques, with the American branch. Some Midwest news came that Hattie Fink, explaining that she had to shorten her name so it would fit on the RFD mailbox, would love to meet her kin.

Reporter Jane Scholl wrote from Fleecum Ranch, Bilk, Texas, to her "Dear, Darlin' Uncle Horace" to wish him Merry Christmas in 1964 and to report that "at this season when Family is all I just can't help settin' down and writin' you all about what's happened to our Southwestern branch over the past forty-two years."

Signing herself Courtenay-Sue Von Phinque Lambert Garcia Cwynwd Brazos Murchison Hunt Weatherford, she reported that "I own outright 3,671 producing oil wells, downtown Dallas, and 99 44/100% of Jim Wells County. But none of it means as much as kinfolk, and I want each and every one of you to come visit me. Not all at once, please. It's just a simple 88-room shack, but I do believe in Texas hospitality and it won't cost any of you a cent except for board, room, and the ranch hands' salaries. Oodles and oodles of love from your dotin' niece. . ."

The gag raged for months, convulsing its participants in the corridors. Newcomers devoted hours of labor to letters of application to the family, carefully tracing their lineage and vying with each other for gaudy details of their personal lives.

Long before the laughter died, the Villets had chosen the Levi Smith family of Vermont as the subject of their in-depth study of "a family." The Smiths are totally innocent of any of the aberrations or extravagances thought up by irreverent staffers whom they never met or even heard of. Grey and Barbara Villet moved to Vermont, rented a nearby house for an entire year, and saw the Smith family almost every day. The results of their efforts produced 325 rolls of film (almost 12,000 individual photographs), thirty notebooks full of notes, and fifty pages, in installments, in the magazine.

At the end of one of the ultimates in saturation and overkill, both Villets and some editors of *Life* wished to publish the study in book form, using many of the pictures and words which even the magazine couldn't absorb.

The Smiths, understandably, gently refused. Enough, they said, was enough.

3

God the Photographer

''The man from *Life*'' became fairly well known, over the course of thirty-six years, to virtually every head of state in the world; all the best quarterbacks and movie stars; the most famous crooks, in or out of jail; astronauts and scientists; politicians, painters, and preachers; Broadway stars and chess champions; and thousands of ordinary citizens whose chief claim to fame was that (*a*) once they appeared in *Life* or (*b*) they didn't appear, after having knocked themselves out to cooperate with the photographer.

''The man''—who had some notable female counterparts in the persons of Lisa Larsen, Martha Holmes, Nina Leen—always appeared draped in cameras, bags, light meters, an air of intense concentration, and a head full of outrageous requests: ''Would you please move your army back two steps for a better composition?'' was actually said by Gordon Parks to the commander of Danish military forces in Copenhagen in 1950; ''I know you've a ruptured hernia, but couldn't you put some ice on it or something and get into your riding pants and boots for just one more picture?'' asked Margaret Bourke-White of Augustus A. ''Gussie'' Busch in St. Louis in 1955; "I know it's expensive to move a whole fleet, but the ships are placed so we can't see the new plane maneuvering among them" was spoken by Ralph Morse to an admiral in the mid-sixties, off Norfolk.

These requests were often delivered through the reluctant mouths of attendant reporters, but the orders came clearly from God the photographer. Their enormity was mitigated somewhat by personal charm and generosity. Most of the men from *Life* could be beguiling, and it helped that they had virtually unlimited expense accounts. After they had finished disrupting armies, navies, and governments, they moved to assault private homes where they were likely to fuse the owner's electrical system, tip over his coffee table, fill his ashtrays with burned-out flashbulbs and film cans, or spend three days instead of the "couple of hours" they had requested. After which they customarily ordered the reporter to "clean up this mess" and then invited the subject and his entire family out to dinner at the most expensive restaurant within driving distance.

Perhaps even more important than charm or money, however, the photographers epitomized the casual arrogance which permeated the entire staff. *Life* was the most important magazine in the world. Anybody fortunate enough to attract its attention should be both flattered and long-suffering. And because it was built on pictures, the lordliest of all its lordly crew was the photographer. Photographers managed to persuade a staggering number of persons that this was true.

In the process they made enormous demands upon themselves. They pioneered tools and techniques which have become standard today in television, advertising, newspaper journalism. They studied electronics and chemistry and physics to expand the limits of their medium and above all they pushed their own brains and bodies and imaginations to the limit in search of "the right picture," "a better picture," "the key picture."

The only problem was, they expected everybody within reach of their voices to do the same. At any gathering of former *Life* researchers, reporters, correspondents, and perhaps most of all subjects, the conversation eventually gets around to a semistrangled, "Do you know what that man made me *do?*"

Reporter Charles Champlin recalls the time he was sent out with photographer Ralph Crane to photograph a herd of prize bulls on the farm of Otto Schnering, president of the Curtiss Candy Company near Cary, Illinois. Schnering had created a model farm built in the style of a Tudor village, and was making a fortune in the artificial insemination business.

"Rudi" Crane envisioned a great full-page picture of all the big

CREDIT: WILLIAM J. SUMITS © TIME INC.

In 1960 Life *summoned its entire photographic staff from all over the world to a conference on latest developments in photographic technique and equipment. Managing editor Edward K. Thompson took it lying down.*

Photographers are: (1) Edward Clark; (2) Loomis Dean; (3) Joe Scherschel; (4) Stan Wayman; (5) Robert Kelley; (6) J. R. Eyerman; (7) Ralph Crane; (8) Leonard McCombe; (9) Howard Sochurek; (10) Wallace Kirkland; (11) Mark Kauffman; (12) George Silk; (13) Grey Villet; (14) Hank Walker; (15) Dmitri Kessel; (16) N. R. Farbman; (17) Yale Joel; (18) John Dominis; (19) Gordon Parks; (20) James Burke; (21) Andreas Feininger; (22) Fritz Goro; (23) Allan Grant; (24) Eliot Elisofon; (25) Frank Scherschel; (26) James Whitmore; (27) Paul Schutzer; (28) Walter Sanders; (29) Michael Rougier; (30) Nina Leen; (31) Peter Stackpole; (32) Alfred Eisenstaedt; (33) Margaret Bourke-White; (34) Thomas McAvoy; (35) Carl Mydans; (36) Al Fenn; (37) Ralph Morse; (38) Francis Miller; and (39) Edward K. Thompson.

money-earning bulls marching up a sloping hillside with Best Bull front and center, then two Next Best Bulls, then three . . . He would photograph them from the top window of a farm silo. He described this concept to Champlin, who was left on the ground to translate Crane's orders to the bulls' handlers.

"The day was raw and windy, the bulls were priceless and neurotic, the handlers were contemptuous, impatient, and eventually, furious," Champlin remembers. "I was down under the silo trying to organize all this and every now and again Rudi would emerge from under his black cloth and shout something like 'Second row, back about two feet,' or 'Get the short bulls farther up toward the front.' I would clear my throat and repeat the order and handlers would say, 'Are you out of your blinking mind?' "

Crane finally got that picture, just short of insurrection.

So did Henri Dauman one day in Union Gap, Virginia, where he had gone to photograph a reunion of the Snead family. Back in the 1800s seven Snead brothers had married seven sisters, and once a year their descendants gathered in Union Gap. They were there when Dauman showed up with reporter Jan Mason from New York but there were so many of them that Dauman decided he'd have to assemble them in front of the local high school and photograph them from its roof.

Instead of being able to enjoy their reunion as they chose, the Sneads and kin were marched to the school yard and ordered to shape themselves into a family tree. Genealogy is hard enough to figure out on a piece of paper, and the Sneads got hopelessly confused trying to find their places and form a design which pleased God the photographer.

"Henri was being very French and a little Napoleonic, and the family kept not quite getting the idea," says reporter Mason. "I spent the whole day running up and down four flights of stairs to get his instructions and then push Sneads around down on the ground."

With similar insistence, men from *Life* persuaded people to chop down trees in the front yard ("We want to really *see* that beautiful window."), move fences, paint walls, put on their Sunday clothes when it was only Tuesday, and stand about for hours while the photographer mended a balky flash unit. Even celebrities were not immune: Actor William Holden, having been photographed in a jungle movie in Hollywood, was busy on another film in London when *Life* decided it needed a cover picture of him to go with the jungle take. A "jungle" was created hastily in London's Kew Gardens, on a Sunday, and actor Holden was persuaded to shave his chest (it had been shaved in the jungle picture), put a knife in his teeth, and crawl toward the camera. With each crawl he hissed past the knife, "I hate you, Mark Kauffman (the photographer). Reporter Ruth Lynam had to repeat the orders on that one, but she considers it nothing compared to what photographer Gjon Mili put Igor Stravinsky through.

"Stravinsky was very ill, but still conducting, and Mili decided to set up all his strobe lights and try to recreate the mood of *The Firebird,* photographing the maestro slightly out of focus, with rainbows of light around his head. It was jolly difficult but we did it. Next day I was home, lying down, and there was a knock on the door. It was Mili. He said, 'I'm not quite sure about that last roll of film, I want to do it again.' I said, 'Darling, you're out of your mind. This man is old and ill, they had to carry him up the steps to the stage.' And Mili said, 'Well, just go and ask him.' And would you believe, he *did it again.*''

Now and again somebody rebelled. Clark Gable once got so mad at *Life* for not publishing a story after he had cooperated for days that he refused to pose for the magazine for ten years. Beatle Paul McCartney once threw a pail over a fence at photographer Terry Spencer in England because he was so furious at having been ferreted out in a summer hideaway. And a barber in Gruver, Iowa, managed to kill a whole story because he preferred fishing to posing for pictures. That story was about an election in Gruver, pop. roughly 150, of five female town councilmen. There was no question, in the forties, of ''councilpersons.'' Photographer Walter Sanders wanted to show the female councilmen, of course, but he also decreed that every soul in Gruver should assemble for a group shot in the local ball park.

''A *Life*-type picture in those days was everyone in town,'' says Hugh Moffett, who was then a reporter. ''Everybody in the state would have been better, but if you couldn't get that, then everyone in town. By gosh I tried, I really tried. One man in town was a paraplegic and we arranged to have him brought to the ball park. But one guy, a barber, said 'I'll be damned if I'll show up. I fish on Sundays.' It rained so hard that day we had to move everybody to the high school gym. They waited around while we rigged up the lights and took the picture. But the barber didn't show up and the story didn't run. Gruver, Iowa, is one of those towns we can't go back to.''

It is not a matter of record that ''the man from *Life*'' ever actually persuaded anyone to have an automobile accident, but there were some near misses. There was Rudi Crane in London, for example, shooting an assignment on ''the new Europe'' in the early sixties. The idea was to show prosperity, well-being, modernity. Crane had once taken a picture of traffic in Los Angeles which was a big success, with car lights blazing into his lens and creating stars in the blackness. He ordered correspondent Bacon and photographers' assistant Frank Allen to find such a spot for him in London, one with the bright yellow sulphur lights which line many heavily traveled roads around London. He further wanted a fairly busy four-lane road, on a curving hill, with some elevation from which he could photograph. Bacon and Allen drove around London for hours one night, finally found what seemed exactly the right spot. There was a four-lane road leading toward Oxford, rows of sulphur lights, and a tube station on which Crane could stand to get his picture.

"We went out about six o'clock one night, Rudi set up his cameras, everything was fine until he suddenly demanded, 'Where is all

CREDIT: JOSEPH KASTNER © TIME INC.

At a photographer's reunion in Gjon Mili's studio during World War II, Herbert Gehr jams a hat onto a grimacing George Silk, left; *Mili,* front center, *picture editor Wilson Hicks,* left foreground. *Eliot Elisofon is behind Mili, wearing his Latin Lover look; Bernard Hoffman is standing, Carl Mydans adjusting his hat, Dmitri Kessel,* far right, *showing off his profile.*

the traffic?' Ordinarily it was a very busy road, on that night for some reason the light traffic was moving smoothly. Rudi turned to me and said, 'Dorothy, go to the police and arrange a traffic jam.' I was so stunned I just stood there, and he said, 'Go on, do something. We need an obstruction. Go cause an obstruction.' "

Crane should perhaps have brought along his own obstruction, as did Mark Kauffman when assigned to photograph the great Christopher Wren churches of London for a *Life* art and architecture story. Wren's beautiful spires, built in the seventeenth and eighteenth centuries, were all but hidden by later, larger buildings in London, and to complicate that hazard Kauffman decided to photograph them not on individual sheets of film but all together on one large multiple exposure. This meant studying all the spires, making a meticulous design on paper of how he wanted them to be composed, then carefully masking the film itself so he could photograph first one church, then another, and end up with five or six individual spires on one sheet of film.

It also meant getting the cooperation of the police, of the National Electricity Board, and an immense amount of equipment. Aided by reporter Anne Denny and Allen, he managed to rent klieg lights from a cooperative cinema company, a powerful generator, miles of electric wire, a flatbed truck to transport all this equipment, and a "cherry-picker" crane in which he could be lifted up above the intruding foreground buildings and high into the air where he could see the Wren spires.

For two nights the team toured London, selecting sites which provided enough space for truck, lights, crane, and a view of the churches. Then they arranged with police to block off the space on shooting night, redirect traffic in streets they blocked.

"It was a fantastic production line," Denny recalls. "We would set up in one position, start the generator, rig the lights, and Mark would sail up in his crane. When he had that picture, the light crew and the lorry driver and the generator would move to the next position. While Mark was packing, getting down from the crane, coming to the next place, we'd be setting up."

The operation went on all night for two nights, with Frank Allen in general charge of logistics, and selecting which all-night coffee bar was best for warming up between photographs. The final picture, of the dome of St. Paul's, was meant to be the central image of the big multiple exposure. But when the crew got there, the dome was dismally dark. Not even the big klieg lights would reach its towering height, so Denny was dispatched to ring up the electricity board, in the middle of the night, to ask if they would please turn on the dome lights for, say, ten minutes. The board could, and it did. God the photographer had even made light.

Back in the U.S. Ralph Morse was one of the masters of the impossible. Assigned to photograph a story of the annual bass fishing derby at Martha's Vineyard, he contrived to illuminate several hundred square yards of beach to make a stunning picture. This effort involved hiring a 250-pound generator, persuading helpful natives to transport it onto the beach, renting two fishing boats and attaching stroboscopic lights on them, anchoring the boats at the appropriate distance off-shore, rigging up wires and circuits and "slave" units (light units which fire when activated by a powerful light source several yards away). When all was in order, he arranged the bass fishermen into a tasteful design, ordered them to "cast," and produced a photograph in which not only the fishermen and the beach were visible but the sea and the surf was itself back-lighted from the anchored boats.

Morse also once bought all the condoms in Gloucester, Mass., to protect his precious film from the waves while photographing the Gloucester fishing fleet. Another time he lighted up the whole of Yankee Stadium to make a historic picture of Pope Paul VI's visit to the U.S. in 1965. While Rome staffers, relieved from much involvement in this unprecedented event, had happy times inventing terrible puns about the "Sermon on the Mound" and "throwing out the first Bull," Morse was furrowing his brow over how to show both the pope and the tremendous crowd inside the stadium.

"There weren't enough strobe lights in all New York City to do it," he recalls. "But I knew the television people were planning to light up the diamond area. That way they could get the main center of action in live color. They didn't really care about the crowd. But when I offered to light the crowd, while they lighted the diamond, we made a deal. I rented about $16,000 worth of equipment, we worked together with the networks to balance their lights with mine, and we all got the whole stadium."

□ □ □

Some *Life* photographers—Carl Mydans, David Douglas Duncan, John Phillips, Alfred Eisenstaedt, Larry Burrows, Margaret Bourke-White—have either written books about their adventures or have been the subjects of books by others. Their exploits are well known and will appear in any *Life* narrative. But many who do not figure in the best-publicized events were pretty memorable themselves. Two at opposite ends of the scale come to mind: Francis "Nig" Miller, a not-quite-tamed man of action, who customarily carried film cans of Bourbon whiskey in one jacket pocket (the rubber sealing lip kept them from dripping), and cans of thirty-five millimeter film in the other; and Fritz Goro, a small and patient German-born perfectionist who could translate the most obscure thought or discovery into meticulous, understandable photographs.

Miller, who inevitably reached now and again into the wrong

jacket pocket, was a slam-bang news photographer who never aspired to lyricism except in his annual Christmas cards, which were photographs of his Australian wife and children in elaborate, sentimental poses. Yet in the end it turned out that Miller had covered more assignments for *Life* (195 closely typed "assignment cards," by the count of *Life* picture editor Richard Pollard) than any other one of the roughly 1,500 photographers who had pictures either assigned by or published in the magazine.

He specialized in dangerous quickies, one-shots, and thankless, grueling group efforts like political conventions. For the 1952 Republican extravaganza he figured out a way to suspend a small camera from his neck inside his shirt, poke the lens through what appeared to be a tie clasp on his neat four-in-hand, and fire the shutter by means of a cable release which went down inside his shirtsleeve and into his palm. Thus armed, he managed to make pictures of the Credentials Committee sessions, barred to photographers, even before the convention commenced, and he sneaked pictures all over the place afterward.

Miller's skill with the concealed camera was used repeatedly on stories attempting to expose illegal procedure in elections, civic administrations, or rootin'-tootin' mountain feuds and moonshiners. He was an expert and he was generous—he would always rig up a "Miller special" for anyone in need. He built one for me, in 1954, into a purse. The body of the camera was bolted to the bottom and fitted with an automatic rewind mechanism which advanced the film after each photo was taken. The camera lens was inserted into what looked like a fastener, one of those fake jewels which often adorn a purse clasp. To activate the shutter, he built a cable release which ran up inside the bag's carrying handles. All I had to do was aim the lens vaguely, from waist level, toward the subject, push the cable release, and then somehow cover up the noise made by both shutter and rewind mechanism.

My mission was to cover proceedings at a Chicago precinct voting booth during an off-year election which *Life* was convinced was about to be stolen by the Democratic political machine. Election fraud is difficult to document photographically but "my" precinct had been chosen because it had a great many poorly educated minority voters who could be influenced easily by precinct bosses on the scene. Some voters wouldn't know how a voting machine worked, some perhaps couldn't even even read the names of candidates. My assignment was to take pictures from outside the voting booth every time more than two legs showed under the curtain which was supposed to preserve the voter's privacy. If there was more than one person in there, hanky-panky was afoot. *Except* that blind voters were entitled to be accompanied inside the booth by one helper from each political party, to read out the names, hear the voter's choice, and make the selection. Thus I had somehow to determine how many blind voters there were in the precinct and make sure that I had more pictures of multiple legs behind the curtain than there were blind persons registered.

I was armed with legal credentials as a poll watcher, credentials provided by a reform candidate's staff, so I was entitled to loiter all day near the booth and also to study the precinct records and count blind voters. From the outset I was worried about two things: first, the presence of the precinct captain, who would have been unhappy had he discovered what I was up to; second, the fact that I had only thirty-six exposures on the purse camera. There was no way I could insert a new roll of film into the complicated apparatus. I couldn't afford to miss, and I couldn't afford more than one exposure on each situation. I got to my post at 8:00 A.M. and tried to watch carefully without appearing to watch. On the very first picture the shutter sounded to me like a thunderclap, the rewind like a motorbike. To cover the horrendous noises I began to cough a lot.

Thanks to Miller's marvelous machine, I had by 2:00 P.M. recorded more photographs of multiple feet than there were blind voters. I took two more shots to make sure and then I fled, clutching in my sweating right hand a big box of coughdrops which the precinct captain had thoughtfully bought "for that terrible cough of yours." One picture actually ran in the magazine.

Miller could also display quite unexpected imagination on quiet stories. He got sent to Geneva, Ohio, in 1954 to cover a quaint gathering of old-fashioned penmen. Twenty-one practitioners of the art in five categories—good business writing, florishing, ornamental writing, engrossing [*sic*], and illuminating—had gathered to rock on the local inn's front porch, look at each other's engrossing and flourishing, and to honor the memory of Platt R. Spencer, whom they called "the George Washington of modern penmanship."

Those were the days of 200-page issues of *Life* in which the staff scrambled around covering everything from garden clubs to treed cats, but even by those tolerant criteria the penmen were a little, well, *quiet*. Miller made the story by sending a reporter to buy a three-by-five-foot sheet of glass, some small brushes, and some gouache paints. He then got the champion penman of all to do his stuff on the glass while he photographed both master penman and his penmanship from the other side. Because of this idea the story ran, the penmen were gratified, the public enlightened.

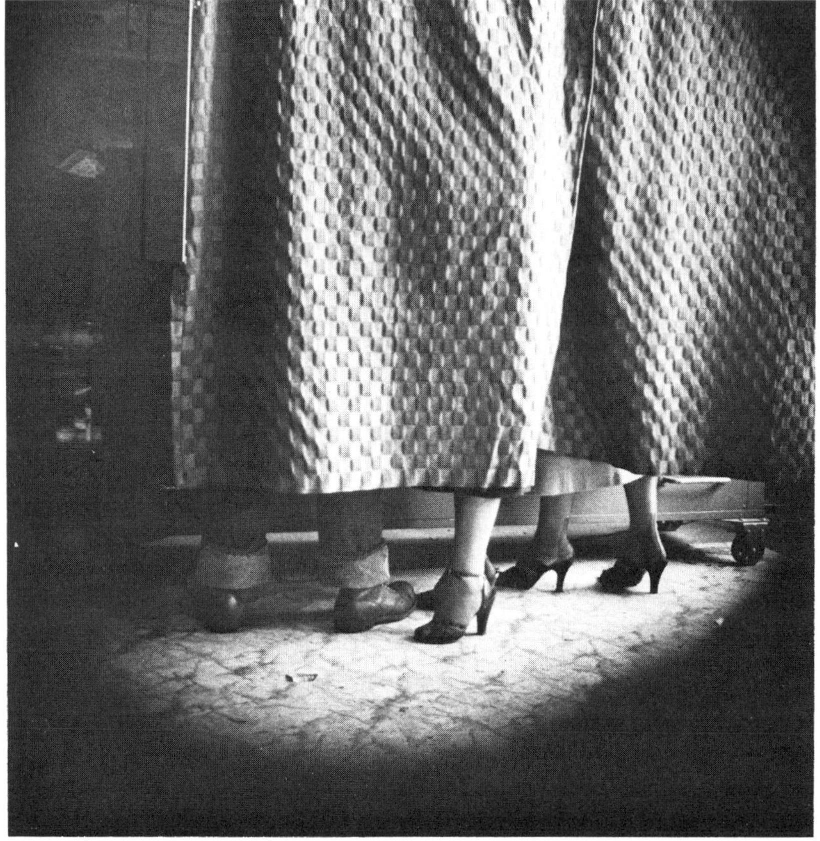

CREDIT: DORA JANE HAMBLIN © TIME INC.

This was the only picture I ever had published in Life. *Using Miller's magic machine, I sure found a lot of feet in the voting booth. The police called me later, advising me to change the lock on the front door of my apartment.*

Miller's temperamental opposite, Fritz Goro, might well have been intrigued by the penmen, but the thought of sneaking a picture, of rushing off to con a crook, of battling it out with militant strikers, would have appalled him. Yet he was quite willing to go off on extended, physically hazardous scientific expeditions and he was, despite the great talents of George Silk, Henry Groskinsky, Yale Joel, J. R. Eyerman, Dr. Roman Vishniak, Nina Leen, and others, probably *Life*'s finest photographer of stubborn nature and of complex scientific subjects.

The "impossible" picture often fell to him: science essays on the nature of the atom, a visual explanation of the electron, the physics of color, how Polaroid film works. Frequently aided by science writer

CREDIT: ARCHIE LIEBERMAN © TIME INC.
Francis Miller displaying his necktie camera at the Chicago convention of 1952.

Robert Campbell, always aided by scientists eager to have their work explained visually to the public, Goro turned out a stream of impossibles. One of his most complex was an explanation of how the laser beam works. The pulsed flash of a laser beam lasts only thousandths of a second, yet it can, among other things, perform delicate surgery, clean marble, detect flaws inside masses, go to the moon and come back with measurements of continental drift.

To make all this comprehensible to readers, Goro had to figure out how to show, on one negative, (*a*) a brilliant light beam, (*b*) a crystal ruby rod which when struck by the light emits a laser beam, (*c*) the laser beam itself, and (*d*) an object receiving the beam. The light flash which produced the laser beam was so brilliant that it required hours of experiment, dozens of filters, hundreds of sheets of film, before Goro got it right. Then the laser beam. Its flash was so fast, so undiffused, that it persisted in being invisible on film. Finally Goro discovered that it was visible in a cloud of smoke, if the smoke was the right density. He and the scientists experimented some more, and built a special chamber into which pulses of burning incense smoke could be introduced. When the tiny blower blew the right amount of incense, the laser beam was visible and the photograph was made. The recipient of the beam in that particular case was a startled-looking rabbit which caught the beam in its right eye. It didn't hurt the rabbit.

□ □ □

It took patience to work on a story with Goro, tolerance to cope with Miller. But there were other gods on the staff who sometimes had difficulty rounding up attendant harp-players. There was a noticeable reluctance on the part of reporters and correspondents to work with some of the most glittering stars: Eisenstaedt, Bourke-White, Elisofon, among others. They demanded so much care and feeding, so much mopping-up and ego-nourishment, that the reporter hardly had any time left to write captions.

Eisenstaedt needed his laundry attended to, his stamps bought, his money exchanged when he dealt in foreign currencies, his meals ordered (though that wasn't so crucial because he usually ate from the reporter's plate, having convinced himself that he or she had ordered a better meal than he had), his transportation and his hotel rooms organized. He was sometimes incapable even of looking out the window to see what the weather was, and rang "his" reporter to inquire, "Is it raining? Should I wear my rubbers?" Much of his helplessness was a pose. It was highly convenient for him. But he posed so relentlessly that attendant reporters ended up basket cases, rebels, or reluctant nannies.

Bourke-White needed her purse retrieved from telephone booths, her hat fetched from hotel suites, her nightly bath drawn, and a daily interpretation of the jokes in "Pogo" ("I don't get it."). She was enormously effective at upstaging or bewitching bigwigs, which was useful, but relentless in her pressure on the peasants. Reporter Bill Pain, working with Bourke-White in Colorado on a Dust Bowl story in the late fifties, was sent firmly to the telephone one night to call the Denver bureau to report that madame's aerial camera had gone bad. There was only one other camera within reach which would serve her purposes, and that one was at Lowry Air Force Base. The Denver bureau was to procure this camera immediately and bring it to her. Pain awakened Denver's Chuck Champlin at midnight, Champlin awakened the air force base, drove through the remainder of the night, and delivered the camera at dawn. The story never ran, but both young men were impressed by Bourke-White's professionalism. They didn't even laugh when she screamed an unconscious pun over the telephone: "This is a matter of life or death."

One of the few reporters whom Bourke-White could not upstage was Lee Eitingon, a cool young woman of dramatic good looks and serene confidence. The two went off together to cover the mass migration of Moslems to Pakistan after the British raj left India, and they were so handsome a team that Ed Thompson cabled them they must be the biggest thing since the Cherry Sisters. Bourke-White for once couldn't get her reporter to interpret because Eitingon had never heard of the Cherry Sisters either. (They were, in case anybody still cares, one of the most disastrous acts in turn-of-the-century vaudeville, described by the Des Moines, Iowa, *Leader* as "an old jade of fifty summers," "a frisky filly of forty," and "a capering monstrosity of 34." An Iowa Supreme Court ruling in 1901 called these descriptions "fair comment" and the Cherry Sisters toured for years thereafter on the strength of their notably bad notices.) Eitingon cherished the cable from her future husband for years, innocently considering it a compliment.

□ □ □

Eliot Elisofon, though capable of climbing mountains, penetrating swamps, paddling about the South Pacific, required at least 50 ccs of flattery a day and kept on about it until some exhausted reporter agreed, "Yes, Eliot, you are undoubtedly a genius." He customarily referred to anyone who accompanied him, from editor to reporter, as "my assistant," and he was fond of writing articles for photography magazines in which he confessed in effect that "I cannot tell a lie, I am the greatest photographer . . .

So convinced was he of this that it was easy in the early fifties to send him a fake letter from Buckingham Palace issuing a command to photograph the young Prince Charles and Princess Anne. Elisofon rented a morning coat and striped pants, put his equipment in order, and turned up in the London bureau for inspection. Because an inflated ego is its own worst enemy, which he almost knew, he asked if the letter could by any chance be a gag. Nobody wanted to own up, but in conscience nobody could tell him flat out that it wasn't. Somebody finally commented that it was odd his letter bore a stamp: "Wouldn't the queen just have a sort of franking thing that says 'On Her Majesty's Service'?" Elisofon ignored this veiled warning, turned up at the palace gates, and was sent unceremoniously away.

To balance the ego-ridden there was a large group known to reporters as "the loves." Several belonged to the Fremont High Mafia, a group of young photographers from Los Angeles who had been trained by Clarence A. Bach, a perceptive and imaginative public school teacher. Bach had enormous groups of first- or second-generation Americans who might not automatically be sent to college, so he decided to teach them marketable skills—manual training, photography. From Fremont High came George Strock, Bob Landry, Mark Kauffman, John Dominis, John Florea, John Zimmerman, Hank Walker, Harold Trudeau, Phil Bath, Walter Bennett. Each time one was hired and made it at *Life,* he loyally recommended one of his buddies. These were good guys, many of whom even carried their own camera bags, something the stars would never do—though, to their credit, the stars often demanded and got full-time assistants to ease the reporters' tasks.

Photographer N. R. Farbman, an intermediate case, was not from Fremont High and would not carry his bags. He desisted from this demand only after an unfortunate episode in the Casbah, Algiers, on a day in the early fifties. He and I were doing a story on a great green cruise ship which had arrived to show rich tourists the exotic life in the smelly native center. We would rush to the top of the hill behind a group of tourists, walk with them down the winding alleys and precipitous steps of the Casbah, and then taxi back and follow another group. On one such descent down crumbling steps, carrying three of his bags, ordered to "get their names but stay out of the picture," I slipped on a shadowed heap of donkey feces, lost my balance, and sat down, hard, on one of his camera bags.

While my head still spun and my teeth hurt, Farb turned around and said, "You're just like the rest of the reporters. Every time I turn my back, you sit down to rest."

Later it developed that I had sat upon his favorite lens, and bent its mount completely out of shape. From that time forward, he carried at least his favorite case.

There were other delightful guys: Jim Whitmore, Larry Burrows, Gordon Parks (though he was accustomed to ask, at intervals, "Hon, did you notice whether I put film in this camera or not?"), Loomis Dean, Bill Eppridge . . .

In a class by himself was Dmitri Kessel, one of the most versatile photographers on the staff and one of the most peripatetic. Kessel was all over the place from Paris to London to Rome to Iran, the Belgian Congo, Tunisia, Spanish Morocco, Lebanon, Kenya—everywhere he went he felt impelled to befriend every human being who crossed his path. He must have paid for more lunches and dinners than any member of the staff except Mr. Luce himself. He also made engaging conversation, referring to a religious gathering as the "Eucalyptus congress," and reminding his friends that some movie star whose name he could not for the moment remember once starred in *The Scarlet Pumpernickel*.

□ □ □

Somewhere between the stars and the loves were the artists, the likes of Gjon Mili, Leonard McCombe, W. Eugene Smith. They could charm, pout, and throw tantrums in several accents and they were usually involved in long-term stories, things involving either

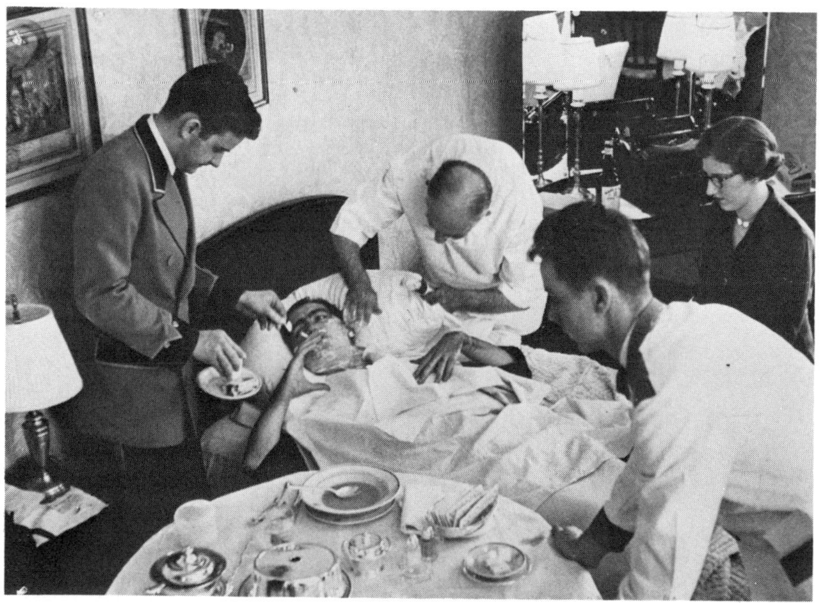

Dreams of godlike life came true for photographer Leonard McCombe in 1950 on a story about a new hotel in Hershey, Pennsylvania. There were so few guests that he had the full attention of waiter, bellboy, barber, and stenographer. Life *didn't print the picture.*

fantastically complex lighting (Mili), several months of staring into space (Smith) or into the eyes and soul of the subject (McCombe).

Few reporters could match their patience on a job. Whenever an assignment came up to work with them there was a churning within the staff. A month with them could be like six months at Alcatraz, but on the other hand a month with them would no doubt lead to acclaim. Virtually everything they ever shot ran in the magazine, and any court jester who had danced attendance, rented equipment, calmed the photographer, turned on the lights, turned off the police, made the rain stop, would be golden in New York when the story was a success. Some reporters faced with the prospect discovered dying grandmothers; others cancelled tickets to the Metropolitan Opera or the World Series. It all depended upon priorities.

□ □ □

There was no question whatever about photographers' physical courage. They dangled from helicopters, crawled into caves, flew into the eys of hurricanes, froze in the Arctic. The dodged bullets—not always in wars and not always successfully—survived beatings and tear gas and banishment.

Carl Mydans covered wars from Finland to the Pacific and back again, survived wartime imprisonment at Santo Tomas in the Philippines and an earthquake in Japan. Larry Burrows risked his life, and eventually lost it, in the Vietnam war for years after the editors tried to make him stop. He had previously been beaten up in Leopoldville, in the Congo, as was correspondent Dave Snell.

Eugene Smith covered thirteen island invasions in the Pacific before he was finally wounded, almost to the relief of his worried colleagues, and sent back to the U.S. Robert Capa, who had survived the Spanish Civil War and World War II, including a landing with the first wave of troops on the "Easy Red" section of Omaha Beach, was killed in Vietnam in early 1954 when he answered a *Life* appeal to fill in there for a month's temporary assignment.

At Little Rock, at the Democratic convention in Chicago in 1968, on freedom marches and picket lines, the photographers took their lumps. During the Japanese May Day riots of 1954, photographers Bourke-White and Michael Rougier were both caught by rioting leftists, as was correspondent John Dille. Rougier, on the ground, was beaten and clubbed but regained his feet and kept on shooting. Bourke-White and Dille, marooned on the top of a *Life* station wagon, worked until the station wagon itself was destroyed by the mob. Dille was almost pushed into the imperial moat by rioters who jabbed at him with nail-tipped bamboo poles, and Bourke-White discovered the next day, at the hairdresser's, that she had more than a dozen small wounds in her scalp, cuts made by bamboo poles and flying glass which she hadn't even felt in the excitement of the moment.

John Dominis, who covered a lot of wars, is astonished today to realize that his most terrified moment came during a small, not very dramatic assignment to cover an oil pipeline suspension bridge over the Missouri River. The pipeline was about a mile long, had started from both sides to link in the middle. His job was to cover the link-up; "Suddenly there I was, supposed to walk about half a mile on top of this pipe. It was about twenty inches in diameter, but only about six inches at the top you could walk on. There was nothing to hold onto. The pipeline guys said to me, 'Just walk, don't crawl, or inch out, or anything. Just walk.' So I walked, but man, that was the longest half-mile of my life."

God the photographer in addition to being brave was also resourceful and imaginative. Michael Rougier, while covering the Korean war, decided to send his combat film to New York in very odd containers—the dry cereal box from which he had just eaten his breakfast was one of his favorites. This mode might, he thought, facilitate shipment at the Korean end and bring attention to his film at the New York end.

Photographers Cornell Capa, Jim Whitmore, and David Lees, assigned to cover a "*Life* Goes to a Party" story in Venice in 1951 were banished from the premises of the palazzo owned by Don Carlos de Beistegui y Iturbi on the grounds that "this is my house and you are not invited to my party." Don Carlos de Beistegui's party was to be in costume, however, so the uncowed photographers snooped around Venice until they discovered what costumes the palace detectives were going to wear that night. They then had their own copies made, hid their cameras in the folds of their medieval robes, and strode purposefully into the palazzo. It seemed discreet to stay out of sight until the party actually began, so they crept into a small, dark room and cowered there until it became obvious that they had somehow managed to hide between the host's bedroom and his private bath. When he arrived to complete ablutions and dress for the evening, they scampered out and onto a balcony hanging perilously over a canal, where they clung together until the coast was clear. Then they photographed a great party story.

Photographer Ralph Morse, assigned to cover the U.S. space program at its inception, became famous for his intricately engineered and technologically perfect pictures of launches, recoveries, and in-flight training. His irrepressible ingenuity is less well known. On one occasion in the fifties he learned that the original astronauts, "the first seven," were going into desert training somewhere in the southwestern U.S. Neither they nor NASA wanted press coverage, but Morse was determined to get it. He guessed that they would use Reno, Nevada as their base and a nearby air force establishment as their transportation point. Thus on a hunch he flew to Reno, found the astronauts in a hotel. They refused to tell him where they were going, but discreet conversation with the hotel bartender indicated a point roughly sixty miles northeast of Reno.

Early the next day Morse rented a Piper Cub aircraft, which he loaded with one-pound bags of flour he had bought at a handy A & P.

"We zigzagged the desert until we spotted a small camp with a tent, and surrounding it in a radius of about a mile were little models of the Mercury spacecraft, made out of cheesecloth on wood frames. I figured okay, this is it, so I told the pilot to fly as low as he could to the nearest highway. Then I dive-bombed the highway with flour sacks, so I'd have a landmark. We flew back to town, I paid him off, rented a jeep, drove back out the highway to my markers, and straight to the camp. When the astronauts helicoptered in, about one-thirty in the afternoon, I was standing outside their tent wearing a borrowed chef's cap, all ready to help with lunch."

Aplomb of quite another order was required of Mark Kauffman when the former British colony of the Gold Coast became the independent state of Ghana in 1957. As the first black African state to achieve independence, it was a big story which attracted journalists from all over the world. There were pictures galore, but everybody knew that *the* photograph, the symbol of the story and of a changing Africa, would be new Ghanaian President Kwame Nkrumah and the Duchess of Kent, the elegant Princess Marina, opening the dancing at the Independence Ball.

To prevent the press from upsetting the stately occasion, Ghanaian authorities decreed that only three photographers would be admitted: one Ghanaian, one wire service representative to provide photos for all, and one foreigner. The foreign press, they said, should settle the question of the third photographer among themselves.

That night at the press camp the argument over the "third man" began at 10:00 A.M., was still raging at 2:00 A.M. None of the usual arguments about *Life*'s importance and worldwide circulation did any good. The Nigerian press was particularly combative, and the fight began to get ugly when suddenly Kauffman, to the astonishment and horror of *Life* correspondent Bob Morse, proposed that the competing photographers draw lots for the post. A neutral delegate was appointed to prepare sixteen slips of paper for the draw, mark an *X* on one of them, ball up the whole lot, and pass the hat.

Kauffman was about the fifth to draw, and to the joy of Morse he drew the *X*. ''My God, Markie, you really took a chance,'' sighed Morse afterward.

''What chance?'' replied Kauffman. ''I've been gambling all my life. A neophyte, asked to do this sort of thing, always rolls the slip with the *X* into a tighter ball than all the others. All you have to do is manage to see and pull the tightest ball, and you've got it.''

Kauffman's picture, of a regal duchess in ballgown and diamond tiara, Kwame Nkrumah in tribal robes, ran for a full page in the magazine and has been reproduced hundreds of times since as a symbol of the beginning of the end of empire.

''It takes more to being a *Life* photographer than just knowing where the shutter button is,'' Morse concluded.

KOMING, or How Many Rivets in a Bridge?

God the photographer had servants by the score. Legions of people were needed to receive and catalogue incoming film, develop and print it, number and file it, lay it out, nurse it into print.

Key persons in the whole complex operation were assignment editors, who chose the photographer for the job, and film editors, who sat day after day peering through magnifying glasses and at small desk projectors to select the best of the color transparencies and the most dramatic or telling of the black and white frames to be printed from each take. *Life* photographers were famous for shooting an entire thirty-six–exposure roll—or more—on a single situation hoping always for a slightly better photo. Thus film editors were constrained to look at literally thousands of frames per day. Peggy Sargent, chief film editor for a quarter of a century, always said she even had nightmares in thirty-five–millimeter frames.

Sargent began her career as secretary to Margaret Bourke-White. When Bourke-White moved to *Life* and into the precincts of the building, she designed and set up her own cozy office with furniture brought from home—Sargent was installed in a hallway outside. It was a good vantage point for meeting people. Before long she became Ed Thompson's secretary, and shortly thereafter film editor. Proprietor Luce, being conducted on a tour of the *Life* premises by Thompson, paused to watch Sargent at work and exclaimed that "she must be the most important person on the whole magazine."She might have been. Years of practice so developed her eye for a photo and her sense of what the photographer was trying to convey that she and her chief assistants, Barbara Brewster, Sigrid Thomas, Miriam Smith, became near-intuitive in their editing. Photographers felt safe in their hands and showered them not only with crazy presents from exotic lands but also with a flow of silly pictures of themselves in action. Their office walls were covered with photos of photographers sitting in bosomy models' laps, reclining nude on jeep hoods with military helmets chastely positioned, mugging in goofy hats, pretending to be driving trains. To be posted on Peggy's wall was to join the in-house Hall of Fame.

Important as these people were, there was another category of employee with whom photographers had to spend most of their days: the reporter, who for years was called a researcher on the masthead. Researcher-reporters, predominantly female, staffed almost every department of the magazine and were dispatched to work with the photographer on virtually every story. There was a vague theory that the combination of male photographer and female reporter created a social unit which was more easily managed and assimilated when the team dealt with people. They could fit as a "couple" into dinner parties, outings, any social occasion. Perhaps that was true, though it has always been my conviction that in those preliberation days it was simply easier for *Life* to convince women to be photographers' handmaidens than it would have been to force men into the role.

Despite the fact that the photographer was God, he remained in thrall, in subtle ways, to the researcher-reporter. It was the reporter who wrote the "shooting script" giving him his instructions. It was the reporter who physically carried the pictures to an editor to show them, who helped provide the words which would accompany them, who checked the names and the accuracy. If the pictures weren't good the story wouldn't run. That constrained the reporter to handmaiden as best she could. On the other hand if the reorter failed to get the caption material, to follow the story through the toils of the office, it would simply expire unseen on somebody's desk. Thus there was a mutual dependence which quickly grew into a love-hate relationship not unlike a marriage.

Love-hate began with "the shooting script," an official communication from "New York" to a photographer anywhere in the world. The script was a summary of the idea of the story; the points to be made photographically; the general length estimated for even-

© TIME INC.

Typical of the irreverent pictures of staffers which graced the walls of Peggy Sargent's office is this shot of photographer Mike Rougier, left, *and correspondent John Dille in Korea. It prompted editor Sidney L. James to quip, "Gee, I didn't recognize them with their hats on."*

CREDIT: GERRY HURLEY RYAN © TIME INC.

Peggy Sargent pins another picture to the "photographers' wall," as assistants Sigrid Thomas, left, *and Barbara Brewster supervise the placement.*

tual publication space (one page, two, four); whether it should be shot in color, black and white, or both; New York deadline time; and any other pertinent and/or useful information the home office had to contribute. Some photographers hated "the script" as much as reporters hated carrying all those camera bags. They threw it scornfully away and shot by instinct, threatening to strangle reporters who insisted on saying, "But it says here in the script. . ."

Other followed scripts slavishly, neatly checking each "assigned" picture as it was taken, and even borrowing layout pads to draw designs of how they thought the story should look on completion.

To understand these disparate attitudes one must imagine a script from genesis to publication. The one to follow is totally fictitous but not atypical.

SCENE 1: An editor reads in the *New York Times* that there is to be a ski race on straw in Heavenly Point, Kansas. Men, women, and children will compete, from age five to age seventy. The straw upon which they will ski will be piled two hundred yards high, and a fence at the bottom will be covered with mattresses to halt the hurtling descent of the skiers.

SCENE 2: The editor hands the clipping to a researcher who has been six months on the job and wants desperately to make good. She takes the clipping, reads, starts writing the script. She went to Vassar and has never been anywhere near Kansas, but she looks it up conscientiously in the *World Almanac*. "Kansas, Sunflower State. Capital, Topeka. Pop. 2,100,000. State Motto: 'To the stars through difficulties.' Admission to the U.S.: 34th. Crops: wheat, cattle." Kansas also has, she notes, "clusters of oil well derricks . . . and towering grain storage elevators."

She sits down to her task. The script will go by telex to the Chicago office, responsible for coverage in Kansas, where a photographer and reporter will be assigned. The message goes out: "for possible lead story want to cover heavenly point kansas ski race. we visualize it as light, fun story with undercurrent of proof pioneer spirit not dead. Americans can ski even without snow if they really want to. for full-page opener would like see skier sailing along on straw pile with hopefully some sunflowers sticking up, cattle grazing innocently unknowing skiers high above them. for support please shoot spectators, possibly standing beside oil derrick with babes in arms, picnic baskets if they plan make a day of it. ender should be winner with proud family and/or fiancee. black and white only please need newyork via packet wednesday good luck best regards."

SCENE 3: Chicago office. The script arrives, is perused by bureau chief and handed to reporter. Problems arise. A phone call to Heavenly Point reveals that straw pile is not two hundred yards high but only one hundred. Will New York settle for such a small pile? It also develops that nobody seventy years old has entered, and that locals riding the straw pile will wear skates, not skis. There has been a shortage of sunflowers ever since Alf Landon ran unsuccessfully for president and the nearest oil derrick is fifty miles away.

SCENE 4: Photographer and reporter arrive from Chicago. The photographer asks, "Where are the sunflowers?"

The reporter says, to sum up, "It beats me. Want me to go buy some?"

Photographer: "Certainly not. That would be cheating. Just get me five skiers, separated pictorially, coming down that straw pile waving their ski poles. Move a couple of tractors down there by the fence, get the spectators into a more aesthetic pattern, and tell them to cheer when I wave my left arm. Oh, and tell them we're from *Life*."

SCENE 5: Picturesque natives on hand. The reporter tries to explain that "New York" thinks they're skiing. It's all very embarrassing, but the *New York Times* said they were going to ski, not skate. Could they, would it be possible, to round up some skis instead of skates?

"Why not?" asks the head native. "We might get into *Life*. How about *That?*"

Whereupon, after a disorganized half-hour, All Ski. Story runs, everybody is happy. Unless of course the story didn't run, which happened all too often.

Scripts always aimed high, were conceived in enormous optimism, and often ended in a dreary series of *caveats:* "do not repeat not hire assistant"; "hold down take, we interested only couple pages"; "need latest October 6." Some became legend. During World War II, when fuel shortages in Britain made it difficult to provide unlimited hot water, patriotic Britons painted stripes low around their bathtubs and promised to bathe in only two or three inches of warm water. Word somehow got to New York that even Buckingham Palace had painted rings around its tubs, and instantly a script was winging its way to London: "Would like photographs of patriotic king bathing in recommended three inches water. Rear view will do."

That one was posted on an office wall until it disintegrated from age. So was another which went to Paris bureau chief John Thorne on the occasion of a summit meeting in Geneva. A New York researcher had thoughtfully drawn up a five-page script which contained meticulous instructions as to just where the president of the U.S. should sit, how Khrushchev should look, where the French delegation should be placed. In brief, a full scenario appropriate for the readers of *Life*. Thorne, who could hardly believe his eyes as he plowed through every word of the Cloud-Cuckoo-Land instructions, sent a succinct reply: "Your telex received. Framing it."

Then there was the matter of the Ainu, an aboriginal race which inhabits the northern islands of Japan, men and women with Caucasoid features, light skin, hairy bodies. At the end of World War II photographer Eisenstaedt was being dispatched to Japan to do a series of stories, including one on the "hairy Ainu." Considerable scholarly research and interviewing had been done by the foreign news staff to prepare a script for this project telling Eisie just which native customs, traditional habitats, social occasions, should be photographed.

The script was worked out in a lengthy staff meeting, and turned over to a researcher to be typed. This young woman, landed with a name she had never heard before, decided that the "Anu," as she assumed the word was spelled, should properly be plural. There thus appeared next day, impeccably typed and neatly mimeographed, about thirty copies of a script directing Eisenstaedt to photograph the "hairy anus."

Amid the chuckles one wise voice was lifted to say, "For God's sake don't let Eisie see this. He'd shoot it as written."

As an ironic postscript, a couple of months after Eisenstaedt had finished the story, *Life* received from the supposedly primitive Ainu tribe a bill for models' fees.

© ALFRED EISENSTAEDT; © TIME INC.

An elder of the Hairy Ainu tribe surveys a hairy bear sacrificed for tribal rites.

□ □ □

After the script was sent and photographer and researcher were at work, each day's "take" went to the lab to be processed and to the desk of a New York researcher-reporter whose task it was to keep track of progress, sort the photos so they made some consecutive sense, study the captions in order to identify all persons therein, and then "sound-track" the entire stack of pictures so they could be shown quickly to the managing editor.

"Sound-tracking" was a meticulous, often nerve-wracking task. Many stories came in late and section heads were eager to be first into the managing editor's office with their piles of photos for the week. Whoever got there first, they thought, might win the most pages in the magazine. Thus they tended to hover, biting their nails and offering gratuitous advice, as some poor researcher was trying frantically to separate stacks of pictures into "roll one, roll two, etc." so as to key them to the captions and make sense of the accumulation. Once that initial sorting was done, the whole stack had to be reorganized so it would "track" as a story, with the most important pictures, events, persons first, then the unfolding action and the minor characters.

Long, complex picture stories could produce one hundred, two hundred big eleven-by-fourteen-inch prints, each neatly marked with photographer's name, date, name of story, and a researcher was expected to have the entire stack always at the ready in case the editor called to say, "I'll look at it now." The stacks were unwieldy, took up enormous amounts of desk and cabinet space, and were hard to remember from week to week. Some researchers had ten or twelve of these stacks lying around, and were supposed not only to keep them dusted but also to recall each salient fact when it came time to "show." I recall a rather large folder marked "moonlit hogs" which reposed on my desk in New York for eighteen months. I never found time to examine what lay therein. I had inherited it from another researcher who preceded me at that desk, and when I moved on I left it for my successor. Years later, all three of us happened to be at the same party and the question of the moonlit hogs came up. Not one of us knew what was in that folder or, for sure, who had photographed it.

Researchers lived in fear of losing or misplacing any of their precious piles, and one day Henriette Roosenburg did—dramatically. She had an enormous foreign news story in careful order on the ledge of a window in the old *Time-Life* building. When the magic moment came "to show," she slid one hand under the bottom print, put the other hand firmly on top, and lifted. This action squirted roughly 198 intermediate prints out of her grasp and straight through the open window. The aerodynamic properties of eleven-by-fourteen prints are extraordinary: they drifted, glided, floated, spiraled, all over Rockefeller Plaza until most of them settled quietly around a very surprised traffic cop thirty floors below.

After sound-tracking and showing, the researcher-reporter had one more vital function to perform—checking. *Life* had at least one checker for every story, upon whose shoulders, however sloping, fell the full weight of factual accuracy. Photographers could shoot blithely, writers could write, editors could edit, but in the end the weight of "truth" with its awesome implications of howling error, libel, lawsuit, disgrace, fell on the checkers. Most field-workers were not in New York when their stories closed, but most had been checkers once themselves so they tried to provide every detail which might be needed, knowing that a colleague would be sitting there late at night studying their captions, reading their reports, and, merciful heavens, dotting every word.

"Dotting" was a sacrosanct function inherited from an earlier generation of *Time* researchers. When a writer turned words in to the copy room, the typists therein made several copies which were distributed to division chiefs, copy editors, managing editor, head researchers—and one copy to the checker. He or she was then expected to establish the accuracy of each fact. To make sure they actually *saw each word,* checkers had to put a dot over it. A black dot with an ordinary pencil was okay for ordinary words. For names, dates, titles, a red dot was required. Green dots were placed over expendable words and phrases which might be later "greened," i.e., added or eliminated, in the final phases of fitting the words to the available space.

Most important of course were the red dots. Only certain high-level sources were accepted for a red dot. *Who's Who* was a red-check source for proper names, although a telephone call to the person in question was an even redder check. The telephone directory, the *World Almanac,* were considered slender reeds but usable in cases of dire need. There was also available the enormous company library with files and reference books stacked to the ceiling, trained fact-chasers to help out on difficult questions. Dates could be checked via the "perpetual calendar" on file there, or on microfilmed copies of the *New York Times* from the year X.

Best of all was the telephone. Accuracy could be established by ringing up an expert, checking three sources against each other, calling a bureau or a correspondent at any hour in any place. Until the checker was sure he or she had run down the truth and the whole truth, nobody's slumber was secure anywhere on earth.

Sometimes this led to some odd conversations. On a day in February 1951, several faithful members of the Grand Old Party met in Boston for a box supper and cheered mightily when a Sioux Indian chief, Ben American Horse, proclaimed, "We hope the White Father will kick out Joe Stalin's Redmen who have sneaked into our tepee." The GOP was delighted with this sally until a couple days later when the communist *Daily Worker* reported that Chief Ben American Horse also believed that the U.S. should get out of Korea. That put the cat among the pigeons, and *Life* wished to determine just exactly what the chief really thought. Researcher Doris Getsinger was assigned to find him, and determine his views. By telephone she tracked him from Boston to a New York hotel, got the hotel switchboard, and opened politely.

"Good evening, I'm calling from *Life.* I would like to speak to Chief Ben American Horse. Yes, the name is correct. I believe he checked in this afternoon. Perhaps you have him under Horse. Under American? Under Chief? He's an Indian, by the way. . ."

Eventually she and the fuddled hotel staff managed to track down the room number, and Gets's awed colleagues heard a one-way conversation which began, "Good evening, sir, that is Chief . . . uh . . . Chief Horse . . . Chief American Horse? What should I call you, sir, Chief Ben. . .?"

In early 1949 *Life* decided to do a "Speaking of Pictures" on all the survivors of the Civil War, Confederates on one page, Union soldiers on a facing page. Researchers spent days in conference between New York and archives in Washington, assembled long lists of names, addresses, ranks, ages. Picture assignments went by telephone and telegraph to bureaus and stringers across the country; dozens of old-timers were coaxed back into their uniforms to pose for pictures. Files piled up in New York, layouts were made. There were inevitable delays: the Civil War had been over for quite a while and more pressing things occupied magazine space. Every two or three weeks word would come that "we're going to run the soldiers" and researchers, acutely aware of the age of their subjects, had to telephone each household to make sure the veteran was still alive. There were almost 100 of them when picture assignments were made, only 68 (50 of them 100 years old or older) when we closed the issue of May 30, 1949. In the interim were untold hours on the telephone, frustrations, and amusing conversations, often with children: "Hello, I'm calling from *Life* magazine in New York. May I speak with your mother?"

"She's not here."

"Oh, is your grandpa at home, or your great-grandpa?"

"Yeah, but he can't walk as far as the phone."

"Oh. Well listen carefully. He was in a war, the Civil War. Which side was he on?"

Long silence, minutes ticking away, and finally the youthful voice on the other end. "Missus? From *Life?* He was on the side that won. G'bye."

Fortunately for the child on that particular call, the researcher rang back an hour later, just in time to head off a spanking from an astonished mother who said, "I thought he was lying to me, a telephone call from *Life* in New York!"

That story eventually ran, but not without one final crisis. The writer wanted to know how many troops were involved on both sides in the drawn-out conflict, and assiduous searches through office sources yielded at least a dozen conflicting, qualified, or estimated figures. One researcher finally telephoned to Douglas Southall Freeman, the celebrated historian and chronicler of the war. Mr. Freeman, called away from his dinner, was nevertheless polite. "When do you need the figures?" he asked mildly.

"Well, um, we're closing tonight. Maybe in an hour?"

"My dear young woman," said the scholar firmly, "these are figures which we have been trying to establish for one hundred years. And you want them in an hour!"

He did, however, ring back with what was called in *Life* "an educated guess," and he did it within an hour: three million.

Checking was not a physically demanding job, apart from the hours it took and the miles walked from desk to library to telephone to desk to library, but it required stamina, persistence, and ingenuity. Writers and editors, faced with the need to make even the most banal occurrence seem important, reached always for superlatives or piquant details and, if they couldn't find them in the assembled newsclips and reporters' files, simply inserted the word KOMING. KOMING was a *Life* word which meant, in short, "this fascinating fact will be forthcoming."

Those who forthcomed it were the researchers. They became quite accustomed to being asked, at midnight, to fill in "there are KOMING rivets in the bridge," or "there are KOMING trees in Russia," or "this was the KOMING Bingo game in history." Obviously on the latter the writer wanted to say "biggest," but he needed a checker to prove it for him.

It was part of the *mystique* that the checker never refused. Back to the telephone, back to the library, back to the files, but find it. Typical of the minor but nagging fact which eludes was a small caption written late one Saturday night by a writer assigned to handle the death of Margaret Mitchell, author of *Gone with the Wind.* Conscious of the fact that Mitchell was a small woman who had written a very big book, he wrote an opening sentence which read, "Last week KOMING-pound Margaret Mitchell, author of KOMING-pound *Gone with the Wind. . .*"

There was little difficulty establishing the weight of Margaret Mitchell, but the book was something else again. There was no copy of *Gone with the Wind* in the company library. No public libraries were open at that hour. Telephone calls to friends who might have a copy proved fruitless. Checkers did manage to find, in yellowing newspaper reviews of the book when it was first published, the number of pages. Inspiration sent them through the files looking for other big thick books which might be comparable in weight. *Anthony Adverse,* which was on the shelves, was pretty close. But how to weigh it? The only scale in the building existed in the medical section, firmly locked at that hour on Saturday night. A phone call to "maintenance" provoked the appearance of a large man with a gun, a flashlight, and a lot of keys. Under his bemused scrutiny researchers weighed *Anthony Adverse* on the medical department scale, converted slightly for the difference in the number of pages, and filled in the KOMING weight of *Gone with the Wind*—two and one half pounds.

That entire operation took three hours of time for a very short caption. No wonder that one night a checker was discovered sound asleep at her desk, head on the copy, with one hand still making neat dots up the wall in conditioned reflex. The same checker was once seen at roughly 2:00 A.M. gritting her teeth and dotting away loyally, punctuating each dot with a muttered "shit, shit, shittety-shit."

No wonder, either, that there was the occasional blooper. A *Life* writer assigned to a story on the fiftieth anniversary of Detroit as an automobile town (in June 1946) began his textblock with the sentence, "Detroit, which was a pleasant, elm-shaded little city of KOMING when the auto came out just 50 years ago. . ."

Then he went home to bed. The checker, either motivated by mischief or dulled by fatigue, dutifully filled in the KOMING and the writer—and readers—were stunned to see in next week's issue the deadpan statement that "Detroit . . . was a pleasnt, elm-shaded little city of 250,000 when the auto came out just 50 years ago. . . ."

Despite such lapses, devotion to duty produced a far higher quota of ingenious action than errors. Reporter Honor Fitzpatrick once sat on a bar stool in Las Vegas and carefully recorded 2,500 consecutive rolls of dice to calculate the odds for a *Life* story on gambling. Reporter Joann McQuiston, assigned to check just how fast the celebrated tides come in at Mont St. Michel, France, armed herself with a stop watch, stationed herself on the very edge of the rocky island on which the abbey of Mont St. Michel is built, and timed the incoming water as it raced across several miles of wet sandy flats. Then, braced like a relay runner, she took off when the water touched the island and strode along with it, measuring her own steps, scattering tourists right and left as she charged toward the abbey along with the rushing water.

"The tide comes in," she was able to report and check, "not as fast as 'a galloping horse,' or 'faster than a man can run,' as some of the books say. It comes in as fast as a normal five-foot-seven-inch human being can walk. A fast walk, but not a run."

Researcher-reporter ingenuity took many forms in response to endless challenge from imaginative photographers, editors, writers. It never even seemed funny to read telex messages back and forth prefaced with phrases like "re essay on the universe," or "for spread on eternity."

Anne Denny in London was told in 1959 simply to "illustrate Charles Darwin" for a story commemorating the 150th anniversary of the birth of the man who invented the theory of evolution. She and Mark Kauffman, plowing through Darwin's works, searched for discoveries or ideas which could be translated into photographs. Quickly one detail leaped out at them: the endlessly inquisitive Darwin had thrust burning torches into earthworm colonies in the dead of night and discovered that the worms were "phototropic," i.e., possessed of an involuntary orientation against light which made them wriggle hastily away from any bright light source.

"Great!" said Kauffman. "All I need is a lot of worms, some plate glass, lights, and we can reconstruct the experiment."

Procurement of glass and lights was simple, but earthworms in central London were not so simple. Denny resorted to the yellow pages and finally found a prestigious dealer in fishing supplies. Did they handle worms? she inquired.

"Certainly, madame, but only in quantity."

"That's marvelous. But how many are quantity?"

"The minimum order is five thousand worms."

Apprehensive over the size and weight of a package of five thousand worms, she took a taxi to the store and found the worms neatly packed in a round cardboard carton about eighteen inches high and ten in diameter. They were heavy, but docile. She carried them back to the *Time-Life* office conference room, where Kauffman had set up elaborate glass tables upon which the worms could be extended, and an antique ship's lantern in which he had installed plates of red and blue glass to test light intensity on the worms' reactions.

The worms did all the right things. They were phototropic as Darwin had said. Red, because it was more intense, bothered them more than blue. But the bright light of a candle flame set them scrambling in all directions.

"It was all fine except for the photo lights themselves," Denny recalls. "They were so hot that the poor worms just fried on the plate glass. We couldn't work with the same bunch of worms more than ten minutes. I kept throwing away murdered worms and worrying about the Royal Society for the Prevention of Cruelty to Animals."

In the end the photos were both dramatic and wierdly beautiful with all the lights and their reflections on wriggling worm bodies. But there were roughly 4,750 worms left over. Denny couldn't bear to destroy them, but she doubted that the store would take them back, so finally she took them home. She had just bought a London apartment whose tiny "garden" in the back was a bleak stretch of hard-packed coal-colored earth without a blade of anything green.

"I dumped the worms unceremoniously out there, sort of said 'good luck,'' and forgot all about them. But those were championship worms; they got in there and did their stuff, and within a year I had a real garden, everything grew like crazy.''

□ □ □

Pure mathematics flummoxed most of the staff, as did esoteric calculations in time and space, but they devised ways to get around it. When John Glenn made his space flight in the early spring of 1962, a writer was searching for a way to make both dramatic and comprehensible the fact that he had circled the earth three times in five hours. The facts and figures were easy to comprehend, except that no earthling could really conceive such a thing. Suddenly the writer realized that Glenn had actually seen three sunrises and three sunsets in five hours, and that he had passed through KOMING Wednesdays in the same brief flight.

The KOMINGS were turned over to reporter Alison Kallman, who quietly proceeded to construct, from balled-up copy paper, her own earth and her own miniature spacecraft. She whizzed one manually around the other several times, marked out the time and place of launch, the time and place of recovery, scribbled things on a piece of paper, and finally looked up and said, ''It was four Tuesdays and three Wednesdays, in five hours.''

Almost exactly ten years before, in London, we had used a faintly similar system to figure out an elusive set of facts. The occasion was the attack of a group of British regular soldiers in Ismailia, on the Suez Canal, against a walled stronghold of Egyptian auxiliary police in retaliation for guerrilla killings of British soldiers. It was a brief, bloody action, played down in the British press, but the London *Daily Express* had bought a set of dramatic photos from Swiss free-lance photographer Rene Groebli. The *Daily Express* played them big, then wished to lay off their own expenses by selling the entire set of pictures to someone else. So they telephoned *Life*'s London bureau.

The *Daily Express*'s picture contact in those days was a canny young woman named Enid Colfer. She and I had had dealings before, and we always went through the same drill. First we made a reservation for lunch at the Ecu de France restaurant, which neither of us could afford except on expense account lunches. There we met, drank wine, ate snails, and came to what we thought a reasonable agreement on the price of the photos for sale. From that point on, we lied outrageously to our bosses. If, for example, we thought Groebli's pictures would probably fetch 1,000 pounds from *Life,* I told New York that the *Daily Express* was demanding 2,000 pounds, and she told the *Express* that *Life* was offering only 500. After a brief exchange of cables and conferences, we almost always achieved the fee upon which we had agreed privately over lunch.

We also fiddled the lunch bill. The Ecu de France cost so much that we always divided the total check, asked for an extra copy, and each of us charged our respective employers for one half, meanwhile claiming the other as a guest. We assured ourselves that we weren't really cheating; we were just getting our money back without causing tremors in the accounting department.

Thus it went with Groebli's photos of Ismailia. They were duly bought, printed, dispatched to New York. Like most photographers working alone, Groebli had taken very few captions. About all we were able to send along was a covering memo: "Groebli's take shows British action against Egyptian auxiliary police in Ismailia, Egypt, on the morning of January 25, 1952. Roll one shows British tanks moving toward Egyptian police stronghold, roll four shows British dead in street . . ."

Fine so far. Many a "pickup" story, i.e., one neither assigned to nor photographed by a *Life* team, failed to make the magazine and we honestly didn't think Ismailia had been enough of a war to win any space. We were wrong. Managing editor Thompson had seen the event for what it was, the opening round of a struggle which was to expel both bulky King Farouk and then the British from Egypt. He had seen the photographs, considered them incomprehensible without far fuller captions, and he had pushed panic buttons all over the skyscraper on Rockefeller Plaza.

My telephone rang first at 4:00 A.M. London time. The message was simple: "Big Ed wants to run Ismailia as the lead story. We've got to have captions, and we've got to have a detailed plan of the action, exactly what happened and when in Ismailia."

There were three more calls between 4:00 A.M. and 7:00 A.M., one telling me that photographer Larry Burrows had been in Ismailia two months earlier and had photographed the city from the air. All the negatives were in New York and there was no time to get them to London, but the London office had a set of contact prints of all the photos. The New York office read me roll numbers and frame numbers and said, "Get the lab into action. Make a copy negative and a print of his aerial, and go to work."

While I mumbled "yes, yes," and scribbled notes on the back of a letter from my mother, the faraway voice added two more important things: "Big Ed means it," and "Good luck."

Even before the lab crew came to work I was at the office scrambling through the filed contact prints. By the time everybody got to work, we had Larry Burrows's aerial photograph enlarged to eleven by fourteen inches, in several copies. Then we got the wagons into a circle: everyone on the staff met to trade ideas, possible sources, ways to approach the problem. A street map of Ismailia would certainly be useful, to identify things on Burrows's aerial and perhaps in Groebli's take, somebody suggested. Perhaps there had been a discussion in Parliament, in which case it would be in *Hansard*'s, the privately published but scrupulous report of debates in the lower house of the British government.

Or, perhaps, there was something on the "telly." British television was then far advanced in comparison with the U.S., and there was a converted cinema in Piccadilly Circus which showed telly news all day long, changing the programs as it received new material. Reporter Monica Horne rushed off to see what they had, plunging, as was her habit, straight across Piccadilly Circus without looking either to left or to right. She is the only surviving practitioner of that art.

Reporter Joann McQuiston and I decided to stay in the office and cogitate. We checked nearby stores for maps of Ismailia. They did not exist. I telephoned the British War Office to request a map and Joann, who had grown up in Egypt, telephoned the Egyptian Embassy. She thought they might help. What they did was hang up. The War Office told me they didn't think they had a map, but that they'd call back. I took the officer's name, and when he hadn't called in an hour I telephoned to him.

"Never mind looking," I lied, "The Egyptians have a map and they're bringing it over, all marked with the action."

That did it. Within half an hour an officer was at the bureau with a map. He said, however, that he really didn't know precisely what had transpired in Ismailia and that he did not know which units of the British army had been involved in the action.

Bureau secretary Nina Joseph, who had been hovering around the fringes of the panic looking for something useful to do, at this point asked if she could have an extra set of Groebli's photos. She would take them to the British Museum, she said, and try to match up visible shoulder patches and cap insignia with those on file at the museum. Nina had, only months before, proved invaluable because a great many of her relatives were in the fur trade and occupied premises in central London which were extremely useful as vantage points from which *Life* photographers covered the funeral procession of King George VI. Hoping that she might also have kin at the British Museum, we shoved the pictures at her and off she went.

By this time Monica Horne was back from the telly to report that many of the televised scenes were near-duplicates of Groebli's pictures, and that the center of the action seemed to be the Bureau Sanitaire, a massive administrative health office in the center of town. Egyptian auxiliaries had lain on the roof of the fortresslike building to fire at British attackers.

We now had Burrows's aerial, a street map which identified its salient points, a brief report from *Hansard* which said the British had used Centurion tanks, and Monica's report about the Bureau Sanitaire. We were clustered surveying these materials when into the office burst Bert Cann, a free-lance photographer who specialized in movies. He was then in his Gilbert and Sullivan period and usually came in singing, "Bow, bow ye lower middle classes."

"Whatcher?" he called out cheerily. Then he saw our faces and stopped dead. "What's up, then? What's lumberin' you lot?"

"Ismailia," we chorused.

"Bloody Ismailia is it? I was there doin' me bloody military service. What's the problem?"

We explained, and Bert bent over the aerial photo and the map.

"This here's the Bureau Sanitaire (he pronounced it abominably). Here's the compound for the British troops. If I was to come up with a tank against'em, I'd 'ave bloody well come in right 'ere."

As his finger traced the route he might have used, we all got a glimmer. There were tanks in Groebli's pictures, and if they were on the road Bert was pointing out, going toward the Bureau Sanitaire, it must have been at the moment of attack. If they were coming away, on the same or a similar road, it must have been the end of the action. As another aid, the *bureau* in the aerial photo turned out to be almost the same size and shape as a small English match box. We put a box on the map, just to see how it looked, and the ceiling light in the office cast a shadow across the match box onto the aerial. Eureka, another clue: there were shadows in Groebli's pictures, and if we could calculate their lengths and angles we would have the information we needed to establish the times of day, and the directions of certain military actions.

Somebody rushed out to telephone Greenwich and inquire what time the sun rose in Ismalia on the morning of January 25, and at what angle. Someone else moved a desk lamp near the map, the aerial, and the match box. We could raise the lamp slowly, calibrating very roughly every hour of sunlight, read the shadows, and match them to the photographs. It took a lot of walking 'round and 'round the desk, turning photos this way and that to copy the shadow angle and length, and it took several dozen lamp-rises and lamp-sets, but finally we thought we had worked it all out. Long before we were finished, Nina Joseph was back from the museum with the British units identified. McQuiston had managed to telephone friends in Egypt to check a few points. Almost all of us had taken half an hour off to go see the telly in Piccadilly Circus.

Bert Cann had a job that evening, but he cancelled it. We were all having too much fun, dancing around our tabletop battlefield in an ecstasy whenever another picture seemed to fall into its chronological place. It took all day and most of the night but finally we felt sure we had it. We went through the whole set of pictures and the whole battle plan one more time, then cabled lengthy captions and a plan of action to New York.

Before another day dawned we had a message from Thompson, who hadn't realized in the beginning what a detective job he had assigned to us. His telex read: "Real swell job on a tough short notice assignment. What you added is difference between kind of a salon job and a picture story that means something. Ed."

5

Clobbering the Competitors

On January, 2, 1954, the world's first atomic-powered submarine, the *Nautilus,* was launched at Groton, Conn. *Life* covered it, of course, and published a lengthy article on the man who nursed it from dream to reality, Admiral Hyman Rickover. *Nautilus*'s launching was not only a news event, it was also a military event, and the magazine from the beginning of World War II until the end of its existence was fascinated by military affairs. Pacific-looking Thompson, managing editor from 1949 until 1961, had been briefly military affairs editor of the magazine and, "because I thought I had something to do with getting us into the war," he brushed aside all company efforts to exempt him. He went off to service in June, 1942, rose to lieutenant colonel in air force intelligence, and came back to the magazine just before V-J day.

Thompson's successor, hulking and handsome George P. Hunt, was a marine in the South Pacific and nobody ever forgot it. There was an office joke that George didn't know for sure whether he was a marine or a painter. He was both, and the contrasting sides of his nature were often in conflict within himself, the staff, and the magazine.

Having duly launched the *Nautilus, Life* went about its affairs until the summer of 1957. It then seemed time to take another look at the rapidly changing world of undersea warfare. Five photographers and two reporters set forth to find out all about it. One of the *Life* teams was the first ever to cross the Atlantic underwater aboard the *Nautilus*'s sister sub the *Skate*. Another team learned about life in a submarine and ventured out of the craft, in aqualungs, to photograph the navy planting mines. In midsummer of 1958 the whole package was ready for publication and scheduled for the issue of September 1; twelve pages of stunning color photographs which included a test launching of the Polaris missile, life aboard a submarine, mines being planted and exploded, the latest in U.S. Navy underwater weaponry.

Then, during the interval between "closing" of color and its actual publication date, came electrifying news: The *Nautilus* had silently and secretly gone under the ice over the North Pole, a feat landlubbers could never even have conceived. Having radioed its triumph home, the sub was bound for Portsmouth, England, and the journalistic scramble was on.

Both London and New York went into flaps which would have registered nine on the Richter scale. London began frantic preparations to send a team by tender to board the *Nautilus* before she docked, to try to interview the crew, and pick up any film the submariners might have taken during their voyage. In the midst of preparations came a lengthy cable from Thompson. Its urgency was telegraphed—pardon the pun—by the fact that he sent it "overhead," that is not on the usual telex connection between New York and the major bureaus. "Overhead" presumably protected secrecy, because it was well known inside the company that any telex message sent "personal and confidential" received virtually instant and widespread distribution by word of mouth.

Thompson had catastrophic news: The *Saturday Evening Post* had made a deal for quite a few thousand dollars for an exclusive interview with the *Nautilus*'s captain, William R. Anderson. The London bureau, Thompson cabled, was to "get down to dockside, interview the hell out of the crew, and beat the Satevepost." Perhaps the unkindest cut of all was that the *Post* man who made the deal, Clay Blair, Jr., had previously worked for *Time* and *Life*.

The staff reacted like Cuby the firehorse to the smell of smoke. London *Life* chief Norman Ross called a staff meeting and what was known forever as "Operation Screw Clay Blair" was born. Because the normal complement of the London office was about five, there was no hope of interviewing enough crewmen to piece together a story good enough to match the captain's own. But there were stringers in every major city in the British Isles. There were also part-time book reviewers, librarians who could wield pencils. There was Nigel Dennis, the distinguished novelist and playwright, who often wrote for *Life* and was a specialist in psychological matters—like, for example, how it might feel to be cooped up in a submarine for six weeks with sixty other men.

Phones rang all over England and beyond, that night. *Time* bureau chief Robert Manning pitched in to help, and persuaded British Railways to provide a special train from London to Portsmouth, via Weymouth, to take the loyal troops of *Life* and bring them back to London again with at least one sailor each in their clutches. Correspondent Anne Denny Angus, a recent bride, was dispatched to London's Fortnum and Mason, famous since the Victorian era for having been able to provide unlimited champagne and caviar at any hour and in any amount, to see to refreshment on the special train. Correspondent Bob Morse and photographer Gordon Tenney went off to Portsmouth to find the tender and get aboard.

Then came another brilliant thought. Why not have a big party for all the submariners at the *Time-Life* building in London? Thus the assembled reporters would have access to the sailors for an entire evening. But a party for sailors requires girls. Again Anne Denny Angus was summoned. Could her husband Archie provide fifty girls for fifty sailors within forty-eight hours? Fifty non-pros?

"Of course," she said, smiling serenely. She then rang Archie.

"Fortunately I had been married only three weeks and I hadn't yet thrown away my little black book," Archie recalls. The book was not his only weapon. He was then stage manager for Jack Hylton, the London impressario who had two theaters playing revue weekly. Josephine Baker was appearing in one of his houses at the time. Hylton was also doing two television spectaculars a month, for which Archie Angus auditioned and provided girls.

"All of them were all right," Angus remembers, "but we also had some rather spectacular girls on our own staff. The most vivid one at the party was Cecily Barbirolli, the niece of Sir John Barbirolli the conductor. She was working in our music library at the time."

Archie set to work calling the head girl of all his various dancing troupes and ensembles. On inspiration he rang a nurses' hostel; on sheer guts he rang some old girl friends. He invited everybody at every rehearsal for every Hylton spectacular.

"I had been to one or two *Life* parties, so I was able to say with remarkable assurance that the girls would find it a memorable occasion," he says. "I found a great deal of enthusiasm. I think in fact we had to reject some applicants, at the end."

While Archie was still on the phone, the swollen *Life* staff boarded the special train and set forth. Official records of the event indicate that there were twenty-two reporters aboard; Anne Angus estimates the figure closer to thirty-two. Midway in the journey the train stopped at Weymouth for lunch. And into the hotel dining room marched the opposition, in the person of Clay Blair, Jr.

Blair made straight for Mrs. Angus, whom he had known in his old *Time-Life* days.

"You're covering this too?" he asked, gratuitously under the circumstances. Then he suddenly noticed how many people were sitting together, lunching together, chatting together.

"How many of you are there?" he inquired.

"Well," scrambled Anne Angus, "we all sort of know each other. This gentleman is from the Birmingham paper, this is Mr. so-and-so from Dublin, this is the *Manchester Guardian* . . ."

Mollified and secure in his contract, Blair boarded a tender at Portsmouth and went about four miles out to sea to intercept the *Nautilus*. So, of course, did *Life*'s Morse and Tenney, and a man from the London *Daily Mail*. Morse was shocked to find Blair sitting with Captain Anderson when he made his way to the sub commander's office. Blair glowered, Morse beamed his most disarming smile, and Captain Anderson thanked Morse for *Life*'s invitation to the sailors. "The boys really appreciate your hospitality," said he.

On shore, *Life*'s envoys captured sailors with the single-minded precision of a trout going for flies. The scene at dockside was wild, but effective. When the special train pulled out there were about fifty submariners on board, being plied with food and drink and questions. From the railway station they were loaded into taxis and taken to the *Time-Life* office. There, to everybody's relief, stood a beaming Archie Angus at the door, 50 BEAUTIFUL GIRLS 50 inside, a combo playing sweetly in a corner, an enormous buffet of chicken, roast beef, salad, sweets, laid out by Fortnum and Mason, and enough booze to float the *Nautilus*.

Interviews begun on railway cars continued on the dance floor. Some of the reporters found they could dance with a sailor and simultaneously take notes over his shoulder. Each had been assigned a subject, not a sailor: safety on board, for example, or daily submarine routine, or the kinds of off-hours education or entertainment provided. Poor Nigel Dennis, who could hardly dance with either sailors or the sub's psychiatrist, was at a disadvantage in attempting to analyze the psychological problems involved in the voyage, and the rest of the male reporters had to buttonhole sailors while they or the combo paused for breath between dances.

It was by any standards a smashing party. The sailors were euphoric and flattered to be feted. The girls were impressed by the heroes of the first subpolar passage. The scrambling reporters, between gulps of rare roast beef and aged Scotch, scibbled frantically in their notebooks and checked frequently with bureau chief Ross and correspondent Morse who were coordinating the effort. Assignments were shifted in mid-party: ''You're getting a lot about safety, are you? Well, then ask more about it. We'll give your original subject to somebody else.''

Long before midnight two men had to be stationed at the front door to ward off hopeful gate-crashers and news-sniffing members of the London press. As a queue of taxis materialized outside, waiting for all those people who eventually had to emerge, a pale and shaken Fortnum and Mason man approached Mrs. Angus.

''I don't know how to tell you, madame,'' he began, his lips threatening to tremble. ''It has never happened to Fortnum and Mason before. Never.''

''What? What?'' asked an alarmed Mrs. Angus.

''We have, madame, run out of drink,'' he confessed abjectly.

''Well, get more! Get a taxi, go to the warehouse, or the store, or wherever, and get more.''

Off went Fortnum and Mason and on raged the party. There were few breeches of decorum. A couple of professionals were apprehended in the ladies' room and summarily ejected. One unfortunate sailor lost his land legs and collapsed atop a full tray of glasses. Within seconds he was plucked from among the shards by two muscular officers, marched briskly out the door, down the stairs, into a taxi and off to his hotel.

There were, mercifully, no bedrooms in the *Time-Life* building. But there was the terrace, and the Henry Moore. One of the proudest features of the building, one of the first to rise in the early 1950s from the bomb craters of World War II, was an airy second-floor terrace with a larger-than-life-size bronze sculpture by Henry Moore. Moore's figure is a buxom lady leaning backward, face toward the sky, supported on her backward-extending arms and bent sturdy legs. She became known to the staff as ''the tired researcher'' or ''lady with piles.'' On the night of the *Nautilus* party she was more, much more. The air was balmy, the skies clear, the great glass doors from the reception hall open, and dancing couples whirled in and out. The copious extended lap of ''the tired researcher'' was easily achievable from terrace level. Some say the bronze didn't cool off for days afterward. All say the cleaning staff next morning found a female guest's long red chiffon scarf tied in an affectionate sailor's knot around the neck of the Henry Moore lady.

Next morning also saw the bleary-eyed assembly of all *Life* staffers and stringers to write up their notes. Even the six-story *Time-Life* building, described by Fleet Street journalists as "the San Simeon of Bond Street" when it first appeared to a dazzled London, was hard-pressed to find work space for thirty-four hung-over typists. Most of the stringers had brought their own portables, and secretaries were shoved over two feet to make way for temporary comrades. If worse comes to worst, most journalists can type on their knees, in taxis, on airplanes. I once managed to write a short textpiece for the magazine while seated on a toilet aboard the *Queen Mary*.

Somehow during the day all the notes got written, stringers managed to file to their own papers and then wearily catch trains for home. Late in the afternoon Ross and Morse called in the regular troops to explain gaps in the assembled material: "This is great about the guys as they actually went under the ice, wondering what would happen if it extended clear to the ocean floor. But meanwhile, what was happening at that moment in the engine room?"

That night and next morning reporters fanned out over central London to track down crewmen at their hotels, ask more questions, fill gaps. In New York veteran writer Paul O'Neil was receiving their thousands of teletyped words, deftly fitting them into a textpiece giving the full story of the *Nautilus* and its exploit.

Clay Blair and the *Post,* having one-upped *Life* at the game of checkbook journalism, fell victim to an efficient demonstration of "industrialized," mass-produced journalism. One man interviewing the captain couldn't get the story as quickly as thirty people interviewing fifty people. Still, the square-off may have been a tie. *Life* put discreet pressure on the navy by pointing out that a man on its payroll shouldn't sign contracts with a commercial organization, and the navy responded by convincing the captain to pose in the conning tower for any and all photographers. The result was a color cover for the *Life* issue which carried the *Nautilus* story and beat the *Post* by weeks. On the other hand the *Life* story may have stimulated *Post* sales; issues of both magazines sold out on the stirring tale of the *Nautilus*.

□ □ □

Part of *Life*'s lead was merely mechanical: the magazine had remarkably high-speed production processes developed at vast expense with R. R. Donnelley. From any start *Life* could beat other magazines to the newsstand. *Look,* never a weekly, opted out of most news races. Very often this didn't show to the casual reader but sometimes it did, dramatically. For example, when John F. Kennedy was assassinated on November 22, 1963, *Life* scrapped several million already printed covers and a dozen pages inside, switched quickly and was on the newsstands with a black-bordered photo of Kennedy on the cover (even the famous red ''logo'' was for once not white on red, but white on black). The issue was dated November 29 but was actually on sale several days before that.

Look was caught with a December 3 issue which had a cover picture of JFK and John-John, and a biggish story inside about the president and his son. The cover billing read 'THE PRESIDENT AND HIS SON'' and hailed the coverage as ''exclusive.'' *Look*'s December 15 issue had a cover photo of Audrey Hepburn and Cary Grant with an upper right headline, called a ''flag,'' which read ''PREVIEW POLL: KENNEDY COULD LOSE.'' Instead of scrapping it and starting over, the magazine hired battalions of temporary workers to paste a black band across those words on the cover. Not until December 31, 1963, did *Look* catch up with the news: a color cover of the White House in the snow, with a cover line ''IN MEMORY OF JOHN F. KENNEDY.''

The *Saturday Evening Post,* always a weekly, went through a series of upheavals and changes of direction in its final years, and occasionally hurled itself at a news story to compete with *Life*. So, occasionally, did *Colliers*.

Managing editor Thompson, asked once to define what he considered *Life*'s greatest competitor, answered bluntly, ''the neighborhood bowling alley.''

''The thing about *Life* was that you had a choice in everything except overriding news. That was not true of most other publications. We could miss some things, choose others. At the end of a year I think we could look back and feel satisfaction that we had covered all the major news events, and not just the hard news—news also in art, in fashion, in science. That's where the bowling alley comes in. We simply were competing with everything else for people's time, for people's attention.''

We were sometimes forbidden to use the word ''look'' in a headline because our type style in some sizes could make the word appear to be the logo of ''the other brand,'' but that was about all. Still, Thompson's businesslike view was not shared by most reporters and photographers. For us the sense of competition was high and fanned constantly higher by pride. We loved running head-on into some other magazine and then trying our best to outwit them. Rapid production time was a distinct advantage, but that was for mechanics and accountants. The real fun was the conception and conclusion of a more imaginative plan, a gaudier approach.

It was often even more fun abroad, where the *Life* teams started at a disadvantage. Even the magic name of *Life* wasn't an open sesame when it collided with France's *Paris Match,* Italy's *Europeo,* London's picture-loving *Daily Express,* Germany's *Quick* and *Der Stern.* Reporter Bacon in London recalls a painful attempt to persuade members of an international underwater conference to pose in a dinghy in a swimming pool to prove some point so obscure she has now forgotten what it was. The Europeans scornfully refused to waste their time on so frivolous an enterprise, but an American expert climbed happily into the dinghy upon request and, next day, offered to do it again. Abashed, Miss Bacon said, "But I didn't dare to ask you again," to which the stout-hearted Yank replied, "I'd do anything for *Life* magazine." Bacon was impressed.

□ □ □

In almost twenty-five years with *Life* I can't recall a head-on with *Look,* but I had one once with the *Post.* It involved the sudden discovery and rescue, by Canadian bush pilots, of a Brooklyn girl named Helen Klaben and a Mexican-American pilot named Ralph Flores who had crashed in Flores's small plane and been lost in the Yukon for forty-nine days in 1963.

When word flashed that they were alive and safe, the scramble was on. I went from the office to Abercrombie and Fitch to buy "cellular underwear" against the arctic cold (it was twenty below zero there); to my flat to pick up some ski boots for which the company had paid on another very cold day in 1950 when I went off to cover an avalanche in Switzerland; and to Idlewild airport to catch a plane for Seattle. There I met West Coast correspondent Wilbur Jarvis and free-lance photographer Laurence Schiller. We flew to Whitehorse, Yukon Territory, Canada. En route we mapped a plan—quietly, because we were sure the plane was full of reporters. I had taken the precaution of telephoning Helen Klaben's mother in Brooklyn before I left, and the plot was that I should rush straight from the airport, sans baggage, and try to con my way into Helen's hospital room as a friend of the family, make a deal for *Life* while the rest of the passengers were getting their bags out, finding hotels, asking the location of the hospital.

At first all went well. I got a cab, explained that I was a friend of the family and had a message from Helen's mother. I actually got into the room and we chatted for ten minutes or so about her experiences and the state of her health. Then a nurse came in, ordered me out, and I made a quick pitch: I was from *Life,* we could pay her

$1,500 for an exclusive story and all rights would revert to her after our one-time publication. We could help her to do a book, offer her our own photographs . . . and . . .

"I have had several telephone calls about this sort of thing," she said. "I intend to have a press conference tomorrow."

The press conference, it turned out, was a series of individual interviews in which Miss Klaben asked the questions, and the questions were all the same: How much? She knew the value of her story, or at least some lawyer did. All night long, while the temperature fell to minus thirty, there was a chaotic queue for the telephone in Whitehorse's best hotel. I pleaded with New York to up its bid to $2,500. Schiller called his agent and tried to make a deal with *Paris Match* to join *Life* and up the bid to $5,000. An Associated Press man with a sinister air informed me that he had $10,000 in his pocket for the story. Weeks later we met to talk things over and he confessed he had been bluffing. The *Saturday Evening Post* had nobody there yet, but they had been on the telephone and their bid was rumored to be $35,000. They were in one of their news moods, checkbook at the ready.

It all got so depressing that I decided to outflank the opposition. I had met, at some point in a very confusing day, a marvelous woman named Flo Whyard who worked for the local paper, the *Whitehorse Star*. It occurred to me that the *Star* probably had covered the rescue and recovery long before any of us in New York had read about it on the AP ticker. I looked up Flo again and we got on fine: my father ran a weekly paper in Iowa at that time, and the snow can get pretty deep out there, too. Flo and I had many interests in common, and of course it turned out that she knew the rescue pilot well, had met and interviewed the trappers and dog-sledders who helped bring Klaben and Flores out. She was also, as are most journalists anywhere in the world, generous with both information and help: after all, her story had already gone to press. She introduced me to some of the crucial bit players in the drama, who were happy to recount their own roles.

For two or three tense days rumors and phone calls and news bulletins flew. Several of us tried to interview Flores, who was in more perilous health than the young woman, and whose highly accented English was very difficult to understand. Miss Klaben had still not decided, she said, to whom to delegate her memoirs. Then came her badly organized "escape" from the rear door of the hospital, a dash to the airport, and a disorderly posse of the press on the tail of the getaway ambulance. Jarvis, Schiller, and I were in the posse, feeling like Donner and Blitzen—and in my case, at least, *Götterdämmerung*—as Schiller ricocheted our overheated rented car from one packed snowbank to another. Somehow we got to the airport, somehow we got on the plane, somehow we fetched up in Fairbanks, Alaska. No "press conferences" there; just a stone wall of "no comment," another flurry of telephone calls, and then another frantic dash through the night to another plane headed for New York. Panting, we proceeded, and photographed the reunion of Helen with her family. Then came the final verdict: Miss Klaben had sold her story to the *Post*.

For *Life* it no longer mattered. Jarvis and I had decided in Fairbanks that he would go back to Whitehorse, overfly the wreck of Flores's plane, try to snowshoe to it on the ground if he could, file a detective job from the site. Between the two of us, we had everything we needed for a story. When word went out from Miss Klaben's agent in New York—his telephone exchange was, ironically, "Yukon"—I asked managing editor George Hunt not to bid again against the *Post*. Jarvis and I could write him a story, for free, in twenty-four hours. In something of a pique over the entire series of events, I headed it "GALL OF THE GOLDEN WEST," but wiser heads prevailed and it ran in the issue of April 12, 1963, as "GIRL BEHIND A FROZEN SCREAM."

The *Post* eventually ran Klaben's story, weeks later, and I got into trouble with the accounting department because my vivid red cellular underwear, top and bottom, had cost thirty dollars each. But that is another chapter.

□ □ □

One of the staff's favorite stories of *Life* dexterity in foiling the competition occurred in San Francisco in October 1965. That month a Pan American stratocruiser, flight 943 from Honolulu to San Francisco, suffered an engine failure at mid-point in the flight. Captain Richard W. Ogg (some of the press called him "The Wizard Ogg") ditched safely into the Pacific near the coast guard cutter *Ponchartrain* and twenty-four passengers, plus seven crew members, bobbed perilously for five hours until they were rescued. The *Ponchartrain* got them all safely aboard, but it would take four days to deliver them to shore in San Francisco. In that four days the rush was on—every newspaper and magazine in the U.S. wanted an exclusive story.

San Francisco bureau chief Richard Pollard found his ear permanently attached to the telephone with New York. "They kept offering me people—about fifteen people—to help. I told them just to send me $5,000 in medium-sized bills, and send me Phil Kunhardt from the Los Angeles bureau."

Life sent radio messages to the *Ponchartrain* offering cash for passenger pictures of the terrifying five hours at sea, the rescue, the trip home. Pollard and Kunhardt dickered for rights to film taken by the *Ponchartrain*'s crewmen, but they were foiled when all those pictures were helicoptered off the cutter to be processed and "pooled"—released simultaneously to all qualified news media.

Even worse, when the *Life* pair with two photographers arrived at the dock in San Francisco they found themselves outnumbered two-to-one by a team from *Colliers,* headed by former Time Inc. staffer Cornelius "Connie" Ryan, later a distinguished war historian. *Colliers,* that month and that year, had decided to make itself a newsmagazine. There were also, of course, a swarm of other reporters, but it was *Colliers* which worried Pollard and Kunhardt.

Pollard had one ace in the hole. He was a friend of the Pan Am public relations man, and had appealed to him for help. The man said he couldn't do much, it wouldn't be fair, but he could manage to contact a passenger onboard the *Ponchartrain*, ask him to nose around among the air passengers to see who might have the best film. He would then, he promised, tell his contact to walk down the *Ponchartrain*'s gangplank immediately behind the passenger with the best film.

As the happy survivors trooped off the cutter, Pollard fixed his eyes on the order of descent. Right in front of the passenger his friend had designated was a French doctor named Marcel Touze. Pollard made for his man. But right in front of Touze, whose camera was not visible, was a Dutch passenger named Hendrick Braat. His cameras hung from his shoulder, and Pollard wondered if somehow the two got out of order in the disembarkation. Hurriedly he ordered photographer Bill Young, who had been assigned to the story, to follow Braat while he bearded Dr. Touze.

Connie Ryan and crew were busily explaining to Dr. Touze about first rights, second rights, guarantees, when Pollard walked up, offered $3,000 in $500 bills to the beseiged Frenchman, and went off in triumph with two rolls of undeveloped Kodachrome film.

Photographer Young meanwhile was in pursuit of Dutchman Braat, who refused to open his hotel door but was willing to negotiate through the keyhole. Young offered him several hundred dollars, Braat held out for twice the price, and eventually Young paid it. By now Braat's film also belonged to *Life*—one roll of black and white, two rolls of Agfa, a German color film, and two rolls of Kodachrome.

By this time it was Friday evening in San Francisco and the magazine had to close 2,571 airline miles away in New York the next day. The first problem was how to get the precious color film processed to see what they had bought. Pollard turned for help to Robin Hinsdale, a former *Life* reporter who at that time was married, lived near the San Francisco airport, and had a three-month-old baby to look after. Exreporter Hinsdale responded to the old editorial urge, however, bundled the baby into the family car and rushed thirty-four miles to the Eastman Kodak processing plant. She got there ten minutes before closing time, and somehow talked the employees into doing a rush developing job—two hours. Shushing the fretful baby, she then drove straight to the airport.

Braat's film was more of a problem. The Agfa, meant to be processed only in Germany, could indeed be done on a rush basis, *Life* was told: it would be ready in a mere three weeks. In the end the California staff turned the Agfa over to Ansco, which could convert it quickly to black and white. Braat's take was a disaster. Some rolls were blank, some fuzzy. One had some lovely photos of Chinese pagodas.

Dr. Touze also had one roll of beautiful pagodas, but the second roll was a winner: beautifully composed, perfectly focused, well-exposed frames of life inside the crashed plane, the rescue, the works.

There was a bit more hanky-panky involving outmaneuvering *Colliers* for some badly out-of-focus pictures taken by a certain Albert Spear, another passenger, and Kunhardt's sleight-of-hand removal of some nonpooled coast guard negatives from an AP office.

CREDIT: WILLIAM SIMPSON, C.S. II © TIME INC.

A Ponchartrain *crewman took this dramatic picture of a rescue craft approaching life rafts and passengers from the ditched Pan American plane. All were saved.*

When news of this series of coups reached New York, managing editor Thompson decided to make the fastest cover switch that had ever been made on *Life* up to that time. On the presses in Chicago, with more than two million copies already printed, was a cover of Anne Boleyn which tied in with the then-running text of *A History of the English Speaking Peoples* by Winston S. Churchill.

At ten o'clock on Saturday night off went poor Anne Boleyn's head for yet another time—and on went a Dr. Touze shot of the Pacific crash-and-rescue scene, backed by nine pages inside as the lead story for the week.

6

The Luce Fellowship

One day last year I put on a bedraggled Burberry raincoat left over from London days and reached absent-mindedly into the pockets as I strolled out the door. In the right-hand pocket, mixed with dust, lint, and the shreds of what must have been a cigarette, was a bit of rolled-up notebook paper. I uncoiled it and looked. It proved to be a set of terse admonishments to myself:

Sell car
Store furniture
Learn Italian

This communiqué must have been written in the spring of 1956, when New York decreed that I should be uprooted from Chicago and sent to Rome. It didn't matter that I had asked repeatedly to be sent back to London, that I was totally innocent of the Italian language, that I was not and never had been a Catholic. Uprootings at *Life* were precipitous and infrequently logical: assistant-to-the-editor James Crider, who spent a lot of his time arranging shifts, had a sign on his door which read "RESETTLEMENT ADMINISTRATOR."

To soften the blow I was reminded that my new job would be

bureau chief, a grand title indeed. That turned out to be rather a minor matter, because I was not only the Rome *Life* bureau chief but also its sole employee. For months I scrupulously made carbon copies of all my work, marked them "file," and then when I had time I got up and filed them. I went back to Berlitz (in almost twenty-five years with *Life* I was always one language behind), studied books about the Vatican, bought a new car, and rented some furniture.

After an appropriate breaking-in period I was even granted a secretary all my own, dispensed from a bureau pool of young women who translated Italian newspapers into English, English business letters into Italian, manned the switchboard, staffed the reception desk, and grappled heroically with the Italian telephone system. My treasure was called Iride Cerabona, which translates roughly into "Rainbow Goodwax," and she could speak Italian, English, French, a smattering of Arabic, and some Swahili. She took over translating, telephoning, filing, and me. She disliked filing as much as I did, and she never got around to it until the "out" box towered over both our heads and threatened to collapse. When it reached this height she would attack the pile for an hour or so, then come to me, covered with the dust which all documents seem to generate upon themselves and ask with exquisite delicacy one question:

"You have labeled the same material for 'file' under 'Cardinals,' 'Vatican,' 'Catholic church' and 'Ye Gods.' Would you please choose one, so I can file them all together?"

Iride's job, and mine, and that of several dozen others at *Life,* was an amorphous blend of researcher, checker, reporter, and correspondent. There were ranks and grades and fine distinctions therein, but the tasks which befell us were largely the same. Each had to become a pure researcher, from time to time, tilling the fields of a specialized subject, scanning every applicable publication, interviewing scholars. We were also expected to cover all kinds of specific, constant, and shifting action—sports, fashion, movies, theater. And each had to pursue the news by whatever means at hand—airplane, riverboat, canoe, or inflated lamb's bladder.

We also had to stay out of the pictures. Correspondent Ruth Lynam, who functioned with *élan* in London, has for twenty years been threatening to write her memoirs. All she has at this moment is the title of her opus: *Sitting in Ditches*. It speaks volumes. Field-type reporters were forever sitting in ditches, cowering behind trees or hidden in their lower branches, diving behind divans, staying out of sight while the photographer worked. Ready, however, at all times to deliver new rolls of film, carry ladders, scribble down names, fend off the police, drive at midnight to put the precious film on an airplane. And, if blessed opportunity arose, take a few minutes to write the captions and the accompanying research.

Within this wide framework there were jobs known as "Luce fellowships." There was no such official designation, but the researcher-reporters invented the phrase to describe the kind of assignment which permitted them to spend months at company expense learning all there was to know about a particular subject. Recipients of fellowships were usually persons whose education and training had made them near-experts in something, or correspondents in bureaus who were geographically close to the object of study. Luce fellows went off on stories which had long deadlines. They were expected to interview scholars, read all available published material, invent ways to convey complex knowledge through imaginative photographs, dramatic paintings, and limpid words. It was an invitation to travel, to study, to learn. The name of *Life* usually opened the doors; the meticulous study of top-notch researchers kept them open.

One source of many a Luce fellowship was an elaborate thirteen-part series in the early 1950s called "The World We Live In." (It was later published in book form and became an all-time best-seller despite the fact that it was mail-order and thus did not appear on best-seller lists which are compiled from selected book store sales.) Each part of the original series was assigned to a reporter and each was given roughly eight months in which to research, evaluate, organize all the available data and see that it was photographed or drawn by artists to include the most up-to-date information.

Science reporter Nancy Genet was given "the sea" and charged with finding out precisely how much modern scholarship had discovered about it. She boned up first by reading all recent publications about sea studies and marine life, then set forth to interview experts at the Lamont Laboratory of Columbia University on the Hudson, the main oceanographic center at that time. From there to Woods Hole, to the Scripps Institute of Oceanography, to the U.S. Geological Survey people, the Naval Electronics laboratory.

She was privileged to meet and work with the top professional people in the field and she picked their brains with enthusiasm. Very early in the assignment she met Maurice Ewing, one of the finest of oceanographers and geophysicists. Tentatively, she requested "a couple of hours" of his time, then kept going back for more. When, several years later, she had occasion to telephone Ewing again on a different matter, she began by saying, "I'm Nancy Genet, from *Life*. I don't know if you remember me . . ." and the scientist broke in gleefully to exclaim, "Of course I do. You're the girl who came for two hours and spent two weeks."

Undersea exploration by means of electronic sounding and drilling devices was then in its infancy, but already it had revealed that the rippling Atlantic and Pacific oceans harbored mountains as high as those on land, depths so bottomless that even Mt. Everest could fall into them and vanish. Oceanographic institutes were studying the figures, examining life on the ocean floor, finding the limits and characteristics of the continental shelf.

Genet, busily studying the facts and figures, woke up on a weekend in 1952 with a sensational idea: How would it be to have somebody do a drawing of the bottom of the Atlantic ocean, as if the water had been abruptly yanked out and the profile of the deep revealed?

"It seems a perfectly obvious notion now, twenty-five years later, but strangely enough at that time nobody had ever done it," she recalls. "I didn't have any idea how, physically, it could be done. But naively I jumped out of bed and got some pieces of paper and started trying to sketch to scale the profile of the sea floor, using the oceanographers' figures. I laid out a rough scale-mileage and started to draw. Almost at once I ran out of space, so I Scotch-taped one page to the first and kept going. I started in the living room, went down a long hallway, and before I had finished from Europe to the coast of the U.S. I was in the kitchen. I spent the weekend crawling along, drawing, Scotch-taping, putting in my best scale of continental shelves, undersea mountains, troughs . . ."

Early Monday morning, feeling a little bashful about her "giant toilet paper roll," she presented herself to art director Charles Tudor and explained her idea. Tudor almost had to forcibly restrain her from unrolling her drawing then and there. It was eighty-five feet long and it would have stretched from the layout room out into the hall, past the ladies', past the gents,' the copy room, the office boys . . .

"We'll get an artist," said Tudor firmly. "They know how to render these things geometrically."

Artist James Lewicki reduced Genet's marathon effort to a clear, comprehensible eight-by-twenty-four-inch drawing called "The Profile of the Abyss," and the editors, thus inspired, had him do another of the floor of the Pacific, flanking the large paintings with other drawings of sea creatures—jellyfish, viperfish, sea cucumbers, sea biscuits, which were beginning to be identified by pioneer diver-scientists.

Other Luce fellowships went to researchers assigned to a later series on "The Epic of Man," also made into a book after publication as a series from 1955 to 1957. Reporter Joann McQuiston was sent from New York on a four-month expedition to discover Neolithic tribes and peoples still existing in remote parts of the earth. After weeks of research in New York, conferences with archeologists and anthropologists, she selected a tribe of Berbers in the Atlas Mountains of Morocco who were alleged to be living as their ancestors had 5,000 years before. McQuiston and photographer David Douglas Duncan flew to Marrakech and bought the smallest Renault automobile they could find, on the theory that if it bogged down in desert or mountain pass they could physically lift it, one end at a time, and extricate it from whatever obstacle it had encountered. Then, armed with bedrolls and camping equipment, water purifiers, food for several weeks, and burnooses, they set forth across both Atlas Mountains and Sahara Desert, camping out at oases, until they achieved the Berber villages set 7,000 feet high in a fertile valley.

Though the twentieth-century Berbers had no written language, no art other than tribal songs and patterns woven into cloth or baked into pottery, no plow, wheel, arch, or draft animals, McQuiston found they could create everything they needed to survive. She and Duncan spent one week simply walking about the villages, observing the spading and hoeing, the shepherds with their flocks, the young men building mud brick houses, women weaving—and letting the Berbers get accustomed to them.

Duncan got wonderful photographs of a New Stone Age society which had survived the millennia, and the twentieth-century Renault managed somehow to survive the journey, though its lights flickered out in the middle of the mountains on the way back to Marrakech, and Duncan had to navigate the narrow passes and dangerous defiles with the aid of a flashlight held out the window by McQuiston. When they took the car back to the man from whom they bought it he simply burst out laughing at their request for a resale price. It was such a battered remnant of what it once had been that they had to give it away.

The Berbers and their picturesque way of life formed the bulk of the magazine's pictorial treatment of Neolithic society, but there was much yet to learn. In the historical Neolithic, for example, what clothing did the people wear, what tools did they use, what crops did they raise? These answers, if they existed, lay in museums or in the work of archeologists. McQuiston's Luce fellowship led her on, this time alone, to Iraq.

The search began in Baghdad, which at that time had two paved streets, no sewers, intermittent flooding by the Tigris River, and an overpowering smell. It also had a fine museum and a dubious hostelry called the Tigris Palace, in which McQuiston installed herself. On her first night there she received the biggest bunch of roses she or perhaps any other reporter ever saw—twelve dozen by conservative estimate. With the flowers came a note: "Dear Miss McQuiston, if you had been in Baghdad as long as we have, you would pardon this liberty. Would you care to have tea with us this afternoon at the club? Please reply to room boy." Affixed to this were five very British names, Geoffrey, Christopher, Brian . . . and of course McQuiston accepted.

Her eager hosts turned out to be sewage engineers hired by the Iraqi government to survey the city and prescribe for one of its most odoriferous ailments. One of them informed her over tea that "Baghdad is quite literally floating upon the most unspeakable *mattah.*" All through the next few days, as she examined every item in the local museum and every uncatalogued artifact in its cavernous basement storerooms, McQuiston kept trying to forget this haunting image of impending collapse into "unspeakable mattah." It was most haunting in the underground storerooms, but she was constrained to go there because persons on a Luce fellowship were not expected to accept just any old Neolithic sickle which might be displayed in a dusty museum case. They had to snoop around among the unsorted items looking for the *perfect* Neolithic sickle.

From Baghdad the trail led to Jarmo, a New Stone Age site then being excavated by an expedition from the Oriental Institute of the University of Chicago. Dr. Robert Braidwood, expedition chief, had put together a team of scientists from many different disciplines—botanists, zoologists, geologists, anthropologists—in one of the first efforts to apply to archeology all the specialized knowledge of related sciences. It was a complex dig, and it could provide answers to many problems for the *Life* series. The artist and writer needed to know, for example, what crops, plants, and trees existed 5,000 year ago at Neolithic sites. They needed some rough idea of the climate, to make an educated guess as to what the people wore. They needed evidence of the shape, size, material of their tools, what kind of houses they lived in. The Jarmo dig was the best current source for such detail.

Thus McQuiston contacted Braidwood, and got a stern reply. He would be delighted to have her see the dig, and members of the expedition would be happy to tell her as much as they could, but their cooperation would cost $1,000 a day. McQuiston knew New York would balk, but she was on Braidwood's side. No archeological expedition in modern times has ever had quite enough time or quite enough money to accomplish what it would like to do, and neither item is budgeted to house, feed, and answer the questions of journalists at the site. After considerable cable exchange and some argument, McQuiston won permission to pay for one day of invaluable assistance. She made her way to the site and, on a dramatic evening inside the expedition's eating tent, was introduced to a dozen international experts in all the scientific fields bearing upon archeological reconstruction.

Dr. Braidwood began by saying, "Miss McQuiston, we are now gathered. You may begin with your questions."

"I was scared to death," she recalls. "And worried about how much time I could have. I started asking specific questions about the climate 5,000 years ago, about crops, about houses. *And they all started having arguments.* I would address a question to the botanist and he would answer, and then the geologist would say 'That's not the way I figure it.' It turned out they had been on the same expedition all this time but each had been off doing his own thing and they hadn't really compared notes. They were working awfully hard, and they'd come back and have dinner together at night but they didn't really discuss. They were making notes and preparing to write their individual reports at the end of the season."

Unwittingly cast as catalyst, McQuiston suddenly found herself persona grata in Jarmo. Perhaps the scholars were fascinated by her questions because they were direct, basic, and cross-fertilizing. In any case, Braidwood suddenly invited her to stay for another few days, for free. If she went off with Hans Helbaek, the Danish expert on paleobotany, the zoologist would ask if he could come along, and the two men would spend hours in conversation on comparative discoveries. Braidwood himself took McQuiston in his Land Rover to nearby Iraqi villages in which houses were similar to those occupied in the Neolithic age.

After about five days, both head and notebook stuffed with facts, McQuiston prepared to leave. Expedition members joked that she was eligible for an honorary Ph.D., and Hans Helbaek suggested quite seriously that it shouldn't be honorary. If she would just go to Oxford University and write a thesis on all she had learned, he said, she would earn a real doctorate.

On the same fellowship, McQuiston was asked to research the Egyptian sections of "The Epic of Man." Her new friend Helbaek introduced her to an Egyptian botanist who knew all about the flora of the Nile valley several thousand years ago, and she found a Scottish woman who had spent her life as an amateur Egyptologist exploring the pyramids, tombs, and inscriptions.

"It was midsummer before I got to Egypt, and the midst of a terrible heat wave," McQuiston recalls. "*Life* always seemed to send us places at the wrong time of the year. But the flora expert was marvelous, and during the hottest part of the day the Scottish lady and I could retire to a cool tomb, drink tea from her thermos, and she would interpret the hieroglyphics on the walls. She also regaled me with stories about all the pornographic papyri which never had been published, and I would sit there with tears running down my face from laughter.''

McQuiston quickly became the best hieroglyphic writer on the staff. Armed with her personal experience and a 646-page dictionary, she took to sending hieroglyphic messages to Lincoln Barnett, chief writer of the ''Epic of Man'' series. Company executive C. D. Jack-

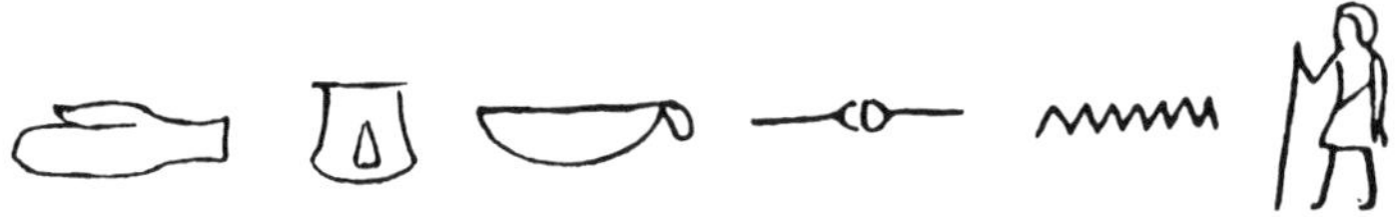

CREDIT: JOANN MCQUISTON AND *f.y.i.* © TIME INC.

McQuiston's hand-drawn hieroglyphic message.

CREDIT: DR. WILLIAM HAYES AND *f.y.i.* © TIME INC.

Dr. William Hayes's more erudite reply.

son saw some of these exchanges and demanded a hieroglyph memo of his own, so McQuiston sat down and painfully sketched symbols which looked like a hand, a jar stand, a basket, a bolt, some water, and a standing figure with a staff. She typed, neatly, that her hieroglyphs ''represent your name'' and should be ''read phonetically rather than literally.'' She also apologized that ''you don't seem to include any birds.''

Jackson, enjoying the joke, took his hand-drawn message to Dr. William Hayes, a college classmate who was then curator of Egyptology at the Metropolitan Museum of Art, and asked for a suitable reply. Dr. Hayes's meticulously drawn three-line communiqué came back (with, happily, a bird or two) and was translated to read: ''The overseer of Scribes, Jack's-son, says to Joann, daughter of Quiston: 'Oh little One, what say you regarding a nice pyramid built for two?' ''

□ □ □

Some fellowships, shifting direction in mid-course, threatened to fall apart at any moment, and involved a high degree of personal discomfort if not downright danger. Correspondent Bob Morse earned several degrees in Middle Eastern politics and modern primitive societies while shuttling from upheaval to upheaval, battlefield to beachhead. Throughout the late fifties and early sixties he bounced around Lebanon, Syria, Iraq, and especially Yemen, of which he remarked, "If you liked the thirteenth century, you'll love Yemen."

He and photographer Larry Burrows, who both later covered the Vietnam war, count as some of their hairiest adventures the frequent coups in the Middle East. They spent two and a half months in Syria and Lebanon in 1958, chronicling the battles for power, dodging sniper bullets, and reporting on the bizarre days in which U.S. Marines charged ashore in Beirut, politely begging the pardon of bikini-clad bathers lounging on the beaches they were assaulting in full combat gear. They were not amused when they got a message from New York that an overkill task force of twelve, headed by Washington bureau chief Don Wilson, would soon be arriving in Beirut to take over the coverage.

Feeling a little de trop, Morse and Burrows decided to try for Iraq. The 1958 shudder through the Middle East had set off an Iraqi revolution in which both King Faisal and Prime Minister Nuri es Said had been brutally murdered, and no correspondents had been able to get to Baghdad since it happened. All Lebanese airports were closed, and no visas were being issued in Beirut for Iraq. Nobody had said anything about the visa situation in Syria, however, so the *Life* team discreetly decamped, having left hotel reservations for the twelve who were to replace them, and rented a car to drive to Damascus.

There a friendly hotel concierge, having been appropriately bribed, produced a taxi driver friend who swore he could take the team 250 miles across the desert, without benefit of road, and deliver them to Baghdad. He said his taxi was in fine condition and that he would accept $200 as pay. The driver was a dubious-looking character and his vehicle even more so, but Morse and Burrows decided to take a chance and a *New York Times* correspondent joined them. After a quick stop at the Damascus bazaar to buy thermos jugs, bottled lemonade, food, and sleeping bags, the small reconnoitering party set forth at 4:00 A.M.

Bored Syrian guards waved their vehicle over the border, never bothering to check whether or not the passengers had visas for Iraq. From then on, for hours, the taxi driver drove and the passengers saw nothing but desert. Now and again the sand was marked by tracks but they seemed to have no pattern. They went every which way, and the driver, scowling, selected one track and pressed on. The vehicle passed an occasional camel, or a Bedouin. At one point they came upon five camels in a group, with no attendant drivers, and the cabbie took a sharp left turn. Morse, Burrows, and the *Times* man looked at each other in anguished silence, praying that the driver knew what he was doing. Finally the *Times* man spoke.

"I'm sure it's very simple," he said. "On all the local maps its says, 'proceed to five camels and turn left.' "

After twelve hours of parching thirst—lemonade is too sweet to quench the desert thirst—and mounting uneasiness, the Syrian taxi and its passengers achieved a real road which, in half an hour, delivered them to the Iraqi outpost of Rutbah, along the route of the Iraq Petroleum Company.

"There the police and the army were not happy to see us," said Morse. "We were promptly arrested, taken to the British rest house. They wouldn't let us make a telephone call or talk to anyone. When we attempted to step outside the rest house, we found rifles in our stomachs. We were held there for twenty hours, during which we were joined in detention by three more taxiloads of journalists who had heard in Damascus that we were trying to get to Baghdad and decided to try the same thing."

Next day, for no explicable reason, the cache of journalists was released and put into a convoy of cars accompanied by two jeeploads of armed soldiers. The entire group, closely supervised, spent two weeks trying to find a story, gave up, and asked to be permitted to fly out. One plane was provided for Damascus, but Burrows and Morse were not permitted to board it. Guards hustled them out of the boarding line, kept them for three hours inside a small, dark room, and then suddenly without explanation loaded both men and their luggage into a jeep. The jeep headed off toward a no-man's land between Syria and Lebanon, and suddenly stopped, unloaded passengers and baggage, and deposited both in the middle of what served as a highway. Armed soldiers took up positions in the low hills which commanded the road and sat there, watching the two *Life* men. It was very hot, and Morse and Burrows sat for another three hours with what little traffic there was whizzing right past them.

"Finally a truck stopped and the driver asked, of all things, what out nationalities were," "Morse said. "I thought, well, this is it, the English and Americans are not very popular in this part of the world in these days. But to my astonishment when I told him he said 'Get on.' It wasn't easy. He was carrying a load of plate glass all held together with a wooden framework. We managed to get our camera cases and overnight bags wedged in front of the glass at the bottom of the truck bed, but the two of us had to ride on top of the glass, trying not to cut our bottoms, clutching onto the wooden frames so we wouldn't fall off. Eventually we rolled down the twisting roads into Lebanon, and Beirut."

Morse and Burrows had, as many a *Life* team before and after them, literally risked their lives and emerged unscathed—but without a story. When their anxieties calmed and their frustrations eased, they could be philosophical about it all: "We did after all learn a lot about police, deserts, guns, politics, violence—and camels," said Morse.

Editor Hugh Moffett, having received a fellowship in French as head of the chief European bureau in Paris, also got one in African travel when he was asked to cover the ninetieth birthday celebration of Dr. Albert Schweitzer in Gabon, Equatorial Africa. He and photographer George Silk applied for visas in Paris and were turned down without an explanation. Somebody said they could get them in Switzerland, so they flew to Geneva. Again they were turned down, so they flew back to Paris. Birthday time was approaching rapidly and, if Gabon wasn't issuing visas that year, Moffett and Silk decided to go without them. They booked seats on Air France and a friendly airport attendant, noting that they had no visas, stamped their passports *situation irregulaire,* twitched a Gallic shrug, and sent them on their way. The plane landed briefly in Lagos, Nigeria, then proceeded to Libreville, capital of Gabon.

"In Libreville instead of visas we got machine guns," says Moffett. "Little boys with machine guns marched us straight to the local cooler. Fotunately I had taken the precaution of cabling from Paris to a State Department type in Gabon that we were going to arrive a little bit *irregulaire*. That man turned up at the jail, by george, and got us out of hock. Then it developed that we didn't have our luggage, our cameras, anything. They'd been offloaded by mistake in Lagos, five hundred miles back up the line.

"With the help of the State Department guy we managed to charter a small plane for two hundred and fifty dollars to fly back to Lagos, get our equipment, and bring it to us. We weren't about to leave Libreville, come back, and try out those machine guns again."

By the time the charter plane got back, bringing the precious cameras, it was 4:00 P.M., Dr. Schweitzer's birthday was the next day, and Moffett and Silk had missed the last plane to Lambaréné, the nearest town to Schweitzer's isolated hospital. Again the State Department man came to their rescue. He owned a single-engine airplane and he offered to fly them. To the harried team there appeared to be nothing whatever below them except miles of muddy water and half the crocodiles in the world, but they made the 100 miles to Lambaréné and offered their volunteer pilot $250. When he protested that it was too much, Silk thrust the bills at him again and said, "That's what we're paying today for charter airplanes. Take it."

Even after they had achieved Lambaréné, however, the travel adventures were not over. Moffett and Silk had acquired a young missionary as guide and interpreter, and they asked him to help them find a boat which would take them from the town to Schweitzer's island. Moffett recalls that there was only one motorboat on the river, run by "a couple of kids about nine and fourteen years old. It had only one speed, wide open, but we chartered it for next morning."

Bright and early next morning, cameras and notebooks and missionary in hand, they rushed to the river and found—no motorboat and no trace of a motorboat. The charter had vanished along with its youthful crew. The missionary attempted to calm his apoplectic companions. "This is Africa," he said, "There will be another boat along . . ."

"We sat there and waited, thinking about the great birthday celebration we were missing, and the good doctor who was so old he might not have another birthday, and then by God all of a sudden along came an *African Queen*–type of vessel, with its motor going *chung chung chung*. We hailed it; it stopped; we got to Schweitzersville at last, and by God we got our story."

□ □ □

So, after many vicissitudes, did the team of Mathilde "Dita" Camacho and Dmitri Kessel, who set forth blithely from Paris in December 1950, to do a little story on the Aga Khan, hereditary ruler of the Moslem Ismaili sect. The Aga Khan planned a three-month tour to his followers in India, Pakistan, East Africa, and Central Asia, with a stop-off in Teheran to attend the wedding of the shah of Iran to Soraya Esfandiary. Camacho and Kessel were to meet him in Teheran, then travel with him and his wife, the Begum, on part of his journey. Camacho rang the Iranian embassy in Paris to inquire what clothing to pack, and was told that "the climate is just like that of Paris." So she packed her pumps, some light and comfortable dresses, and off they went.

Once in Teheran they discovered that the Aga Khan wasn't there because the wedding had been postponed—Soraya had come down with typhoid fever. Just as they were packing up to go back to Paris, word came that the Aga Khan and a friend of Kessel's at the court had arranged for the pair to be guests at the wedding, whenever it was rescheduled. They were delighted: the shah was young, handsome, glamorous, and his bride was movie-star beautiful. The wedding was definitely *Life* material, the stuff of grand spectacle. But what to wear? They flew off to Beirut, then the glittering capital of *haute* everything in the Middle East, where Kessel commissioned a tailor-made tuxedo which never fit and Camacho bought a yellow damask silk dress which she called forever after her ''mother-in-law dress.'' It had elegant long sleeves, a modest round neck, and the general shape of a potato sack.

Properly if not elegantly clad, the pair returned to Teheran and whiled away the time making friends at court, interviewing and photographing political leaders just to have the material in hand for possible future need. The wedding finally took place on February 13, 1951. Camacho duly noted that the Aga Khan and the Begum attended, that the Iranian queen mother dropped a handful of real pearls on the heads of the bridal couple, where they mingled with candy pearls symbolically sprinkled by less affluent guests. She also apologized for ''skimpy captions'' because despite her Beirut finery she had to cover the wedding ceremony ''peeking from the doorway behind the master of ceremonies and another court official while Kessel was inside shooting.''

The Aga Khan then announced that he was going to Karachi, and the team prepared to follow him. But conflicting orders came from New York: Forget the Aga Khan and do a major takeout on Iran as a nation, including a close study of the bristling border with the Soviet Union. Camacho and Kessel by now had suitcases full of accessories appropriate for a royal wedding, but nothing at all for camping in near-zero temperatures along the border.

Sighing at the latest abrupt shift in their current fellowship, they cabled New York to please send them anything they could dig up in the way of background material on the country, anything they knew about the border. Camacho also borrowed some thick stockings, some ill-fitting boots, and a lambs' wool vest from friendly U.S. Embassy women who were sure she would never survive the trip without them.

The team acquired a car and a husky Armenian driver named Henri to help with the equipment. They also acquired an Iranian army officer who had very little English, but fluent French, having attended the French West Point, St. Cyr. Camacho and the officer had no problems whatever communicating with one another, but some difficulties arose over social arrangements. On the very first day, as their little expedition pulled out east of Teheran toward the border, the officer suggested to Camacho that, since they would be traveling and working together for several weeks, they should get married. He already had one wife, he confessed, but another would be permissible under Moslem law and, he made it clear, quite desirable.

When Camacho demurred and pointed out that she eventually had to go back to her job in Paris, the officer offered generously to divorce her when the trip was over. That too, he said, was quite permissible under Moslem law and occasionally desirable. As a final gesture, he grandly said that if there were any children, Camacho could keep them. The marriage would be only "for the duration."

In such a situation not even Kessel could help his teammate much, and besides he had his own preoccupations. He was born in Russia and he could understand perfectly the loud-speaker broadcasts which howled through the night from the Soviet side of the border to the Iranian one. Most of the messages were propaganda, but one chilling announcement proclaimed that "two spies disguised as journalists are operating along the border. If you see them prowling around, shoot at sight."

Camacho, the acutely uncomfortable apex of the isosceles triangle, drew upon a large store of natural diplomacy to ward off the suitor without offending him—he was, after all, a crucial element in the success of the mission—and to protect Kessel by never letting him out of her sight so he could inadvertently stray across the border onto the Russian side.

The juggling act went on for an agonizing six weeks with very little compassion from New York: Don't worry about a thing, came one message, tell Kessel to buy two cases of vodka and for food you can just catch a sturgeon and squeeze it and get caviar.

All along the route, fighting off real wolves and cold, the team camped out in military posts. There was usually a wood-burning stove but often as not it had to be extinguished because the smoke was worse than the cold. In posts where there was a bed it was turned over to Camacho and then the men slept on the floor. If Camacho had to go to the bathroom in the night she was escorted by a soldier carrying an oil lantern and a rifle, stumbling down long paths to a hole in the ground. She went three weeks without taking off her clothes, much less having a bath, and on one occasion in which the group found a civilized home with a real family and a real bath in the courtyard, she was put off by the curiosity of her hosts. "Just as I was starting to peel off layer after layer I noticed that the door to my room was slightly ajar and there behind it an absolute column of wide eyes—papa, mama, all the kids, lined up to survey this foreign lady peeling."

Her suitor the officer, she swears, never changed his clothes in the entire six weeks. Perhaps he didn't have another set. By the time the assignment was finished and the officer bidden a grateful farewell, Camacho had dispatched 117 pages of typewritten captions and Kessel had taken more than 5,000 pictures. After all that, a total of three

CREDIT: DMITRI KESSEL © TIME INC.

Dita Camacho and her Iranian escort-suitor, strolling through snow on the border between Iran and the Soviet Union.

pages ran in the magazine on the shah's wedding, and eight pages—plus a cover—on Iran.

And our bedraggled heroes finally got back to Paris, four months after they had left for a nice quiet little story on the Aga Khan. Only the most informal poll has been taken among former Luce fellows, but it seems clear that Camacho and Kessel hold, at least, the Central Asian championship.

7

Twenty-three Lines of Forty-three

Of all the unsung heroes and heroines on the magazine, the in-house writer heard perhaps the least music. Deprived of the dogged but often delightful task of actually covering stories, these toilers were handed the reporters' or correspondents' reports, photostats of picture layouts, a handful of newsclips, and set to work.

Not the lightest of the crosses they bore was being asked what they did for *Life*.

"I write."

"You write? Write what? It's a picture magazine."

A close observer would note, however, that each picture had a caption, each page or spread had a small chunk of text. So many *Life* people came from newspapers that it was a matter of pride when they learned to say "caption" instead of "cut-lines," "textblock" instead of just plain "copy." *Life's* captions and blocks were meant to accompany, explain, sometimes even justify, the photographs themselves. They had, by logical decree, to "read out" of the photos: some reference to the pictures as well as the subject of the story had to appear in the first line or two.

Writers' orders always came, as if to computers, in numbers: "twenty-three lines of forty-three," or "five lines of eighteen." Into which "character count," meaning numbers of letters and spaces per line, they were required to cram all the applicable facts, a certain amount of evocative color, and "*Life* liveliness."

I'll never forget the first time I was permitted to try it. Ed Thompson asked if I thought I could put what he described as my overweening regard for the British Empire into a caption of two lines of 120. Of course, said I. On about the ninth attempt I managed it, and triumphantly I carried my whole two lines to his office. It then developed that what he really meant was could I identify about two dozen members of the British royal family and their noble kin, from left to right, in two lines of 120 and also express in the same space my regard for what they had wrought. Most of them had titles even longer than their names. I no longer recall just how this project all came out, but I cannot forget hacking away at the same two paltry lines for almost one entire day.

Layout was the problem. Pictures had precedence, words had to fit into the scraps of space left over. Furthermore, everything had to "square" upper left and lower right, with no unsightly white space at the end of a line. Dozens of people learned how to do it quite well, wearing out whole shelves of *Roget's Thesaurus* in the process, grappling with long names in short spaces, craftily making private lists of long and short words which meant roughly the same thing so they could be hurled into some breach some late night without the trouble of looking them all up.

One copy editor, Charles Elliott, became so fond of obscure words that he made a list of about ten of them every week on a file card, thumb-tacked the card to the wall by his desk, and set himself to get every single one of them into that week's issue of *Life*.

If textblocks were hard, captions were hell. The magazine style for many years was to use a "bold," or capitalized lead-in, to each caption. The bolds served as minor headlines and attention-getters for readers who hadn't yet learned how to "read" a photograph. Often they ran to such idiocies as "MAN WITH CIGAR at left is ward boss so-and-so," or carefully paired things like "PROCESSION'S END brings the troops and bands . . ." and next to it, "DAY'S END blazed with celebrational fireworks." Writers hated them, but editors defended them on the basis that they helped the reader understand salient points or piquant details in the photos which might otherwise have been overlooked.

As a mechanical aid to the daily discipline of writing to count, the magazine provided special copy paper like graph paper, with the entire page marked off into ten-letter segments. It saved a lot of time.

Immediately upon completion of his exercise in discipline, the writer trudged off to deliver his masterpiece to the copy room for typing and distribution. There ensued about half an hour of calm, followed by shot and shell from all directions. First usually was the researcher on the story, who almost always had a quarrel with some particular fact or word, and who was almost always correct. Fixing the copy to his or her satisfaction of course altered its length, one way or the other, and entailed some rewriting. Next would come a summons to the office of the copy editor, who was for most of us for two decades Joe Kastner. Though the entire office functioned on a first-name basis and the air of genial democracy was entirely genuine, there was still a delicate pecking order: researchers and checkers went to the offices of writers; writers got up and went to Joe Kastner; everybody in the place went to the office of the managing editor at the drop of a summons.

Kastner's manner with writers was mild and devilishly clever. His opening line was usually, "This is okay . . ." long pause . . . "except that I don't think it tracks, right in here." Or, "I really don't like this sentence. I don't know what I would like, but this isn't it."

While the writer squirmed, Joe's blue eyes wandered from the copy to the end of his pencil, out the window, off toward the closing schedule for the day, and finally back to the writer's face. Then frequently followed a gentle interrogation. "Do you know any more about this? Could you get the reporter to dig up some more stuff?"

His final words were, "Well, run it through again. Call me when you've finished, and bring it straight here."

Kastner's position was clear. "If I didn't trouble the writers, I wasn't doing my job. If a writer turned in a good story, I wanted to make it a very good story. If it was bad, I had to make the writer save it, if he could."

His most devastating blow was the simple remark, "This is boring." That one was calculated to send any writer screaming out of his office in a fury which often expended itself in considerably improved copy.

Kastner's techniques and psychology were impeccable. He had been one of *Life's* first writers and he bore the added distinction of being one of the few persons in the shop who could understand the mumbled instructions of both Henry Luce and Ed Thompson.

He got his own training from the magazine's first managing editor, John Shaw Billings. Billings always said that he wanted to keep *Life* "like a summer theater, in which everybody is expected to turn his hand to whatever needs doing." He believed that everyone should

© TIME INC.

Copy editor Joseph Kastner, left, *and managing editor Joseph Thorndike chastise an errant colleague in the old* Time-Life *building on Rockefeller Plaza.*

have fun putting out the product, but never should be permitted to take himself too seriously.

As part of the "summer theater" concept, he once took the whole original staff on a mid-week "weekend" to Chicago to visit the Donnelley plant. Young writer Kastner had just completed captions and textblocks for a story on Texas. His headline said simply "TEXAS" in enormous type, with the subhead, "IT IS BIG." Though he didn't consider these words exactly lyrical, Kastner was fascinated to see them actually appearing on paper as the presses rolled.

"I stood in front of those machines, with the great rolls of paper running through, four forms, eight pages, great foot-high gas flames roaring underneath to dry the ink, and *there was my creation coming off* . . . 'TEXAS,' 'IT IS BIG.' I couldn't tear myself away. I could have stood there all day and watched.

"I remember Billings saying to me later, 'I knew it was a mistake to let you see your words like that. Now you'll begin to take yourself seriously.' "

That general tone and attitude remained forever. It was company policy to inflate and deflate individual egos as they seemed to require it. George Hunt, twenty-eight years old when he went to *Life* from *Fortune* magazine, was made coeditor of the art department along with Margit Varga. He had written a book about his war experiences in the Pacific, *Coral Comes High,* he had written articles for *Fortune,* and he was a painter. When a *Life* story came up on Giotto, he wrote the textblock. It was his first effort on the newsmagazine, and his editor was Kastner.

"He took my copy, called me into his office, and said 'Look, I can't find anything wrong with this.' He put it through, straight through, and I was walking around on air. But he also said, 'You wait. Just wait.' Then came the time to write the black and white page on the life of Giotto and I wrote it with full confidence. I turned it in to Joe, and boy did he rip that apart! I revised it, rewrote it, rewrote it again. He really took me over the coals."

Above Kastner, or any other copy editor, still loomed the managing editor himself, whose initials were required upon any piece of copy meant for publication. Still, the scrawled "JK" at upper right was an enormous lift. One fledgling writer, faced with the illegible "JK" for the first time, asked veteran writer John Stanton what it meant. Stanton looked at it hard, peered over his glasses, and said, "Three of those, and two Wheaties boxtops, will get you an EKT [meaning the approving initials of Ed Thompson]."

After the agony of captions, textblocks, checkers, came that bane of the writers' existence, the headline. In this, all forces conspired against the writer. Managing editors and art directors seeking effective display were unmoved by writers' problems in accommodating the necessary words to the available space. Photographers would have been happy to have their products cover the entire page with no words at all. Researchers cared more about fact then imagery. Writing moles in their cages doing twenty-three by forty-three didn't have much clout. Now and again irresistible force inevitably met immovable object. On one such occasion a writer was summoned to do a headline on a story about an upheaval in Guatemala. Bernard Quint, the art director, had laid out a beautiful spread for which the headline was to consist of three words in descending order at the upper left hand of the page: three words whose count was laid out for five, four, and three characters. Dismayed, the writer began to calculate. Even if "Guatemala" were hyphenated, which it could not be, it wouldn't fit. Nor would "upheaval" or "revolution." In wordless apprehension the writer turned and looked for help from the colleagues surrounding him. There were never fewer than ten people in a layout session, all hanging over the backs and shoulders of the managing editor and art director.

Help came in the person of correspondent Ken Gouldthorpe. Perhaps emboldened by the fact that he had just breezed into town from Paris and was still feeling giddy, Gouldthorpe grasped the problem at a glance, decided that the art director was being capricious in laying out such an impossible head, and said in a very loud voice, "FINK WILL FIT." Those three words would have fit, pretty nearly. After a moment of silence, Quint was persuaded to change the layout to accommodate a more amenable headline space.

Writer Chuck Champlin, on one of his first headline marathons, didn't have such good luck. He was assigned a story on the marriage of Marilyn Monroe and Joe DiMaggio and he achieved a brilliant head: "A DIAMOND IS A MAN'S BEST FRIEND." Unfortunately it didn't fit, and the art director and managing editor refused to change the layout to accommodate it.

Problems of this nature created, in a corridor which connected the managing editor with the copy editor, a weird scene late on every closing night. Most of the magazine had been finished and dispatched but there were always three or four headlines which wouldn't fit, which someone didn't like, or which some poor writer had been unable to produce. Like farmers rushing to the aid of a neighbor who had broken his leg, writers congregated to "help with the chores." All those who had finished their own work wandered down to headline alley and pitched in. There were six or eight available typewriters; the free company liquor had been open for some time; it was the end of a hard week; most people were too hopped-up to want to trudge home to bed.

Thus the group effort to produce a headline began. It always reminded me of the joke about an infinite number of monkeys with an infinite number of typewriters who would, in an infinite number of days, write *Hamlet*.

Particularly odious were headlines for a spread, most of which had to "jump the gutter," that is cross the centerfold where the staples were. *Life* style decreed that one could never break a word across the gutter. The head had to fit perfectly on both the left- and right-hand pages.

One night at least six of us were struggling with a head for General MacArthur's funeral. The photo showed the funeral cortege proceeding down Seventh Avenue, past Pennsylvania Station which at that time was being demolished, or about to be.

Typewriters clattered with abortive efforts:

AN OLD SOLDIER SAYS FAREWELL . . . no.

GLOOMY DAY FOR A GLOOMY PROCESSION . . . no, too long.

OLD SOLDIER PROCEEDS . . . no.

FINAL FAREWELL TO A WAR HERO . . . pretty banal.

FLOURISHES FOR A FURIOUS . . . no.

WE SAY GOODBYE . . . no.

HIS COUNTRYMEN SALUTE . . . no. Nobody in the whole picture was saluting. A lot of them weren't even looking.

Finally, writer David Snell arose from his Underwood with a shout of triumph. "I've got it, I've got it," he said. "And it fits"—LEAD US NOT INTO PENN STATION. Unfortunately, somebody lost courage and that headline never ran.

Young writer Jordan Bonfante was more fortunate. He was landed late one night with the impossible task of relating, in one textblock and one headline, two wildly incompatible photographs whose shapes had intrigued the managing editor. On the left was a horizontal photo of a semicircle of young pianists playing in a group recital. On the right, facing this picture, was the vertical semicircle of a radar dish. The shapes were lovely, but how on earth to wed them in words? Perspiring freely, Bonfante produced a short textblock which was adequate to the problem. But he simply couldn't get a headline.

Luckily for him, George Hunt was in one of his fey moods. George sometimes worried that maybe he was too pedantic for the public, and occasionally he issued an order that he wanted crazy headlines. Bonfante, having been told that it was one of George's crazy weeks, went back to his desk and produced a gem: "GET YOUR PLANET-PICKING PARABOLA OFF MY PIANO." The words didn't make much sense but they sounded funny, so Hunt initialed them, and they ran as written.

From these epic battles with space and the typrwriter, *Life*rs emerged with strange little tics. I catch myself typing imaginary headlines with my fingers on the car steering wheel while on long drives. Dave Snell once told me that he dreams in headlines while having a nightmare. Joe Kastner has found that he cannot play Scrabble: "I look at all those letters, and it makes my head hurt."

□ □ □

Beyond the headline, beyond the checker, beyond the copy editor and the managing editor and any number of kibitzers, there loomed for the hapless writer one last hurdle: the final fit.

Words, sentences, paragraphs, even individual letters, had to fit the space assigned. Despite all the careful counting, the juggling, the thumbing of *Thesaurus,* captions and textblocks persisted in coming out half a line long, or ten characters short once they had finally been set in type. This disaster was heralded by a phone call from the copy room, inquiring politely, "Could you come down for a minute?" Adding or subtracting at this point was called "greening" in office jargon, because it was done with a green pencil to indicate that the changes were for space, not fact. Armed with a green pencil, the writer trudged down the back stairs, was handed his words in computer-set lineage, and set to work to fix them.

© TIME INC.

Managing editor George Hunt struggles with the "fit" on his editors' note aboard the Churchill funeral flight. He is using Life's *special triple-spaced and calibrated copy paper, designed to make the writer's task easier.*

One of the copy-room women, a southern belle named Virginia Sadler, who was the cheeriest person on the floor despite a tragic confinement to a wheelchair, was particularly adept at coping with "greens," and she was horrified one night to see a new girl mark copy with the terse instruction to "green two or three characters, some small."

The order became a joke among writers, but its implication was horrendous. One night Robert Wallace, one of the stars of the writing staff, received instructions to "green two or three, some small," on a headline which read OF HORSE AND FOOT.

He could possibly have greened "and," so the head read OF HORSE, FOOT but then the whole cadence would be lost. He could have greened "of," maybe, and left the head HORSE AND FOOT. But this lost not only cadence but also meaning.

In frustration, Wallace sat down and typed neatly, on the lined and measured paper, the following reply:

Of land and sea
Of ant and bee
Of cock and hen
Of pig and pen
Of fish and bait
Of love and hate
Of rave and rant
OF COURSE I CAN'T

A small layout adjustment solved the problem that time, but normally submission was inevitable for the writer. Nobody could argue with type despite jokes about type-stretchers and type-shrinkers. Things had to fit and the writer had to make them fit.

Some writers were notoriously fast, others slow. The first master of what became known as the "four-minute textblock" was A. B. C. Whipple, who later became managing editor of *Life's* international editions and still later an editor in the books division. In his writing days, Cal was the terror of the checkers. He seemed never to read anything they gave him. Instead he made up, from his endlessly inventive brain, whatever came to mind. It often bore little resemblance to established facts.

Despite all this, he was considered by the editors the most amenable writer on the magazine. Thompson recalls that he would call Cal in to talk over a brief piece of copy and would begin by saying, "Now, Cal, right here . . ." and before he could finish the sentence Cal had vanished, shouting over his shoulder "I see what you mean, Ed."

"Half the time," Thompson says, "I would finish my sentence just because I had started it. By the time I had finished, Cal was back with a totally rewritten version of his textblock."

At the other extreme was Marshall Smith, for years sports editor of *Life*. Smith ran a tight ship of young reporters, referring to his operation as "Smith's School for Boys." Routinely he shoveled off the married ones to some other department: in his view one was married only to the magazine, and young men with wives were thus undependable. Smith's school for boys produced many a notable story and even more notable parties, but when Marshall himself sat down to write it was instant crisis. He froze at the typewriter. Hours, days, weeks would pass as he grappled with a long piece. He tried everything from booze to Turkish baths to loosen up, but mostly they didn't help. Everybody on his floor learned to tiptoe around while Smith was "with textpiece."

There were always star writers who seldom had to bother about twenty-three lines of forty-three: Lincoln Barnett, Robert Coughlan, Paul O'Neil, Ernest Havemann, etc. These stars were given almost unlimited time to produce long articles for the magazine, and those who wanted to do their own reporting were permitted to do so. They worked a lot harder than a lot of staffers ever thought they did, and most of them were as scrupulously punctual as the lesser toilers over captions.

Now and again, of course, somebody got hung up. Shana Alexander managed to dilly-dally for seven years over an assigned article on Marlon Brando, with some support from Brando himself, who once refused to see her after she had trekked at *Life*'s expense all the way to Tahiti for an interview. Shana did, of course, write quite a number of other things as the seven years crept by.

The cliff-hanger of all time was provided by dapper Robert Coughlan, a veteran who was once described by one of the magazine's text editors as the best article writer in the U.S.

Coughlan had a formidable subject, "The Search for the Historical Jesus." Still, he had had formidable subjects before, and he had always delivered. He had also always one-upped every male on the staff by sheer sartorial splendor. Paul O'Neil wrote wearing his "lucky" sweater, a tattered remnant of what it must have been before either moths or dogs got at it. Dick Meryman wrote with ruffled hair and a tangle of tapes and snippets of transcriptions, surrounded by reels of Scotch tape with which to piece together his bits. Marshall Smith wrote with an ice bag clutched to his head. Keith Wheeler paced the halls, muttering. Dick Oulahan roamed around swearing off both cigarettes and liquor. James Mills vanished from the office, to commune with himself and his contacts. Almost ever other male writer, on whatever level, wore the Thompson uniform: tie and jacket off, shirt sleeves rolled two flips from wrist to mid-arm.

Robert Coughlan, on the other hand, never had hysterics, never used a tape recorder, never wore a sweater in the office. Furthermore, he never took off his tie, never unbuttoned his shirt collar, never rolled up his sleeves. He had been seen, by almost everybody, typing away calmly with his jacket on and his cufflinks gleaming.

"A man in such perfect charge of his personal elegance must be in equal charge of his writing" decreed then–text editor Ralph Graves. He had not a qualm about Coughlan, nor did John Thorne, editor in charge of the special year-end issue on Christianity of which Coughlan's piece was a major part. In any issue of *Life,* but particularly in the specials or the double specials which closed the year, pages went to press on an expanded schedule. Early forms closed weeks before the publication date so they could be printed and set aside to await binding. Graves and Thorne scheduled Bob Coughlan's piece for the earliest form. Coughlan didn't make it.

Graves and Thorne pressured somebody else into producing a story early so it could close. They told Coughlan he could have another week. He was grateful, and he was still typing. He looked cool, unworried. His extra week passed, then two weeks, then three weeks. By now issue editor Thorne was anything but cool and unflappable. He rushed into Graves's office one day and announced that Coughlan had *locked his door.*

Nobody ever locked his door at *Life.* Such behavior was considered aggressively unfriendly, insulting, selfish, and furthermore implied illicit sex on company time. It was much better form to slip off to a nearby hotel, carrying a Manhattan telephone directory in a flight bag as "luggage," if the need for a nooner became imperative.

No such suspicion devolved upon Coughlan, so Thorne proceeded to the locked door and banged on it. He reported back to Graves that Coughlan was annoyed by this unseemly interruption, and said that if the editors wanted the article on Jesus he was not to be disturbed again. Also, no phone calls.

Deadlines came and went, and finally Thorne was driven to surreptitious surveillance. Coughlan's office was at the end of writers' row, and next to it on the inside corridor was an empty researcher's office with a high window which gave onto Coughlan's cage. Thorne discovered that if he climbed up on the vacant researcher's desk, stood on tiptoe, and tilted his glasses to strengthen them, he could see the page number of the sheet in Coughlan's typewriter.

Carefully and silently he tiptoed in, craned, memorized, and clambered down. Coughlan was really working, he reported to Graves. One day he said, "He's on page twenty-eight." Next morning he reported excitedly that, "He's on page thirty-two." The euphoria didn't last: next morning, with terrible sadness, Thorne reported that "Coughlan's back on page twenty-seven." There matters rested for days, until Thorne rushed into a Graves story conference to shout, wild-eyed, "Coughlan's got his tie off!"

Eventually, having run out of every deadline in the endless arsenal of a tolerant magazine, Coughlan finished the piece. It was excellent, and it ran. Yet it remains a milestone of sorts.

"I am sure," says Graves, "it is the only story in the history of *Life* which closed on a crash news deadline when the most recent information contained therein was two thousand years old."

Cuckoos in the Studio

''Studio photography'' has a nice quiet upper-class ring to it. The words conjure drapes, carpets, discreet lighting, imaginative backdrops, and a resident genius photographer with eloquent hands, endless creativity, and probably quite a lot of temperament.

So it must have been with Canadian portraitist Karsh, from whom *Life* often bought photographs. Or Philippe Halsman, who created in a studio his famous photograph of Salvador Dali in which he out-Dali-ed even the maestro. Halsman somehow persuaded Dali to leap into the air—repeatedly—his waxed mustaches flying, and then took his picture while airborne amid a welter of sheets of flying water and sailing black cats—both of the latter flung into the air and into the picture when Halsman shouted ''*allez!*'' to a swarm of assistants.

So it was also that Gjon Mili, the master of motion, made some of his spectacular multiple exposures of dancers, stopping them in motion with stroboscopic flashes yet permitting them to execute a full fluid movement in a series of blending and overlapping images.

These men worked mostly in their own studios and seldom darkened the door of the *Life* studio, which was neither nice nor quiet nor even upper-class, except in its utility. *Life*'s studio looked like an abandoned—and possibly condemned—gymnasium in a building in the west fifties. It was vast, grey-walled, dusty, echoing, and for years un–air-conditioned. It would have been the perfect setting for a nineteenth-century madhouse which in fact it was, give or take a century.

On any given day there could be a full-scale boxing ring set up in one corner, waiting for Muhammad Ali to turn up and spar for the sports photographers. Somewhere to the lee of this would be, say, the battle of Waterloo, carefully reconstructed with hundreds of toy soldiers and yards of papier-mâché backgrounds, waiting for photographer Yale Joel and a brace of consulting professors and researchers to capture the action in living color for a history series, or a *Life* spectacular on great battles. Several yards from Ali, beyond the battle of Waterloo, hygienically separated from the sweat of combat by nice clean drapes and sparking equipment was the *Life* kitchen set up to do Great Dinners, among other things.

Over toward the door, in the area nearest to the freight elevator, was an expanse known loosely as "the zoo." This was where photographers like Ralph Morse, Mark Kauffman, Eliot Elisofon, brought their wild animals—alligators, gibbons, kangaroos, steers.

And around the periphery of the working floor were ladders, step or fire, up which everyone could flee should Ali, the cooks, the soldiers, or the wild animals suddenly turn menacing.

All manner of mania went on in the studio. Ralph Morse once brought in quite a large alligator—such items can be rented, in Manhattan, by a diligent search of the Yellow Pages—to take a picture of a pop singer whose latest hit song involved New Orleans and an alligator. It seemed logical to put singer, musicians, and alligator into the studio for a knockout full-page page photo of a singer and a song which were headed for the top of the charts. The singer grasped his guitar, straddled the alligator, the combo started to play, Morse focused—and then the strobe lights flashed.

There seems to be something about strobe lights which infuriates animals. The docile alligator suddenly went mad and roared around the studio snapping its impressive jaws at everything and everybody. Some fled shrieking up ladders; a few hardy souls poked at the rampant beast with anything handy. He, she, or it—nobody had sufficient courage or curiosity to establish which—chewed one leg off a tripod and was working on the ladders when the alligator's keeper had the presence of mind to find a two-by-four and swat it a good one on the top of the head. This calmed the beast so that a muzzle could be slipped on and the picture-taking proceeded.

Philippe Halsman invented and executed the famous photograph of "Dali with cats" in his own studio, then sold the best picture to Life. *The cats and the water were thrown and photographed twenty-six times before Halsman got the right composition. Here are some near misses: Dali getting ready; water covering Dali's face; an unwanted secretary in the background; a flying chair blocking the artist's face.*

The lights had the same effect on what appeared to onlookers to be at least a half-ton steer. That particular effort was for a year-end special issue on food, one essay of which was to show the progress of a new-born calf from barn to feed lot to slaughterhouse to wholesaler-retailer and table—in the process accounting for the high price of beef on the table. Eliot Elisofon was assigned to photograph it, but he flatly refused to run all over the countryside to do so. He decreed that in order to have perfect lighting conditions and control—the story was to be in color—it would have to be done in the studio in New York.

Reporter Clara Nicolai was appointed handmaiden to Elisofon on this occasion. After days of telephoning, she found a farmer in Duchess County who raised Angus cattle and had animals of all ages which he would transport to New York, for a fee. She then found an animal hostelry in Manhattan which advertised that it could house "everything from a flea to an elephant." That done, she set about getting the props, which for this particular assignment included one rolltop desk with chair, a spittoon, a red barn door, several bales of hay, a section of post and rail fence, a cattle trailer and ramp, feeding trough, two bags of oats, meathooks on a traveler, a butcher's showcase, a chopping block with appropriate knives and cleavers, and six male models to take the parts of the cowboy, feeder, commission man, agency man, meat packer, and butcher—all with appropriate clothes.

Procurement of male models provided the giddiest moment for Nicky because the rodeo happened to be in town and a couple of calls produced "twenty great big hunks of cowboys with boots, rodeo belts, hats, and all. I didn't know whether to look at their biceps, or maybe their teeth, so I just chose three of the ruggedest-looking ones . . ."

On the appointed day the farmer arrived with his truck, his son, and the half-ton steer. He had decided that they must photograph "the big boy" first because he was likely to lose 100 pounds a day in the hectic atmosphere of Manhattan and the farmer wanted to take him home as soon as possible. When they arrived at the studio the freight elevator was firmly lodged on the ground floor, its operator having been struck down by a germ. Undaunted, Nicolai figured out how to run the thing. She did close her eyes and shrink into the corner as the steer came aboard, but somehow she managed to get it up to the fourth floor. Cowboys, hay bales, barn door, lights, and photographer all were in place and "the big boy" was led onstage. He stood calmly enough at first, with photographer Elisofon crooning to him about how beautiful he was, and what long glorious eyelashes he had. Then the strobes went off and the steer went off. He shot from behind the barn door as if from a gun, galloped all over the place in wide-eyed panic, nostrils flaring, knocking things over, depositing in his nervousness what we used to call "cow pies" all over the studio. Everybody chased him—the farmer, the farmer's son, the three cowboys, reporter Nicolai, and photographer Elisofon. Everybody, that is, except city-bred Tony Triolo, the studio assistant on the assignment, who had never before been close to anything larger than a dog. Tony fled up a ladder to the balcony and refused to come down until somebody got "that wild animal" out of there.

The farmer, wisely, had brought along some tranquilizer injections and with the help of the cowboys he managed to administer quite a large dose. Almost instantly the "wild animal" turned into Ferdinand the Bull, but there still remained the mess in the studio. Elisofon ordered Triolo to clean it up, and Triolo shouted from the balcony that he hadn't been hired to "clean up bullshit" and anyway he didn't know how to.

"Go to a hardware store," said Elisofon. "Buy a garbage can with a tight-fitting lid, buy a shovel, and buy some sawdust."

This Triolo eventually did; all the actors got back into place, and the picture was taken. If examined closely today, it reveals the tranquilized condition of poor "big boy": his tongue is all but lolling out, his eyes more dreamy than normal. He lost 200 pounds on that one traumatic day, Nicolai recalls, and Triolo may have lost ten himself.

One would hardly think that simple stories on food could produce much derring-do, but even food *not* on the hoof inspired a lot of shenanigans in the studio. Elisofon, a passionate amateur cook, who once wrote a book called *Food Is a Four Letter Word,* was known for such imaginative creations as a whole story called "Cooking on Ice." For this epic he had persuaded an ice concern to freeze food inside giant blocks of ice and then produce another ton of the stuff which he could garnish with dishes of fruit, glasses of parfait, crisp salads, and the like.

When the ice arrived at the studio it developed that the chunks were too big and awkward to be slid into the elevator. Photographer Elisofon became apoplectic as his story began to trickle away, and a rather large crowd gathered outside on the sidewalk to peer at what appeared to be real food locked into square glaciers. Finally, husky icemen were produced who could carry the story upstairs. Two Time Inc. maintenance men arrived with enormous mops to swab the decks while the pictures were made, and Elisofon shot frantically against time as the entire modern living staff slipped and slithered across the floor to adjust dishes and glasses on the unstable melting surface of the ice blocks. One picture involved a scooped-out watermelon filled with fruit and garnished with rosebuds. Reporter Jeanne Stahl's primary task was to keep squeezing drops of water on the roses with an eye dropper as the strong studio lights evaporated her previous efforts. With her other hand she kept the watermelon on an even keel as the cracked ice which surrounded it melted faster than the ice block on which it rested.

At the end of a long, hard day, the only casualties were two parfait glasses which slipped off a melting glacier and shattered on the floor.

Less harrowing, but somewhat more complex, was a story on "How to Carve Six Roasts," which ran in the December 17, 1961 issue. Food expert James A. Beard was hired for this, as well as Max

O. Cullen of the Meat Institute. These two did most of the carving for the cameras. But the story also involved drawings by *Life* artist James Lewicki which were to show the inner bone structure of a roast before it was carved, and thus guide the hands of less-experienced carvers than Beard and Cullen.

Now a classic problem arose. How was Lewicki to know the precise inner structure of a leg of lamb, a suckling pig, or half a cow? How indeed except through the magic of X-ray. The whole gory problem ended up being hauled into the office of Roberta Jones, head lab technician for the Time Inc. medical department. The unflappable Miss Jones, who spent many a summer vacation with camera and alpenstock investigating ruins around the Mediterranean, hardly batted an eye. She photographed the roasts, one by one, on fourteen-by-seventeen-inch sheets of special X-ray film and developed the negatives herself. The important factor in X-ray exposures is the thickness of the part to be photographed, so she went around holding up bits of raw meat to various parts of her colleagues' anatomies and calculating the exposure therefrom. A leg of lamb has about the thickness of a big man's shoulder, she decided, and she X-rayed it thusly.

From her meticulous work came all the details artist Lewicki needed. There was one poignant footnote: The suckling pig, which had to be X-rayed on two film sheets which were then spliced together, had suffered, at some time before its demise, two broken ribs which went untreated because nobody knew they were broken.

The standard food stories—how to carve, how to serve, food production and cost—had become a bore to most of the staff and probably to the majority of the readers before Eleanor Graves took over the modern living department in the sixties. Having exacted from managing editor Hunt a promise that she wouldn't have to do food, Eleanor launched herself into a series on interesting houses, pop sociology, imaginative furniture, and the like. Then one fateful day she was summoned to Hunt's office and told that the game plan had changed. *Life* needed some food stories.

Faced with necessity—nobody liked saying ultimatum around there—she agreed. But only if, in the tradition of the magazine and every department in it, she had a free hand to make it the best food coverage in the world. To which end she asked, and got, a pair of pros who had never been known as food specialists—photographers John Dominis and Mark Kauffman. Free-lancer Fred Lyon joined the crew later.

Rising to the challenge, good eaters Dominis and Kauffman repaired to the studio with Mrs. Graves. There they spent days deciding how to approach their task. From the conferences came consensus: they would begin with a great picture, and progress from that to the

Great Dinner. After one big, beautiful, saliva-invoking closeup of the meal's central dish, they could follow with a complete menu. Though not an earth-shaking idea, it was a new approach for a food series and a departure from earlier *Life* style which had tended rather toward "40 desserts for 40 days," all spread out like a midwestern church supper.

One of the first of the Great Dinners series featured *paella*. Professional cooks under Eleanor's supervision prepared the chicken, shellfish, rice, and vegetable dish, and added the saffron which gave it not only flavor but also color. All went well until Dominis focused his eight-by-ten ground glass view camera on the succulent end product.

"Rice is funny stuff," he noted for the first time. "Some of it gets kind of wrinkled and looks, well, just *homely* in a closeup."

"I had no idea what the detail of a really big closeup photograph would do to a dish," Mrs. Graves reported.

In the end she and Dominis spent hours with tweezers, auditioning each grain of rice and placing the handsomest individuals into the foreground of the picture. When all was in order with the beautiful rice up front, they shot, then fidgeted while the color lab developed the transparencies. Out they came eventually and with them—horrors—an uninvited guest at the feast. Eleanor Graves remembers it as a cockroach; Dominis thinks it was a fly. In either case this bit of verisimilitude settled on the rim of the dish in the first photographs, then moved to a more comfortable and no doubt more rewarding position right smack on the food for later ones. There it remained, unseen by the transfixed Great Dinners creators, for the entire picture session.

Whether cockroach or fly, it looked to both editor and photographer "as big as a shrimp" on the huge photos, and the entire production, cooking and rice and tweezers and all, had to be repeated the next day in the studio.

One of the many criteria for Great Dinners was that they had to look good as well as taste good. This required endless ingenuity, experimentation, and imaginative backgrounds. One of Eleanor's favorite dishes was lemon soup, but by her own admission "delicious lemon soup in a bowl looks like . . . well, like maybe a lemon milkshake. Not very inspiring." To jazz up the picture, they decided to put the soup in a beautiful silver tureen, carefully sprayed with beads of cool-looking "perspiration," and photograph it against a background of whole eggs, the other main ingredient in the soup. Eleanor, the photographer, and lab assistants spent hours selecting, washing, and gluing into egg cartons a background "wall" of the lovely shapes.

When all was in order the lights went on, the photographer started to focus, and the eggs started dropping out of the cartons and smashing on the studio floor. The heat of the lights had melted the glue holding the eggs in place. At this point two gallant studio assistants stepped forth with a suggestion: they could suck all the eggs dry and glue in only the very light shells, holes backward.

"And there they sat, those lovely guys, solemnly sucking ten dozen eggs and spitting out the contents into buckets," recalls Mrs. Graves with awe. "It almost made me sick just to watch, but they did it. We got our beautiful egg background and the men took the buckets of egg goop home to feed their dogs."

On one memorable occasion, while shooting barbecued Cornish game hen, the crew managed to set fire to Mark Kauffman's studio and had to evacuate the premises while New York City firemen dealt with the Cornish hen, the barbecue, and the studio.

A photograph of enormous hotdogs proved so provocative that Gore Vidal and Beverly Pepper in Rome made an official request for permission to use it as the cover of their *Myra Breckenridge Cookbook.* Request denied.

For a full page called "Pears Made Perfect," the Great Dinners genii strung up each individual pear on a string, hung dozens of them in precise design, and then shot through a scrim which made the whole set-up look like a painting and which also disguised the strings.

All of this required hours, even days and weeks of work, and considerable expense, but produced one of the most popular series the magazine ever ran. Mrs. Graves, Dominis, and Kauffman loved every minute. If they decided to do a Mexican dish, they were entitled—nay, constrained—to eat at all the best Mexican resturants in Manhattan in order to select and perfect a single great dish and an accompanying menu. Nobody ever told them to hurry, nobody ever refused to pay for their exploratory dinners. Eleanor learned early on that she had to prepare every single menu at least once in her own kitchen, so she could present the entire thing like a battle plan, with explicit directions about how and when to do what. Her husband Ralph, no cook but a connoisseur, happily ate four or five editions of the same Great Dinner before it was pronounced ready for the magazine, and he recalls that his wife was so overwhelmed by the success of the series and the resultant expectations of anyone invited to their home for dinner that for months she refused to cook for guests. On company nights in this period they customarily sent out to Chez Pearl Wong and dined grandly on sent-in Chinese cuisine.

Part of the series' success was of course Eleanor's determination to achieve perfection. Now and again she was defeated by the fact that some dishes refuse, stubbornly, to look delectable. Such was the fate of *osso buco,* which everyone loved to eat but couldn't bear to look at, close up. Time after time they photographed it; time after time they rejected it for publication.

One break-through of the series was the insistence that only real food be photographed. The first cook hired for the project was a veteran of women's magazine cookery and always used shaving cream for whipped cream, marbles for cherries, cigarette smoke for steam. These were time-honored traditions in food photography, but for *Life* they would never do.

This cook departed, to be followed by a German woman who wore a severe air and a Mary Poppins hat, and who came accompanied by her sister. These two were hard at work on a Great Dinner one day when reporter Alix Kerr rushed into the studio with two plastic bags, containing the still-pulsing liver and kidneys of a skid-row derelict who had recently expired and been taken to a city morgue for autopsy. The cooks surely must have noted, but not recognized the significance of, a model of the human body which had been reclining for days on a special catafalque in the studio. Photographer Ralph Morse and science reporter Kerr were working on a story about medical breakthroughs in the replacement of parts of the body. Aided by medical experts, they had assembled and arranged in the proper position all the replaceable parts except the kidney and the liver. Having arranged with New York City authorities to lend them these organs at the first opportunity—they couldn't keep them for more than a couple of hours, because by city law no body can be buried without all of its parts—Morse and Kerr had been sitting around chewing their nails and waiting for four days. Finally the telephone call came, reporter Kerr leaped into a taxi, and returned triumphant.

The precious organs were a little too bloody and messy for a neat *Life* picture, however, so Kerr repaired to the kitchen to tidy them up. When the startled cooks learned what they were they turned white, then red, then white again. The chief cook put on her Mary Poppins hat and announced that nothing would induce her to work in such a place. Storming out, she was followed by her sister. It took concentrated cajolery, a raise, and a couple of weeks to get them back to the studio.

A well-kept secret of the studio was how well the Great Dinners staff dined after a photograph session. There was feast after feast as they ate up the finished product, usually accompanied by a select guest list invited over from the main building. On one day even Muhammad Ali ate genially with the staff, after his manager had advised them please to put away the liquor and even the wine, because his man is a teetotaler.

That exotic occasion was surpassed quite by accident late one night, and was unrecorded except in photographs taken by the participants. These photos appear here in print for the first time.

It all began when, as part of a special food issue which also involved the big steer, the editors decided to produce a feature called "How to Improve your Kitchen." With the help of a home economics expert from Cornell University, the idea was to select an average kitchen, reproduce it in the studio, and then chronicle in photographs some suggested improvements possible with the expenditure of, say, $200 or $500 or $1,000.

For the "before" picture they selected a pleasant Greenwich Village kitchen belonging to friends of staffer Jozefa Stuart. Reporters Laura Bell and Clara Nicolai spent days measuring and sketching the size and shape of the Village kitchen; the size and position of window, sink, stove, refrigerator; and taking a precise inventory of every bottle, can, container and utensil in the kitchen, together with its locale. All this was faithfully reproduced in the studio down to such details as whether the original kitchen had had on its shelves a can of Bumblebee tuna or Chicken of the Sea tuna.

When all was in order the first photographs were made. Then, with the Cornell expert and the staff dancing attendance, an expert carpenter, who happened to be Van Wyck Brooks's son, crafted new sets and kitchen refinements. With each new configuration all the pots and pans and kettles and bottles and cans had to be arranged in the new setting for the next day's shooting. The reporters worked day and night—days with Elisofon, nights setting up for the next day's take. One late afternoon, because of snafus in the lighting system, they finished early and knew they would have to try the same picture again next day. Thus no need to rearrange the pots and pans, thus a night off.

Feeling in a "whee" mood they did what just about every other *Life* reporter did on an unexpected evening off: they called in at the Three Gs, an Italian spa on West Forty-eighth Street which was home away from home to everyone from managing editor to office boy.

Once ensconced at "the Gs," warmed and sustained by friends and familiar surroundings, one tended to ignore the passage of time. By about eleven o'clock the group had dwindled to reporters Nicolai, Joann McQuiston, Jean Strong, and Valerie Vondermuhll. At this hour they were ravenous but the cook there always went home, perhaps in self-defense, at about 8:00 P.M. In vain the ladies pleaded with the waiter to admit them to the kitchen where they would be happy to stir up their own spaghetti. The waiter was sorry but adamant. He hadn't the right to let strangers into the kitchen.

Suddenly Nicolai remembered the studio, the kitchen, the set-up for next day's shooting. Her companions recall that she actually shouted "Eureka!" before leading them over to the stores. There were greens in the refrigerator, liquor bottles on the shelves, wine in a fiasco, packages of spaghetti yearning to be opened, and even a can of clams for clam sauce. Two hours later, blissfully full of goodies, the group set itself to washing up and making order. Everything was easily replaceable on the shelves except the can of clams. There was no other, and where could they buy clams even in Manhattan at 1:00 A.M.? Inspiration struck again—they fished the empty can from the garbage, carefully soaked its label off, then glued it back on upside down and set the can back on the shelves wrong side up with the opened top well hidden.

While this was going on McQuiston, rummaging around in the murky background, came upon several trunks of costumes. None of them dreamed that the studio also had costumes, but there they were, including several frilly and irresistible ballerina's tutus. Now once upon a time reporters McQuiston and Nicolai had both attended Barnard College, and one of Barnard's great annual events was Greek Games, with modern dance.

Naturally they had to don the tutus and give a demonstration for the benefit of reporters Strong and Vondermuhll. Off with everything, on with the tutus, which lacked several inches of closing in the back, but no matter.

Nicolai recalls what followed with awe.

"I was the prize dullard in modern dancing at Barnard. It took me three months to get promoted from a horse to a swan, which was the most it had ever taken anybody. But that night Joann inspired me. We did classic ballet; we did modern dance; we did everything. All very ladylike . . ."

Except that they got carried away by the presence, in the studio, of an enormous white paper background draped from the ceiling to the floor and strewn with beautiful-yard-wide pillows. It was the set-up for some complex studio photo the next day, but the dancers found it irresistible. They cavorted all over it in their bare feet, leaving grubby footprints, and even did high kicks which left some footprints at incredible heights up the back of the paper. At roughly 4:00 A.M. the program ended and the ladies of the ballet went home to bed.

Next day, photographer Henry Groskinsky arrived to do his set-up shot, took one horrified look at the paper backdrop, and rushed back to the *Time-Life* building to report to lab chief George Karas that *somebody* had had an "orgy" in the studio. There were "nude female footprints," he reported, all over the backdrop and even up the

© VALERIE VONDERMUHLL

Danseuses *Joann McQuiston,* left, *and Clara Nicolai do their stuff in the studio.*

wall. While Karas was still checking to find out which photographers had keys to the studio that night and could have hosted the orgy, Nicolai got wind of the inquiry and turned herself in.

She explained to Karas exactly what had happened, offered to do whatever possible to make up for the inconvenience to Groskinsky. She could hardly finish for the roars of Karas's laughter.

"Forget it," he said. "And above all DON'T TELL HENRY. He's having such a wonderful time thinking about that orgy . . ."

9

Manners, Morals, and Lawsuits

In the heady pursuit of a picture which electrifies, a story which titillates, a headline which sings, journalism can go agley.

Sometimes *Life* did.

One of its more innocent breaches of propriety occurred in 1952, when the popular feature ''*Life* Goes to a Party'' included two pages on a quaint new folk diversion called the ''fumble party.'' The event took place in Denver, Colorado, and *Life* noted happily that its host was ''the owner of a piano company'' and the guests included ''a state senator, the granddaughter of a former U.S. senator, and the daughter of an oil company president.''

What could be more respectable than that? Well, the game could. A fumble party, it turned out, involved a sort of blind man's bluff for grownups in which one player was made ''it'' and sent from the room. Then the room was plunged into darkness and the guests exchanged clothing with each other, arranged themselves in any manner they saw fit, and ''it'' was summoned back to fumble around and identify people. If ''it'' guessed right, the unmasked temporary transvestite was made to be "it" and if "it" guessed wrong then he or she had to submit to some cute punishment like a dunking in the family shower.

The Denver bureau, which sometimes felt itself at a geographical disadvantage in the hot competition for space in the magazine, had perhaps oversold the story as the beginning of either a trend or a fad.

When the fumble party story arrived in New York, eagle-eyed Marian MacPhail, chief of research, spotted it instantly as a journalistic Molotov cocktail. All that fumbling around in the dark, girls giggling over trying to zip the flys on borrowed pants, and, horrors, what research described as "a tangle of bodies, arms and legs" on the floor. She went straight to managing editor Thompson and got the story killed.

But it didn't stay killed. Within days Thompson and MacPhail happened to be away simultaneously on business or vacation trips, and the mantle of management fell on assistant managing editor Maitland Edey and assistant research chief Muriel Hall. Edey and Hall, innocents both, accepted this odd game not only as perhaps a fad but also as perhaps of sociological significance: an innocuous effort to make contact across the emotional void left by the end of World War II, the estrangement over Korea?

Whatever their reasons, they ran it. Instantly the roof fell in. Readers flung down their pens in frustration and telephoned. Important members of the board of directors sallied forth from their ivory towers to the *Life* editorial floors to register their complaints. Alarums and confusions rattled the building and there were dire rumors of firings. To the credit of the organization, nobody was fired and the furor died down.

Seen from the permissive vantage point of the seventies, those were strange days. In 1952 some stern Puritan mores were in force, and an unofficial "morals committee" ruled the pages of *Life*. Head man of the morals committee was an insouciant Irish-American named Bill Gallagher, possessed of twice his own weight in charm and the dirtiest mind on the magazine. It was his proud boast that it took a dirty mind to run a clean magazine, and he proved it every week. Everybody adored him, and when he died not of the cirrhosis of the liver which he had so diligently courted but of cancer, our only comfort was that Bill had to the end persuaded the doctor to give him his daily infusion of booze intravenously.

Assisting Gallagher were Marian MacPhail and copy chief Kastner. It was they who had to point out to young Andrew Heiskell that he couldn't say, of heiress Barbara Hutton falling down on a ski slope, that the lady had left "a million-dollar hole in the snow."

Writer John Stanton once was handed a spread on which were combined two weddings: Rita Hayworth to crooner Dick Haymes and, on a facing page, the marriage of Baron Robert Silvercruys, the Belgian ambassador, to Rosemary McMahon, widow of Senator Brian McMahon. The impropriety of this juxtaposition of events was obvious to all, but poor Stanton had to describe it. He labored mightily, and produced twin headlines which pointed up the difference in the two weddings: "DIGNITY RULES . . ." on one page, "HOTEL PRESS AGENT PRESIDES . . ." on the other. He also was careful to describe the Belgian ambassador as aristocratic and silver-haired, and he marched off to the copy room with his masterpiece. Within ten minutes he was back, gloomy and dragging his feet.

"It turns out," he reported, that you cannot say of any aristocratic, silver-haired bridegroom that he has 'an erect posture.' "

Double entendres were the joy of the staff and the bane of the morals committee. Someone was always having to explain to someone else that we couldn't say "MAYOR'S WIFE HAS HER FIRST AFFAIR" to headline a story on a respectable woman's first formal dinner in the mayor's mansion; or that a caption on a young couple looking over mattresses (for a story on home furnishings for the modern living department) should not read "Mrs. so-and-so turned this one down because she prefers a hard one."

Almost all of these gaffes were inadvertent and some were very funny. On one occasion *Life* ran an article about Thornton W. Burgess who wrote a series of nature tales for children. One of Burgess's most popular creatures was a rabbit. Readers, who wondered if Mr. Burgess had somehow pirated the popular "Peter Rabbit" from Beatrix Potter, demanded an explanation and demanded further to know who had illustrated Mr. Burgess's books. A *Life* writer in charge of that week's letters column turned out an explanation and was making her way to the copy room when suddenly her own lines rang a warning bell: the final sentence read, "As for the illustrations, there was no intent whatever to make Mr. Burgess's Peter resemble Miss Potter's Peter."

Convulsed by what she had wrought, she stood giggling by MacPhail's door when assistant managing editor Roy Rowan strolled by.

"What's so funny?" he asked, and then he grabbed the copy paper, made a quick pencil alteration, handed it back, and went off down the hall laughing his head off. He had changed the sentence to read, "As for thc illustrations, there was no intent whatever to make Mr. Burgess's Peter resemble Miss Potter's cottontail." Needless to say, neither version of that gem ever appeared.

Even more prudery prevailed in the pictures. Though *Life* prided itself, particularly under Thompson, that it never altered or retouched a photograph, its layout artists routinely took up air brushes to neaten up animals defecating in backgrounds, soften the extremes of décolleté, and zip up flys. Artist Matt Greene once spent several hours removing the navels from a line of chorus girls. Greene also once very cleverly grafted a whole new rear end onto a British steeplechase horse. Morals were not involved in this one—just mechanics. The editors wanted to run it as a full-page picture and the photographer, eager to get the horse landing on its nose after having misjudged a jump, had cut off its rear. Researchers were sent to the picture collection to audition horses' rear ends, and artist Greene selected a near match and put the steeplechase horse back together again.

Taste involved far more than sex and related subjects, however; everyone was trained to keep watch for, say, a picture of earthworms which might turn up immediately opposite an advertiser's full color photo of delectable spaghetti. A most engaging picture of aquatic animals cavorting about, batting each other with their flippers, was thrown out of the magazine at two o'clock one morning—despite the fact that it had closed six weeks before and was already printed in Chicago—because the lead for that week's issue was the Thalidomide scandal and the tragedy of babies born with deformed "flipper" limbs.

Similarly, one frame of the famed Zapruder movie film of the assassination of John F. Kennedy was never printed in the magazine because by unspoken agreement it was too agonizingly gory.

But all other lapses and breaches of taste were as nothing compared to the clamorous elopement in 1960 of Remington typewriter heiress Gamble Benedict and her Romanian-born boy friend, Andrei Porumbeanu. *Life* didn't instigate the romance, but it certainly sponsored the honeymoon.

The story began when Gamble, nineteen years old and the ward of her grandmother, "Gammie," eluded family surveillance and slipped off on a freighter to France with thirty-four-year-old Porumbeanu. The pair clearly wished to marry, but there were complications, most notably the fact that Porumbeanu was already married and had two children. *Life*'s first story of the romance ran in the issue of January 25, 1960, and included eight pages of pictures of "Gambie" and "Gammie," Porumbeanu's Romanian army officer father, Andrei himself during his service in the U.S. Air Force, some former suitors of Gambie, and a few snaps of the runaway couple cavorting in Paris night spots. The magazine was careful to point out that Andrei was not, as had been reported, grandma's chauffeur, but instead a man with a mixed career as translator, student, and air force enlisted man.

Just a week later, however, *Life* reported an "Idyl of Love Interrupted," with pictures of a disconsolate Porumbeanu in Paris and a bereft Gamble in New York. Apparently on orders from grandma the French police had plucked the pair from a Paris taxi and hauled Gamble off to the Tribunal for Children, where it was decreed that she was subject to French laws protecting girls under twenty-one. The court put her into the custody of her older brother Douglas, and she was whisked back to New York.

Then one day a lawyer purporting to speak for the couple called upon *Life* editor Hugh Moffett at the office. Moffett, a Chicago-trained journalist whose free-wheeling style and aggressive news sense were copied by a whole generation of *Life* reporters, was intrigued by what the lawyer had to say. All that business about court orders and a divorce for Andrei had been smoothed over, the lawyer said, and Gamble and Andrei were going to get married. They were a little short of cash, however, so how about if *Life* would pay about $6,000 for an exclusive story on the wedding of the century and help everybody keep it quiet until the deed was done?

Moffett, who prides himself on not being able to pronounce names like Porumbeanu (he always called Princess Paola, wife of Belgium's Prince Albert, "Payola"), went straight to managing editor Thompson. In Moffett's recollection Thompson was all for the story though he balked at the idea of paying for it, and he balked even more at the price. Thompson on his part recalls that the money was only for "expenses" and that he was "carried away by the enthusiasm of my colleagues." There are always at least two versions of any famous *Life* tale, sometimes four or five. Little defensive coloration operates in these conflicts of memory, and no desire to deceive. The truth is that all memories are faulty, and those of people in the kaleidoscope of weekly, daily, often hourly events of breaking news are even more so.

In any event the deal was made and a wedding date set in New Jersey. Reporter Norman Ritter of the Washington bureau was put in touch with the couple and in charge of Operation Elopement. The New Jersey effort failed because of relatively rigid laws and time-consuming formalities, so an SOS went from *Life* to the Atlanta bureau. Enter Charles Osborne, who at that early stage in his career was accident prone. He got orders to draw "quite a lot of money," fly to Raleigh, North Carolina, and snoop discreetly for a small town in which a couple could be married in the shortest possible time with the least possible annoyance about blood tests, publicity, and parental consent. In Raleigh he rented a Hertz car and began canvassing. At regular intervals he reported to Richard Stolley in New York, who was running what was called "The Tower" in any far-flung operation which involved constant coordination.

Osborne rejected the beach resorts and Pinehurst as good spots for a quickie marriage and finally ended up in Piney Woods territory. One town which both he and New York thought might work out was in the throes of a "new broom" political clean-up, however. The local bartender broke the news to Osborne as gently as he could: "This town is shut down. Every town in North Carolina now requires a blood test and a wait."

Sighing, Osborne headed south and eventually fetched up in Dillon, South Carolina. There a clerk at city hall allowed as how they could do the job in twenty-four hours but not one minute sooner. Osborne persuaded the suspicious clerk that he was negotiating on behalf of a friend, and couldn't they at least start the paper work so his friend could be married the next day? The clerk said he'd try, and Osborne raced back to call The Tower with the good news. All they needed in Dillon was signatures and the wedding license would be issued.

In the middle of the night the happy couple, reporter Ritter, and photographer Philippe Halsman checked into Osborne's motel. Os-

Gamble Benedict Porumbeanu shared her honeymoon with photographer Don Cravens, standing, *and reporter Terry Turner. The knee at extreme lower right belongs to her momentarily ignored bridegroom, Andrei Porumbeanu.*

borne already had photographer Don Uhrbrock in tow, but Halsman had been dispatched to shoot a color cover, his specialty.

As dawn broke over Dillon the prospective bridegroom became fretful and started making lengthy telephone calls to a lawyer somewhere near Charleston, asking if there wasn't some way to hurry things up.

"This may have contributed to a certain breach of security," Osborne now reckons. "Our little party had already aroused some curiosity in the motel, and somebody probably listened in on some of those phone calls. By the time I thought I should go pick up the license, I decided to take Uhrbrock's car instead of mine, just in case somebody had spotted mine. When I got back to city hall the steps had a totally different population from the usual southern town square. Or from the afternoon before. There were a lot of guys with cameras slung around their necks, a lot of rented cars, a lot of reporter types. I went in and got the license. Then I strolled out as nonchalantly as I could, and drove back to the motel by circuitous routes."

On arriving at the motel he found two things: a near-manic Halsman, and a note from Uhrbrock saying that he, Ritter, and the couple had decamped for North Carolina. P.S., they had taken Osborne's rented Hertz car.

Halsman's dismay was caused by the facts that he hadn't been able to shoot a cover while hiding in the motel, and that he had another job in New York that night. He demanded to be delivered immediately to Fayetteville, North Carolina, and put on a plane. Osborne had time only to call Stolley in The Tower and report that Ritter had "kidnapped my goddam story."

Then he climbed into Uhrbrock's rented car (from Avis) and headed for Fayetteville as if for a fire. Halfway there a car pulled out ahead of him to pass, he turned on his signal to follow, and saw two cars coming toward him in the other lane. He also noted that the car he was overtaking was *backing up* on the highway.

"That didn't seem much crazier than anything else that had been happening, it was sort of dreamlike when we impacted," he recalls. With Halsman twitching by his side, he leaped out for a quick exchange of license numbers, addresses, insurance details, and off again toward the airport. Halsman made his plane and Osborne went around the corner to Avis. There an attendant tut-tutted at the smashed grille, lights, front end, and noted that Uhrbrock, when he rented the car, had not initialed the little box on the form which permits anyone else to drive it. Almost as an afterthought, he informed Osborne that the North Carolina State Highway Patrol was looking for this very car, which had been reported stolen.

With enviable eloquence, Charlie somehow persuaded the agent to take back the damaged car and rent him yet another. "I made a big speech about *Life,* and then I slipped him fifty bucks, or something, and called Stolley."

From The Tower he got instructions to proceed—slowly—toward Asheville, North Carolina, near where Ritter, Uhrbrock, and the couple had abandoned the Hertz car—Osborne's—and hopped onto a small charter plane. The plane was necessary, The Tower hinted, because the opposition, meaning the whole rest of the panting press, was closing in and threatening *Life*'s exclusive. From Asheville, it later developed, the wedding party decamped to Hendersonville where a justice of the peace married them. And from there, with still another charter plane and still another *Life* crew, they had gone off to a chummy honeymoon somewhere in Florida.

Charlie Osborne never saw Gambie and Andrei again, but he was handed a package of film of the wedding ceremony itself and told to fly to New York with it, immediately. But to do so, he had to drive from Asheville back to Atlanta to get a plane. On the way, as he reached the no-man's land on the North Carolina–Georgia border, very late at night, he noted that his gas gauge read zero.

"My future life passed before my eyes. If I ran out of gas there was no way to get to Atlanta in time to get a plane to New York. If I didn't get to New York the magazine would close without the story. My career would be finished. I would be black-listed in the entire world of journalism, forever. Even if those mean mountain men in the area didn't do me in while I was trying to get to Atlanta."

Then came his first break in thirty-six hours: an open filling station. He caught a 7:15 A.M. plane which landed in Newark, battled his way to Manhattan and got to the office—except the office wasn't there anymore. During the time he'd been in Atlanta Time Inc. had moved from Rockefeller Plaza to a new building on the Avenue of the Americas. This meant a trudge to the reception center, identification of himself, instructions on how to find the *Life* floor and the right offices. Moffett wasn't even there, he had flown to Milwaukee to cover the primary election which pitted Kennedy against Hubert Humphrey, after which Humphrey made such a long speech that Moffett missed his plane to New York.

Osborne didn't really care much. He had survived what amounted to auto theft, one accident, one kidnapped story, near-firing, peril among the mountain folk, two rented cars, a plane trip, lost sleep, and untold wear and tear on his nervous system. He was dreaming of a couple of drinks and lunch with some old buddies, and a long, long nap in a comfy hotel room, when Dick Stolley appeared looking stern.

"Ed Thompson has given me direct orders for you. You are to go directly back to Atlanta. Do not stop, do not pass go, do not collect two hundred dollars. Just get off the premises."

Ed Thompson was in fact barricaded in his office. Gambie's grandma had learned about the whole gambit, and half the process servers in New York had been loosed to serve summonses on anyone who had anything to do with spiriting away her granddaughter and helping her get married.

Osborne didn't know this. He dragged his tired bones back to floor level, back to the airport, back to Atlanta. He hadn't seen or telephoned his wife for sixty hours and just as he settled down to recount his adventures the phone rang. It was New York telling him to move his car away from his house and get it out of the neighborhood. By then his very own car seemed the only one south of the Mason-Dixon line which he hadn't driven during the days of his ordeal. He ignored the order.

The flight, marriage, and honeymoon ran as a cover and seven pages in the April 18, 1960 issue, with a headline which said "ON ROAD WITH THE ROMANTIC RUNAWAYS." There were pictures of Gambie and Andrei, beaming, as they applied for the license. The pair was shown toasting the start of their honeymoon, snacking in the motel, frolicking in the Florida sea and trying on hats. There was even a shot of the bride pretending to hack up a red snapper for family dinner. There were pictures of Andrei's first wife, an outraged "Gammie," and a few other bits.

All of it was calculated to palpitate the hearts of America's reading public, but it misfired.

Moffett, unrepentant still, says, "The first story, when they were together in Paris, cheered everybody up. But this one, when they made it legal, annoyed everybody. Especially advertising people, and the rest of the press whom we beat to the story. And of course, Judge Horne, who had issued a court order against the marriage. Judge Horne thereupon ordered a grand jury investigation."

Reporters Ritter and Stolley and editor Roy Rowan testified, and then Moffett himself: "I'd never been before a grand jury before, and it's a bit like a pit where the lions eat the Christians, or one of those doctor's operating rooms where the students sit around to watch how the doctor does it. The state's attorney was up there, throwing questions at me. I was a terrible witness. I said we didn't usually investigate weddings to see if they were legal or not, we just covered them. Our lawyers wouldn't let me say what I wanted to, which was 'Never trust a lawyer when he says something is all smoothed over.' "

In the end the jury returned a no-bill and Moffett went personally to Judge Horne to apologize for having inadvertently helped defy a court order. Thus the episode ended. It left such a bad taste in many *Life* mouths, however, that three years later there was a near revolt on the part of staffers asked to write a lead story on that year's romantic uproar, the Liz Taylor–Eddie Fisher–Richard Burton triangle on the set of *Cleopatra* in Rome. There were loud moans of "another Gamble Benedict story," and in the end a rather more savage attack on the love-struck trio than they might have received had the other memories not been so strong.

Ed Thompson is quoted by some as having provided his own half-rueful and half-defiant explanation of the whole affair with a single sentence, "Once a year we indulge in an orgy of bad taste."

Life was, inevitably, sued now and again. Sometimes these were nuisance suits brought by persons who thought, correctly, that the magazine would prefer to make a minor payment than to suffer litigation costs. Sometimes the litigants had just cause: Once, shortly after the bikini had reached North American shores, *Life* ran a picture of a young woman wearing one and writer Bob Wallace thought he detected on operation scar on her abdomen. He sat down and tapped out a light-hearted caption the gist of which was that girls who wear bikinis should not have stomachs "like beat-up golf balls." The flaw, however, turned out to be in the photograph and not on the girl. She had never had an operation in her life. *Life*'s in-house head lawyer, John F. Dowd, quietly settled damages out of court.

A far more formidable problem for Dowd was what became known as "the case of the non-Italian." It began when photographer Paul Schutzer, who was stationed in Paris, decided that there was a special brand of highly pictorial *machismo* in Italian men. Each time an assignment took him to Italy, he wandered around taking pictures of them arguing in traffic jams, mooning at pretty girls, admiring themselves in restaurant mirrors, having their locks adjusted in barber shops. Because this was considered rather a hobby of Schutzer's, and not an assigned story, he never had a reporter with him and he never bothered to take captions. His pictures were appealing, however, and eventually they were laid out for several pages.

The photostats of this layout landed on my desk. "There are no captions," I was told, "but you lived in Italy. Just write something about the men."

I plunged in with gusto. One of the pictures showed a tall, curly-haired, Mr. Universe type happily flexing his muscles. There wasn't a doubt in my mind that here stood one of those proud *fusti* whose conviction it is that their mere presence creates unbearable joy in female hearts. I wrote a caption which said something to that effect, and the story closed.

A few days later, lawyer Dowd came in to tell me that not only was this *fusto* not Italian, he had been to Italy once in his life. He was a professional man, an American, and Schutzer had caught him purely by chance during his holiday. The man was threatening to sue, although neither his name nor any other name had appeared in the caption, and despite the fact that being called an Italian didn't seem to either of us as ipso facto offensive. Dowd finally took the offended tourist to lunch, offered apologies, and assured him that it would never happen again. No money changed hands except from Dowd to the restaurant owner.

Several months later, the Rome bureau sent in a story about an Italian woman who had written a book about Italian men in which she asserted, among other things, that some of them weren't so great in bed. The bureau enclosed pictures of the author, but as the story was being laid out somebody said, "We really should have at least one picture of a typical Italian man."

Somebody else remembered Schutzer's take of a year or so before, so they sent to the picture collection and had the whole set of prints delivered. And of all the Italian men Schutzer had photographed, dozens of them, which one did they pick? Of course. Now we were not only describing him as an Italian but we were also implying that he was a lousy lover. Before you could say "Jack Dowd," the man was on the telephone again. The second story closed in an entirely different section of the magazine, and neither Dowd nor I had known a thing about it until we saw it in print. Whereupon we went straight to the picture collection in the dead of night, plucked out the offending negatives (against all the rules) and ceremoniously burned them in an ashtray. Then Dowd arranged an out-of-court settlement for about $7,500.

Perhaps the tourist shouldn't have been so hasty. He might have got a lot more had he bided his time and appeared, say, on the cover of a book about Italy, or on the jacket of a *Time-Life* record album. Even after his negative had been destroyed, Jack Dowd got a call from David Scherman, editor of the big book called *The Best of Life*, wanting to put the famous photo into this permanent collection of *Life*'s great pictures.

"But that time, at least," sighs Dowd, "the non-Italian didn't run."

□ □ □

The litigation level at *Life* was, on balance, quite low. This was thanks greatly to the checking system, but also to a genuine desire at all levels not to libel anyone, and to the skills of Dowd, Gabriel

"But we're from 'Life'!"

DRAWING BY COBEAN; © 1951, THE NEW YORKER MAGAZINE INC.

The New Yorker *teased, but* Lifer*s loved it. This 1951 cartoon was cut out and pasted to many a bureau door, with the faces of bureau staffers expertly affixed to the bodies of the men and woman in the original cartoon.*

Perle, and others. Their approach was hard-nosed, practical, reasonable. Dowd was one of the best journalism lawyers in the U.S. He read every word of a borderline story, stayed through the night to keep watch on the really tough ones. When he found something potentially dangerous he asked the managing editor, "Are you sure you want to say this?" If the answer was "yes," he would sometimes suggest a slight change of wording, sometimes make an educated guess and warn, "This might cost you $10,000, is it worth it?" If the editor's answer was still "yes," Dowd said okay and went on to the next problem.

One of his favorite witnesses, at any trial in which she could be involved, was reporter Helen Fennell. Fennell could spellbind a jury with her description of the checking process. All the different colored dots, the telephone calls to experts, the endless trips to the library to hunt up facts. After a performance by Fennell no jury within the sound of her voice was willing to believe that the magazine had erred on purpose.

Sometimes, reversing its field, *Life* fought suits on principle when it would have cost less simply to pay. One such was filed by the National Football League on behalf of two Philadelphia Eagles players. *Life* had run a story saying that the Eagles' playing conduct was unnecessarily rough and mean, and staffers had interviewed a battery of one-time opponents who were willing to testify that this was true. The football league, deciding it couldn't afford to ignore the charges, sued. *Life,* deciding that its story was correct and not libelous, decided to fight. The trial was held in Philadelphia, where *Life* staffers and their star witnesses dined regularly at Bookbinders. "The normal professional athlete can consume three lobsters and four steaks per meal. Our witnesses were eating us out of house and home," recalls one survivor.

The magazine lost that suit, primarily because on the queries it had sent out to bureaus and stringers while researching the story it had used the subject title "dirty football." The jurors decided that this indicated that *Life* had made up its mind before gathering all the facts, and awarded the two Eagles $5,000 each.

On a far more important case, fought all the way to the Supreme Court, *Life* won. This involved, of all seemingly banal things, a play called *The Desperate Hours,* and the subtle legal concept of privacy.

Privacy has some meaning to all trained journalists and to lawyers, but "the invasion of privacy" has never been codified, has no well-defined limits. It is often whatever a judge or a jury decides it is.

In the case of *The Desperate Hours,* writer Joseph Hayes based a novel, a play, and later a movie on the experiences of a suburban Philadelphia family held prisoner in their home by escaped convicts. Between the time of the event itself, 1952, and the presentation of the play, in 1955, the victim family had sold the house and moved to another state, in an effort to forget. When the play opened in Philadelphia, somebody suggested to *Life* that they take the actors back to the home where the action had taken place, and photograph them there in scenes from the drama.

It seemed a good gimmick for a different kind of theater story.

Both the new owners of the house and the actors were willing, and the *Life* team went eagerly along. The story ran in the issue of February 28, 1955, under a headline "TRUE CRIME INSPIRES TENSE PLAY." There were no photographs whatever of the real family, though they were named in the text—and cited for their "heroism" in a crisis.

At this point the family sued Time Inc., because of the *Life* story. Their primary complaint was that the play was inaccurate: In the drama, duly reconstructed in *Life*'s pictures, one convict was made to mistreat the young son of the family, another made sexual advances to the daughter. Neither episode was true, the family charged, but instead of suing the playwright they chose to sue the magazine. They could not sue for libel because the *Life* story was entirely favorable to them and to their behavior under stress. So they sued for damages for invasion of privacy.

In its initial hearing, the suit found sympathy from a jury moved by the nervous problems of the mother of the family. The jury believed that her discomfort had been aggravated by publication of the *Life* story about the play, and awarded the family $250,000.

Ed Thompson, managing editor at the time, feels that "We could have settled. On appeal the judges kept cutting down the sum initially awarded. It would have cost us much less to settle but we decided to try to *make* the law here, to fight a landmark case, to try to help codify the whole business of invasion of privacy."

The legal battle went on into 1956, and up to the Supreme Court. By that time *Life* was represented by Harold R. Medina, Jr., of Cravath, Swaine, and Moore, and the family had hired as their lawyer Richard M. Nixon. Reporters who covered the Supreme Court proceedings wrote that "Nixon the lawyer and Nixon the eternal candidate struggled one against the other." They praised Medina for his low-key, detailed exposition of the coverage given the 1952 incident and the cooperation of the family in talking to the press at impromptu "press conferences" in the front lawn of the family home.

Eventually the Supreme Court ruled that the *Life* story had not invaded anybody's privacy. After vast expense and effort, Medina and *Life* won and helped make journalistic law.

□ □ □

More terrifying in some circumstances than a libel suit is a copyright infringement, which at even a modest one dollar per infringement is expensive on seven million copies. Worst of all is an injunction. If for any reason an injured party can get a temporary injunction against publication, he can force the magazine to stop the presses, take out the offending material, and throw away hundreds of thousands of dollars worth of paper and time.

Often the key principle in an injunction is property right—clear ownership of something which the publication is attempting to use. One of *Life*'s hairiest adventures with the law arose over just such a violation and involved Charlie Chaplin.

The time was the forties, the scene was Hollywood. Chaplin was filming *The Great Dictator* and he had closed the set to all journalists. Everybody knew Chaplin was making himself up as Hitler, and every magazine and newspaper in the U.S. was aching for a picture. Twenty-three-year-old Dick Pollard, on his first *Life* job, was ordered to try to get one. He and photographer George Strock managed to find a Chaplin film cutter who, for money, would turn over a single photographic frame from the cutting room floor and hand it over. The frame he offered was tiny but Pollard and Strock got a good print and sent it off to New York—with a message which stated clearly that the negative had been stolen and, if printed, would be actionable at law.

Competition was always fierce inside *Life,* and picture editor Wilson Hicks grabbed his precious actionable photo, raced to managing editor John Shaw Billings's office with it. Chaplin as Hitler went into the magazine instantly as "Picture of the Week." Instead of telling Billings the picture was stolen, Hicks sent a wirephoto copy of it back to California, via the Associated Press, and deadpanned a request to Pollard to "clear it; get Chaplin's approval." Chaplin not only didn't clear it, he also got a Chicago judge to issue an injunction, and he sued *Life* for $1 million.

Then a lot of things happened at once. Several hundred thousand copies of the offending picture, already bound into magazines, were temporarily stopped and stored while a new "Picture of the Week" was locked onto presses.

Pollard was called onto the carpet by Hicks, who charged, "The picture was stolen. You're in trouble."

"But I told you it was stolen. You still wanted it," protested Pollard.

There then ensued a brief but nasty exchange of opinions of which of the two gentlemen involved was more likely to be fired for the offense. Pollard left the office sure that it would be his head which rolled. Had it ended there, the legend of *Life* might have ended too with the Chaplin suit. But it didn't. Hicks relented and retracted all his threats; Pollard was sent off on a holiday to Laguna Beach to remove him from the sight of any Chaplin lawyers who might be snooping around and connect him with the case. Chaplin and the company reached an amicable agreement in which magazines bearing the already printed stolen picture could be distributed, and he dropped the suit in return for a promise that he could himself select and lay out eight or ten pages on his new movie when it was ready for release.

Repercussions of this incident were felt for years. Reporters were trained carefully on property rights and copyright. In 1966 Alfred Eisenstaedt and I were sent to photograph Chaplin's comeback as writer, director, and composer of *A Countess from Hong Kong,* starring Sophia Loren and Marlon Brando. We thought all arrangements had been made before we left New York, but once we got to London it developed that the maestro had balked. Nobody from *Life* on his set, he proclaimed. After endless hours of negotiation aided greatly by Sophia, we got permission on one condition: Chaplin himself would approve every single photo sent to New York, and if he disapproved of a negative it had to be destroyed. This unprecedented request sent me fuming to the nearest telex machine but to my astonishment New York agreed. At that moment in 1966 I never had heard about the great Chaplin picture theft, but the man who answered my telex was then picture editor in New York—Richard Pollard.

Chaplin's request set a bad precedent. Both Sophia and Brando decided that they, too, should have approval of every print. And I was forced to destroy several hundred negatives which could one day have formed part of a priceless record of the great clown at work on his last movie.

Because I couldn't bear to burn them or cut them to bits, I simply marred each negative by scratching across the emulsion side with one end of an unbent paper clip. I tried to keep this desecration from Eisenstaedt, and I was aided enormously by a fortuitous sensation in the British press. Somebody, months before, had stolen a champion racing greyhound, artificially altered its coloring, and had been making a fortune racing his disguised dog under an assumed name at tracks around the country. While we were in the midst of *A Countess from Hong Kong* the dog was found, and was the subject of headlines for days. Eisie was fascinated, and he hardly even noticed my sessions with the paper clip because he was so busy trying to puzzle out why anybody would name a dog after a bus.

□ □ □

The final arbiters of taste, propriety, and privacy on the magazine should have been, and perhaps were, the readers. Yet they remained quite cool to the kind of story which caused lawsuits or strife within the shop. The Gamble Benedict story for example does not appear on the list of stories which brought 500 letters or more. We often got more than that from people who objected to liquor ads.

A few years before the Gambie caper a rather minor article called "How to Have a Bone Dry Basement" drew 4,138 letters. It was surpassed only by a previous one on "A Defiant Bear Cub Is Killed," which drew 4,336, virtually all in virulent protest. It is a truism in journalism that readers seldom react violently to stories of man's inhumanity to man. But let somebody beat a bear cub, trap a baby seal, net a bird, and the wrath of the nation pours in by every post.

By comparison to the bear cub's 4,336, for example, the *Life* story on the My Lai massacre brought 1,278 letters. One of the first of what became known as "the horrors" was shot by Wallace Kirkland in 1944 and showed a circle of hunters closing in on a cornered fox and clubbing it to death. That one drew 3,625 letters and some particularly vituperative words. Almost as many—3,237—poured in when *Life* ran its second "birth of a baby" story in April 1938. That one, four pages of explicit photographs and drawings, was considered so daring that the editors wrote letters to all the then-650,000 subscribers explaining that the story was made necessary by "the almost universal ignorance of the problems of motherhood and childbirth." Still cautious, they then bound it into the centerfold of the magazine and explained to readers that the four center pages were "easily removable if you wish." To keep children from seeing them, of course.

Despite this, the all-time biggest letter-getter was a 1942 article on homemade hats. More than 5,000 readers, almost all women, wrote for more information. "How to" or medical stories always drew well too, things like "Mystery and Misery of Backache" (1,012); "Rising Fortunes of U.S. Bone Setters" (1,162). Chief editorial writer John K. Jessup once loosed the hornets about his ears by suggesting, in an antigambling editorial, that the thoroughbred race horse is a stupid, inbred beast.

In defense of the reader, it must be noted that although scenes of discrimination, brutality, deprivation, seldom moved them to write in thousands, quite specific pleas for help always brought results. Gordon Parks's moving story of Flavio, an undernourished boy in a Brazilian *barrio,* drew only 501 letters when it ran as a straight story but 2,595 letters three weeks later in 1961 after a follow-up story which was a thinly disguised cry for help to save Flavio.

Separate lists were kept of stories most frequently requested in reprint form. These lists reflect the readers' use of *Life* material either as educational aids or as small albums of big pictures they wanted to keep. Among the most popular on the reprint list were the series on Ancient Greece, Ancient Rome, Ancient Egypt; John Dominis's photos of the Great Cats of Africa; the Great Dinners series; articles on "How the Computer Gets the Answer," "How to Keep Your Volkswagen Alive"; Lennart Nilsson's "Life before Birth"; and, on a different level, an article about how Truman Capote wrote *In Cold Blood,* and a textpiece called "Marilyn Monroe's Last Interview."

When asked to participate in the production of the magazines, the readers deluged us. In March 1970, for example, *Life* announced a photo contest. Both professionals and amateurs could participate, the rules said. There were three categories of pictures—landscapes, faces, and action—and two requirements: the pictures must never have been published anywhere, and they must have been taken in the year 1970. Prizes totalled $80,000 and the winning photos would be published in a special year-end issue.

From March, when the announcement was made, until October, when the polls closed, 40,000 individuals had all but swamped the building with 500,000 pictures. The response staggered the in-house "judging staff," which found itself for weeks unable even to sort and catalog the avalanche of photos, let alone judge them. The net result, for the magazine, was a fine year-end special on photography and a warm glow across the land in the bosoms of winners and runners-up. The judges were unanimous in their opinion that most of those 40,000 people who sat down and sorted out their pictures, printed them, sent them in, did so not so much for a slice of the prize money as because they wanted others to see their work and they wanted to say, "I was in *Life*."

□ □ □

Photo contests and reprint requests apart, the most intimate link most readers had with the magazine was through the letters department, headed for years by Mabel Schubert and staffed by seven correspondents and six secretaries. This department opened, read, sorted, and passed along each week's take to a letters editor who then selected and excerpted the most salient and/or amusing ones to be printed in each week's letters column. Though the letters to be printed were selected on the basis of their eloquence, their pertinence, or their provocative questions, the balance was maintained: i.e., if the mail ran five to one against a certain story, the letters column had one "for" and five "against," or as near to that balance as space allowed.

CREDIT: RALPH MORSE © TIME INC.

Editor Phil Kunhardt tackles the job of examining the thousands of pictures submitted in Life'*s 1970 photography contest.*

Over the years the letters department and the constant readers-and-writers developed a pen-pal rapport. By policy every letter was answered, but some of those who wrote weekly just to be friendly had to settle after a while for an annual Christmas card. One fellow from Boston, according to Mabel Schubert, wrote three times a week for as long as she could remember. One woman insisted upon sending the letters staff her "personal scrapbook" which included, among other detritus, several pairs of old socks. Most alarming of all was a woman who kept mailing in local news notes about her hometown politicians and neighborhood gossip and finally wrote to say she was forwarding to the magazine her "life's savings." Panicked, the letters department called the mailroom and said, "Please keep an eye open for somebody's life's savings."

"They're already here, we think," reported the laconic gentlemen of the mailroom. Schubert rushed to the sub-basement, took one look at a battered suitcase closed, tied with rope, sealed with wax.

"Return it," she decreed. "Return it this moment, unopened, to sender."

Sometimes the flood overwhelmed even the letters department. The bear cub story response landed upon Jo Sheehan, who had been assured that the job of letters editor was sometimes tedious but never taxing, and who was appalled on her first day at the desk by piles, bundles, stacks, mountains of letters. Office boys trundled them in to her in the equivalent of supermarket shopping carts.

It was the same on the week that Harry Truman defeated Thomas Dewey for president in 1948. A swamped office boy trundled his cart into one of the news areas and said, "What shall I do with these?"

"What do you usually do with them?" inquired an amiable reporter.

"Well, usually they go to letters. But you see there are about four more carts downstairs, and some of these are telegrams, and . . ."

The intrigued reporter picked up the first telegram, addressed simply to *"Life,"* and opened it. It said: "To the Editors. Dewey will win, you say? Nyyyyyaaaaaaaaaaaaaaaaaah."

Readers also got very upset if ever they were spoofed by *Life*. They were correct, I think. Our general attitude did not lend itself to spoofing. In 1964, the 400th anniversary of the birth of William Shakespeare, I was assigned to write a piece on the long-running controversy about the precise identity of the Bard of Avon. I read a dozen books written by persons who thought the "real" Shakespeare was Francis Bacon, or Christopher Marlowe, or the Earl of Essex, or the Earl of Oxford (this the most reasoned case, presented by, among others, writer Charlton Ogburn, Jr.), or a group of English Jesuits or maybe even a mysterious nun called Whateley. It was fascinating reading and it made a lively textpiece.

When it was over, however, I was struck by the fact that scholars can take the same set of facts—particularly if they are skimpy—and turn them to a myriad hypotheses and conclusions. Just for fun I sat down one night and wrote a short *Life* report proving, by use of the Shakespearean scholars' techniques, that Henry Wadsworth Longfellow had written the works attributed to Mark Twain. I showed the piece to some colleagues, who did me the courtesy of laughing, so eventually *Life* published it under the headline MARK (YE) (THE) TWAIN. I also took pains, I thought, to give away the spoof twice within the first two paragraphs.

The next thing I knew, the mailboys' armored cavalry approached my door. I wince when I remember the letters: "You are the sort of person who would write in *Jack and Jill* magazine that there is no Santa Claus"; "What wretched snobbery! And what historical inaccuracy!"; "You took the nation's most famous humor novelist and trod his name to dirt"; "I submit that you are a fool. I would use a stronger term but why go after a piss-ant with a sledge-hammer?"; "At least no one will question who wrote your crap." Etc.

To their credit, most of these outraged readers signed their letters. I answered the most virulent of them myself, on the theory that the loyal troops of the letters department should not have to mop up after me. With the help of Tom Prideaux, I also drew up a form letter to be sent to professors of English and American literature who had exploded with fury: "Given your academic credentials, I can only think that now *you* are pulling *my* leg."

That particular joke refuses to die. At least twice a year somebody forwards to me a student letter asking for more information on the "Longfellow-Twain controversy." I answer them, more briefly as the years pass. I know that they say in the theater "satire is what closes on Saturday night," but it was the one thing I missed at *Life*. My regret is not that I tried to do it, but that I didn't try again. And again.

10

The Back of the Book

There was a great deal of banter about "the front of the book" versus "the back of the book," with accompanying friendly jibes about which was more important to the total product. The front of the book dealt with "hard news," the most important or disastrous of the week's events at home and abroad, and the back of the book dealt with everything else—sports, science, fashion, art, movies, nature, religion, plus any oddments which a newspaper would have called "features."

It was a rather pleasant in-house rivalry, because although the precious lead story went most often to either domestic news or foreign news, it could also on occasion go to sports, on a hot pennant fight or the Mickey Mantle–Roger Maris race against Babe Ruth's home-run record. It could go to religion on the occasion of an assembly of the World Council of Churches, to art, to fashion when an earth-shaker like Dior appeared on the scene.

These occasions were relatively rare, however, and the back of the book scored most heavily on covers. Week after week the front of the book people got the lead story, but the back of the book people won the coveted cover space, perhaps because fashion models, movie stars, and sports heroes tended to be more photogenic than politicians, generals, and victims of natural disaster. Despite the fact that an enormous majority of *Life* readers got their magazines through the mail, newsstand appeal was deemed important and the cover was its come-on.

Covers always closed days ahead of the rest of the magazine, to allow for printing time, and lead stories closed fast, so the front of the book people always accused the back of the book people of having very soft lives indeed. All ''back'' stories were predictable, was the charge. Their reporters always had weekends free, never—well, hardly ever—had to go hurtling off unexpectedly on airplanes to cover fast-breaking events.

Still, the back of the book had a panache all its own, much of it created by a trio of formidable and colorful women: Sally Kirkland, fashion editor; Mary Leatherbee, movie editor; and Mary Hamman, modern living editor. (Hamman was succeeded by Eleanor Graves of ''Cuckoos in the Studio.'')

Kirkland, Leatherbee, and Hamman ran free-wheeling operations, semi-independent of the bureaucratic inner organization. All were hyperactive and intensely vocal. Not one of them aspired to be managing editor, but there were days in which they seemed to manage the managing editor, proclaiming their opinions on everything from domestic politics to the wisdom of a landing on the moon. They brooked little interference from any quarter if they had to see the top boss about something critical like hemlines, movie stars, or a breakthrough in foam furniture.

Thus they were appalled to discover, in the mid-fifties, that they were being upstaged by a ''French woman'' who appeared frequently in the office wearing a low-cut black dress, a black hat, and a mysterious air. The mystery woman dominated the attention of managing editor Thompson for what Kirkland, Leatherbee, and Hamman considered exaggerated amounts of time. They didn't mind being kept waiting while Thompson laid out stories on revolutions, earthquakes, and political conventions. This was the sort of trivia with which the magazine was forced to deal, and anyway they were all allowed into the layout sessions, if they wished, to offer their advice. But when Madame X arrived they were excluded. Neither they nor anybody else ever discovered exactly who she was or what was her mission, though the prime theories became that she was (1) a publicist, (2) a journalist, or (3) a spy. (Thompson later revealed that she was Lady Hulton, wife of the proprietor of Britain's *Picture Post,* a lady fascinated by layout.)

CREDIT: HERBERT ORTH © TIME INC.

The floor was always the best place to spread out Life *pictures for layout. In this art department session in 1950 George Hunt,* left foreground, *consults with art editor Margit Varga,* center, *and reporter Jane Wilson. Standing in background are writer Bob Wallace and art director Charles Tudor (in vest); at right are reporter Valerie Vondermuhll and assistant managing editor Maitland Edey.*

For days the back of the book troika bided its time and brooded. Then it struck. Kirkland, Leatherbee, and Hamman all got dressed up as Madame X in identical low-cut black dresses, identical black hats, identical lipstick-smeared teeth, and flounced into Thompson's office to demand his total attention. They got it.

The back of the book did not lack its own kind of drama. Fashion editor Kirkland, who came to *Life* from *Vogue* in 1947, completely reorganized fashion coverage. She was quite willing to do the sacrosanct Paris showings, and she won a gold medal from a grateful Italian government for her attention to the Rome shows, but she roamed far afield to discover exciting trends and materials, new designers, and exotic parts of the world. *Life* suddenly was full of stories about campus fashion, practical U.S. switch-about clothes, gorgeous Greeks photographed against crumbling Corinthian columns, Italian style-setters standing on patterned mosaic floors and in medieval courtyards. Fashion became a pictorial feast and a good trip around the world.

Sally always moved with a retinue and a list of requests as long, and as imperious, as Queen Victoria's palace orders for the week. European bureaus trembled at her approach, and even the Iron Curtain fell over backward on schedule when she decreed it. In 1967, for example, she decided to do a big color essay on Hungarian fashions. To colleagues who found the notion bizarre, Kirkland explained that Klara Rotschild was the most famous couturier in all of Eastern Europe and she lived in Hungary. Besides, Kirkland said, Hungarian fashions were so modern, so imaginative, that they would astonish the West.

That they did, when the story was published, but it is possible that Kirkland and Co. astonished Hungary even more. Mme. Rotschild, contacted in advance, had agreed to the story and had cooperatively produced a dozen professional models to wear her clothes. She had, however, blocked out only one day for the photography session. Fashion photography in Hungary at that time apparently consisted of a series of models braced like relay runners to change clothes, dash into a corner, be photographed with a quick flashbulb, and then back to the starting line to change and rush in again. In addition, their presence was required after one day at a state-sponsored fashion show in Bulgaria, hundreds of miles away. In East Europe, models, like Olympic shot-putters and ballet dancers and opera singers, are employees of the state. When they are needed to make a state appearance they must go.

Kirkland and her retinue—London photographer Norman Parkinson, his assistant, Paris bureau correspondent Nadine Liber, an interpreter, a driver—needed far more than one day. They wanted to pose the models and the clothes on location, outside the magnificent palaces and bridges and churches of Budapest, in the countryside, wherever they could show modern styles against a historic background. They appealed to Mme. Rotschild, who could do nothing about the models but who could leave samples of her clothes at the disposal of the *Life* crew.

At this point Kirkland, Liber, and Parkinson took to the streets, with their interpreter, and politely approached every pretty girl they saw, asking if she would be willing to put on some gorgeous clothes and pose for a picture. About two dozen girls said they would, and they kept a date with Kirkland in her hotel suite. While the interpreter struggled and Kirkland waved her long arms around, the girls grasped the idea of the story and accepted with enthusiasm.

All of them showed up on time, one of them embarrassingly early. Photographer Parkinson wanted to shoot one handsome costume, and its model, at dawn on the Danube. They made a date to meet at a nightclub at 3:00 A.M., with plenty of time for an estimated 3:45 A.M. sunrise. At midnight Kirkland and Liber proceeded to the nightclub to reserve a table and wait out the time. To their horror, their model walked in at about 12:15 with an escort. Had she made a mistake about the time? Could they hold her there until 3:45A.M.? Communication was difficult. Kirkland spoke English and a little French. Liber spoke French, English, and Russian. The model spoke only Hungarian. Her escort spoke Hungarian and German.

For an hour Kirkland played for time, smiling and chattering aimlessly. For another half-hour Parkinson told the longest joke he knew. It involved some turtles, and complicated pencil sketches, which he made as slowly as he could. The model and her escort seemed reasonably amused, but still the time didn't pass quickly enough. Through all these painful minutes Parkinson's assistant, Barry Weller, was wandering purposefully through the nightclub, eavesdropping on other people's conversations. Finally he pounced upon a man who seemed to speak both German and English, and he asked if the gentleman could help in a delicate situation. The gentleman could, and did. Escorted to the command table, he listened to photographer Parkinson's problem in English. Then he translated it into German for the model's escort. The escort translated it into Hungarian, and the answer went back through the same tortured channels to the photographer.

The volunteer interpreter looked baffled, annoyed, and then philosophical. "She says yes, she will wait and pose for the picture," he eventually translated. "Personally," he added, "I think you are all insane."

Insanity is as insanity does, though, and Kirkland was as able to cope with it as to provoke it. When she sallied onto a beach on Majorca in 1953, wearing shorts, a policeman ran up and screamed his disapproval of her costume. The Spanish were pretty stuffy in 1953. Kirkland couldn't understand a word the policeman said, but she understood his gestures all right. Thumbing frantically through her dictionary, she managed to ask haltingly, "Where can I buy a skirt?", and ten minutes later she emerged from a nearby shop with two meters of checked gingham tastefully draped and tucked around her narrow waist.

Without the powerful presence of Kirkland herself, a lot of the rest of us were judged insane while loyally attempting to follow her instructions. The Paris bureau's Stanley Karnow, now a syndicated columnist, once found himself on a Time Inc. fashion assignment and had to tuck both feet firmly under his chair when he looked down and noticed that his socks didn't match. I, within one ten-day period in Paris in the early fifties, was banned from Dior, expelled from Schiaparelli, and made the laughing stock of Balenciaga because I there had referred to the preliminary version of a rather grand dress as the "first draft." The Dior episode was minor, arising from the fact that I had inadvertently dropped on the salon floor a silly note from a friend in the office. To the Dior house detectives—fashion houses in Paris employ more security officers than the Waldorf Astoria, to keep other houses from stealing their styles—it looked like an ominous code and an attempt to pirate their clothes. The Paris bureau's Nathalie Kotchoubey managed to extricate me from that morass and get me reinstated the next day.

The Schiaparelli escapade was more serious. I went to the famed fashion house with photographer Nat Farbman, whose job was to photograph the procession of models as they made their way down a very narrow path through several rooms crowded with fashion reporters, buyers, and retail representatives. To get a picture of the entire ambiance, Farb had to climb up a metal staircase at the end of one long skinny room, and to stay out of his pictures I had to hide behind a door at the other end of the room. All went very well at first. I could see the models, through a crack by the hinge of my door, read the number which each model carried in her hand, and match it to the list of clothes which had been handed out to all the spectators. I could tell which ones Farb was photographing by noting the light of his flashbulbs as they exploded from his staircase onto my door.

Busily scrunching, scribbling, peeking, I became suddenly aware of loud hisses from the staircase. Farb was out of film, and the only reserve supply was in a camera case which lay at my feet, behind the door. As I peered out in his direction he looked quite frantic.

Under normal circumstances I would have taken out a roll or two and thrown them to him. Most *Life* reporters had great accuracy up to twenty yards. But the solemnity of the whole affair, the seriousness of a fashion show, the whole French *thing,* had upstaged me—the way the French always hope that it will. I couldn't just throw film across all that *grandeur*.

There was however, I thought, the perfect set-up for a delicious minor joke. Hurriedly I snatched a page from my notebook, carefully I drew a quite legible number 138, and then I sashayed off down that narrow models' path myself, carrying my number in my right hand as the models did, carrying Farb's film in my left hand, trying hard to copy the special models' walk.

Schiaparelli was not amused. I was ejected, forthwith, but not until I had got quite a good hand from some folks I knew in the front row, from *Women's Wear Daily* and the Paris *Herald-Tribune*.

A few months later a new Kirkland assignment hit Paris, this one calling for "exciting, unfamiliar faces" instead of the usual models. Again Nathalie Kotchoubey rushed to the rescue and rounded up a group which included an unknown seventeen-year-old starlet named Brigitte Bardot. Bardot was assigned to a pair of white lace Capri pants, which were then just becoming the rage. Kirkland herself had selected the form-fitting pants, but when she saw in New York the pictures of Bardot wearing them, with nothing underneath except a pair of brief white panties, she was horrified. Cables went out to pack up the pants, ship them to New York, and have them rephotographed. There, at Sally's direction, they were chastedly lined and put upon a model less well-moduled than Bardot.

Sad to say, my brief brush with the fashion world had no spin-off whatever in personal elegance.

□ □ □

Unofficial aider and abetter of the fashion department was *Life* movies' Mary Leatherbee, sister of Broadway producer Josh Logan. Mary came to the magazine after a spell as a World War II bomber ferry pilot and the notable exploit of having once flown a plane *under* the Golden Gate bridge. She never lost that impetuousness—or skill. She and Sally were chums, and Leatherbee joined as many fashion expeditions as she could, serving as antic companion, helper, and loudest laugher of all at every disaster which occurred.

In her own department, Leatherbee was like the month of March: sudden storms, brilliant sun, showers, wind and fury, rainbows. When troubled she paced the halls like a caged leopard, and she never hesitated to barge into any story session anywhere on the magazine to express her opinions. Off on a project of her own, she was fearless. When she went to cover Cecil B. DeMille's *The Greatest Show on Earth* at the Ringling Brothers Barnum and Bailey circus quarters in Sarasota, Florida, she insisted upon getting up on the ropes with the female acrobats and participating in their aerial ballet—just to get the flavor of the act.

Two years later she was down in the depths off Nassau, Bahamas, to check on Walt Disney's production of *20,000 Leagues under the*

Sea. Leatherbee had never worn an aqua-lung in her life, but for two weeks she all but lived in one, with mask and flippers, peering over the shoulder of the chief diver as he wrote messages in yellow chalk on a special slate and showed them to the actors and the prop men. She surfaced every forty-five minutes to replenish her air supply, and between surfacing and observing the action she helpfully held some live *langoustes* and shoved them off in the right direction when it was their turn to "swim on."

About midway in the assignment, when she discovered that the weights on her waist made it difficult for her to swim back up for her vital air supply, she complained to a professional diver who checked over all her equipment and then advised her to take off half the weights. He then said, casually, "You know about taking a deep breath before you come back up, don't you?"

Mary confessed that she didn't, and asked why she should.

"Because if you don't," he said, "your lungs might rupture."

CREDIT: ALFRED EISENSTAEDT © TIME INC.

Life*'s entertainment department celebrated Christmas in 1963 with the closing of a special issue on the movies. Theater editor Tom Prideaux is on the floor, movie editor Mary Leatherbee in the chair. The others,* from left, *are: Dora Jane Hamblin, Richard Oulahan, Ann Guerin, Chris Welles, Mimi Kan, and Laura Bell.*

From the time that assignment ended, Leatherbee never again donned full diving equipment, though she did take up snorkeling.

Frequently the performances of *Life* staffers on movie assignments rivaled the performances of the stars themselves. Leatherbee and photographer Richard Avedon once persuaded Marilyn Monroe to get dressed up as everybody from Theda Bara to Jean Harlow and Marlene Dietrich to pose for a series of color pictures, and Leatherbee sweet-talked Paul Newman, James Garner, Gower Champion, and Buddy Ebsen into getting themselves up like Keystone Kops and leaping off cliffs onto the California sand for a 1958 entertainment special issue.

Perhaps her finest hour, however, was talking Cary Grant into imitating Charlie Chaplin for a 1963 movie special issue. Grant flatly refused, at first, and Leatherbee, from her desk in New York, kept him on the telephone for a full hour. She subjected him to sweet reason, fierce argument, finally tears of frustration, until at last Grant capitulated. With the great Grant in the bag, she then had little trouble talking Tony Curtis into dressing up as Rudolph Valentino, Dean Martin and Frank Sinatra into playing Roman charioteers, and Bob Hope and Bing Crosby into hamming up a scene of a 1930s style gangland shoot-em-up.

When Leatherbee herself got out to Hollywood for the picture-taking, Grant met her all dolled up in Chaplin baggy pants, cane, mustache, and derby, and solemnly handed her a package which he said contained an award for her telephone call, "the most memorable performance of the year." Inside the package was an Oscar.

Reporter Bob Morse and photographer Brian Brake should have had Oscars that year too, for their feat in producing the only "double gate-fold" cover *Life* ever ran (a double gate-fold looked like a normal cover but actually unfolded, twice, to spread an enormous 31½ inches). The scene was a movie studio in Tokyo. Morse and Brake had been assigned to cover the entire Asian film industry—in India, Hong Kong, and Japan—for a special issue on the movies. While they were in Tokyo they got a picture of one of Japan's biggest stars, Toshiro Mifune, who was then making a quickie science fiction film in which he wore batlike wings and was strapped to a blue backdrop illuminated by a golden light. Behind the masses of camera crews, grips, spare sets, was a reflecting pool about eighty feet long. With the golden light on Mifune and the rest of the sound stage in semidarkness, camera and crew and equipment were silhouetted and reflected in the pool.

Brake and Morse knew it was a spectacular picture, but they were unprepared for what followed. On an otherwise peaceful Saturday afternoon a cable came from Leatherbee in New York: "You have been selected to shoot the first double gate-fold in *Life*'s history." What she wanted was the Mifune picture shot again, this time in a slightly different proportion and on a big camera, to fit the special shape of a 31½-inch-wide cover. The prospect was exciting, but a phone call to the studio revealed that (*a*) Mifune had finished that picture and was very busy on another one, (*b*) the reflecting pool had been demolished, and (*c*) an entirely different movie was being shot on that sound stage.

Because no one on *Life* was ever permitted to say "we can't," Brake and Morse promptly made an appointment to meet and talk to the head of Toho studios. Quite aware that, in Japan, the bigger the delegation the more profound the effect, they rounded up every soul in the Tokyo bureau to go with them.

Toho studios had collected a rather impressive delegation themselves, headed by the president, and the two groups spent an hour bowing politely to each other and sipping tea. Morse waxed lyrical about what an honor it would be for a Japanese studio to have the cover on America's biggest magazine, and hinted at the discomfiture of gilded Hollywood if Tokyo got the big play. Brake described what wonderful pictures he had made of director Akira Kurosawa, one of Japan's finest, who had made many films for Toho.

Throughout all this the president of the studio remained appropriately inscrutable, and said only that he would take the matter under advisement. Bowing in all directions, the *Life* delegation left the room. Agonizing hours later, the word came down: "Okay, we'll do it." The picture being shot on that sound stage was halted. Sets came down. The reflecting pool was reconstructed. Mifune's new picture was halted for a day while he got back into his bat wings, was strapped to the backdrop, and suspended there for hours under broiling lights.

Brake got his picture, even though the studio public relations man hinted darkly that the whole thing had cost Toho studios $100,000. As the *Life* team walked away from the set, a white convertible whizzed past them bearing a beaming Mifune, who waved and shouted "thank you" as he sped away.

□ □ □

Similar derring-do was required of another back of the book section, sports. Sports and military affairs were virtually the only all-male departments on the magazine, and the young men of sports were noted for their exuberance at office parties. Phil Kunhardt, before he became an assistant managing editor, once seized a fire extinguisher in a moment of gay abandon and aimed it down a corridor past an elevator bank. To his consternation and that of a dignified Time Inc. executive who was riding in one of the elevators at the time, the car stopped, the automatic door opened, and the executive got the full load of foam in his face.

When they weren't letting off excess energy in the office, the men from sports expended adrenalin in imaginative ways to cover routine events. In 1959 Chicago bureau chief Roy Rowan assigned sports' Jack McDermott to think of a new way to cover the Indianapolis 500. The "Indy" had been for years the site of flaming, fatal crashes, so McDermott and Rowan decided to use 1959's coverage in part as a protest against the carnage.

McDermott went off to Indianapolis several weeks before the Indy to research carefully just where and how the fatal accidents had occurred. While he was there he arranged for credentials, press positions, and motel rooms for the big *Life* staff which would be covering the 1959 edition of the race.

On the day before the 500, a task force from New York and Chicago arrived. Photographer Stan Wayman spotted a souvenir salesman, just outside the speedway grounds, who was waving skull-and-crossbones flags at prospective buyers. This callous appeal to the blood-lust of auto-racing fans struck Wayman and his colleagues as the perfect opening picture for their story. Wayman took the picture and off everybody went to have a loud party in Roy Rowan's motel room. Buoyed by the fact that they all thought they had the precious story "opener" in the bag, the sportsmen whooped it up with fireman's hats, skull-and-crossbones flags, loud music, and even louder jokes. Photographer Wayman took a roll of pictures, just for fun.

Life's 1959 Indy coverage appeared in the issue of June 8 under the headline "BEWARE! THE INDIANAPOLIS 500 AGAIN PROVES DEADLY AND THE CASE AGAINST IT GROWS WITH THE TOLL." The story ran for four pages, including one page with a drawing of the speedway and an indication of where its fatal accidents had occurred. Under the drawing were small pictures of the twenty-seven drivers who had been killed there from 1911 until 1959. The text also mentioned the twelve mechanics and five spectators who had been killed during the running of the Indy.

Immediately several advertisers for tires, gasoline, sparkplugs, etc., cancelled their contracts with the magazine. A columnist who wrote for an Indianapolis auto-racing magazine charged that *Life* had faked the opening picture: that souvenir salesman, the columnist said, was outside the football stadium, not the speedway.

Life publisher Andrew Heiskell, Indy-bound to save the company bacon if he could, gathered up all the negatives and prints of the entire story and was able to prove beyond doubt that the skull-and-crossbones salesman was at the speedway.

It was a full year before the outraged automotive advertisers could be coaxed back into the fold, but at least Heiskell didn't have to explain away any photos of staffers cavorting about waving the flags and wearing firemen's helmets. In a minor Watergate, somebody had tactfully removed all the impromptu party negatives and prints from the stack before Heiskell picked them up for his trip.

The Indy story was a case in which *Life* not only covered the news but also made it: discussion of the blood-letting and danger of auto racing ran high for weeks after in the press and in public discussion.

In quieter ways other back of the book departments also made news while covering it. When the art department heard that French painter Raoul Dufy was checking into a Manhattan hospital for a week, they asked him if he would stay over for another week or so and paint some pictures of New York especially for *Life*. Dufy agreed and ended up spending three weeks in the city. The art department's Jane Wilson, fluent in French, toured the city with the artist and with photographer Gjon Mili. They took Dufy to Brooklyn Bridge and fended off interfering drivers and pedestrians so the maestro could paint. When he wanted to do Times Square he drew such crowds of gapers that Wilson and Mili had to hide him inside a car parked at a vantage point. Almost immediately a policeman descended, but when Wilson explained the project the cop agreed not to give them a parking ticket. He would have to make them move, he said, if a difficult crowd gathered. So Wilson and one of Mili's assistants lounged at the side of the car, shifting themselves so as to obstruct the pedestrians' view of the famous artist at work without obstructing the artist's view of Times Square. That particular painting was actually finished inside the doorway of a vacant Broadway store, with Dufy perched on a stool working on a little table which the art department had thoughtfully provided.

In the course of these adventures, back of the book people got acquainted with an enormous number of glamorous and famous people. News seldom strikes repeatedly in the same place, but famous figures in theater, movies, art, sports, were the subjects of more than one story and they and the *Life*rs became well acquainted. Want to talk to Agatha Christie? Lillian Hellman? Andrew Wyeth or Joe DiMaggio? Christian Dior? Frank Sinatra? Somebody in the back of the book always knew them well enough to ring up and put you through.

Life readers got the special benefit of these special friendships, but sometimes story subjects did too. Some graduates of Stephens College in Columbia, Missouri, for example, must still cherish the memory of the day Errol Flynn turned up as a photographer's assistant. *Life* photographer Peter Stackpole, assigned to do a story on a sorority in a midwestern college, had been directed by his script to Columbia and he was on his way there when he bumped into old pal Flynn at

CREDIT: HANSEL MIETH © TIME INC.

The misanthropic monkey first ran as a Life *Miscellany picture in January 1939 and was printed seven more times in the magazine, four times in other Time Inc. publications. He definitely said something to the readers.*

© MICHAEL LIEBERMAN

The Miscellany page, which ran at the end of the magazine for years, celebrated the discomfiture of everything and everybody. Amateur photographers and readers doted on it.

the Los Angeles airport. Flynn had just had both a fight with his wife and several drinks. When he heard where Stackpole was going he thought it would be a real gas to go along. Once the pair got to the college Stackpole went about his business, Flynn kept in the background trying to make the proper motions of an assistant photographer, and he kept the brim of his hat pulled well down. At an appropriate moment he revealed himself, to squeals and screams, and then everybody had a glorious two days at the sorority house.

Then there was *Life*'s Ruth Lester, who never left the precincts of the office except to go on vacation with her husband, but who had a running correspondence with dozens of the country's best free-lance photographers and most stellar amateurs. Ruth was presiding officer of one of the most popular features of the back of the book, the final page which for years closed the magazine: Miscellany.

On the Miscellany page year after year appeared pictures of baboons up to their lugubrious eyes in muddy water, seemingly legless horses, upended bullfighters, kids doing crazy things, flaked-out dogs, unlikely juxtapositions of billboards and human activity—in short, any photograph at all which brought either an instant laugh or a startled "What on earth is *that?*"

Readers loved Miscellany, Ruth loved Miscellany, the writers loved Miscellany. On that one final page headlines and captions could be as antic as the pictures themselves. A child playing the piano, with what appeared to be a yowling cat seated on the keyboard, could be "ONCE MORE, WITH FELINE"; a family dog carrying a stack of cups and saucers on its nose could be "OLD DOG TRAY"; a rabbit standing on its hind legs while a classroom of small children covered their hearts for the pledge of allegiance could aid a "HARE-RAISING CEREMONY." Miscellany was fun for everyone, and there was an added bonus: Ruth Lester kept a scrupulous card file of all Miscellany contributors. If nobody in the whole office had a contact to an elusive celebrity, he or she just might turn out to be an amateur photographer, in which case Lester had undoubtedly corresponded with them and would be happy to ring them up.

Other categories in the back of the book could include just about anything, and many were little-disguised attempts to capture famous people in unfamiliar roles or poses. One such assignment fell to reporter Jane Howard, who had just made something of a name for herself amongst the staff by leaping out of an airplane while covering a story on amateur parachutists. She landed in a tree. Jane was assigned one day to track down twenty or thirty prominent Americans who had interesting hobbies, then script a story about them.

Appalled at first, she applied herself to interviewing everybody on *Life* who might know such a person, then examining the enigmatic clues buried in biographies in *Who's Who*. She got to meet everybody from publisher Alfred Knopf to tennis star Althea Gibson, from Ralph Bunche to David Dubinsky to Elizabeth Arden. She didn't become a name-dropper as the result of all this, but she still likes to recount the day she met with members of the Golden Thimble Club at Gypsy Rose Lee's apartment. Assembled for a session of sewing, embroidering, and quilting were Gypsy herself, her sister June Havoc, Faye Emerson, Celeste Holm, Georgia Southern, and Britain's Hermione Gingold. Suppressing her fascination at the cast of characters, Howard took scrupulous notes until she was undone by the irrepressible Gingold.

"Good heavens," shrieked the comedienne, staring at her embroidery pattern, "I seem to have embroidered a very rude word in Arabic."

11

"Gambling Money" at the Top

Extravagant was a word often used in reference to *Life,* and in its larger sense the term was applicable. In the narrower sense of mere money, the magazine was always schizophrenic. Virtually no expense was spared in pursuit of a better product, and personal austerity was far from the rule. But one never knew when the purse strings would suddenly tighten and beady-eyed accountants would inquire if everybody on the whole floor really needed a personal copy of three New York newspapers. These bursts of miserliness were known as paper-clip-counting periods.

As a general rule, while expenditures to provide a picture went unquestioned, personal charges got a good hard look. A London correspondent once hired a shepherd and his entire flock of sheep to arrange themselves picturesquely across a British hillside and never heard a peep from New York. Yet when, very shortly thereafter, she bought a pair of rubber boots to wade through the muck on the moors, the office reimbursed for only half the total expense.

There was a slight amount of head-shaking about the chartered jet for the Churchill funeral flight, but managing editor Hunt was able to persuade the money men that the flight saved more than it cost, in cutting down production time. On the other hand, the scrapping of almost an entire run of the magazine in November 1963, to substitute a new cover and virtually an entire issue on the Kennedy assassination ran close to $1 million and there was no murmur of dissent from any quarter.

Abraham Zapruder, the amateur photographer whose color movie of the assassination scene was used twice in the magazine, eventually received $150,000 from *Life* for exclusive world rights to the photos both as stills and as movie footage. The decision and the price both came about from a genuine desire on the part of Zapruder and *Life* to tie up the precious film tightly so that it could not fall into the hands of unscrupulous profiters. Yet in the same week Hunt balked at an estimated $10,000 which would have bought a similar exclusive story on Lee Harvey Oswald's wife, baby, mother, and household effects. That decision was primarily a moral one: Hunt refused to "pay any money to an assassin or to his family."

There apparently was also a moral issue involved in somebody's mind only days later when an exhausted staff of about fifteen who had worked night and day on a special "John F. Kennedy Memorial Edition" (not the weekly magazine, but a special issue for newsstand sale) sat down to eat the first real meal any of them had seen in almost two weeks.

The meal was laid on by Jeanne McInnes, an executive secretary not known around the shop as a big spender, and she was seen to beam as staffers who had lived on salami sandwiches and cold coffee for days sat down to real food on real plates with real silverware. Their bliss was short-lived: almost before they had time to digest the food they were informed that they'd have to pay for it, because some watchdog had decreed that the catered meal had not been officially authorized.

Perhaps the system was designed to keep everybody off balance and a little wary.

One general rule was "never pay for a story." And yet in 1959 when the shah of Iran was about to be married (again) I got instructions to offer $50,000 for a world exclusive on that event. The deal fell through because a spokesman for the court let it be known that anything under $250,000 would not be considered. Still I felt no compunction whatever about offering the fifty grand and protesting that if we had to share with any other news medium we would lower the bid. Similarly, the Rome office made far-in-advance deals with influential local photographers to pay fixed amounts of money for the privilege of photographing important papal events. Also, nobody on the magazine flinched when, to do a story on Pan American's new flight from New York to Teheran, associate editor Kenneth MacLeish made one round trip to "case" the story and then assistant editor Robert Campbell and photographer Leonard McCombe made *two* round trips to cover it.

On another occasion the indomitable Moffett and Kauffman managed to hire three airplanes in the same day to take one picture. It

CREDIT: TONY TRIOLO © TIME INC.

Half a ton of office equipment and photographic supplies were neatly laid out near hangar 3 at Kennedy Airport to be fork-lifted aboard Seaboard's chartered jet for the Churchill funeral flight.

was just after the war, and General Eisenhower and his brothers were having a family reunion. They hadn't been together for years, and they decided to go fishing in northern Wisconsin. The Secret Service had warned everybody off and forbidden the approach of any nonofficial boats. So Mark Kauffman took off in a charter plane, hoping to photograph the brothers from the air. He had instructions to telephone Moffett in Chicago, as soon as he had the picture: as usual, it was a tight deadline and New York was waiting.

"I sat around the office all day and didn't hear from him so I hired another plane in Milwaukee to go find him. Find everybody. Finally I got a call from that plane, and they said they'd been to the fishing island, and 'there ain't nobody there.' I figured I would kill Kauffman. If I ever saw him again. Then all of a sudden he walks into the office, says 'Hi, chief,' and I say 'Where the hell have you been and didn't you have a dime?' It turned out that the first plane he hired couldn't get low enough to photograph the brothers, so he rode that one back to some airport and got another plane. He made it, the second time, but in the meantime my scout plane had been and gone and hadn't seen a soul. Mark had even shipped his film to New York, but I was so mad that he hadn't called that I was still giving him hell in the taxi we took home. I had a suitcase with me, I can't remember why, and in all the shouting and yelling I forgot and left it in the cab."

If the no-payment-for-a-story rule was flexible, the no-graft rule was rigid. On this point the company could be stern indeed.

Any member of the staff caught taking money, goods, or any other under-the-counter remuneration, risked instant dismissal. I remember in the mid-fifties when photographer Miller and I discovered, quite by accident, a marvelous new ride in a Chicago amusement park. People got into little cars, on tracks, inside an enormous barrellike structure and were then whirled around, up and over. Nothing on earth would have induced me to ride in the thing, but it made a fine full-page color shot. The Italian inventor-owners of the ride, conditioned by the mores of their homeland, promptly dispatched a case of whiskey to the office. Miller and I dispatched it back to them. The donors sent it back. After about five trips from the Loop to the suburbs, the case was getting pretty tatty and we yielded to the inevitable. We threw an office party and confessed all to New York.

No doubt there were similar episodes here and there, but the policy was clear. No graft and no free-loading. I once flew around the world with Conrad Hilton on a story about his "instant America" hotels (my colleagues called me "Connie's Boswell" during that period), and was constrained by *Life,* not by Hilton, to pay my own way on the commercial airliners which carried the Hilton party. As if that wasn't enough, I had to battle fiercely with the Hilton organization to receive and pay my own bills in the Hiltons at which we stayed en route.

On that same trip, I charged the company for a couple of hairdos and some emergency repairs to an evening dress. These charges were challenged, and I still have a yellowing Xerox of some nameless defender's memo to accounts: "The three items of personal expense which you have questioned were unavoidable in view of the pressure of time and the necessity of making a fitting appearance. During her trip around the world with Conrad Hilton she was kept very busy, and was representing *Life* in the center of a rather posh crowd. Dodie normally does her own hair and her own needlework. [Not true, but at least I did not normally charge them to the company.] When on the road, it has never been her practice to charge off such items, and it is not *Life*'s intention to start honoring such claims. These are extraordinary expenses arising from extraordinary circumstances . . ." Thank you, nameless defender.

Chief eagle-eye on foreign expenditures was for years a man named Bill Hoeft, who in addition to being an expert accountant was also a clean-minded boy scout. To save company money, he customarily invited foreign bureau staffs to *breakfast* on his forays around the world. Most of us disliked this practice because it forced us to arise earlier than usual, and deprived us of the sort of sybaritic lunch or dinner we expected from visting New York executives. We plotted successfully against Hoeft one time in Paris by booking breakfast at the Hotel Meurice, one of the more outrageously expensive hostelries, and by ordering in advance all sorts of exotica including caviar. He had to borrow money from us to pay the bill.

On the other hand, photographer Nat Farbman, Swiss stringer Steve Laird, and I once could have saved the company some money by sharing one double bed on a hotel in Vals, Switzerland. The town had been all but demolished by an avalanche and that one double bed was the only one left for hire when we arrived to cover the disaster. We climbed into the lone bed gratefully, having shed nothing but boots and parkas and overcoats. It was so cold that the water in the toilet was frozen solid. Farb also took off his tie, mainly so he could play the proper gentleman each morning by smoothing his hair with his hands, neatly knotting his tie, and calling out cheerily, "Anyone for breakfast?"

At story's end our hotel bill was about twelve dollars, which would have gladdened Bill Hoeft's heart, but how on earth could we face his widened eyes if we explained that we had all slept together? In the end it seemed prudent to persuade the hotel to give us three separate bills, and to overcharge the company by twenty-four dollars.

I can't remember whether or not we bribed the manager for the three bills. Bribes were, occasionally, mandatory: for museum guards who helped move lights during late-night shooting, for all manner of workmen pressed into extra service, for policemen whose "no loitering" orders included photograpers on quite legitimate business. We normally described these expenditures, on expense accounts, as "gratuities" or "charities." but if the sums got really big we called them "scaffolding."

Reporter Jozefa Stuart, in Italy to help with a *Life* series on ancient Rome, found museum cooperation fantastic once enough small presents had been handed around. "We built enough 'scaffolding' on the Rome series to cover the John Hancock building and save all its windows," she recalls.

Almost always, however, scaffolding and charity paid off handsomely. Marian MacPhail and Bill Gallagher, fellow members of the morals committee, had another smaller bond. It was Gallagher's job, in the years before regular air shipments, to deliver a *Life* packet each Saturday evening to the Twentieth Century Limited for transport to Chicago and the printing plant. After each week's delivery, Gallagher submitted a bill for twenty or thirty dollars to MacPhail. Finally one day she asked him what it was for. Gallagher said that he gave the head porter on the baggage car about ten dollars for each trip, and five dollars to the porters on both cars adjoining it—with the admonition that if anything went wrong they should go get the *Life* package and deliver it.

For years the twenty or thirty dollars was charged and paid. Then came a night when the baggage car was unaccountably unhitched in the yards. An alert porter dashed through the stranded car, grabbed the *Life* packet and got back on the train carrying it himself. Even more dramatic was a night when a blizzard stalled the Twentieth Century Limited en route to Chicago. When the news came to New York there was panic. Twenty-four pages of photos were in the packet on the train. Sunday morning came and went, and no packet. Sunday noon came and went. An emergency staff began preparing a second packet with duplicate prints and layouts, but about 4:00 P.M. a man from Donnelley rang to report that a black porter, very cold and very tired, had turned up at the plant with the envelope. The engine and one car had finally limped into the yards, and Gallagher's men delivered the goods.

□ □ □

Life expense account stories abound, most of them absolutely true. Among the best-loved is that of photographer Bob Landry during World War II. For months his accounts came in listing a minimum of five dollars per day for taxis. Finally someone noticed that he had been on an aircraft carrier in the Pacific for the entire time. A stiffly miffed request from New York to Landry for "explanation" brought a bland reply: "You should see the size of this thing."

Edward K. Thompson in his reporting days was sent off on short notice to the Panama Canal to cover a Pan-American conference from 1:00 P.M. to 1:00 A.M. and a conference on defenses of the Zone from 7:00 A.M. to 1:00 P.M. He drew and spent a fairly large advance from the office but when he sat down to make out his report could not account for about $200. So he simply added an item for "canal tolls" and the account went through unquestioned.

Photographer Wallace Kirkland, dispatched to the far north, bought a fur coat and listed it openly on his account. The item was denied. When it came time to make out the next month's account Kirkland did it with special care, signed it, and attached a laconic note: "Hidden in here is one fur coat. Try and find it."

In a similarly arctic situation, I got a flat turn-down on my request to be reimbursed $60 for the cellular underwear I wore to the Yukon in pursuit of Helen Klaben. Having felt both enterprising and virtuous by saving the company the $1,500 they had originally offered for her story, I was filled with rage when the expense account came back. Rage was quickly followed by wonder, however: the accounting department said that I could either yield up the underwear to Time Inc., or keep it and pay them half the original price. Now who in thunder was going to wear my underwear next, and why, and where was Time Inc. going to store it until it was needed again?

Our expense account forms at that time were a livid green. The effect was magnificent as I stapled the red underwear to the green form, folded it carefully, and shoved it into an interoffice URGENT envelope. As a final protest I safety-pinned a note to one baggy knee: "Herewith underwear. I would have had it washed, but did not wish to cost the company another 25 cents."

This cause celebre went eventually to the big chief of editorial expenditures, who invited me to his office, chatted for a few minutes, and then bade me farewell with an invitation to "collect your goddam underwear from my out box, will you?"

In late '58 Calgary, Canada, correspondent Ed Ogle, who worked for both *Time* and *Life,* found himself in a rented car with the option of hitting a moose or driving into the brush off the road. He chose the latter, came to rest against a small spruce tree, and ruefully reported to New York that the damage to the car was more than local insurance allowed. This time there was no argument. Agreeing that nobody should mess with a moose, the company paid.

Entertainment expenses, perhaps because they were incurred largely by advertising and management staffs, were seldom questioned. Photographer Kauffman, when he found himself unaccountably out of pocket after a story, invented "surprise parties" in which he claimed to have entertained all sorts of people who certainly would have been surprised had they known it. "Entertainment" was in effect the "scaffolding" of the upper classes.

Mark, the reporters, the correspondents, got a lot more fun out of their occasional largesse than did the admen—mainly because they could distribute it in better places and to more deserving people. Hugh Moffett, who had gone off to Korea as a war correspondent, was wounded and found himself on a hospital train in Japan with about $100 worth of company money in his pocket.

"There were all these GIs on the train, and I couldn't even for Chrissakes walk. But I could look, and at one place we stopped there was a fruit stand. Apples, peaches, all kinds of stuff. The GIs didn't have any Japanese yen but I did—what the hell, I worked for *Life*—so I pulled out all my yen and said, 'Go buy that fruit stand. ALL OF IT.' That was my finest hour."

That kind of entertainment became a matter of pride even to the accountants. Science reporter Nancy Genet blandly filed for reimbursement for "one pregnant rabbit, three chemistry flasks, 30 circus tickets," and was amazed that nobody even telephoned her to hear what it was all about. The charges came, in fact, as a result of an assignment to Notre Dame, with photographer Eugene Smith, to do a story on the world's first germ-free lab, built by a team headed by Dr. James Reyniers. At story's end both Smith and Genet wanted to do something to thank the staff for its help and patience. The story itself would be enough for Dr. Reyniers, but what about the others? Then Genet overheard some of the lab assistants discussing the circus, which had just come to town.

One man said wistfully that he would love to take his kids, "But at those prices?" That did it. Smith and Genet threw a circus party that they, at least, will never forget. The pregnant rabbit and the chemistry flasks were incidental, needed for photographs, not for grateful repayment of help rendered.

In one final affectionate recollection of the germ-free lab and its men, the very French Ms. Genet recalls that she arrived in Indiana pronouncing Notre Dame the French way. "One look of scorn told me what a *faux pas*—I mean what a booboo—I had made."

Similarly, London correspondent Anne Denny had no repercussions from her charge for 5,000 earthworms, but she encountered a classic example of *Life*'s schizophrenia when she was dispatched to cover the second landing of the *Mayflower* in the mid-fifties. A precise replica of the original vessel had been built in England, and a volunteer crew, clad in seventeenth-century costumes and determined to grow realistic beards en route, was to sail her across the Atlantic. Everybody at *Life* was calm and secure about coverage, because on board the second *Mayflower* as crew were former assistant managing editor Maitland Edey and photographer Gordon Tenney. Infrequent radio reports from onboard, sightings at sea, charted the progress of the small sailing ship as she churned steadily through the waves.

Then one day a horrid truth dawned in New York: If the ship got all the way in, even though Edey and Tenney had an exclusive on life aboard, every other news medium would have the story of its arrival and the edge of the exclusive would be irreparably blunted.

Reporter Denny, a weekend sailor and member of a notable nautical family, was summoned and told simply "Find the *Mayflower.*" The ship was then roughly a week away from the U.S. coast, precise position unknown. *Life*'s idea was to hire something—anything—find the craft, photograph it at sea, and hopefully take off Tenney's film and Edey's account of the voyage. Denny and photographer Peter Stackpole, an expert sea-going man and underwater photographer, shot off to Bermuda and set about the search. Then came the conflicting cables from New York: first, "Find it. Spend anything you have to." Then, within hours, "Don't go hog wild. Maybe you could find someone to share expenses." Next day, "Charter a helicopter. Charter a boat. Don't forget to hire a good navigator." Within hours, again, came a *caveat:* "Hold down the charge if you can."

Denny and Stackpole began by trying to charter a boat from Bermuda. They could go out, maybe find the *Mayflower,* photograph her, take off the film, and go back. But logistics interfered. Charter sailboats were available, but if the *Mayflower* was, say, a three-day sail from Bermuda it would take the *Life* team at least a day and a half to intercept it at sea and while they were sailng back to Bermuda the *Mayflower* itself would be headed for the beach and the assembled press. Airplanes seemed in order. Denny went to a navy base in Bermuda and won permission for the *Life* team to ride a navy plane out to search. The first day the weather was so bad nobody flew. The second day they couldn't find the *Mayflower*. On the third attempt, there it was, in Denny's words "a miracle, this tiny boat, like a toy, on the vast ocean. We swooped over it with the door of the plane off, Pete and I roped together and both of us roped to the inside of the aircraft. It's one of the most frightening things . . . we went down low and there they were, with their beards and seventeenth-century clothes. I could see Mait and Gordon, but they and all the rest of the crew looked if they hated us. Part of the *ethos* of the whole sail was to do it as the first *Mayflower* had done, without radios and aircraft and the lot. I wished that we had a sign saying 'We're from *Life,*' but we didn't have one. We did get a good check on their position, from the navy pilot. They were about three days out, we figured. That night in the hotel I got a third set of cables. One said "Don't spend too much," and within two hours another one trumpeted, "At all costs do this, get them."

"We made one more flight, and on this one I think they recognized Pete dangling out of the plane. At least they didn't look so mad. We were very depressed as we flew back, though. There didn't seem to be any way to get to them. Then, as we hovered over St. Georges, Bermuda, we saw two U.S. Navy destroyers that hadn't been there before. Pete said maybe they were going back toward Virginia, and maybe he could go with them and intercept the *Mayflower*. The moment we landed I beat it to a telephone, called the navy, and told them the whole story. They were great. They said they'd take Pete but they were sailing in half an hour.

"Then there was the problem of the speed limit in Bermuda. Mostly they use horse cabs, but even the motor cabs are limited to fifteen miles per hour. And we had twenty-four miles to go, in half an hour. We bribed taxi drivers, chewed our nails, got to the hotel. No camera bags ever got packed so fast. They were literally pulling up the gangplank when we got to the destroyers. Pete and I threw his stuff onboard, and off they went.

"It ended happily. The destroyers intercepted the *Mayflower,* Pete got his pictures from the sea. He got Tenney's pictures and Edey's text and everything. When the *Mayflower* actually docked, the magazine was out with a color cover and the whole story inside. The rest of the press covered the landing, but we were *out*. And bless *Life,* they paid for Pete and me to fly down and meet the crew, and hand them each a copy of the magazine."

□ □ □

Whether from habit, osmosis, or temperament, members of the staff were as schizophrenic about money as was the magazine. Dozens of them departed each year on expensive vacations to exotic outposts of civilization, but at home they thriftily used the weekly house organ, *f.y.i.,* to try to sell each other everything from used cars to "one pair ladies' overshoes, worn once, size 9, best offer." These ads were free, the ensuant haggling awesome.

No one would haggle, however, over a definition of the greatest extravagance of the magazine: the expenditure of time and energy on stories which never appeared. *Life* people had half a dozen key phrases or punchlines designed to telegraph universal and often painful truths, but the one best calculated to send everyone into knowing chuckles was "It didn't run."

Every single person who ever worked there has a favorite story of near-killing personal effort, of imagination, of derring-do, which somehow ended up on the cutting-room floor. At staff gatherings they tell these wild tales to one another and as the suspense mounts everybody begins to wait for the fatal line: "It didn't run."

"Gambling Money" at the Top

For years one of the in-house wall decorations was a photograph of reporter Jane Estes, looking outraged and astonished in equal measure and saying, "What do you mean, three-quarters of a page? We shot it for an essay!" Outsiders never could understand how funny it was.

Waste is inherent in all creative enterprises, but there were periods at *Life* in which it became exaggerated. Ed Thompson, who presided in years when the magazine was rich and fat with 200-plus–page issues, brooded about the fact that in the news sections the magazine often assigned ten stories from which to select only one to publish.

"Hard news is perishable," Thompson says, "and we had enough money then to gamble on possibilities rather than probabilities. When a rare possibility came off, it was a great coup. We also had a lot of intrastaff competition, grabbing for the available space. The result was a lot of assignments that probably shouldn't have been made. I never worried about the waste of money. I was more concerned about the waste of human effort, of a very fine staff trying hard . . ."

I once spent two months examining the condition of British coal mines and miners, sped to my task by the fact that Mr. Luce had made a trip to Britain on the same ship as Mr. Churchill, and the latter was alleged to have said that if Britain could mine 10 percent more coal per annum her immediate postwar problems would be solved. When my "script" was completed, and approved by both *Life* and the British Coal Board, it turned out that I couldn't cover it because no women were allowed in coal mines. Photographer Carl Mydans, who was accustomed to much more glamorous assignments than this one, spent almost as much time as I had on the job and worked even harder. In the process he became fascinated by the sight of slag heaps in the sunset. He saw them as the shape of female breasts thrusting into some immutable future. Despite this vision, and months of effort, the story never ran.

Years later the London staff set forth to chronicle the inside story of "the City," the banking heart of London, then still financial capital of the world. To accomplish it they won difficult permission to photograph Rothschild's, where gold bars were poured, and the Bank of England, the Old Lady of Threadneedle Street herself, where no outside photographer had ever been. On that great night in 1959 photographer Larry Burrows was on his first major essay and he approached it with such zeal that his lights blew the fuses on the entire electrical system of the Bank of England. All the burglar alarms, the complex safe-sealing mechanisms, the lights themselves, went off. *Life* was never allowed back and the story never ran, because at that crucial moment the pound fell. The City was in trouble, and New

York decided that perhaps London was not, after all, the financial capital of the world.

Everyone has a horror story, but among the more horrendous is that of correspondent McQuiston when assigned to cover the flood in Holland in 1953. It was the most disastrous flood since the Germans destroyed the dikes in World War II, and the U.S. Army rushed a fleet of two-and-one-half-ton amphibious trucks, known officially as DUKWs and as ''ducks'' to the troops, from German bases to Holland. McQuiston and photographer Farbman made complex arrangements to join a ''duck'' rescue convoy to cover the story. Their particular amphibious vehicle was well back in the line, and five minutes after they got aboard Farbman decided he should be in the duck at the head of the column. He got out, ran with as much of his equipment as he could carry, and just as McQuiston prepared to follow him with the rest, the convoy moved out.

''My duck had twelve crewmen and me—number thirteen,'' McQuiston recalls. ''Six were German, warmly clad in American equipment. Six were Dutch, just boys about eighteen, with no warm clothing, no army rations, no socks, just wooden shoes. I had no food, but I was wearing an ancient fur coat which should have been condemned by the board of health. Early in the evening our duck got stuck on a submerged picket fence and we couldn't move. A violent, hideous, cold storm came on. I tried to share the Dutch side of the duck but the Dutch boys were so cold that they all snuggled up to my coat, wooden shoes and all, so I fled to the warmer German side.

''Eventually I had to go to the bathroom, and there was nothing to do but try to balance my very cold behind over the side of the duck.

''Next morning we managed to get unhitched from the picket fence and went on. We floated through villages on the level of the second floor. Corpses of animals kept drifting past us—no humans, thank God. There were fantastic pictures, but I had no cameras. That afternoon, late, our duck caught up with the convoy and I saw Farb. I got out and ran like hell, carrying the rest of his gear he had left behind.

''It turned out, after long two days and one very long night, that he had seen less in the head duck than I had seen. My eyes were so swollen from exposure that I had to dictate captions to Pepi Martis, the Paris driver, who had taken us to Holland in the company car.

''When we got back to Paris, we discovered that none of our pictures had been used in the flood story. Neither had those taken by people from the London office. We heard that Peggy Sargent was so furious that she burst into tears. After all that agony just nothing. . . . It didn't run.''

All managing editors grappled with the ''non-run'' problem.

George Hunt, who followed Thompson, abolished departments as entities and appointed three assistant managing editors to handle separate sections of the book in an effort to cut the waste. By his reckoning he did.

"When I took over, I think we were batting about twenty-five percent. When I left I think we were batting over eighty percent. I'd say we were that good."

This was a welcome economy of staff time and effort, but money saving was another matter. Proprietor Luce always became personally involved in budgetary matters, and at one time during Thompson's era as managing editor he asked, casually, "If the pinch were on, you could lop a million dollars off the top, I suppose?"

Thompson's reply was, "Harry, I could lop a million off the bottom—for rent, light, heat, mandatory raises, that kind of thing. But I couldn't spare the top million. That is gambling money."

By the time managing editor Ralph Graves took over, in 1969, there was no more "gambling money." Graves was constrained to slash everywhere—on staff, on overassigning, on all the frills. Corre-

CREDIT: PETER STACKPOLE © TIME INC.

Editors Thompson, center, *and Hunt,* left, *with picture editor Ray Mackland, examine mockups of fourteen different* Life *covers to select one. In this as in other matters, the system was wasteful but results were excellent.*

spondent Bacon in London saw the result perhaps more clearly than did the loyal troops at home: "Once *Life* started to economize, we couldn't do it. It wasn't the kind of magazine you could run and also save money. I remember one of the hijack stories. A plane had finished up in Cairo and was burned. In the old days we would have had a team in Cairo, another in Beirut, one in Tel Aviv, in Damascus, teams everywhere. But we couldn't and we didn't. What ran on the cover I think was a black and white picture from the Associated Press.

"Without the waste, *Life* could never be so good."

12

Fun and Games

If I have read properly the nuances of Brendan Gill's account of life at the *New Yorker,* then most of the brilliant moles of that magazine, who seldom even spoke to each other, would have loathed it at *Life.*

Gregariousness was the most common quality among the highly diverse personalities on our staff, and the urge to congregate expressed itself in the coffee line, around the water cooler, in endless story conferences, other people's offices—and parties.

To outsiders, most *Life* legends revolved around office parties and the gaudy, noisy nature thereof. There were parties for departing and homecoming correspondents and photographers, parties for promotions, parties for those celebrating ten, fifteen, or twenty years on the staff. Parties for departments whose members had just closed a special issue or a difficult essay. Parties, it was said, to celebrate the changing of a light bulb.

Farewell festivities for staffers going off to glamorous assignments also brought showers of gifts—new suitcases, tennis racquets, inflatable canoes, portable bars. One secretary was presented with a lawnmower for no reason at all except that she was sailing to France on the good ship *De Grasse.*

For years there was an annual bash called "*Life* Out" which involved an entire day of softball, golf, tennis, boating, dancing, and general horsing around at a near-Manhattan country club rented for the occasion. Christmas parties raged on every floor and often in each department on every floor, with elaborate buffets provided by the company and bars set up all over the place. A Rockefeller Center hairdresser who had many *Life* clients was dragged off in a rush of Christmas cheer to survey this scene and fifteen years later he still speaks with wonder: "I never saw so much food in my life, or so many people having so much fun."

One Christmas, celebrants in the *Life* text department looked out their windows across Fifty-first Street and almost smack into the eyes of Equitable Life Assurance employees at their own party. They looked pretty staid over there, so editor Jack Newcombe seized a can of the white spray we had just used to put snow on our tree, and after a brief rehearsal he managed to write clear across the windows, backward so the words would be legible across the street, "YOUR ACTUARIAL TABLES ARE PHONY."

There was a startled moment and then arm motions indicating that we smart-alecks should wait a moment. After a pause for preparation, eight Equitables lined up behind their own windows and elevated flash cards which said, "READ LOOK."

□ □ □

Part of the particular clubbiness of the *Life* staff stemmed from a peculiar work week. For years, many worked a Tuesday–Saturday week, a schedule which cut them off from the normal sociability of weekends with normal people. Each work week began, as did each day, deceptively: slowly and quietly. It was not an early-to-work office. Anyone seen wandering about at 9:00 A.M. was assumed to have been there all night, battling a difficult closing or a tough textpiece. Most trickled in from 10:00 A.M. on, on a highly flexible schedule which they organized themselves on the basis of how late they had been the night before, what they had to do that day, and the emergencies arising from sheer existence in New York City.

Mornings were devoted to conferences and newspaper reading, some layout sessions, but the writers often didn't get down to serious work until around 4:00 P.M., when they got final layouts, and their evenings tended to stretch on and on. As the day built late, so did the week. Saturday night, when the news sections closed, extended well into Sunday morning. Commuters made hotel reservations, certain that they would miss the last train. Manhattan staffers released at

2:00 A.M., 4:00 A.M., banded together in groups of two or three to brave the dawn and share both taxis and the safety of numbers for the trip home. These nocturnal wanderings caused confusion in the minds of other night-prowlers and taxi drivers. I remember one chill grey morning when a colleague and I caught a cab at Seventh Avenue and Fiftieth Street. As we clambered in, the driver turned with a slightly raised eyebrow and asked, "You girls work at the Taft Hotel?" I was too startled to reply, but my companion did. "Yes," she said, "she takes the even floors and I take the odds."

For years *Life* staffers made dinner dates and theater engagements with a routine disclaimer: "If I don't have to work." Even Sundays were a loss, more often than not, because people who didn't get home until 5:00 A.M. were still asleep when the Sunday brunch parties gathered. Gradually we came to refer to our non-*Life* friends as "civilians" and gradually we ceased to see them. After a few years of this we were so removed from the mainstream of civilian life that being dismissed early on a Saturday night was a sentence to loneliness.

One of the saddest of all Saturday night stories belongs to Leon Jaroff, a former *Life* reporter who is now a *Time* editor. Jaroff, who had been working night and day, was given not only Saturday night off but also the entire day. He woke up at a decent hour, stretched, and lay quite still thinking of what to do with all this glorious free time. First he had a leisurely coffee, then he bustled off to the basement laundromat, entrusted to it all his best white shirts, and went back upstairs to read the *New York Times*. When he went back to get his shirts he found that some inexplicable malfunction had sprayed black oil all over them. So he decided to get his car and have a nerve-soothing ride in the country—but some unknown assailant in the parking garage had slammed into his car and jammed a door. Then the girl with whom he had made a date called to cancel out. Desperately he called another girl, took her to dinner, and she was violently ill in his car all the way home.

At eleven o'clock on a Saturday night, Jaroff was home alone with a bashed and smelly car, dirty shirts, and no company. In desperation he picked up the telephone and called the office.

"Isn't there something I can do?" he asked. "Anything at all? Can't I just come up and see everybody?"

This schedule-enforced isolation from the rest of the world, plus the close working relationship of photographers and reporters, inevitably created some office romances. A few flaming affairs were well known and gossiped about, but their existence seldom interfered with daily operations. Most staffers chose simply to accept and then ignore them. As far as I know, nobody ever made up a box score of romances divided into affairs and marriages, but I would wager that the marriages equaled the affairs, if brief and boozy one-night stands are eliminated.

□ □ □

To make the whole cockeyed work week more palatable, and incidentally to keep the help on the premises as effectively as possible, the company knocked itself out to think of helpful things to do. Office boys sharpened writers' pencils, a special window was set up in the accounting department to cash personal checks and sell stamps. There was a travel section which expertly arranged airline tickets to everywhere, a medical department for annual checkups and routine distribution of cold pills, immunization shots, and hangover remedies. The library would locate out-of-print books and borrow them for the use of writers and researchers, then be responsible for getting them back from whence they had come. At Christmas time a section of the mailroom moved up from the sub-basement to an editorial floor to wrap packages, calculate postage, and mail employees' parcels. For years people tossed personal mail casually into the office "out" box and helped themselves to typing paper, carbon paper, Scotch tape, envelopes, typewriter ribbons, copies of daily papers, and carried them home. A copy-room worker named Rachel Tuckerman routinely passed among us on Saturday night gathering up copies of the *New York Times* because she kept two dogs in a small Manhattan apartment and found that neither would perform vital daily functions upon any material other than the austere *Times*. Some fortunate folks with fireplaces discovered that the office grease pencils made marvelous fire-starters and routinely filched them by the boxful from the office boys' supply cupboards.

Perhaps the ultimate in paternalism was the free, catered, Saturday night dinner. There had long been free company liquor on closing night, designed to keep people in the office, but it developed that some people, especially the bosses, would have a drink or two and then vanish for a long leisurely dinner. This was most annoying to writers and checkers, so the decision was made to bring dinner in. Caterers arrived with silver platters, china, napkins, bowls of salad and fruit, mobile serving tables with great gleaming covers over roast chicken, roast beef, ham, ribs. Apronned and chef-capped, they brandished gleaming knives and served enormous portions.

This amenity proved less successful with *Life* staffers than with their free-loading friends. More and more *Life*rs went outside to eat and more and more of their chums, people on other magazines, even tourists off the street, came to eat on Saturday night. On one notable occasion an office guard on the ground floor was approached by three strangers who inquired, "Is this the place that has free food tonight?" After a few years of this, and fruitless attempts to police the eating queue, the dinners were abandoned.

Not so the office lunch. All activity on *Life* floors ceased about 1:00 P.M. every day as staffers trooped out in groups of two to six to have a cozy couple of hours together. These lunches were usually truly working sessions, to discuss upcoming projects or make plans, but the urge to sociability extended them to the full two hours tolerated by management. On special occasions, three hours were tolerable.

Given the ritual quality of the office lunch, eating establishments were of supreme importance. Some of the affluent went regularly to "21" or Toots Shor's, and a French-speaking contingent liked Louis XIV. But most ate at cheaper, smaller restaurants in the neighborhood: Madame de Winter, the old Chateau Suisse, the old Stockholm, even the cavernous Headquarters. Gradually one of the favorites became the Canton Village, a Chinese place with a vast upstairs and a marvelous manager named Pearl Wong. Pearl and her husband Jimmy grew particularly close to a large *Life* group, and passed around free stingers when we least needed them.

When on one dreadful day word passed that the Canton Village was changing hands and Pearl and Jimmy were leaving, there was panic at the magazine. After a number of harebrained suggestions and false starts, a group of *Life* people agreed with the Wongs that the best thing to do would be start their own restaurant, with the financial help of their loyal fans. Assistant managing editor Ralph Graves canvassed the *Life* floors asking for a $500 investment from each. There was an instant scramble to participate, and one rigid rule: not more than $500, or one share per customer. There were other investors among Pearl and Jimmy's friends, including theatrical designer Irene Sharaff, director Sidney Lumet, and a group of TV journalists, but the main impetus came from *Life*. Quite apart from affection for the Wongs and Chinese food, few on the magazine could resist the prospect of being able to remark, casually, that "I own a piece of this Chinese restaurant, see . . ."

The money was raised quickly but then came complications. The new establishment had to be within five or ten minutes' walk from the *Time-Life* building, it had to be adaptable to a Chinese kitchen, whose equipment differs greatly from, say, a French or Italian kitchen, and it had to be in a building which wasn't to be torn down in about ten minutes. Half of midtown Sixth Avenue and its environs was being destroyed at the time for new high-rise buildings. Many urgent meetings and corridor conferences later, a *Life* committee of two called upon the president of Time Incorporated, James A. Linen, to ask him if he could intercede with his friend Laurance Rockefeller to try to find Pearl a suitable site. In one of the most high-level small property deals ever executed in Manhattan, the two titans of business put their heads and their staffs together and found, in the sprawling fief of Rockefeller Center, just the right spot.

Stockholders of what became Chez Pearl Wong, Inc., descended proudly, salivating the while, upon the new premises on West Forty-eighth Street. Quickly we learned several things: Pearl didn't give away stingers any more; being a stockholder did not guarantee one a table; we had invested our money very wisely. Since those days Pearl's has moved yet again, victim of the wrecker's ball, to further east on West Forty-eighth Street but former *Life* people still congregate there, and Ralph Graves still writes and mails out the annual stockholders' report to Pearl's most devoted clients.

One place *Life*rs never ate, if it could be avoided, was that otherwise beloved institution the Three Gs, right across the street from the old *Time-Life* building. One dodged through traffic and plunged down five or six steps to be greeted by some notably abject wall paintings of the Bay of Naples, some beaten-up tables, and all one's friends. The drinks were bearable, the service execrable, the ladies' room grungy, but it was our pub. Correspondents and photographers just off airplanes went to "the Gs" before they went to the office, if it was after 6:00 P.M. Everybody kept the Gs telephone number in his little black book, and the Time Inc. operators quickly learned to ring the Gs if the person wanted was not in his office. Early thirsters in groups of two, or four, grew to globs of twenty or thirty as the customers themselves moved tables around, hoisted chairs over backs, found always another six inches for another friend. Even during the social hour, bigger was better at *Life*.

Head floor waiter at the Gs was Angelo, who had a booming laugh and a caressing voice. He had been deported a time or two, accused of illegal entry into the U.S., and he had no real concept of any other kind of entry. I remember joining a huge group at the Gs after having been out of the country for two or three years, and when Angelo brought me my drink he hissed into my left ear, "How did you get back in?"

"I jumped ship," I hissed into his right ear. Angelo quivered with joy and patted me approvingly on the shoulder.

When the Gs expired—before *Life* did, perhaps we should have

CREDIT: JOE SCHERSCHEL © TIME INC.

An ordinary night at "the Gs." From left: *Jack Newcombe, Peter Stackpole, Clara Nicolai, Valerie Vondermuhll, Joann McQuiston, Matt Greene, Beatrice Dobie, Marilyn Wellemeyer* (foreground), *Monica Horne, Hugh Moffett, Gene Farmer* (*with mustache*), *and Lee Hall,* standing.

taken it as an omen—a group of Time Incers bought the bar and transferred it lovingly to the second floor of another Italian restaurant nearby. A rumor that somebody from *Life* had bought the ladies' room door, to possess the telephone numbers scribbled on the inside, turns out to be exaggerated.

□ □ □

Now and again, despite the general euphoric atmosphere, somebody got fired. The pain of the victim was paltry compared to the agony of whoever it was who had to deliver the blow. Once in the late forties the reluctant executioner did her duty and then impulsively invited the fired researcher out for a drink. This young woman did not usually drink, so the two martinis she imbibed hit her hard. What then transpired led to an office adage: Never fire anyone on a Saturday.

The Saturday in question was before the days of free company liquor, but there was drink available all the same. It was then customary in the domestic news section to deposit a large coffee can on a central desk and to drop into it quarters or half-dollars as thirst loomed. Male editors, and the more flush of the the writers, were expected to put in dollar bills. When enough cash had accumulated to buy a bottle of cheap whiskey, a shout went to Connie D'Amato, newsfront secretary, to ''call Kelson's.'' Kelson's was a liquor store just around the corner, conveniently open at all hours. It had a delivery ''boy'' of considerable age who wore an ankle-length coat, a battered hat, and moved at a snail's pace. Eventually he shuffled in, deposited a brown paper bag, and a committee counted out the money. Before he shuffled off he always touched his hat and said, ''Have a nice time.''

Usually before he had even achieved the portals of Kelson's once more, the first bottle was exhausted. So once again the coffee can rattled, and Connie D'Amato was back on the phone. She had on her desk one of those metal telephone number gadgets with an alphabet on the right and a dial arm with which she could select the correct letter, then push a button to make the thing fly open. One of the familiar laments of a Saturday night was Connie's, ''No matter where I push this stupid thing, it flies open to Kelson's Liquor Store.''

As the ''evening of the firing'' wore on, the fired researcher became less and less well-adjusted to her new status. Having peacefully passed out briefly on an editor's couch, she suddenly socked in the eye a solicitous male who had come to see how she was feeling, and then armed herself with a seltzer bottle and set about demolishing the glass partitions which separated one cubicle from another. She was abetted in her efforts by one or two other women who decided that they, too, had grievances against management.

Most people tried only to stay tactfully out of the way, but when the fired researcher decided to jump out the window they launched a frantic and successful search for a psychiatrist who might be able to quell the disturbance. This gentleman was met at the elevator, escorted to the scene of the action, and he stood for a perceptible while surveying it all.

Finally he spoke. ''Can you tell me please,'' he asked, very politely, ''which one is the patient?''

*Life*rs recount this tale with relish. The elevation of one account of outrageous behavior to a kind of group syndrome is of course dubious, but the fact is that energy and exuberance were the stuff of the staff, and their occasional lapses into excess were forgiven.

□ □ □

Next to the urge to congregate was the urge to decorate. Every office in the place had its individual decor, from the customary tourist posters and scrawny geraniums to wry admonishments: "If it isn't worth doing, it isn't worth doing well," or "Kindly restrain your enthusiasm." Copy editor Kastner brought in roses from his garden and placed them beside an ancient typewriter which looked as if it had been dropped from the top of the building. He used a nice new machine, but the sight of the battered wreck on top of his bookcase had an admonitory effect on writers trudging into his presence to be judged.

One of the more off-beat wall decorations belonged to Valerie Vondermuhll, who found her name so colorfully garbled on letters from readers that she began to post them: Valerie Vonden Muhil, Galerie Vondermuhll, Ondernuhwl, Vonderbuel, Van Den Polh, Yodernuhll, Valeries Vondermuhij, and, from faraway Italy, an epistle posted to Signorina Wonder Mule.

Perhaps best of all, in the old building, was a cell-like enclave inhabited by writers David Snell and Charles Champlin. Snell came to *Life* from several years as writer and cartoonist on the *New York World Telegram* and Champlin was fresh from college, but they were kindred souls. Their office became known as the "Hotel Plunge" because they had plastered all its walls with headlines clipped from New York papers: "Hotel Plunge Claims Life of Unknown Man," "Hotel Plunge Fatal to Mother," "Hotel Plunge Snuffs Out . . ."

Inside the Hotel Plunge there was no end of marvels. On one wall an ancient hand-crank telephone concealed a radio from which poured, at appropriate hours, Beethoven and Mozart. On another was an immense diagrammatic chart of the U.S., abristle with multicolored pins. Affixed to its bottom was the cryptic notation, "This map indicates the location of the pins."

On Snell's desk was the personalized rubber stamp of "Miss Agatha Fangquill," a prim and contentious personage who sprayed the area with stamped notices: "Miss Fangquill wishes to point out that this violates company policy"; "The person(s) responsible for this will report immediately to Miss Fangquill in Room 318"; "Miss Fangquill was not fooled by this"; or "It has been brought to my attention that certain ones among you ______. This will not be tolerated. (Signed) Agatha Fangquill."

Snell also had a stamp which proclaimed, in Old English lettering, "First Unitarian Church of the Holy Trinity," and another in the most rubbery of circus-poster type which indicated "RUBBER STAMP APPROVAL." He was fond of dropping remarks like, "Well, this is a sight for sore ears." He found the quiet presence of owlishly spectacled Champlin a daily boon. Champlin had his own brand of whimsy. Dispatched once as a very new reporter to investigate some now-forgotten crisis on Wall Street, he got back to the office without the guts of the story but with a wide-eyed account of how some brokers spent their days sailing paper airplanes out of windows. Sure he would be fired for not getting what he was sent for, he wrote a wryly witty account of his day, entitled, "Little Flyer on Wall Street," which helped win him rather quickly a writer's post on the magazine.

The Hotel Plunge disappeared in *Time-Life*'s move from Rockefeller Plaza to Sixth Avenue, as did some tasteful snakes somebody had painted all over the heating pipes, but the new building inspired even higher feats of individual decor. The new building, conceived with a quite sensible theory of inner and outer corridors and easily movable interior partitions for quick expansion or contraction of working space, was considered austere by the staff. It also swayed disturbingly in the wind, and some of its movable inner partitions didn't quite meet. The staff proudly referred to it as "the only building in New York without wall-to-wall walls," and then proceeded to pass memos, photos, or telex messages between the nonconnecting walls instead of getting up to walk to the appropriate office via the corridors.

There was also the bust of Lincoln. Nobody, to my knowledge, knew where it came from or who had brought it but there it stood, palpably white and torsoless, on a little stand. And every week it sported a new necktie. In any month Honest Abe went from four-in-hand to Ascot to bow, in a riot of colors, with never a trace of the identity of its haberdasher.

One of the oddest phenomena of the new building was what became known as "the Cadwalader effect" because it seemed to transpire most frequently in the office of Mary Helen "Bebe" Cadwalader, then in charge of a weekly feature called the "*Life* Guide," a list of often resistible events far and wide among the aspiring tourist cities of the U.S. When Cadwalader's door was opened abruptly the ceiling panels rose, with a sigh, and when the door was closed they sank, making an unnerving clatter. Batteries of engineers and building superintendents were summoned to observe the Cadwalader effect, but they never found a solution.

Perhaps it had something to do with air conditioning, because the new building was designed to operate entirely without real air. All windows were sealed and all employees dependent upon a forced-air system which cooled or heated ostensibly on command. The news bureau's Thomas Carmichael created a bit of folklore by announcing that he, personally, intended to occupy the building armed with a canary in a cage and a large brick. When the canary keeled over, he said, he would hurl the brick through the window. On the night when the lights went out in New York, in 1965, many of us wished that we had a Carmichael brick. A telephone call to maintenance, asking when we should evacuate the building, produced only the suggestion that we "buy a canary." Everyone did survive that night, including *Life* editor Thomas Griffith, who quipped that he had "caught the eight o'clock candle" to trudge thirty flights down the emergency stairs.

There were other decorative effects inside the new building. Somebody discovered that the lightly seated ceiling coverings, made of sound-absorbing panels, were highly susceptible to sharply-thrown pencils. If properly launched and vigorously thrown, a pencil would embed itself into the ceiling panel and stay there, defying gravity, for months. The practice was frowned upon officially but it proliferated in the wee hours of any closing night. Ceilings of almost all "bullpens"—areas in which several people worked together—bristled with pencils, in all colors.

So also bristled the community dartboard. This object, which conformed to all the specifications of a proper English pub dartboard, was installed in a large open area which housed both domestic and foreign news in the new building. Everybody from the resident workers to casual passers-by picked up a dart and had a go whenever there was a free moment. The dartboard's appeal was enhanced by the superimposition thereon of a large picture of some unpopular international figure. General de Gaulle was a big item for awhile, as was Portugal's dictator Salazar. Fidel Castro played the board for maybe a week, Mao appeared now and again, also Franco, Syngman Rhee. The late Senator Joe McCarthy enjoyed a highly punctuated resurrection for a long time when somebody found a stack of big pictures of him and changed them daily. Richard Nixon had maybe the longest run of all, but he had to be replaced frequently owing to the energy of the throwers when he was on the target.

□ □ □

No matter how long the day or week, there were always long pauses during which one set of workers was marking time while another dealt with its segment of the total process. Some used the time wisely—Keith Wheeler insisted that he had written an entire novel, in less than a year, while waiting each week for his copy to be typed, distributed, and edited.

Most used the time for jokes and pranks. Layout men made funny montages with photostats—Holland's late Queen Wilhelmina riding her bicycle atop a telephone wire reaching across bleak midwestern prairies was one of their masterpieces, as was the famous picture of Lyndon Johnson hoisting his shirt to show his incision. Instead of the incision, the layout men had superimposed a view of machinery as complex as a computer.

Correspondents and news bureau communications desks spent the time making up silly cables and sending them to chums around the world. Once when I was sent suddenly from Rome to New Delhi to try to intercept the Dalai Lama on his flight from Chinese troops invading Tibet, correspondent Bob Morse produced a gem: "Dodie's gone to Delhi to dilly with the Dalai." When the cardinals in conclave in Rome in 1958 were having difficulty getting their smoke the right color (black for "no decision", white for "we have elected a new pope"), the London office telexed a helpful willingness to "transship one red Indian or two girl guides." When shortly thereafter London was staking out Buckingham Palace awaiting news of the queen's *accouchement,* Rome advised firmly that "there will be no repeat no smoke."

Most spare-time jokes were far more elaborate. One example will suffice: Once upon a time there was a reporter named James Goode, who was an antique car buff. His passion was shared by reporters Jane Scholl and Anne Denny, the latter of whom once got to do a *Life* story about antique cars and took to signing all her telex messages "cadooga" instead of "best regards." Together, the three aficionados perused obscure personal ads for the sale of ancient Packards and Locomobiles, Stutzes, Metzes, Stanley Steamers.

On one glorious day, Goode found an ad for a 1933 Pierce Arrow owned by a retired parson in Westchester County, New York. The car was for sale for only $600. But, woe, on the very same day Goode was dispatched to Bermuda on a story. He implored Denny and Scholl to go look at the car, buy it if it seemed to be worth $600. So excited was he that he also begged them to drive it to the nearest telephone booth on the highway, place a telephone call to Bermuda, rev up the Pierce Arrow motor and let him hear it, via telephone. He also took time to give them a three-page, single-spaced memo about what to look for in his new-old car: it should have matching luggage covers in the back; it should have a special kind of headlights. He appended some warnings: "look for rust under the running boards," "check that the rear bumper is intact."

Armed with their memo, Denny and Scholl proceeded to the minister's house in Westchester and asked to drive the Pierce Arrow. The minister refused to let them even start the engine, but the two were not deceived. There was *rust* under the running board. The matching bud vases were missing. The upholstery was tattered. The car was a mess. They said thanks but no thanks and started driving back to New York. All the way they thought "what a shame!" but then, gradually, a gorgeous joke dawned.

Once back in New York, they enlisted the help of David Snell, who just happened to know about a record store which had a ten-inch disc which repeated the sounds of an ancient car motor straining to start. It coughed, it snorted, it refused, it finally made the unmistakable "kapocket kapocket kapocket . . ." of a real vintage car. Record in hand, Denny and Scholl were ready to act.

Their joke, however, had to be researched as carefully as a story. If they were to pretend to telephone Goode in Bermuda, from a telephone booth on a highway, they had to duplicate the sounds of quarters, dimes, and nickels, going into a toll phone. Researcher Scholl, who had a charge account at Abercrombie and Fitch, went over there to audition bronze bells. To her delight, she found that they had bells which would do the job. She bought them, went back to her desk, and rang up the switchboard to explain the plot. A Time Inc. switchboard girl was to pose as the "international operator" and Helen Fennell was to be the local operator on the call.

When all was in order, hours later, the Time Inc. switchboard placed the call. Fennell broke in to ask, "Mr. Goode? Mr. James Goode? Long distance calling from New York." Then, "Deposit your money please." Jane Scholl rang her Abercrombie and Fitch bells to the precise total of $3.45 and then Fennell came back to say "thenk you" and Anne Denny got on the line.

"Jim!" she exclaimed. "We've got your car, and it's a beauty. We did have to spend a little more than you thought. You said six hundred dollars and we paid fourteen hundred, but believe me it's worth every penny . . . and Jim? Jim? Do you want to hear the motor?"

At this precise moment Snell turned on the coughing and spluttering record, so Goode could hear his car almost start, hiccough, and finally turn over. As the nice "kapocket" started, Denny said soothingly, "Isn't that great?"

Then her tone of voice changed. "Jane!" she screamed into the telephone. "Jane, no no no, not *backward!*" And the sound of a very large CRASH. At which point the Time Inc. operator broke into the call to say, "I'm sorry, your three minutes are up," and she shut down the line.

From Bermuda, Goode made outraged calls of protest: "Two girls are out there on the highway freezing in this winter weather, and you have cut them off!'' All he ever got in reply was, ''I'm sorry, sir, long distance recommences at eight o'clock tomorrow morning.''

Desperately, Goode cabled thanks to his erstwhile friends in New York, and promised them a lunch at Voisin. He flew home a day early from the Bermuda story to behold his vintage Pierce Arrow, and found himself the subject of several feature stories in New York newspapers whose reporters had heard about the elaborate gag. At first he was too angry even to speak. Then he thought it over and smiled a very broad smile.

''It was,'' he said, ''the best-researched and best-executed joke I have ever been the victim *of*.''

13

LIFE with EKT

One man more than any other put his personal stamp on life at *Life:* Edward K. Thompson of St. Thomas, North Dakota, self-professed hick (not true), self-professed slob (he was Phi Beta Kappa at the University of North Dakota), one of the magazine's first stringers and employees, and its fourth managing editor, from 1949 until 1961.

EKT, as he signed himself on memos and copy, ran the shop in its most glorious days and transmitted both his style and his professional standards to everyone who worked for him. A tall man with light blue eyes, neat blond hair and a cherubic face, he looked a bit like Winston Churchill, a bit like Dwight Eisenhower, and a lot like every round blond baby one had ever encountered—if one could imagine that baby with a big cigar in its face and gleaming white shirtsleeves rolled halfway between wrist and elbow.

His style was low-key calm, his standards rigidly high. He wanted nothing but the best and he intended to get it at any cost to himself, the company, and the staff. He is still at it, as founder, editor, and publisher of *Smithsonian* magazine. In his *Life* days nobody heard him raise his voice except in song, laughter, or a summons to one of his assistants. He liked shouting for the help instead of using either the telephone or the inter-office squawk box. Even his wrath, when aroused, was quiet. But awesome. One withering glance from those blue eyes would uncurl permanents and sizzle seersuckers.

He was a master of picture journalism and a most inarticulate editor. His conversation in layout sessions consisted mainly of grunts and gestures, incomprehensible to everyone in the room except his art directors, Charles Tudor and Michael Phillips. Researchers summoned into the presence to show a story were unnerved as he whipped through a three-foot stack of pictures in three minutes, winnowing the ones he liked from those he didn't, winnowing again for a final layout, commenting all the while in what sounded to his anxious helpers like the lyrics to some North Dakota Indian rain dance. Now and again he would stop, point at a face on a photograph, and demand abruptly, "Who's that?" Woe to the researcher who didn't know.

Each such show-and-layout session ended with Tudor or Phillips vanishing to his lair clutching a handful of pictures, a fistful of sketches for layouts, and the rest of the group standing nervously in the corridor outside asking each other, "What did he say?"

Even in one-to-one conversation Ed mumbled or was elliptical. Copy editor Joseph Kastner, who had known him since 1937 when Thompson first came to the magazine, found him "uncommunicative." When EKT became managing editor he instituted a system of rotating "Monday editors" to run the magazine while he had a day off. The implicit hint was that whoever performed best on Mondays might get to be the assistant managing editor. Kastner alone of the rotating fill-ins didn't want the job. He kept telling Ed that, and getting no response. Nor could he get any hint about what Ed really wanted him to do.

Weeks went by and one night both men were bidden to a staff Christmas party in the RCA building. Thompson asked Kastner to stroll over to the party with him, through the underground concourse of Rockefeller Center, and Kastner was aquiver. This might be the big moment. As they walked Thompson remained silent, so Kastner took matters into his own hands.

"My guess," he said, "is that you want me to continue to be copy editor."

Thompson turned just a little over his shoulder, started to say something, and right at that moment the two men arrived at a revolving door.

"By the time we got through it," Kastner says, "Ed had given his answer, and I never heard it."

Ralph Graves, the weekly magazine's last managing editor, worked for Thompson for years and seldom understood fully what he said. Graves took it as a challenge: "Ed's total lack of communication kept everybody off balance. He had no trouble whatever making up his mind, and no trouble not explaining it. So none of us ever forgot that we had a job to do."

When he did communicate, EKT's medium was the calculated insult. First exposure to this treatment was disturbing to the delicate, but within months staffers began to treasure his put-downs as if they were Bronze Stars. Joann McQuiston got a star early on. In the late forties she occasionally rode the same subway as Thompson did and she was stunned one morning when he strode past her at the exit and inquired mildly, "How many peasants have you kicked today?" She had no idea what he meant until she realized that she was wearing stylish knee-high leather boots, very new in New York at the time. In translation from EKT-ese, what he had really said was, "Don't you look chic today?"

Shortly thereafter McQuiston found herself again on the same train with Thompson. She decided no conversation was required, and she got off the car only to wander absent-mindedly in the wrong direction. The boss followed her, wordlessly took her by the shoulders, turned her around, and aimed her in the direction of the *Time-Life* building. Then he ambled off. Within an hour McQuiston found herself busily sound-tracking pictures in his office. Thompson was looking at pictures, sketching rough layouts, making his usual grunting noises, when suddenly he turned to McQuiston and thrust a small note into her hand. She backed away three steps and read it. It said, "You are now in Room 29–01."

Two of McQuiston's colleagues once approached EKT's office with an editorial problem and paused politely outside the door to inquire, "Do you have time to see two ladies?"

"Certainly," proclaimed Ed. "Where are they?"

Months went by, in my case, before I achieved the honor of an EKT insult. I had heard him drop them on others, especially one night when Gene Farmer stormed into a layout session with a totally extraneous problem which involved a pet gorilla that had died in a zoo. Thompson dealt deftly with the problem and then called out to his friend Farmer, as he left the room, "Try not to drag your knuckles on the floor."

My very own insult was ticking away somewhere, I felt sure, and then one glorious day it came. Months before, I had been sound-tracking a story for then–managing editor Joseph Thorndike in the presence of EKT, my immediate boss Irene Saint, and the usual com-

Layout's version of EKT as all *the chiefs of staff was not technically perfect. "It was their first attempt," says Thompson, "and they hadn't quite mastered the art of collage."*

mittee. I was very new and trying hard, so when a messenger walked into the office with a box for Thorndike I ignored the interruption and pressed on relentlessly with my running commentary on the photographs as Thorndike went through them. I certainly didn't notice that he looked at his watch, or that he looked at the suit box. Roughly forty seconds later Thompson glared at me: "If you would please

When EKT went to war in 1942, Life*'s layout room made a montage for his party. The original of this photostat of President Roosevelt vaulting over EKT's back was about three by five feet.*

leave the room, Thorndike could change his shirt and get to his dinner party.''

I fled in disorder and all evening brooded over what seemed unfair criticism of my behavior. Then came the day of payoff. EKT had been made managing editor and his secretary rang to tell me to come immediately to his office.

''With what story?'' I asked.

''I don't know,'' she said. ''Just come. And go straight into his room.''

I walked terrified down the long, long hall, went into the office, and there sat Ed nude from the waist up, behind his enormous desk. He was puffing a cigar, wearing his most beatific smile.

''Just thought I'd give you a treat,'' he said, ''because you were so frustrated at not being able to watch Thorndike change his shirt.''

The day I knew I'd really made it, though, was the day EKT decided to send me to Paris instead of to London. Bureau assignments were much cherished in the early fifties and I had been promised, I thought, a post in London. I couldn't wait. McQuiston had been promised, she thought, a post in Paris. She couldn't wait. Then in a Quixotic gesture Thompson switched our assignments. We were both aghast, but I much more so: Joann was fluent in French, I could barely manage *la plume de ma tante*. Perhaps made overconfident by EKT's shirtless joke, I stormed into his office to announce that ''You can't do this to me. I don't speak French.''

His simple reply, delivered without a smile, was, ''What makes you think you speak English?''

I went to Paris.

□ □ □

No compendium of picturesque Thompson insults can explain the fanatic loyalty of his staff. That was made up of a dozen other qualities, not the least of which was *his* loyalty. One of the best-known inhouse EKT stories revolves around the ''our next president'' blooper in *Life* in 1948. The magazine's editors, like most other editors, believed that year that Thomas E. Dewey would demolish Harry S. Truman in the November elections. *Life* was closing a preelection story about the final days of the campaign, for an issue which would be on the newsstands and in mailboxes just before voting day. This is a tricky situation for journalists, but writer Ernest Havemann felt quite safe as he tapped out a caption for a picture of Dewey campaigning in California: ''The next president travels by ferry boat over the broad waters of San Francisco Bay.'' Checker Ruth Adams, a tough and skillful veteran of many a political story, objected to the wording—''Let's at least wait until he's elected . . .''—and asked Havemann to change it. He refused. Adams then went to Sidney L. James, division editor in charge of domestic news, who also refused to change it. Adams considered going over James's head to Thompson, but she didn't do it.

Shortly after the magazine hit the stands, Truman had been elected. *Life* looked foolish and the proprietor himself was considerably upset. In an elevator, Luce asked Thompson who had written the caption. EKT declined to reveal the name because, "I had passed the caption and considered myself responsible."

This gallant intervention actually served the researchers, who were responsible for "fact," even more than it did Havemann. When word got around, the checking staff took up a collection to buy EKT an orchid, which he loathed, and a high-pitched dog whistle which they labeled carefully "researchers' whistle, to be used only by EKT." (It was also EKT who changed the masthead designation from "researcher" to "reporter.")

When for some reason he couldn't draw the lightning himself, he did what he could to make amends. Once Luce became annoyed about *Life*'s coverage of "the sack dress" and criticized fashion editor Sally Kirkland's judgment. In passing along Luce's objections to Kirkland, Thompson noted that "I have already bawled him out."

EKT always knew a lot more about people in the office than they thought he did. Beatrice Dobie, who began her career as a part-time copy reader and rose to London correspondent and head researcher for the books division, had just won her way into the foreign news section when she was summoned to his office to help show a long and complex story. The layout session dragged on and on, and when it ended she and the other researchers gathered up the stacks of pictures to go back to their desks. As they left the room Thompson called out, "Bea, if you hurry you'll just have time to make the six o'clock mass at St. Catherine's." Dobie, who had no idea that he even knew her name, let alone the fact that she is Catholic, has never entirely recovered from her surprise.

□ □ □

He was always among the first ones into the office in the morning, often the last to leave. He wasted a lot of the time in between because EKT was accessible at any hour of any day to listen to a problem. He would listen to the newest researcher with as much attention as he did to Luce, though he expected researchers to be more brief about it. He was the most unflappable man on the magazine and he thrived on emergencies. We could all see his spirits rise when there was a late news break on a Saturday which might stretch the long day into an even longer night.

Led by Ed, we all developed a taste for emergencies. Any sudden overwhelming event—a war in the Middle East, a hurricane in Kansas, an earthquake in Peru—sent the staff into instant action without orders, requests, or even, at first, a plan of action. Each individual calculated quickly where and how he or she could fit into what would eventually become a plan, and rushed to do what was most urgently needed. Correspondents became couriers, copy girls did research, researchers sent out for sandwiches, writers took film to the lab. We all felt so much like firemen that a favorite gift for any beloved bureau chief was a fire chief's helmet.

As the Thompson style of loyalty and informality came to pervade the premises, so did his taste in spare-time *divertissement.* The latter included, notably, singing, roughhouse, and pick-up ball games in the corridors. Late Saturday nights in the layout room always ended with EKT leading the singing. He favored hillbilly gems—"Git up off'n the Floor, Hannah, Them Hogs Has Got to Be Fed," or rousing Protestant hymns like "Love Lifted Me" and "The Old Rugged Cross." He sang abominably, but with infectious pleasure. Those who could actually stay on key learned to shift when he did—usually at the end of each phrase—and those who couldn't happily added their own cacophony to his.

After one late-night trip to California, during which a hostess coaxed EKT and fellow-caroler Ralph Graves from their seats to a front cabin lounge "so the other passengers can sleep," California bureau secretary Pat Roache bought a pitch pipe and presented it to Thompson and Graves. The pitch pipe was ceremoniously produced each Saturday night thereafter but it didn't improve the quality of the singing much.

Singing became a popular between-chores activity at the office. From New York it spread to the bureaus, where it was customary for any departing reporter, photographer, or chief to be serenaded at his farewell party by every member of the staff. A number called "Plucky Lucky Lindbergh" was almost mandatory at these events, as was some parody of a Gilbert and Sullivan tune. The new *Time-Life* building in London was launched with a ditty called "We've Got a Loverly Bunch of Architects," sung—sort of—to the tune of "I've Got a Loverly Bunch of Coconuts."

Some members of the staff actually could sing. David Scherman and Edward Kern were fine on Gilbert and Sullivan, as was Harvey Loomis, known around the halls as Nanki-Poo because he had once sung the role in a Blue Hill Troupe rendition of *The Mikado* at Hunter College.

Thompson also invented a roughhouse called "the children's hour," in which either he or an amenable researcher knelt behind an unsuspecting and earnest employee and then the accomplice pushed,

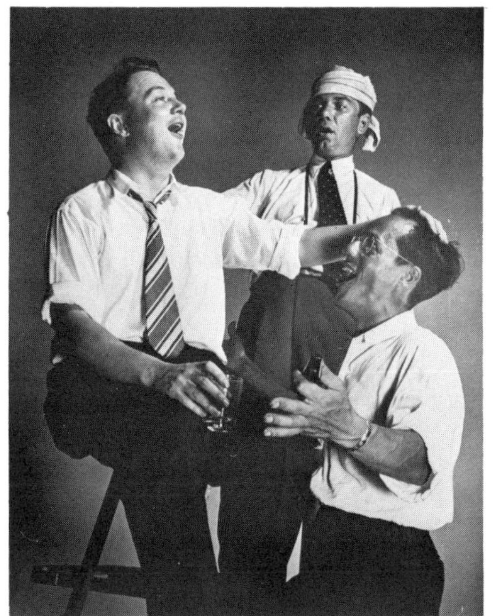

© OTTO HAGEL; © TIME INC. © TIME INC.

Left: *Thompson in full song,* left, *with his hand on the head of photographer Dave Scherman. Photographer Tom McAvoy is in background.*

Right: *On Thompson's fiftieth birthday the staff gave him a rocking chair and Dmitri Kessel sat in his lap.*

sharply, upending the victim of the prank. After four or five such episodes everybody decided the game was too rough, but the mere shout of "children's hour" was for years to send everybody scrambling to get his or her back firmly and safely against a wall.

Physical activity abounded. Baseballs, footballs, soccer balls, Frisbees, flew around bullpens and long corridors and there were hula hoops, bongo boards, yo-yos, all over the place. EKT was an inept ballplayer. He once attempted to hit a softball with a broom, missed the ball entirely, and knocked out a corridor light fixture with the broom. The occasion was a celebration of the birth of his first grandchild, EKT III.

He also had, in the terms of the professional sports reporters on *Life,* "soft hands." he loved to play football but he had some trouble catching the ball. One night in the layout room sports reporter Jack Newcombe threw him a pass which bounced straight off Thompson's fingertips and out an opened window in the old *Time-Life* building. It was thirty floors from the ball game to the street, straight down, and after a startled moment everybody rushed to the window and leaned out to see where the ball would land.

Down, down it went and when it finally hit the brightly lighted sidewalks of Rockefeller Plaza it accomplished what witness Newcombe describes as "the all-time, all-league, all-world record for a first bounce—it went at least twenty feet up in the air."

Six feet away from the impact point stood a yellow cab. Its passenger door was open and the passenger, a gentleman, had both feet out of the door and on the street as he leaned back to pay the cabbie. Then the football hit and sailed up into the night air. It didn't touch the cab or the passenger, but as Newcombe and Co. still peered down the two legs and feet disappeared abruptly back into the cab, the door slammed, and the taxi sped off into the night.

On the night that Thompson smacked the light fixture, a maintenance man summoned to survey the damage looked around and said, "Mr. Thompson, I didn't see a thing." Nor did anybody see a thing, officially, on football night. Nobody ever told on anybody, and Thompson's exuberance made him tolerant of everybody else's. After foreign news section reporters had closed a mammoth story on the wedding of Princess Elizabeth of England they were sitting, exhausted, amid heaps of captions, cables, memos, newspaper clippings. Somebody decided it would be fun to burn up all the unnecessary pieces of paper, so they shoved the furniture aside, made a bonfire in the middle of the floor, and set about dancing around it whooping like Indians. In mid-dance EKT walked in, took one hard look, and walked out again. He didn't tarry, but on the other hand he didn't issue orders to cease and desist. He was equally equable when foreign news flew its special martini flag, in a bracket mounted over the bullpen door, and had a "pour" for all hands. These sessions often ended with the men playing sexy rhythms on upended wastebaskets while one of the women performed the dance of the seven veils.

That was the kind of party Thompson favored. He liked office high spirits to break out spontaneously like a forest fire, rage out of control briefly and memorably, and then expire. He hated formal, organized things like *Life* Out and the Christmas party. He was also only mildly enthusiastic about the big annual event of the sixties, a semiformal occasion on which staffers of all three editions of *Life* were bidden to the grand ballroom of a Manhattan hotel for an evening of speeches, entertainment, dancing, elaborate food and drink. This event, organized under the aegis of Thompson's successor, managing editor George Hunt, became known as "the Hunt Ball" and despite its elegance was not overwhelmingly popular with old-timers. For one thing, each employee was assigned a specific seat at a specific table instead of being allowed to seek out his cronies in peace, and for another thing the formal atmosphere was not as conducive to spontaneous fun as were the untidy corridors of home. The Hunt Balls did produce memorable reunions of far-flung staffers, and one year a sensational men's fashion show starring male employees.

Thompson in his era tried to kill both *Life* Out (because the trip home from a suburban country club after a day of celebration was dangerous) and the Christmas party because "after every one of them I got telephone calls from wives saying, 'What have you done with Joe Blow? He didn't come home last night.' " He won on *Life* Out, lost on Christmas because the personnel department "felt it was therapeutic for the staff to get drunk once a year and insult the bosses."

His attitude was colored, undoubtedly, by his experiences at the first two *Life* parties he ever attended. The first was in November 1937, on the anniversary of the first issue of the magazine. In those days *Life* did a lot of business with the Black Star photo agency, and

CREDIT: WALTER DARAN © TIME INC.

Photographers Alfred Eisenstaedt, left, *and Gjon Mili were stars of the men's fashion show at the Hunt Ball of 1959. People who knew Mili well bragged that they were intimate enough to call him "Gjack."*

Black Star bought a huge ice cream cake from the fanciest ice cream parlor in New York and sent it over. The party consisted of eating slices of cake, period.

Only a month later all was different. This was *Life*'s first Christmas party, fueled primarily by liquid loot from then–movie writer Joseph Thorndike's Hollywood contacts. *Life* in its earliest days regularly published a picture story on "Movie of the Week," and Thorndike wrote it. Grateful producers and directors swamped him with free liquor and he decided to make it all available to the staff for Christmas. Thompson, "unaccustomed to orgies," went off on his lunch hour to pick up a Renoir print he had bought as a present for his wife, and returned to find the office in total disorder. Researchers were kissing writers, insulting editors ("an unsavory group," Thompson recalls) and generally misbehaving. The offices were then in the Chrysler building and EKT had somehow to get himself and his print down from the fifty-first floor to the subway, catch the crosstown shuttle, get to Penn Station, and ride to Long Island. When he got into the elevator it took him two floors past ground and delivered him into the arms of the maintenance employees of the Chrysler building who were having their own rip-roaring party. They welcomed him, fed him, drank him, and when he finally escaped he had developed a lasting resistance to office Christmases.

□ □ □

There was one area in which EKT never joked at all: the integrity of the photograph. Fakery or alteration in any form was anathema. He would not permit air-brushing—except perhaps to zip up flys—and he wanted always a "full negative print," that is a print to its natural borders, so if it were to be "cropped" (cut) anywhere for editorial effect he would do it himself. He insisted that the staff get original prints from wirephoto negatives because the quality was better and whenever he spotted a set-up picture—all the members of a committee, for example, lined up with one of them presenting a handshake or a plaque to another—he remarked mildly, "Wasn't the photographer lucky to be there right at that moment?" Then he tossed the picture into the wastebasket.

He was the first to spot the "heart rendering baby" in its first incarnation in wartime Shanghai, as a fake. Long after the picture had been published (he was not managing editor at the time) he sent for the entire set of pictures and saw on the contact prints a series of photographs made before the one which was printed in *Life*. On these earlier shots there were clearly visible the adults who had picked up the bedraggled child, set him down on some railway tracks, and left him there a few minutes to cry with fear and make a famous pictorial document of human suffering in wartime.

It was he who issued the edict that no repeat no reporter should ever appear in a *Life* photo. Not even if the photographer begged and pleaded for "just any old body" to step into a picture to give it scale or a human presence. He fired photographers for faking, and thundered at reporters who helpfully pushed shutter buttons for photographers who were using more than one set-up camera and requested an extra finger. In his rigid view, reporters were reporters and photographers were photographers and he would brook no crossing of the line.

One of his proud boasts was that he never looked at the back of the photograph. That meant that he didn't want to know, while selecting pictures for the magazine, which photographer had taken them. *Life* pictures were always stamped on the back with the name of the story and the photographer, the date, and a set number. Many distinguished free-lancers used the same system. But Ed was not to be swayed by the glamor of the great names. He looked at the print, not the credit.

Occasionally there was hell to pay for his purity. Two, five, ten expensive *Life* men went out on a story and then EKT would cooly lay out an opener, or a spread, using photos from AP, UPI, sometimes even an amateur. If the prima donnas complained, as they sometimes did, all he ever said was that he picked the best pictures.

Even more splendid than usual, Thompson stopped to make final decisions with assistant art director Mike Phillips before going to Washington to the Eisenhower inauguration festivities in 1953.

If they continued to argue, he reminded them that he was the managing editor. On one famous occasion, the triumphant return of General MacArthur to New York (after he had been fired by Truman), *Life* staked out about twenty-five photographers with accompanying assistants, reporters, beaters, and bearers, and EKT not only ran a service picture as the lead but also chewed out the entire staff for not having taken better pictures than the wire services did.

On the other hand, given basically dull photographs on an impelling news event, he could lay them out with enormous impact. At the time of the Soviet invasion of Hungary in 1956, *Life* wasn't able to get a team in, and film out, in time for the first week's coverage. Thompson had nothing but a pile of wire-service prints, most of them shot from basements, out windows, behind barricades, as photographers tried to stay out of the crossfire and also get some image to send back. Almost all the pictures were of Soviet tanks, and gradually a plan grew in EKT's mind: he laid out a spread of tanks, tanks, tanks, looming larger and larger across the big display space, producing a stunning pictorial presentation of the naked power which was crushing Hungary.

Watching EKT lay out a story like that was a lesson in picture journalism.

Watching him fend off "the business side" was a lesson in editorial freedom. He permitted no *Life* advertising salesmen to intrude upon the editorial floors, and once a year accepted a call from the advertising director to inquire if it was okay to drop by and wish the managing editor a Merry Christmas. He, all of us, had a few friends on "the business side," but the only time their side consulted with our side was on the selection of covers. Because covers presumably helped sell the magazine they were considered advertising, and the business side could have its say. If EKT would listen.

□ □ □

Thompson ran the magazine before the rise of women's liberation or the black revolution of the sixties, and during a period in which *Life*'s editorial stance was Republican. It is an indication of staff regard for him—or of his cool inscrutability on such matters—that people who were Democrats thought that he was one too, secretly, and people who were Republicans were sure he shared their conviction.

The few blacks on the staff assumed he was on their side, and the women had no complaints. It was axiomatic that Ed thought women couldn't write for the magazine, though he denies this, and it was axiomatic that he placed photographers on the top of the pole and expected everyone else to serve them. He was the first, however, to bawl out a photographer who was beastly to his reporter, and the first to insist upon a general atmosphere of respect and equality. He never used bad language in the presence of either ladies or gentlemen, and during his regime the attitude of the female staff became, "Okay, boys, hold my coat, light my cigarettes, and respect my mind."

Most *Life* women believed, correctly, that they had among the best jobs in journalism. The hours were sometimes horrendous but the pay was good, the companionship rewarding, the experience exciting. Some reader surveys showed that the magazine wasn't as popular with women as it was with men, and this bothered the business side. Delegates from business kept nagging at EKT to elevate a woman to writing status in the text department, or to try to groom a female assistant managing editor. At one point Luce even announced to Thompson that "*Life*'s editors hate women."

Thompson was so stunned that he was even less communicative than usual. When he pulled himself together he reminded Luce of four women department heads: Sally Kirkland of fashion, Dorothy Seiberling of art, Mary Hamman of modern living, Mary Leatherbee of movies. Plus Marian MacPhail, head of research; Lee Eitingon, assistant picture editor; and Nancy Genet, assistant science editor. And a battery of women correspondents in the field. *Life*, he told Luce, was "a veritable hotbed of feminism."

He further insisted that he never took sex into consideration when assigning people to bureaus or to jobs within the house. There may be argument on the point but I, for one, believe him. Among my souvenirs is a scrap of yellow telex paper which is the end of a message sent from Rome to New York in 1957. It contains my instructions on how to intercept an air passenger who had some film which might interest *Life*. Our customary sign-off on telex messages from abroad was "albest" and then the signature. For some reason mine got garbled on that message and turned up in New York reading "ALBERT HAMBLIN."

EKT cut off the bottom of the message, drew a neat pencil line to "ALBERT" and mailed it back to me in Rome with a short typed message: "Dear Albert: I guess I didn't need to convince anyone that there was no reason why a woman couldn't do a good professional job in Rome. EKT."

14

The Chase

Perhaps the story *Life* loved most was The Chase. A really good one combined all the classic elements—spectacle, human drama, derring-do, overkill, lots of opportunities to charter things, a race against the competition. As an added fillip, it usually gave at least two desk-bound New York editors a chance to engage in duel by deployment. Because chases by their very nature move in and out of neatly designated areas of responsibility, at least two chiefs could send out their own Indians and then happily play my-guys-will-outwit-your-guys. This inner competition, much cherished on the magazine, led to an extraordinary amount of predawn telephoning and flurries of cables which were more fun for the chiefs than for the Indians.

One of the wildest of all chases began on Monday, January 23, 1961. On that day a 20,000-ton Portuguese cruise ship, the *Santa Maria,* bound from Curacao to Port Everglades, Florida, hove to off the island of St. Lucia in the Caribbean and lowered a lifeboat. Into it clambered half a dozen men who started to row slowly toward Castries harbor. Late diners and portside loafers watched the lifeboat draw near and then saw, to their horror, two wounded men and a handful of very excited sailors shouting in a language which English-speaking St. Lucia couldn't make out. While the sailors yelled and the crowd gaped, the *Santa Maria* steamed off at full speed and vanished over the horizon.

Finally one of the crewmen summoned his few words of English and shouted, "Pirates! We have been taken by pirates."

Alarm signals flashed in all directions from St. Lucia that night. A British frigate which had been anchored in St. Lucia rushed off in pursuit of the fugitive cruise ship. Two U.S. Navy destroyers and eight land-based aircraft rushed from Puerto Rico and Trinidad to join the search.

I arrived at work at the usual time next day and was told by foreign news editor Gene Farmer to go straight back home again, pack, get to Idlewild airport, meet there photographer Art Rickerby—whom I did not know, a fact which was to become poignant a few days later—and proceed to Port of Spain, Trinidad.

To my mumbled, "What? What?" Gene only snapped, in his best harrassed executive fashion, "No time. You just git, git . . ." and he shoved a little packet of AP ticker copy into my hand. In the taxi from home to the airport I read it. The *Santa Maria* had sailed from Lisbon on January 9 and had an uneventful passage. A few days later it picked up some third-class passengers at Guaira, Venezuela, and on the island of Curacao. They were all men, and they came aboard carrying their hand luggage. These "passengers" shortly revealed themselves to be rebels against the regime of then-dictator Antonio Salazar of Portugal. Their leader was a swashbuckler named Henrique Galvao. At a signal from him the men pulled pistols and submachine guns out of their suitcases and took over the ship, killing one officer and wounding two others in the process.

The legitimate captain was a prisoner in his cabin. There were about three dozen American passengers on board the ship. Nobody knew where Galvao was headed or what he had in mind. Clearly he intended to use the captured vessel to protest against the Salazar regime, but where did he plan to go with it? Trinidad seemed a likely place to start the chase.

Rickerby and I met at the airline ticket counter and shook hands politely. During a long delay before take-off we both confessed to an old desire to see and hear the famous steel bands of Trinidad. And we regretted, though not as much as we would later, not having had time to rummage through our wardrobes for something more appropriate to the tropics. We were both clad in New York's winter wool. With boots.

By the time we got to Port of Spain there was a neat little pile of cables at the hotel. Farmer wanted Rickerby to try to get aboard a destroyer. He advised that correspondent Ed Shook and photographer Bill Ray were enroute to Trinidad and told me to "decide how best to deploy the *Life* forces."

There was also a cable from Roy Rowan: "please send shook and ray to st. lucia in view of fact destroyers not now expected trinidad." Rowan was domestic news editor, which meant that his department was now in the act and that Rowan had, apparently, just one-upped Farmer.

Then came two more cables from foreign news's Farmer: "hank suydam and joe scherschel arriving san juan puerto rico today," and "in view fixed sighting reportedly about four hundred miles north of amazon river mouth hadn't you better get to belem [Brazil] fastest? That looks like nearest big port and it would take rowan's grumman goose exmiami three days to make it. You can hire seaplane there . . ."

I hadn't the faintest idea what "Rowan's Grumman Goose" was all about, but it was clear that Farmer was alarmed and wanted his Indians to step more smartly than Rowan's. And it might be wise to charter something just to appear alert.

In between cables, Rickerby and I spent a day in a Trinidad taxi rushing from the navy base to the airport, checking rumors, trying to pry from Washington a confirmation that Rickerby had a Defense Department clearance and could, indeed, be taken on a navy ship or airplane. In the course of that hectic day we paid several calls on the navy base public information officer, Commander Maurice Currie. He was courteous but noncommittal. The fact was, neither the British nor American forces had been able to find the *Santa Maria.* She was sighted at last by a Danish freighter, and a wag at the navy base posted a hand-lettered sign which said, "Have no fear, the Danish merchant fleet will watch over you." Rickerby and I also covered a press conference given by the British commander of a frigate, the *Rothesay,* which had been in St. Lucia when the lifeboat came ashore. The commander had been sipping tea at the time, with the local governer.

By the next day Shook and Ray were at St. Lucia interviewing the crewmen from the *Santa Maria* who had gone ashore in the lifeboat. Rickerby had wangled himself a ride on an observer aircraft looking for the ship, and I was trying to find an airplane to get me to Belem. There was a scheduled Pan American flight three days later but that seemed hopelessly far away. I have a copy of a cable to Farmer in which I reported rather plaintively that "charters difficult because british west indies viscounts grounded for check and they using all extra aircraft in emergency. they offer request loan dakota from british guiana at dollars 200 per hour but plane couldn't be here before friday.''

By next morning Rickerby still had not come back from his reconnaissance flight. I had no idea where he was, and I got a call from another reporter who said that one of his friends had gone out on a navy reconnaissance plane and was told that they might not come back to Trinidad, to Puerto Rico, or to the Western Hemisphere at all. They might instead go to Dakar, Africa.

Then photographer Ray, who was supposed to go back to New York from St. Lucia, decided instead to go to Recife, Brazil. He wasn't going to get off the story just because New York had told him to. My ''deployment'' was in total disarray, and the rumors were flying: the *Santa Maria* had been sighted heading for Cuba; it was heading for Angola; it was heading for somewhere in Brazil.

As if there weren't enough, early morning messages from Farmer instructed me to try to find a stringer photographer from Jamaica, named John Hlavacek, in Belem. He might be useful. There was also a photographer from Venezuela, named Charles Tasnadi, who might be in Belem. Find him. The cast was thickening as fast as the plot.

Finally on Friday a plane materialized and the assembled press galloped for it. The flight from Trinidad to Belem was fascinating and terrifying by turns as we skimmed the tops of jungle trees and all but touched wheels on vast muddy rivers. Belem, however, was less than enchanting, being filthy, noisy, and menacing in a nonspecific but quite convincing way. I had been instructed to go to the Grande Hotel, where I found a whole string of new URGENT cables from New York. I also found Rickerby, whose plane had deposited him there after a fourteen-hour flight during which they never saw the *Santa Maria;* and *Life*'s Suydam and Scherschel, who weren't supposed to be there at all. I did not find Tasnadi or Hlavacek. Late that afternoon I called on the American consulate to see if there were by chance messages from the missing men. Consulates and banks were our best contact points during chases, because everybody needed another visa or another $1,000 about every four hours.

By next morning, January 28, Rickerby and I decided Belem was a bad deal. Suydam and Scherschel were there. It was ridiculous to have two teams in the same city, and the latest rumor was that the *Santa Maria* was headed further south. We separated to try to get plane tickets, met at lunch, and this time Suydam and Scherschel joined us. They had tickets to Recife, they confessed, but they had decided instead to go to Rio. They would give us their Recife tickets. Because Suydam was one of the Machiavellian characters on the magazine—he belonged to a group known as the Rover Boys—I wondered then, and I still wonder now, just what his ploy was. But again there was no time, Rickerby and I had to "git."

Recife was heaven after twenty-four hours in Belem. There, too, home was the Grande Hotel, the name seems as ubiquitous in Brazil as is the Excelsior in Italy. Recife's Grande was bursting with at least 250 journalists from all over the world, who not only occupied all the rooms but also set up command posts in the lobby, on the roof, and slept, some of them, in the corridors. There were deafening conversations, in six languages, twenty-four hours a day. The telephone service was appalling. One AP reporter placed a call to New York and was told to wait *un momento.* He waited for seven hours, but he couldn't leave the phone and do anything else because every twenty minutes the pleasant-voiced operator rang him back to repeat, reassuringly, *un momento.*

The taxis were driven—when they ran, which was rare—by a fraternity of blithe philosophers who regarded each flat tire, broken axle, or exhausted battery as a conversational opening which could be expanded into a day-long examination of the human capacity for surviving natural and mechanical disasters.

My phone rang only once, the first day in Recife, and it was New York saying that Paris bureau correspondent David Snell happened to be in Africa on a story and might be dispatched to Recife to join our group.

"From Africa?" I screamed, and they told me to look at a map. They were right. He was a lot closer than anyone else.

By Sunday morning, January 29, events and bodies were coagulating. The *Santa Maria* was anchored about fifty miles off Recife, while rebel Galvao dickered with the U.S. Navy, the Brazilian government, and the Portuguese. At this point a new and imposing figure entered the scene: Portuguese General Humberto Delgado. Delgado claimed that he had won the Portuguese elections of 1958 and was the rightful ruler of the nation. He had been defrauded of his position by Dictator Salazar and had been living in exile in São Paulo, Brazil. But now he was on his way to Recife to join Galvao on the *Santa Maria.*

Also on its way to Recife was one of Farmer's more mysterious cables. It read, in part, "You should know we have attempted make very odd deal through stringer garcia of caracas [Venezuela] to guarantee exclusivity on photographic material off santamaria . . ." The "odd deal" included two journalists from Venezuela, Robert Miller and Charles Tasnadi—that same mysterious Tasnadi for whom I had been searching ever since Belem. These two, Farmer cabled, had top-secret connections and could contact General Delgado and go with him to board the ship. "Beyond that," Farmer's cable read, "deponent knoweth not what all this may produce."

When Farmer resorted to "deponent knoweth not" I knew somebody's Indian was in trouble. Probably me. By this time *Life* had in Recife photographers, Ray, Rickerby, and Scherschel, reporters Snell, Suydam, and Hamblin. Hlavacek had turned up and wanted to be helpful. The unknown Venezuelans, Tasnadi and Miller, loomed on the horizon. Logistics were getting complex and tempers short, especially about 3:30 every morning when my alarm went off and I had to get out to the Recife airport to ship the day's film by air express to New York.

Sending air express packages in unfamiliar countries is always an adventure, but Brazil was special. In the first place, Portuguese is a somewhat offbeat language, and in 1961 the people on duty before dawn at the airport spoke not a word of anything else. The man in charge of the air express desk at the Recife airport was always sound asleep at 4:00 A.M. The first time I went, I had to shake him awake. We had a half-hour conversation in pidgin Italian, French, English, and my five words of German, and in the end he simply shrugged his shoulders, opened a drawer, handed me a waybill form, and went back to sleep. I found that I could make out the Portuguese wording with a little study—air express waybills are pretty much alike everywhere in the world—and that the noise of his typewriter, when I used it, did not disturb his slumber in the slightest. From that first morning on I simply went in, got out the form, typed it up and signed it, left the envelope of film and a tip, and went back to the hotel—provided the taxi could make it all the way. I don't know who woke up the air express man when it was time for the plane to leave, but somehow all of our packages got to New York.

Monday, January 30, I devoted to (*a*) trying to send radio-telegram messages to various U.S. citizens on board the beleaguered ship, several of whom had managed to get messages out to their next of kin and might be willing to recount their experiences for *Life;* (*b*) scraping up $150 in a hurry for Bill Ray, who found a small airplane he could charter to overfly the *Santa Maria* and photograph it; and (*c*) finding Miller and Tasnadi. I located them at last, late at night, only after Hank Suydam had sidled up to me in the hotel bar to say he had encountered a pair of journalists he thought were phonies, pretending to have a deal with *Life*. His interruption was distinctly inopportune because I was at that moment deep in discussion with some navy public information officers who were scheduled to board the *Santa Maria* next day with an American admiral aboard the destroyer *Gear-*

ing. One of the PIOs was an enlisted man who had just agreed, for $50, to try to pick up film from passengers on the ship and get it off and into my hands. He would also try to find a passenger named Nat Logan Smith who had indicated that he had written a piece he was willing to sell.

By this time the assembled reporters, all 250 of us, were very busy trudging up and down the Recife waterfront trying to charter boats. The *Santa Maria* was out there in the mist, out of sight but large in the mind, and the Recife Regatta was in spate. Intrepid reporters who were afraid to drink the water in the hotel were willing to risk oceans of it onboard a tugboat, tuna boat, lobster boat, sailing skiff, anything that would float. Dozens went charging out through the night trying to reach the ship. Recife fishermen whose reported net annual income hovered around $400 had got together and decreed that a single charter trip out to the *Santa Maria* and back would be $500.

Life's first vessel weighed anchor late Monday with Snell, Rickerby, and an interpreter aboard. That expedition hadn't come back yet on Tuesday morning when the destroyer *Gearing* set forth carrying Admiral Allen Smith, a Brazilian officer, and my bribed enlisted man to rendezvous. Also on board were about 100 newsmen, including Suydam and Scherschel.

Miller and Tasnadi, our Venezuelan cloak-and-dagger boys, scorned the *Gearing* expedition on the grounds—quite correct, as it turned out—that nobody from the press would be allowed to leave the destroyer that morning. I saw off Suydam, Scherschel, and the *Gearing,* sent an air express packet, and again found Bill Ray on my doorstep. This time he wanted to borrow my little aluminum suitcase because he knew this mad French photographer who was going to parachute onto the deck of the *Santa Maria* that very day and he needed a waterproof bag for his cameras in case he . . . well . . . um . . . somehow missed the ship. Praying silently that it wasn't Ray himself who contemplated this desperate effort, I handed over the bag and went to rout out Miller and Tasnadi. They, in turn, yearned for a boat of their own to try to reach the ship. They didn't have any money but I liked them both and they seemed to speak all the appropriate languages, so I forked over $600—prices were already rising—and off they went to the waterfront.

New York at this point instructed me to find "a cost-sharing few others" to defray the expense of the Miller-Tasnadi mission, and I asked New York to radio the ship: "urgentest get radio message to captain telling him two men from caracas carrying credentials signed personally delgado attempting reach him will approach in fishing vessel within 24 to 30 hours will identify themselves by flashing three shorts and one long, then interval, then repeat signal with mirror or flashlight.''

The next forty-eight hours remain a sleepless blur. Because Brazilian fishermen showed reluctance to accept female passengers, and because cables came from New York about every half-hour, and because I always throw up in small boats, I decided my post was ashore. Armed with powerful binoculars, and with a note pinned to my hotel room door indicating my whereabouts, I took up vigil on the roof of the Grande Hotel.

I did not see the dramatic moment—it was too far away. But it did happen that, in the midst of tense negotiations between the American admiral and the rebel Captain Galvao, two small planes circled the *Santa Maria* each disgorging one parachutist. The first man, dressed in a professional-looking rubber suit, leaped and missed, and was fished from the sea by a small boat which put off from the *Santa Maria.* He, lucky man, was taken aboard and Galvao, who obviously liked his swashbuckling style, invited him to lunch.

The second parachutist, clad in chino pants, a white shirt, a borrowed Brazilian parachute, carrying my aluminum suitcase, climbed slowly out on a strut, braced his foot on one of the plane's wheels, and leaped into space. His chute opened more slowly than expected so he fell fast, missing the ship completely. As he hit the waves he sank perilously deep. When at last he surfaced, he saw a gig from the destroyer *Gearing* headed for him, and tried frantically to swim away from it.

Gasping, gurgling, struggling in the warm water he kept shouting, ''No, no. Other ship, other ship.'' Relentlessly the gig bore down however, and to his horror the parachutist saw sailors lined up on the rail of the destroyer with high-powered rifles. Photographer Charles Bonnay of *Paris Match* was convinced they meant to shoot him if he didn't cease from flight and get meekly aboard the gig. Only later did he discover that the sailors were simply ready to protect him from sharks if there were any about.

''I wanted to fall closer,'' Bonnay explained later. ''But the chute is very fast. I fall fast. I head for the water because I know I break myself if I head for the ship.''

While all this drama was going on, Snell and Rickerby turned up at my command post on the roof, looking green. They reported total failure of their mission with the fishing boat, and stumbled off to bed. The navy enlisted man from the *Gearing* turned up with several rolls of passenger film, which he had concealed in his socks to smuggle them off the *Santa Maria,* and he reported that he and other public information types had taken some good pictures of the passengers and negotiations on board. These pictures were to be "pooled," made available to all the media simultaneously. I had hoped to one-up the rest of the press by getting my man to write good captions—so that everyone might have the photos, but *Life* alone would also have names and accurate information. My man had done his job impeccably—but unfortunately the piece of paper on which he had written the captions had blown out of his pocket as the *Gearing* steamed for the port.

There was no time to mourn. Farmer was back on the cable with:

> doubtless you've heard of this but orshefsky [the Paris bureau chief for *Life*] just phoned that french parachutist delamare dived into ocean and been uppicked by santamaria so hes aboard presumably taking pictures stop agent louis dalmas who staying your hotel we understand sold ttvv rights to ccbbss stateside and still rights to various european clients but has not sold still rights unistates stop he wants to hear from us first stop contact dalmas soonest and see how land lies bearing in mind this maybe more stunt than picture story but also bearing in mind delamare in position to get the last night out for the passengers if hes any good with still camera stop this should be balanced against what you think other prospects are for getting on board and so far chatham radio has no contact on my two messages stop however eye unknow what you all up to tonight so have to defer your judgment stop suggest you try check this out with dalmas and start at one thousand down if this seems to be gap we cant plug otherwise stop if that unworks go up to twenty five hundred top guarantee but its up to dalmas to convince you that this thing is going to produce visavis what you think youre getting elsewhere so be tough as you can stop you might try using phone after seeing him although eye had no luck on that today good heavens the flying enterprise [another, earlier saga of the sea] was nothing but we trust you kid best.

Armed with these limpid instructions, I put down the binoculars and went off in search of Monsieur Dalmas. Of course Farmer didn't know what we were "up to tonight." *We* didn't know what we were up to tonight: except that Miller and Tasnadi, at least, were headed for the ship with their three shorts and a long signal carefully memorized, and their mirror and flashlight at the ready. Their trawler bounced and lurched through the sea, running without lights for secrecy. There was nothing to look at actually except a Japanese crew of three who fascinated the reporters with their skill at tying knots with their feet and their teeth. Virtually everyone on board was desperately seasick. Three hours out from Recife the newsmen caught a glimpse of a smudge of light on the horizon, a stationary light indicating a ship at anchor. In two more hours the trawler crept within three miles and the light turned into a ship looking tiny on a moonlit sea. Closer, closer crept the trawler, and even the sickest of the reporters staggered to his feet.

Then, inexplicably, without waiting for our Venezuelans to give their signal, the Brazilian trawler captain turned on a huge searchlight and pointed it at the *Santa Maria.* Startled faces appeared over towering rails, and the newsmen shouted frantically into the night, in English and Spanish and Portuguese. In vain they produced their credentials and waved them aloft—press cards, White House press passes, Venezuelan police cards, American Express, Diners' Club, Amoco credit cards, passports, anything. To no avail. Lazily, disdainfully, the ship—now renamed the *Santa Liberdad* by Captain Galvao—started her engines, turned her stern with a flounce toward the trawler, and steamed away at what seemed many, many knots per hour.

Our trawler limped back into Recife about 8:00 A.M. Wednesday, February 1. By then I was back from the airport and on the roof again. Miller came to me in a state of high excitement. General Delgado himself had arrived in Recife. Miller would go see him immediately, and if *Life* would charter just one more boat, he was sure they could get aboard. By this time I had reached a fine state of "Oh, what the hell?" so I handed over another $600. The plan was that Tasnadi would rent the same trawler—its crew at least knew the way—Miller would line up Delgado, and at 10:30 the group would set forth again. Nobody had had any sleep, but it didn't seem important.

By this time news came that the *Santa Maria* was steaming toward Recife. Supplies on board were running short, tempers even shorter, and Captain Galvao had headed for land. He was sailing slowly, however, and dickering with Brazilian authorities to grant asylum to himself and his men as political protestors, not pirates. At least the Recife Regatta wouldn't have so far to go to intercept the ship.

Just as the main plot began to work itself out, the *Life* plot raveled. Unbeknownst to the Venezuelans and to me, Hank Suydam had overheard part of our planning conversation, and had dispatched a friend to head off General Delgado and prevent his rendezvous with Miller and Tasnadi. His motives for this should perhaps be viewed generously, though it is difficult. Perhaps he felt that the Venezuelans weren't "the real *Life* team" and that he could produce a dramatic coup by outwitting them. At the time, however, Miller and Tasnadi and I felt a bit like Charlie Osborne back in South Carolina, that Suydam had attempted to "kidnap our goddam story."

Again in company with a "cost-sharing few others," the Venezuelans set forth for the *Santa Maria.* They were completely baffled because General Delgado hadn't kept his appointment. This time, however, they got close enough to the ship to identify themselves, with a megaphone. Galvao ordered a rope ladder dropped, and Miller climbed aboard to present his credentials. They were accepted, and he went back to summon photographer Tasnadi aboard. When Tasnadi was safely up the ladder, Galvao's men ordered the trawler to pull away. This created outrage and consternation among the "cost sharing others," with complete justice. But Galvao's men at the rail were armed. The trawler pulled away.

All that afternoon, as the *Santa Maria* inched closer and closer to port, Tasnadi took pictures and Miller interviewed crew and passengers. They were there for a brief but ugly insurrection of third-class passengers, mostly Spanish and Portuguese, who had not been treated with such consideration as had the Americans in first class. There was pushing and shoving, a man thrown through a glass door, a dramatic confrontation between Galvao and the insurrectionists. By late afternoon Tasnadi had a story and was desperate to get his film off the ship and on its way to New York. Galvao was reluctant to let anyone leave, but Miller finally persuaded him that the only way to get his side of the story to the world's press was to let him leave the ship and begin filing. He gathered up Tasnadi's film, his notes, and waited for the next fishing boat to approach.

Ironically, the next one on the scene had been rented by another contingent of journalists who included Suydam and Scherschel. The *Santa Maria* threw a ladder over the side so Miller could climb down to the fishing boat, but before he had stepped on the first rung, *Life*'s enterprising Joe Scherschel had sprung from fishing boat to bottom rung and was clinging there desperately waiting to climb up and board the ship. Somebody—versions vary—shouted orders to stop Scherschel, somebody else gave orders to take the fishing boat away. Scherschel clung stubbornly to his swaying ladder for fifteen minutes while his colleagues photographed him and Miller shouted at him to get the blankety-blank down and off there.

When some semblance of order had been restored, Scherschel got reluctantly off the ladder, Miller climbed down, and rode back to Recife under what he called "blast-furnace gazes" from the frustrated journalists on that boat.

My ecstasy at receipt of Tasnadi's onboard film—now a clear *Life* exclusive—impelled me to beg Miller to go back to the *Santa Maria* one more time and take Dave Snell and Art Rickerby with him. General Delgado had sent an irate message to Miller—"Where were you?"—and gradually we had pieced together the perfidy of Suydam. Within an hour we had the general, his secretary, Snell, Rickerby, Miller, and me all safely sipping tea in my hotel room. What turned

CREDIT: CHARLES BONNAY, BLACK STAR

Captain Galvao, head bent, surrendering his hijacked ship in Recife, Brazil, in 1961. At lower right is General Delgado getting out of car at dockside.

out to be the last entry in the Recife Regatta set forth in moonlight. This time the party didn't have far to go—the *Santa Maria* was anchored about one inch outside the three-mile limit. General Delgado identified himself from the small boat and climbed up the rope ladder to be embraced by Captain Galvao. Their revolution had failed, but the two comrades in arms appeared not to notice it. Miller, Snell, and Rickerby followed the general up the ladder and went straight to work.

When nobody turned up at the Grande that night I went to bed about 2:00 A.M. At roughly 4:00 I was awakened by banging on the door. There stood a small, polite Brazilian fisherman. Wordlessly he handed me half a sheet of yellow legal-sized paper upon which Snell had written, "Please give this man $600. Love, Dave Snell."

It turned out that the general and his secretary, who had been constrained by her skirts and spike-heeled shoes to stay in the bouncing fishing boat while the general went aboard, had no desire whatever to spend the night on the *Santa Maria.* Miller and Tasnadi, Snell and Rickerby, were even more determined not to leave the ship. In the impasse, the general apparently feared that if he and the secretary returned alone to Recife he might have to pay the charter fee. "I am a chief of state," he informed Snell icily. "I do not handle money. You will pay for the boat, and please do so while I finish dictating a statement."

Snell just didn't happen to have $600 on him at the moment, hence his hurried note to paymaster general ashore.

On Thursday, February 2, the *Santa Maria* came into Recife harbor. Captain Galvao still refused to tie up at the dock, as he harbored dreams of being permitted to refuel and sail away to carry on his revolution. The passengers thus had to be debarked in skiffs and tenders.

Life now had, however, Tasnadi's and Rickerby's film. I had concluded a successful arrangement with Monsieur Dalmas for U.S. rights to the take of Delamare the daring parachutist, and we had shipped his film to London where the bureau had complex instructions to meet a stewardess in the "reporting room, building 221, London airport" to receive it, transship to Paris, and there Orshefsky would pick what he wanted for *Life.* We also had coverage of the disembarkation; we had passenger Nat Logan Smith's account of life on board; we had the passenger film smuggled off by my enlisted man. We sent an overjoyed cable to Farmer in New York: "modestly speaking we really tore up the pea patch have virtual exclusive all film onboard and every other angle blanketed."

All of the *Life* troops were booked out of Recife to Rio de Janeiro on a 6:00 A.M. flight Friday, February 3. We were to spend the day in Rio neatening up our reports, captioning the film, getting ready for a midnight flight from Rio which was scheduled to arrive at Idlewild at 6:00 A.M. Saturday. That would provide little sleep, but a whole day of work in the home office to close the story.

That was the night, February 3, that the blizzard hit New York. Our Varig Airlines jet took off from Rio on schedule. I clutched an enormous package of film, captions, text. Near me in the big plush seats were photographers Rickerby, Scherschel, Ray, and about twelve new best friends from AP, UPI, the *Toronto Star;* we got pretty chummy on chases. Some of us slept, fitfully, until 6:00 A.M. I woke up then because we seemed to be landing. I looked out the window at—palm trees. Acres, oceans of palm trees. Stunned, I punched Rickerby and pointed out the window.

We were back in Trinidad.

It wasn't quite daylight when we trooped wearily down the airplane steps. Airport attendants said there was a delay in New York. Nothing very serious, a lot of snow, a few hours delay . . . in the meanwhile would the ladies and gentlemen be so kind . . . and they waved us toward a palm-fringed building near the control tower. Inside, in what looked like the recreation hall of quite a good summer camp, were arrayed row upon row of cots. They seemed neat and clean; some were occupied, some were not; we stumbled toward them in the semidark, groping and apologizing and finally sinking mindless, without a care for night dress, toothbrushes, or anything else, into exhausted sleep. I remember putting my precious package under the pillow for safety.

Something—perhaps ESP from Farmer in New York—awakened me less than three hours later. I groped through the shuttered gloom toward the door, back to the control tower, to inquire about take-off time. The man on duty shook his head. No hope for today, he said, all New York and New Jersey airports were closed. Snowed in, and still snowing. Why didn't we all, he suggested, enjoy beautiful Trinidad and stop worrying?

By this time one of my colleagues, I have forgotten which one, appeared at my elbow and we looked at each other with consternation. We had with us a great *Life* coup and we were stuck in bloody Trinidad with the magazine destined to close that very night. Together we plunged from the office and ran like maniacs over the tarmac. Surely somewhere, somehow, there must be a plane going to the States. If not to New York, maybe to Dallas, to Washington, to Miami. They couldn't be having a blizzard in Miami.

Sure enough, eventually we found a Pan American cargo plane headed for Miami. We implored the crew to take us with them, but they said it was against the rules. They listened patiently to our whole long story and finally said they could take the package of film, captions, text, but no bodies.

"None at all? Not even one?" we pleaded.

Well, the pilot said a bit dubiously, sometimes when he carried animals as cargo he was permitted to carry also a keeper.

"How big an animal?" we asked. "A chicken? A crate of chickens? Some birds?

No, not really, he said. Something bigger.

"A cow? A calf, maybe?"

Maybe, he said. That did it. Waving our thanks we rushed to the nearest taxi, plunged into the countryside, and after almost an hour managed to buy a nice looking calf for forty dollars. Neither calf nor cab driver displayed much enthusiasm for our project, but we were desperate. I held the calf's head on my lap, stroking it gently, while my colleague dealt with the taxi driver. We arrived in triumph at the cargo plane, only to be turned down again. The pilot looked genuinely sorry, but he couldn't take our calf and its keeper. I don't know what had really happened, but his official explanation was that his cargo was airplane propellors, and a calf tramping around in the fuselage might damage them.

This left nothing to do except entrust the precious package to the pilot and set about calling Miami and New York. Someone else took charge of the calf, and I regret that I never learned its fate. The phone calls took hours. While more fortunate companions got up late, ate breakfast, proceeded to the swimming pool, we sweated in phone booths screaming instructions about where and how to intercept our film and story.

When finally all that was done, I walked to our early-morning dormitory, visions of baths and toothbrushes dancing in my head. My path was blocked by a very small, very upset Trinidadian.

"Madame," he said, his voice choking with aggrieved propriety, "you have . . . you have spent the night with sixteen gentlemen!"

I was even more speechless than he. I had not, it is true, counted the gentlemen, but I considered "spending the night" a gross exaggeration of the innocent exhaustion of the hours between 6:30 and 9:00 A.M. that day.

"We were all directed by airport authorities toward that . . . uh . . . those . . . quarters," I said firmly. "I am sorry if you are upset, but there was a certain amount of confusion. We were going to Idlewild, you see, and . . ."

He never let me finish. "Follow me," he snapped, and he led me back to a registry desk. He then reached up, plucked a key from a rack, shoved it under my nose, and proclaimed: ''This is your room for tonight. You will sleep there. You will select one gentleman—only one—and you will sleep there.''

Now it was my turn for propriety aggrieved.

''You mean . . . ?'' was all I could choke out.

The small man glared, nodded, and shook the key at me. Meekly I took it, meekly I collected my baggage, meekly I moved to my new room. I spent the late afternoon with the gentlemen at the pool, deciding whom I should honor with an invitation to what had proved to be rather palatial quarters with two huge beds, a bathroom, and a palm-fringed veranda.

In the end, I chose Rickerby. I had noticed on the plane that he was the only photographer who didn't snore. Besides, I remembered my mother's admonitions years ago about always being accompanied home by the gentleman with whom I had gone out. Rickerby and I had started this thing together, albeit as total strangers to each other, and we would end it together. I explained this to him, in private. He was appalled but gallant, and the two of us played out an embarrassed Alphonse-and-Gaston scene for the bathroom both that night and the next morning.

The next day Varig managed to move us as far as the Dominican Republic, and there we played roulette in Trujillo's fancy gambling joints while our colleagues in Miami, New York, and Chicago managed somehow to close a lead in the magazine with the material we had worked so hard to get. By the time we finally got to New York, late on a Monday afternoon, the first issues of *Life* were out and on the newsstands.

Years later Snell and I were reminiscing about the chase for the *Santa Maria* and he said, ''Do you have a favorite quote of all time?''

I thought I did, and I thought I knew what he meant. We both retired to our offices to plow through the files of carefully stored notebooks, and we both produced the very same quote.

It was rendered to us in Recife, by a U.S. diplomatic official whom I believe should be nameless, on a fateful afternoon when nobody knew what was going to happen next or how we should proceed. I quote herewith from the oficial:

''This is the moment of truth, as Hemingway said. Anything can happen. Captain Galvao has to decide to be or not to be. Meanwhile, the patient isn't getting any better.''

With that kind of help, how could any journalist fail?

Merciless Mechanics

Many of *Life*'s most strenuous efforts, wildest exploits, cherished memories, came straight from the most prosaic of sources—exigency. The merciless mechanics.

To begin with, we could not cover a story from a distance, reading wire-service reports and interviewing each other at the bar of Shepheards Hotel in Cairo or the veranda of Raffles in Singapore. We had to have photographs, and to get them one had to be there. This was step one.

Step two was getting the photographs physically on an airplane, with captions enclosed, so that they would arrive in New York in comprehensible form. Somebody had to take them to the plane, get them on, get them off at the other end, deliver them to the office.

We were, we often told each other (sometimes at the bar of Shepheards or on the veranda of Raffles) really in the transportation business. Time itself, and airline schedules, loomed far larger in our lives than did literary quality. We ran around like nuts covering what we could get in the time allowed, got it on the plane, and prayed. This urgency applied most specifically to the news staff and to correspondents in the field. The non-news departments normally had time to cogitate at length, to develop their stories rationally and calmly. For the rest of us, a switch from propellor planes to jets affected our lives far more than the collapse of a government. In the fifties when one airport after another altered its schedules to accommodate jets, bureaus all over the world stayed up nights reorganizing their workload. Every day's schedule was pointed to ''making the plane'': the switch to jets actually altered the daily routine of many a *Life* bureau.

The big envelope in which we dispatched our efforts was called ''the packet,'' and ''making the packet'' was an article of faith. It was invocation, prayer, and affliction. Whether carried lovingly, dangerously, resentfully, to the nearest airport it contained the end result of all our work, the precious parcel of our combined efforts and hasty scholarship.

The bearer of the packet thus became a highly important member of the team, a colleague. Mechanics contributed mightily to the cherished ''democracy'' of *Life*. Probably the most celebrated packet-bearer on the magazine was Pepi Martis of the Paris bureau. Pepi is an Austrian who had done some time in the French Foreign Legion before he joined Time Inc. at the end of World War II. His title was driver, but he quickly became also guide, photographers' assistant, chief packet-carrier, interpreter, factotum. Pepi spoke four languages, stuttered in all of them, and preceded each sentence with a loud ''Jesus Christus!'' The phrase was accompanied by a resounding smack on the front of his balding head with the palm of his very clean right hand.

He owned the best and most battered ''foreign correspondent's raincoat'' in the entire Paris bureau, plus a tatty blue beret which he always swept off with his left hand as he entered the holy precincts of the office. He could find roads, restaurants, hotels, with a facility and a taste that Michelin would envy, and he could also set up tripods, attach miles of wire, calculate photographic exposures, and even push the shutter button if necessary. He was polite, friendly, and equal to any celebrity whom he encountered. He once advised a recently deposed monarch in Estoril, Portugal, to ''move over a little to the left, Kink, or you won't be in the picture,'' and on an occasion in Paris when he was introduced to General Eisenhower he was so enthusiastic that he threw an entire armload of flashbulbs and electrical wiring into the air to shake hands. Pepi and the general shook solemnly amid the sound of crashing glass.

Perhaps most important of all, Pepi never missed a packet. One early morning he heard on the radio that a New York–bound plane had crashed just outside Le Bourget airport in Paris. Without even bothering to wake up his bosses, Pepi hopped into an office car, found the wrecked plane, found the *Life* packet which had bounced free from the debris. He rushed with it to the air express office, got a new waybill, put it on the next plane, and then went back to help rescue workers at the crash site.

So beloved was this man that the *Life* Europe staff once took up a collection to buy him a trip to New York. There he was such a social success that at one point, consulting the little black book he carried in his upper left vest pocket, he had to inform the publisher of the magazine that he didn't have, unfortunately, a single luncheon date free during his stay in the big city.

There were other Pepis, like Giulio de Angelis in Rome, who looked so much like a *commendatore* that bureaucrats always assumed he was one. Giulio could arrive at Ciampino airport half an hour late, fix an entire airline with his imperious stare, and halt flights in their screaming tracks while he got his packet aboard. There was Wilhelm in Bonn; and Imai in Tokyo, who has since risen to be office manager. There was Alan Clifton in London, a pale frail office boy of about sixteen when we first knew him, who had such a genius for spiriting late packets onto airplanes that at one office party he was made to kneel and be dubbed The Earl of "Any Packet?."

Among the other colorful packet carriers were the Shanghai office's two Changs. The bureau used two cars, a Dodge and a Plymouth, and bureau chief Roy Rowan took to calling his drivers Dodge Chang and Plymouth Chang. When the Communists took over China and the bureau retreated to Hong Kong, one driver—Plymouth Chang—went along. The only car that went along was, however, the Dodge. "So Plymouth Chang became Dodge Chang and it was all very confusing," Rowan recalls.

□ □ □

To facilitate the transshipment and rapid handling of these precious parcels, *Life* designed and customarily used a fire-engine red envelope, eleven by fourteen inches. On its already strident outside were affixed large labels, in a variety of colors, proclaiming PRESS MATERIAL and DO NOT OFFLOAD and HOLD AT AIRPORT FOR LIFE PICKUP. Special customs brokers, most notably Vinnie Mancusi in New York, made the "*Life* pickups" and rushed the envelopes to the office. Every now and again the labels were redesigned for even more startle value. After one such new issue New York received a red envelope totally covered with the new labels. Inside was a one-sentence message from correspondent Scot Leavitt in Texas: "Send more labels."

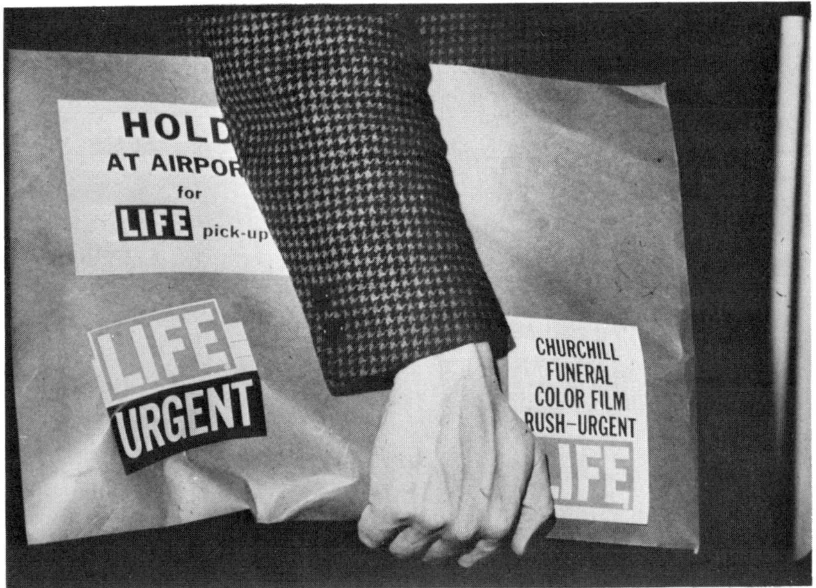

© TIME INC.

The "Packet"—bright red envelope—hopefully not offloaded and impossible to lose.

For special occasions like coronations or state funerals, when instant identification was of the essence, the red envelope was replaced by an attention-getting new one: colored stripes, or zigzag patterns. These were meant to be recognizable at one hundred yards by hired motorcycle couriers, foot runners, and taxi drivers charged with finding *Life* staffers in immense crowds and complex traffic situations. For the Rome Olympics of 1960 *Life* and its sister magazines acquired, through the good offices of *Sports Illustrated*'s Andre Laguerre, about forty St. Louis Cardinals baseball caps so that reporters and taxi drivers who didn't speak each other's languages could at least identify each other in the confusion and make the dash to office, airport, and packet.

Now and again there occurred an impasse which demanded improvisation. One such happened to photographer James Whitmore on a sultry summer day in the late 1950s in Rome. He was assigned to photograph the scene of the beatification of Mother Seton (later to be made a saint, in 1975) inside the sprawling Piazza San Pietro, and he knew that he had to have his film back in the office by 12:45 P.M. or it wouldn't make the packet. He got his picture, but when he tried to get out of the piazza his path was blocked by about 100,000 people, jammed together crying and praying and screaming.

His colleagues in the office, calculating the minutes, began to panic. Jim was never late: where was he today? With about three minutes to go he burst through the door panting, tossed three rolls of film to the nearest secretary, and sat down. Whitmore, one of the most meticulous of men, never appeared without every blond hair in place, each crease in his trouser legs razor sharp. That morning he looked as if he had interrupted a dog fight and lost.

"What happened?" we all asked.

"Niente de male," he said. (Jim spoke the best Italian in the bureau.) "I couldn't get out. So I kicked a Swiss Guard in the shins and they *threw* me out, hand over hand, over their heads."

It was Jim again, not many months later, who thought up the device with which we made the packet when Pope John XXIII was crowned on the little balcony under the cupola of St. Peter's. This event occurred during one of those changes of airline schedule. We had no jets in Rome, but they had them in London. To make the New York closing deadline we absolutely had to make a 1:00 P.M. flight from Rome to London, and there the jet to New York. Pope John was scheduled to be crowned at high noon, and Ciampino airport was by the most sanguine of estimates twenty minutes away. Air express normally required one hour to process a packet. We were caught in the classic time bind, but if we missed that plane we would miss an entire issue of the magazine.

Giulio de Angelis, the Pepi of Rome, did his act first. He went out to Ciampino and registered three packets, complete with waybills, the contents to be added at the last moment. He even paid in advance, an act which went against every instinct of his Italian heart.

In the office we laid on four fast Fiat cars, one for each photographer, and we obtained special passes to park them just outside the Piazza San Pietro, motors revved, ready for the dash to the airport. Then we had a council in the office.

None of the photographers could go around kicking Swiss Guards on that day, because it was impossible to see Pope John from the piazza itself. He was a short man, and he would be almost invisible from piazza level. The photographers had to get up high, on top of the graceful arms of the Bernini colonnade, so they would have a clear shot toward the balcony, the cupola, the clock, the moment, and the man. We had managed to get permission for all of them, but to achieve their positions they had to get to the Vatican six hours before the appearance of the new pope. Even climbing up to the Bernini colonnade, from inside Vatican City, took at least half an hour. How were they going to get back down again, fight through the crowds, give their film to the waiting drivers?

We sat in gloom on the office floor—as usual there were more people than chairs, for a crisis. Suddenly Jim said, ''If there were some way we could throw our film down, from the top. If we could have catchers down below, at piazza level . . .''

''The film would get lost,'' somebody else said. ''they jostle, down there. It would just get trampled and ruined.''

It was an idea, though, and we all applied ourselves. What if we made cloth bags to hold the film? And tied the bag to a rope, and fastened the rope to a stick, and the photographer would just plop the film into the bag, throw it over the side, and a special messenger down below snatched it out of the air and ran to the car?

That's what we did. We bought four brooms and sawed off their handles into convenient lengths, bought four lengths of thin strong rope about forty feet long, stitched up four white cotton bags large enough to hold about four rolls of film, and the photographers tucked all this gear into their camera bags. On the day of Pope John's coronation we assembled at the office at dawn. There were the three office drivers, a new man hired for the day, and four ''catchers.'' We went straight to the Piazza San Pietro, saw the photographers off in charge of their Vatican guards, positioned the catchers, the cars, and two reporters. We also left with the photographers the customary Vatican survival kit: sandwiches, wine, thermoses of coffee, and empty bottles with large mouths and secure corks. One of the hazards of Vatican coverage was that neither food, drink, nor hygienic facility was available to a man staked out on top of the Bernini colonnade.

Iride Cerabona and I went back to the office to watch the proceedings on Italian television. We knew where each photographer was and we intended to write captions from the screen and telex them to New York. Nothing at all happened from 7:00 A.M. until about 11:00. Shortly after that there was a stir on the TV screen. An official emerged onto the balcony to drape what looked like a Persian rug over the parapet. As the camera panned we thought we saw Dmitri Kessel setting up his tripod between two rather obscure saints on top of the colonnade.

At high noon a functionary came out. But no pope. I looked at my watch. Twelve-five. Twelve-ten. Twelve-fifteen. I could hear the airplane engines at Ciampino. I could hear the presses clanking in Chicago. We were going to miss the plane. Then, miracle, two tiny figures appeared on the balcony, and after them a dozen papal functionaries. Cardinal Deacon Canali announced in a trembling voice that ''we have a pope,'' and John bowed his head slightly to receive the towering triple crown. The piazza exploded with shouts and cheers, Iride crossed herself, and I wanted to do the same.

Then came the second miracle: a strange white streak which plunged from the colonnade to the piazza on the TV screen.

"Kessel!" shouted Iride. "There goes Kessel's film."

Within seconds there were three more streaks. The white bags were on their way to the catcher, the car, the packet, the airport. The race to the airport was epic, and the brand-new driver turned in the most spectacular performance of all. There is in Italy an unwritten law that persons transporting pregnant women or wounded citizens to hospital may charge through red lights, exceed the speed limit, terrorize the neighborhood, by signaling their emergency: They put a white handkerchief out of the window, lean on the horn, and GO. Our new driver had provided himself not only with a white handkerchief but also with a compliant nephew and a fake bloody bandage. He wrapped bandage around nephew, extended hankie out window, wore out his battery with the horn, and achieved Ciampino airport in a dead heat with the three office drivers who actually had a head start.

We made the packet, the plane, and the magazine. There was a very nice party in the office afterward, with toasts to Pope John, the photographers, and the new driver.

Sometimes, of course, we missed the packet. That didn't mean necessarily that we missed the plane. In cases of dire emergency a driver or a correspondent could save the situation by thrusting the big red envelope into the hands of a pilot (usually reluctant), a stewardess (less reluctant), or a passenger (usually flattered and fluttery, but willing), and then telex New York that the customs broker should meet the plane, find pilot, stewardess, or passenger, grab the packet, and run. As a final last resort, the reporter could board the plane in person and hand carry the packet to the office.

This was the "courier" system, which had a piquancy all its own. Correspondent Bob Morse, covering the Lebanese civil war of 1958, found himself with several rolls of precious film shot by photographer Larry Burrows and no way of getting them out of the country. He and Burrows had watched U.S. Marines come ashore, had covered all the action, but then the Lebanese clamped on tight security and refused to let any film out of the country until it had been developed, printed, and censored.

There was nothing to do except find a U.S.-bound passenger willing to carry the *Life* film in his baggage. Morse and Beirut stringer Abu Said began a tour of the big hotels looking for a likely tourist. Finally at the Riviera Hotel they found a man headed for Paris.

Would he take their film? He would, but he demanded as his price "hotel accomodations in one of the best hotels in Paris."

"Fine, fine," said Morse. "But I must cable Paris to meet you, ship the film, make you a hotel reservation. What is your name?"

"Sydney Carton, of London, England," said the man.

"You're kidding," said Morse.

"If you want to make jokes," huffed the traveler, "forget the whole thing."

"No no, no," stammered Morse, "I was just surprised."

Thus it was that *Life*'s film got to Paris, to New York, and to a lead in the magazine, and passenger Sydney Carton lived it up in a suite at the Plaza-Athenée in Paris.

"It was I'm sure a far, far better thing he did that day than he had ever done before," noted Morse.

Similarly, then-secretary Helen Fennell in Atlanta found herself stuck with several rolls of film shot by Francis Miller on Tallulah Bankhead. Not exactly Tallulah herself, but places named the same. Miss Bankhead had sued some commercial organization for having the temerity to use "her" name on a product. There was, she said, only one Tallulah and she was it. Fennell and Miller had been running around the South finding other uses of the name—including Tallulah Falls, Georgia, which local lore claimed was the source of the star's name when her parents stopped there briefly en route to Alabama. Miller had photographed the falls, a couple of Tallulahs in graveyards, and rushed to the airport. But Atlanta in those days had no facilities for handling press materials at midnight, so Fennell had to give the film to a pair of passengers headed for New York.

Then she telephoned Bob Girvin, at that time head of the news bureau, to tell him the film was on its way. Girvin, feeling his oats as a big wheel and dubious about Atlanta secretaries, launched into a detailed analysis of the perils of couriers, the difficulty of finding them at New York airports.

"You won't have any trouble finding these ones," said Fennell. "I gave the film to Abbott and Costello."

Sometimes, as Girvin knew, the courier was harder to find than the film. In at least one case the staff found the film and never did find the courier. The story was the sudden, shocking shut-down of the crusading newspaper *La Prensa* in the early fifties by Argentine Dictator Juan Peron. *Life* was eager for any pictures its Buenos Aires staff could get out of the capital, but it was an era of severe censorship and actual physical danger for Argentine journalists. After the closing of *La Prensa* there was only one cryptic message from

Buenos Aires to New York: "The man with the stick has what you want."

Man with the stick? Newsfront head researcher Irene Saint and foreign news's Valerie Vondermuhll puzzled over it together. Stick. Pilot? They set their researchers to checking all airline schedules from Buenos Aires to New York. They sent stake-outs to Miami, to Washington, to Idlewild. Pilot after pilot was pounced upon by *Life* people as he climbed wearily out of his aircraft. No film, however. Saturday night came and went, that week's magazine closed, and there was no story from Argentina.

Sunday morning, Vondermuhll, an avid track-meet fan, turned to the sports section of the *New York Sunday Times* to see what had happened the day before at a winter meet in Madison Square Garden. One story jumped out at her: "The Rev. Robert 'Bob' Richards, just back from the Pan-American Games . . ." Richards was then the U.S.'s leading pole vaulter, and he had been in Latin America. THE MAN WITH THE STICK.

Vondermuhll called Saint and the two of them began the search for Rev. Bob. Just to make sure, they also divided up the names of all U.S. pole vaulters who had competed in the Madison Square Garden event, and started to track them down. Saint had a family contact at the Garden box office, who was able to get the names of hotels the athletes used. A dozen phone calls later, it appeared that all had checked out and scattered toward home.

All day Sunday, with the help of the tireless Time Inc. switchboard, the two women pursued their men. Somebody said that Bob Richards often went to Philadelphia to visit friends after a meet. Calls there finally located a pole vaulter, but not Richards. Vondermuhll called Richards's home in California and got a neighbor who squealed, "Oh, that will be Bob calling his wife." But it wasn't, and his wife hadn't heard from Richards since the Pan-American games. Maybe, she said, he had stopped to see a friend in Hershey, Pennsylvania, and she provided the friend's name and telephone number. A call to Hershey, and the friend said, "I'm expecting Bob to call me, I'll tell him you want him."

In the midst of all this, Time Inc. operator 25, who had been bearing the brunt of the in-office telephoning, called Vondermuhll to say she was going off duty. "But don't worry about a thing," she added, "keep on asking for operator 25, I've explained the whole problem to my replacement. Be sure to tell me next week how it all ended."

Finally at 7:30 P.M. Sunday the Rev. Mr. Richards rang from a telephone booth in Grand Central Station: "I understand you've been trying to reach me."

After listening to the whole story, he had to reply a rueful no. He had no package for *Life*. "I sure wish they had given to me," he said, "in spite of all the confusion and censorship down there nobody checked any of our luggage. I would like to have helped you."

Two or three days later the mysterious film turned up, as if by magic, on a desk in the picture bureau. Nobody knows how it got there; nobody ever saw a man with a stick.

□ □ □

Mechanics dictated one of the other cherished traditions of the magazine, the "Chicago closing." This simply meant the expedition of a task force from New York to the Chicago bureau to develop film, lay out, write, and close a late-breaking story to hurry the product to the printer. It was first used for news coverage coming in from the Far East: Film could be intercepted and processed in Chicago to save all the flying hours to New York and then back again to the Donnelley plant in Chicago.

Later, Big Ten football games, played on Saturdays in the Midwest, were closed in Chicago, as was occasionally the Kentucky Derby. National political convention stories often closed that way.

Each such occasion threw the Chicago bureau staff into a nervous tizzy. It was all a lot of fun, the excuse for a big party and a glorious family reunion of staffers who hadn't seen each other for a while, but the event also always brought a managing editor, a copy editor, a high-powered art director, and other brass into the limited confines of the office. Their presence put everybody on the *qui vive* and the office was a shambles when it was over. Once Hugh Moffett thought it would be nice to provide some fine Iowa melons as a treat for the staff during closing hours, and had them flown in. This nice homely plan was completely upset by Thompson, who found them just the right size and heft to be hurled like footballs around the office. Some of his prospective catchers, butter-fingered or preoccupied, fumbled the melons and watched aghast as they exploded on desks, carpets, and corridors.

Film editor Peggy Sargent, who usually didn't go to Chicago closings because she preferred to stay home in New York with her husband Paul, was pressed into service once during the Korean war. Some important take was coming in late and Sid James, then news editor, conceived the idea of intercepting it in Minneapolis and processing it on a charter flight from Minneapolis to Chicago. Darkroom chief Frank Scherschel got a flying darkroom together. Peggy Sargent was to edit the pictures. The small crew assembled with their charter aircraft at the Minneapolis airport, the darkroom was put aboard, and everybody settled down to wait for the incoming craft.

Estimated time of arrival came and went. The temperature in Minneapolis dropped farther and farther below zero. Somebody had to keep going to the telephone to tell Chicago ''not yet.''

Finally, to the cheers of the staff, a plane's lights winked over the snowy airport. It landed, reversed engines, skidded a bit, taxied over to the terminal. As James, Scherschel, Sargent, and Co. pressed their noses to the frosty window panes, out climbed one small Chinese man. He had no package of film, and he turned out to be a stowaway.

While part of the staff attempted to calm Scherschel, who was showing signs of apoplexy, others went off to telephone Chicago again and tell them to go ahead with an alternate story because the Korean film had not arrived. Someone else went to find the charter pilot and ask him to start his engines and take them to Chicago.

By this time however the hangar doors had frozen, halfway up and halfway down, and nobody could get the plane out. It was a gloomy group that stood around waiting for an emergency crew to come and thaw out the doors, get the plane out, and fly back to the non-closing in Chicago.

Mechanics helped enormously in establishing the names and reputations of a whole generation of *Life* writers. One of the layout problems had always been arranging editorial material around advertising, particularly the half-page ad which left a tall, skinny space for some kind of editorial content. It was a very awkward space for photographs: one managing editor joked that the only picture which really would fit it would be a one-legged man hanging on the side of a cliff. Canny staff photographers often tried to shoot tall thin pictures in the hope of getting an extra half-page in the magazine, and sometimes the space was filled simply by running a column of small photographs one on top of another.

Managing editor Hunt decided to fill those awkward halves or thirds with words instead of pictures. Thus was born the ''front of the book'' section directed by David Scherman, who had been photographer, correspondent, writer, and editor. He hired Richard Schickel to write movie reviews for that space, Melvin Maddocks to review books, William Zinsser to turn out amusing columns on any subject which appealed. Extending the idea a little farther, Hunt began assigning words for the ''trailing half'' page of text which began to follow everything from straight news stories to the ''Closeup,'' a section also administered by Scherman.

These spaces provided small bylines for ambitious staffers willing to try to write them as an extra effort, and they quickly became popular both with readers and reporters. Many writers—Jane Howard, Gail Cameron, Chris Welles—got their first bylines because of this adjustment to stories laid out for "a page, two halves, and a half." About the same time, Mr. Luce decided he wanted an editors' note, further personalizing the magazine, and Loudon Wainwright thought he would like to try writing a column. His "View from Here" was an instant hit, and Hunt and Ralph Graves talked Shana Alexander into writing a column on alternate weeks, "The Feminine Eye."

One of the most imaginative assaults upon merciless mechanics involved the queen of England, "the dummies," and a near civil war in the office. The occasion was the visit of Queen Elizabeth II and Prince Philip to Canada and the U.S. in the autumn of 1957. The queen's Canadian sojourn had been spectacular: pomp and ceremony, Canadian mounted police, uniforms and medals galore, but the U.S. leg of the trip looked as if it might turn out to be pretty much of a snore. There was only one interesting gimmick—the queen and her husband, sports fans both, were going to be guests of the governor of Maryland at a Maryland–North Carolina football game at College Park on a Saturday afternoon in October. That, in itself, might merit one picture in "World's Week." But if somehow we could get the queen's comments about this strange new game . . . find out what she said as she watched . . .

Planting a listening device into the special royal box was the first idea, but in those pre-Watergate days bugging devices weren't as sophisticated as they were shortly to become, and anyway the security officials wouldn't hear of such a thing.

Next somebody thought of what was then called a "shotgun mike," a sensitive microphone which could be aimed accurately toward a small area yards away to pick up conversations. That device, carefully tested in advance, proved unsatisfactory.

Don Wilson, then head of *Life*'s Washington bureau, had an inspiration. There was a school in Washington for deaf mutes, complete with teachers who were highly skilled lip-readers. How about hiring a couple of them, setting them up in a special booth directly across the football field from the queen and her party, and having them watch her through high-power binoculars and read her lips as she commented on the game?

Two experts from the school agreed to take on the unusual assignment. The lip-readers became known, in quite rude but friendly shorthand to the staff, as "the dummies." They were equipped not only with binoculars but also with tape recorders, so they could repeat the royal party's words as they were uttered. There was to be a movie camera which would record as much action on the field as possible while remaining fixed on the faces of the queen, the governor, and their party. As if all this weren't enough, four other *Life* people were assigned to cover the football game itself, communicating with the central control post by walkie-talkie. Thus the reporter scribbling captions in his notebook could possibly connect a play on the field with a remark made by Her Majesty.

All went well, if hectically. The lip-readers picked up the queen asking her hosts, before the game started, "How many men are on a team?" Later, watching a huddle, she asked, "Why do they gather that way?" Still later she required an explanation of the scoreboard with its baffling numbers indicating downs, yards to go, score, time remaining.

She was catching on fast, but the lip-readers impressed the *Life* people even more. "The moment I heard one of them use the word 'scrum,' which is a British rugby term almost unknown in the U.S., I knew those guys were on the ball," recalls Hugh Moffett. "They read on her lips a word they probably didn't even know."

Some difficulty arose now and again because the lip-readers' pronunciation was not immediately recognizable when distorted by tape recorder and walkie-talkie. As the game and the day wore on the reporters began to wonder if, once they got back to New York, they would be able to unscramble all the tapes, film, movie takes, their own notes, and fit the story together.

As it turned out, they could, but not until they had overcome some fierce inner-office interference. Nineteen fifty-seven was well into the era of elaborate Saturday night dinners served inside the office, and as the film was being processed the work crew and the lip-readers sat down to enjoy the feast. Suddenly somebody noticed an atmosphere of distinct chill around the premises of foreign news editor Farmer, and an aura of alarm around that of managing editor Thompson.

Thompson, it developed, had known little about Operation Lip-Read and Farmer, the staff's leading Anglophile, had known nothing at all. He took the whole strenuous effort as a case of flagrant *lèse majesté,* an affront to Her Majesty, to the British empire, and to himself. He had transmitted enough of this disapproval to Thompson to throw the whole project into some doubt. Thompson ordered the staff to watch every foot of the movie coverage, to check the movies and the tape-recorded quotes again with "the dummies," and to match every still photograph with every episode on the movie film and every quote on the tape.

It was a crushing assignment after a long day, but everybody pitched in. Word also went out to Don Wilson, who by this time may have regretted ever having had the inspiration, to stand by in his office to receive final copy by telex, and then to read it, word for word, to Maryland Governor Theodore McKeldin, the queen's host for the game.

All of this eventually got done and the work of the lip-readers was exonerated. McKeldin confirmed every quote, and on the third running of the movie film even the checkers thought they could see the words frame themselves on the queen's lips: "My, it's exciting" and "Why does that man [the center] leave the huddle first?" Prince Philip was even easier to "read." By the second half he had become an expert and when he saw a Maryland back take off on a long run toward a score, he yelled quite *visibly* to all in the darkened projection room, "Oh man, look at him go!"

It was 6:00 A.M. Sunday before the survivors of Operation Lip-Read walked out into the dawn. After all their work they had achieved only two pages in the magazine, but they were inordinately proud of those pages. A highly ingenious plan had worked, and *Life* got an authentic British comment by a well-informed woman on a wildly popular American game, a comment which would otherwise have remained completely unavailable.

None of the reporters who worked on the story can remember the score. For them, and for the lip-read queen who may have forgotten it, here it is from *Life,* October 28, 1957: Maryland 21, North Carolina 7.

16

Cloak-and-Dagger Stuff

The exposé, a venerable and commendable institution of journalism, was pursued at *Life* with sometimes limited skill but with unbounded enthusiasm. Reporters and photographers dressed up like hippies lurked on street corners hoping to capture a drug peddler; Italo-Americans got themselves done up as mourners and crashed mobster funerals hoping for a sneak shot of a *capo mafioso* or a bit of mumbled gossip mingled with the condolences. Other intrepid types posed as poll watchers in Chicago (election fraud), text book salesmen in Alabama (racial discrimination), stock brokers in Illinois (the Louis Wolfson attempt to take over Montgomery Ward in the mid-fifties). Correspondent Nadine Liber of the Paris office once posed—absolutely convincingly—as a Persian princess to get out of Iran carrying *Life* film of the Shah's celebration in 1971 of the 2500th anniversary of the Peacock Throne.

Among the most enthusiastic devotees of the exposé were George Hunt and Gene Farmer. Hunt and Farmer were such different types and personalities that they sometimes had difficulty even communicating with each other, but they shared a love for the cloak-and-dagger stuff. Hunt approached it as a holy crusade, and set up a special office-within-the-office to specialize in it. Farmer's approach was less formal but more devious: He went in for secret knocks, locked files, code names, and, on one memorable occasion, armed guards patrolling the premises and scaring the wits out of the female reporters.

Farmer usually called his capers ''operation skullduggery,'' or ''get the bastards,'' and he sometimes engaged in intrigue for the sheer fun of it all. Those of us who worked with him in London watched with amusement and amazement as he went about complex machinations to buy the memoirs of Klaus Fuchs, the German-born atomic spy then locked up in a British prison; intercept Andrei Vishinsky, en route from the United Nations to Moscow when Stalin died in early 1953, and bribe or persuade him to defect; run down hints of chicanery in the football pools; and lay to rest a rumor—unfounded, as it turned out—that some dastardly traitor was mixing crab grass into the turf of the Lords' cricket pitch.

Farmer was abetted in many of these efforts by Andre Laguerre, then *Time*'s London bureau chief and former wartime press aide to General de Gaulle. Everyone not included in their plots enjoyed teasing them. On the night of the projected Klaus Fuchs manuscript delivery the two stood tensely inside Laguerre's darkened office, peering intently though the slats of a Venetian blind down toward the back door of the neighborhood pub, the Coach and Horses (renamed by the staff the Jaws of Death). There a former cellmate of Fuchs was to deliver a ''brown paper parcel'' at an appointed hour. Two or three of us tiptoed to the closed office door, opened it stealthily, and made raucous machine-gun noises which sent Farmer and Laguerre six inches into the air. Their contact didn't show up that night, but I don't think it was because he heard our machine-gun noises.

Vishinsky didn't defect, either, but a lot of Farmer's efforts paid off. One of the magazine's real coups was exposure of a plot by the Dominican Republic's then-strongman Rafael Trujillo to kidnap, smack out of the heart of New York City, an anti-Trujillo Columbia University professor named Jesus Maria de Galindez.

Galindez disappeared on the night of March 12, 1956. Instantly there were dark rumors and a strange story about an American pilot who had helped spirit Galindez away—probably to the Dominican Republic itself. As the story first broke in the newspapers it was all a little hazy. Nobody knew where Galindez was, whether or not he was still alive, or how exactly he had been spirited out of the country.

It was a story *Life* was uniquely fitted to handle, with its network of correspondents, stringers, sources all over the world, with its pa-

CREDIT: WALTER DARAN © TIME INC.

Editors Gene Farmer, left, *and Hugh Moffett, looking like fugitives from the "Monty Python" show, prepare to prey on the perpetrator of something pejorative.*

tience and its money. The air of international intrigue appealed mightily to both Farmer and managing editor Thompson. A staff of five or six people in New York went straight to work on all the rumors: Had a plane taken off secretly from a New Jersey or Long Island airport on the night of the disappearance of Galindez? Had a man been transferred by ambulance from one plane to another in Miami, at night? Had there really been a pilot named Gerald Murphy from Oregon who had allegedly flown the plane, fitted with extra fuel tanks?

Staffers and stringers fanned out to check all appropriate airports and their records, study flight logs, track down with manufacturers and airports what private planes had been fitted with extra fuel tanks during the crucial period. Friends and relatives of Pilot Murphy were found, interviewed, consulted. *Time* magazine's Jerry Hannifin in Washington, a pilot, helped with contacts to the FBI and the State Department. *Life*'s Alison Kallman, also a pilot, worked on possible flight plans and checked them against every nugget of information anyone else dug up.

By December 1956 there had been no further word of Galindez. Murphy was dead and *Life* had begun getting mysterious telephone calls from people with Latin accents. Some pretended to be Cuban or Dominican journalists and publishers, seeking information from *Life* to help them with their own investigative reporting of the murky affair.

Not until February 27, 1957, did the magazine run its first long story on the Galindez case. By then staffers had studied flight logs until their eyes nearly fell out, examined hundreds of photographs gathered up from airports from Long Island to Miami, gone though all the known biographical material on Trujillo, on Galindez, on Murphy. As prepublication pressure built up and the mysterious telephone calls increased, Farmer went to Thompson and requested permission to hire private guards (whom he always called "Pinkertons") to protect the office, the staff, and the assembled materials. In due course two burly strangers in civilian clothes, with strange lumps showing here and there on their anatomies, turned up in the building. One set up guard on the elevator bank leading to foreign news, the other lurked near the premises of the section itself.

"We were never sure just who 'the Pinkertons' were, but their lurking presence was much more terrifying than strange visitors and Latin-accented telephone calls," one of the women remembers. "We were glad when it was over and the guards withdrawn."

The February 1957 *Life* story explained in detail, with documentary evidence, how Galindez, a Basque refugee, had been abducted in New York and flown to the Dominican Republic by Gerald Murphy. Murphy was subsequently employed by the Dominican airline. When he, too, disappeared, the Dominicans said he had been killed by a fellow pilot who then hanged himself in a Dominican jail. *Life* expressed disbelief.

This lead story not only reported the news but also made it. The Galindez case became a cause celebre, an international scandal, and portions of the *Life* story were picked up and repeated in newspapers and magazines all over the world.

"The Pinkertons" vanished shortly after publication but everybody involved in the story knew that eventually Trujillo would strike back. His playboy son "Ramfis" was alleged to be even angrier than his father over the exposé. He also was much more sophisticated.

When the backlash came it was handled with intelligence. The Dominicans hired Morris Ernst, a liberal New York lawyer, to make his own examination of the evidence, of *Life*'s coverage, and to evaluate them. By early summer of 1958, more than a year after the story, the Ernst report was published. It concluded that there was "not a scintilla of evidence" which could connect the disappearance of Pilot Murphy with that of Galindez. Ernst's most telling point, in refuting the *Life* evidence, was that Murphy could not have made the abduction flight's final leg, from Tamiami airport in Florida to the Dominican Republic, within the time span assigned to it by *Life*.

Publication of the report required an answer from the magazine, and the burden of reply fell upon company lawyer Jack Dowd and foreign news assistant editor Marilyn Wellemeyer.

"I was not terribly happy being assigned to the Ernst report," Wellemeyer remembers. "The French Fourth Republic was toppling in May 1958, de Gaulle was returning to power. *Life* was covering the story in a big way and I had spent several years of graduate study learning French history and French politics. I wanted to be involved in that. But instead I had to nitpick the Ernst report, and I hadn't even been in on coverage of the original story on Galindez."

Nitpick she did, however, all night long with Jack Dowd. The crux of their problem was the flight from Tamiami airport. Together they called Miami and put the full staff and stringers to work checking the airport one more time, going over the logs, watching for those telltale fuel tanks.

About dawn they got the word: an airport attendant, when he was being interviewed by one of Ernst's investigators, had for some reason given him the wrong time. When *Life* checked back, he corrected his error and the *Life* story remained valid.

The answer to the Ernst report was printed on June 9, 1958, under the headline "COSTLY WHITEWASH OF BLACK CHARGES," and said that *Life* stood by its earlier reportage and the facts. It challenged both the Dominican Republic and Lawyer Ernst to sue. Neither did.

The final story ran less than a month later, on July 7, 1958, and it vindicated *Life* fully. The FBI, which had been investigating Pilot Murphy's disappearance at the request of his family and of Oregon Congressman Charles Porter, had just released a notebook, a piece of paper, and a pilot's log found in Murphy's Dominican apartment after his death. Both paper and notebook bore the name of Jesus de Galindez, and the notebook also mentioned German Ornes, another Trujillo enemy. The pilot's log recorded a flight to the Dominican Republic but had been entered a week earlier than the one *Life* had reported—quite a logical cover-up for a man who might have been involved in a kidnaping.

Life, refusing to exult, printed the details under a headline "MYSTERY, CONTINUED," and the subhead "New Evidence Links Murdered Pilot to Galindez." The *New York Times* was more direct: "The belief that Gerald Murphy was linked to the Galindez case is now proved."

□ □ □

Under George Hunt the exposé became a programmed, specific section of the magazine. He startled his closest staff on one of the first meetings after he became managing editor by announcing that "we are going to restore to journalism the techniques and the fulfillment of Lincoln Steffens."

Hunt, brought up on Steffens, was as idealistic as his idol. He set up an investigative department which was officially listed as "News Projects" but quickly became known to the staff as the "Department of Spooks." The spooks were given total freedom, total support, and all the time they needed. Head spooks were Sandy Smith and William Lambert, both of whom came to *Life* after distinguished careers on daily newspapers. Lambert had won a Pulitzer Prize, a Heywood Broun Award, and the Sigma Delta Chi Award; Smith was one of the best-known crime reporters in the U.S. Heading the staff for administrative purposes was Russ Sackett, no slouch as a spook himself. They carried the burden of investigative reporting for almost ten years, abetted frequently by veteran *Life*rs Paul Welch, Keith Wheeler, and James Mills.

Their stories came in a flood: a study of homosexuals, which was one of the first serious approaches to this subject in a national magazine; stories of corruption in the Bahamas, Miami, the state of Louisiana (Governor John McKeithen flew to New York charging "smear," and after having examined *Life*'s evidence went back home again announcing that he was going to clean up the state). They did articles discussing the financial dealings of Roy Cohn, late of the Senator McCarthy, Cohn, and Schine road show; attacked Senator Ed Long of Missouri for misusing his Senate investigative committee for the benefit of Jimmy Hoffa; and ran an all-out crusade against New Jersey Congressman Cornelius Gallagher and his connections both with an alleged Cosa Nostra *capo* named Zicarelli and a 1963 soybean scandal.

One of the most clamorous of their cases involved Supreme Court Justice Abe Fortas, a long-time friend of Lyndon Johnson and perhaps too close a friend of financial manipulator Louis Wolfson, once described by a financial writer as "the biggest corporate raider of all time." Not long after President Johnson nominated Fortas as chief justice, *Life* published a Bill Lambert story which challenged Fortas's ethics in accepting (though he later repaid it) a large sum of money from a Wolfson Family Foundation charitable organization, in advising and doing favors for Johnson after he took his seat on the Supreme Court, and other things. Justice Fortas was facing a not-entirely-friendly Senate Judiciary Committee at the time, and in the end his appointment as chief justice was blocked, partly as the result of the *Life* attack. Fortas also resigned from the Court.

All this was pretty high-level stuff researched by experts. It was not readily achieved by the average eager aspirant to the cloak-and-dagger world on the magazine. I once spent a good part of three days hiding in a sand trap on a golf course in the south of France, in about 1950, trying to get pictures of King Leopold of Belgium, whose throne was toppling. And about eight years later in Italy I pretended to be a rich American tourist in search of antiquities, so I could meet and deal with some genuine tomb robbers and antiquities merchants. That adventure was marvelous until the Italian policeman who was posing as my "French expert" suddenly pulled a real gun from a real holster and pointed it at us—all of us, me, the traffickers, my friend the contact man. I was never so frightened in my life.

Reporter Sam Jaffe once spent a very cold, wet hour standing on a street corner in Manhattan with the upper left shoulder tab of his raincoat unbuttoned and hanging down as a signal for his "go-between" to mobster "Three Finger" Brown. He would have minded neither the rain nor the failure of his mission so much had it not been in full view of his gleeful colleagues in the *Time-Life* building who had made the "hot tip" telephone call to him themselves, including the instructions about the shoulder tab.

Correspondent Bob Morse wasted several days trying to find master spy Kim Philby in Beirut to offer him $5,000 to write a piece for *Life* on the royalist side of the civil war in Yemen. Philby never turned up in his familiar watering places, or even at his "newspaper" office, because between the time Morse was told to find him and his final admission of failure, Philby had slipped away to the Soviet Union and the whole story of his incredible spying career was leaking out.

On an even hairier occasion, Morse was dispatched to Baghdad, Iraq, after strongman Kassem had been murdered in yet another coup. Everyone in the Mideast knew that Kassem's bloody murder had appeared, live, on Iraqi television, but the coup leaders refused to release any photographs of the event. They also said there was no film record of the television broadcast itself. Morse, who boarded a press plane from Beirut to Baghdad with little hope of getting anything, ran around Baghdad for five hours with two pickup photographers and found little to photograph except armed guards surrounding the television station itself and strutting soldiers in the streets. Then he had to leave, to get back to Beirut and at least file some words on the situation in Baghdad in time to make the magazine.

"At the airport I was approached by three very unsavory-looking characters who said they had pictures shot from the television screen of the murder of Kassem. They were prepared to sell them for one thousand dollars which I didn't have, but I had my personal checkbook. I was very nervous about all this, sure it was a trap and they were probably secret agents. However, I said I'd look at the pictures.

" 'Not here!' they said in alarm. 'In the toilet.'

"In the toilet? That sounded even more ominous. But we sure didn't have any other pictures on that story. So, sitting on a toilet seat in one of the cubicles, I looked at the pictures. They had only eight exposures, in negative form, and all I could tell was that there were images on them. I made out a personal check for one thousand dollars and ran for my plane.

"Once I got aboard, I decided that New York was going to think I had either gone mad or was drunk. So I had about five drinks, went to work trying to write some text, and shipped the whole thing off to New York.

"On Sunday a cable came in saying that five 'good' pages had closed on Kassem. I bet that's the only time anyone ever produced a *Life* lead sitting on a toilet seat."

While experts like Sackett, Lambert, and Smith were winning Pulitzers and things, the likes of Sam Jaffe, Bob Morse, photographer Bob Kelley, and I were making points for the Laurel and Hardy Award. Kelley and I should have won it, in 1949, for our performance in what was known as "the five-percenter scandal."

In the late spring of that year the *New York Herald-Tribune* published an exposé on a man named James V. Hunt who had set up an office in Washington to help manufacturers and jobbers win government contracts. He purported to be well-connected in congressional and executive circles, and he could use his influence to help all comers sell their wares in Washington. He was in short an influence-peddler and he charged 5 percent of each contract as his fee. In those relatively innocent, preinflation days, 5 percent seemed a lot and "the five-percenter scandal" caused roars of outrage across the nation.

The initial break belonged to the *Herald-Tribune,* but there was a special angle made for *Life:* As one of his very convincing ploys, Hunt had lined his office walls with photographs of himself standing beside, shaking hands with, being embraced by, very important people. All suitably framed and autographed to "Dear Jim," of course. There were three photos of President Harry Truman with "Jim," one of Major General Harry Vaughan, Truman's military aide; there was "Happy" Chandler, and Senators O'Mahoney, Brewster, McMahon. It was a cast of hundreds, so the *Herald-Tribune* said, but it had published no pictures of the pictures on the wall.

Thus I was dispatched from New York to Washington with orders to get into James V. Hunt's office and get pictures of the pictures. The photographer was to be the Washington bureau's Robert Kelley. Kelley and I first took a stroll over to the office, sans either camera or notebook, to look things over. We probably called it "casing the joint." Hunt's suite of offices, with his name on the door, was closed, firmly locked, and dark through the opaque transom. It was fairly high in an office building, maybe the twelfth, fourteenth floor. There was a doorman on the ground floor, a receptionist, and a man running each of the building's elevators. When we inquired about Mr. Hunt, we were told that he was in a private clinic being treated for an attack of nerves.

The rest of the day we spent cruising past the office building taking pictures of it, taking pictures of Hunt's home in the suburbs, and the private clinic in which he was staying. That night I called Ed Thompson and, terrified of the great man's wrath, said there was no way to get into Hunt's office.

"It's all closed, locked, Ed, and there's not a soul inside," I said. "The only way to get in there would be to break in."

Thompson's reply was succinct. "Try," he said, "to make it trespassing, not breaking and entering."

"What's the difference?" I quavered.

"Sixty days," said Thompson. Then he hung up.

Kelley and I, both appalled, went straight to the *Life* Washington bureau chief, Eddie Jones. We explained our dilemma and he gave us $100 in $20 bills. He also told us to buy a bottle of Scotch, a bottle of gin, and some paper cups. Maybe, he said hopefully, there would be a cleaning lady who enjoyed a nip at night. Or maybe the transom of James Hunt's door was both low and easily opened . . .

We bought the booze, pocketed the money, and repaired to Kelley's cubicle for a conference. We decided to wrap up a tripod, a couple of cameras, a lot of film, and some lights, into a nice neat parcel which we would label "Office of James V. Hunt, Room . . ." whatever, I no longer remember the number. Then we would trudge over to the building, ask to be taken to the right floor, and "play it by ear"—a favorite *Life* phrase.

We got to the building between 8:00 and 9:00 P.M., when nobody was on duty on the ground floor except the night elevator man. He was completely unmoved at the sight of us, and just motioned for us to sign a check-in book on a table. We signed, as I recall, "Bob Girvin" (then an assignment editor) and "Sid James" (then domestic news chief), who perhaps were out of favor with us at the time. Then, clutching our parcel and our liquor, we got off at Hunt's floor. We had to go hunting for the head cleaning lady, a motherly black woman upon whom we descended like postulants to the mother superior. In our still-almost-honest stage of this operation, we poured o to her our whole story. We wouldn't do any harm, we might lose ou jobs if we didn't succeed, it was already a scandal and we were only trying to defend the people's right to know . . .

Politely she heard us out, and firmly she shook her head. "I don't know anything about all that, and I'm sorry for you young folks if you get into trouble with your boss. But I'm paid to make sure these here offices are clean and that nobody gets in here that doesn't belong in here."

She then bade us goodnight. She didn't want a drink, and she didn't want the twenty dollars which Kelley proffered in a trembling hand with a request that she forget she had ever seen us. We walked off wandering through endless corridors, while the high-minded chief cleaning lady finished her chores and departed to another floor. Then we tiptoed back to Hunt's office door.

Sure enough, the transom was open and it didn't seem impossibly high. I suggested to Bob that if I crouched down, and he stood on my back, maybe I could stand up high enough to boost him high enough to grab the transom supports and get in. It didn't occur to either of us to wonder how he would get out.

While we were in the midst of this operation, with muffled mutterings of "take your shoes off" and "why do you have such a slippery back?", an elevator door opened about six feet to our rear, and a Western Union messenger walked out. He looked quite surprised.

"Tell him we're acrobats," murmured Kelley, but my mind didn't work that fast. I think all I said was something like, "Heh, heh, lost our keys . . ."

The Western Union boy shoved his little yellow envelopes into my hand, glared, and departed. The elevator man glared too: Bob Girvin and Sid James were some strange types. Kelley and I shoved the telegrams over the transom and sat down to think and pant for awhile. At this moment we both heard approaching footsteps and an odd clanking noise.

"The night watchman," hissed Bob. "Come on, run, follow me." I didn't know where we were running to, until Bob led me into the men's room and ordered, "Stand on a seat. Leave the cubicle door open but stand on the seat so he can't see your feet under the door. And keep your head down."

We stood on those seats for what seemed an hour. The night watchman came in briefly, flicked the lights on and off, and left. We could hear him jangling around outside, all the keys, flashlight, probably even a gun. As his sound faded slowly we resumed breathing. We also opened the Scotch.

When all seemed quiet we crept out of the men's room and back to that transom. Only to hear the ominous jingle approaching again. This time it was between us and the men's room so we bolted for an exit door and a fire escape. We sat out there for quite a while, too scared even to ask each other if night watchmen kept bullets in their guns. Finally we opened the exit door a crack, peered back into the building, and the man had vanished. Instead of the jingle we heard the aspirate wail of a vacuum cleaner at full throttle. Was it our incorruptible friend again, or perhaps an underling? It was, thank heaven, the latter.

The outer door of James V. Hunt's suite was wide open, exhaling a blast of fresh air from what must have been opened windows inside. The inner door was still locked, but the vacuum cleaner's driver was very young, smiling, and cheerful. Bob divined at once that she would be sympathetic to love. He instructed me to douse us both with Scotch—over the shoulders, behind the ears, not down the gullet—and to kiss him quite a lot, after putting on more lipstick.

It was one of the least romantic "kiss me" orders I ever received, but I did as I was told. When we were appropriately lipstick-smeared and smelly, he led me by the hand to the open door.

"Good evening," he proclaimed. Kelley has one of those innocent, blond, blue-eyed far-western faces, and he has beautiful manners. The cleaning lady didn't exactly shut off her machine, but at least she looked up, and she smiled.

"Sir?" she inquired.

"My girl friend and I work for Mr. Hunt," he said, holding out the big package with Hunt's name written all over it. "But we forgot and left our keys in the car downstairs and we have to deliver this. Could you let us in, just for about half an hour's work?"

The young woman looked us both over, sniffed a bit, smiled a slow smile, and said, "You could go down and get your keys . . ."

At this point I made my only intelligent contribution of the evening.

"What about your wife, then?" I asked Bob, feigning panic.

Kelley almost kissed me for real, right that moment. The cleaning lady laughed, winked, refused the twenty dollars which Bob had in his hand, and said to both of us, "You never were in here tonight, you hear?"

We heard all right, but Bob wanted to make sure that she did too. The moment the door of the inner office swung open and the cleaning lady tucked away her keys I got my instructions.

"Get on that couch, there by the door, and jiggle it until I tell you to stop."

"Jiggle it?"

''Jounce it. Hard.''

While Bob unwrapped our package, set up his tripod, plugged in the lights, got the cameras ready, I was just jouncing. Then he hissed, ''Come in,'' and I rushed into the inner sanctum to help move lights, take down captions as he photographed the photographs on the wall.

We probably were inside thirty minutes, though neither of us has a clear recollection. We moved some photos of Harry Truman to get better closeups, I counted the number of pictures in each row, and the number of rows, and paced off the size of the room as best I could.

Then we were finished. I turned off lights while he packed equipment, and we were about ready to tiptoe out again when my memories of Agatha Christie came flooding back.

''What about fingerprints, Bob?''

''Omigod,'' said he. We went straight back in and spent another half-hour using some tatty Kleenex, and the tail of Bob's shirt, to mop everything we could remember having touched. The faint wail of the vacuum cleaner had moved far down the corridor.

Then we went out, closed the door carefully—and wiped the doorknob with Bob's shirttail—and walked down two flights of stairs to baffle Hercule Poirot. There we paused to consider the next move. The crucial thing was to get the precious film out of the building. What if the elevator man had figured out we were taking pictures, and demanded the film? What if he called the cops? What if the incorruptible cleaning lady had dropped a word to some security man we didn't even see?

''Give me the film,'' I said. ''I'll put it down my front.''

''That will take care of one roll,'' said Kelley, with singular lack of gallantry. ''What shall we do with the rest of it?''

For answer I snatched it all, walked down another floor, and hid our entire take under about four inches of sand in one of those tall floor ashtrays outside the elevator. The ashtray had been cleaned that night and even raked. I was sure it wouldn't be touched again for twenty-four hours.

Then, totally without film, totally sober despite the way we smelled, totally in shock from our brush with cloak-and-dagger, Kelley and I rang the bell for the elevator at about floor eight. A man we had never seen before opened the door, commiserated with us for having had to work so late, and didn't even pay attention as we countersigned Bob Girvin and Sid James on the registry book. We emerged blinking into a hot, humid Washington near-dawn and even before we found a taxi nerves had done us in. We began at a canter, switched to a lope, concluded at a dead run to get to the office. Once there we rang Eddie Jones, only to hear from his wife that "He's been so worried about you two, so scared, that he passed out half an hour ago."

We also nearly passed out next day when we had to go back to That Building and loiter near the ashtray on the eighth floor, watching endless traffic of honest toilers going to and fro about their business, snatching with snakelike hands to extricate our film from the sand when nobody seemed to be looking.

Our story ran as a four-page lead in *Life,* but with no photo credit whatever in the front of the book. Just in case there might be repercussions, I was sent to Colorado for a couple of weeks' holiday with my vacationing family, and Kelley was I think dispatched on an assignment to Florida. About a month after our adventure Kelley was

These were the pictures on James Hunt's wall. The photograph ran in the lead story in Life *on August 1, 1949.*

sitting peacefully at his desk in the Washington bureau when the phone rang and a voice at the other end said, "This is the FBI." Bob told me that the receiver fell straight out of his limp hand, bounced on the floor, and when finally he retrieved it the voice said, "A friend of yours has applied for a job with us, and he's given you as a reference."

Read It and Weep

There were certain stories we all dreaded. They befell us as regularly as the equinox and the IRS, as relentlessly as the climacteric. There was something almost touching about their fidelity; we knew when we were about due for one.

Heading the list were the farm story, the weather story, and the animal story. That was in the U.S. Abroad, these categories were generally replaced by "the Americanization" of something or other—Paris drugstores, Tokyo nightclubs, London pubs, the Vatican—or "European prosperity," or "the reaction" story, the latter a round-up of pictorial reactions to some U.S. event the precise meaning of which was frequently obscure to foreigners.

Farm stories were assigned regularly from New York, and most of them ended up in the Chicago bureau. Farmers, in New York's view, were forever (*a*) making too much money, (*b*) not making enough, (*c*) saving the world's hungry, (*d*) goofing off with their ill-gotten subsidies at winter resorts and country clubs, or (*e*) *other*. There was a persistent dream in New York that the real America must exist out there somewhere; the heartland, the strength and insouciance and productive know-how which made this nation great, ahem.

The trouble was, the perfect example was hard to find. And New York often sent the wrong people to find it.

One-time Chicago bureau chief Hugh Moffett once found himself in unexpected possession of photographer Leonard McCombe, a British-born rising star whom New York had dispatched to Chicago because McCombe wanted to "do a farm." Moffett loaded him into the car, drove south from Chicago, and was only mildly upset when McCombe buried his nose in a novel instead of surveying the countryside.

Down around Bloomington, Illinois, Moffett stopped to call on a county agent to get expert guidance on the best farms in the area. Armed with some addresses, he started the rounds. McCombe refused even to get out of the car. He would look out the window, brood a bit, and remark, "That's not the kind of farm I want."

Patiently Moffett drove to another county, found another agent, and this one volunteered to take his own car and lead them around. But not, he said, today. It was late Friday afternoon and he explained that people in those parts didn't work on Saturdays and Sundays. This alarmed McCombe, but not Moffett. He said that since they couldn't bother the agent on a weekend he guessed he'd go back to Chicago to attend a big party photographer Wallace Kirkland was giving. McCombe asked to be dropped somewhere in eastern Illinois, and Moffett promised to be back on Monday morning to continue the search. He would have done so, except that the first telephone call he got on Monday morning was from assignment editor Girvin in New York, laughing his head off and saying, "Moffett, you've met your match. I've got this Englishman sitting here in my office and he says you were unable to *find a farm*."

More than ten years after this episode, *Life* sent Bayard Hooper, a New Englander, to cover the Iowa State Fair. Presumably he could bring the eastern viewpoint to this big, gaudy, dusty, smelly, and quite exciting event. Hooper returned to the Chicago bureau with his own rueful version of what had transpired. He had, he said, approached with great courtesy a farmer-looking type in the fair's cattle barns.

"Excuse me, sir," he said, "can you tell me how many gentleman farmers there are in Iowa?"

The man looked him over carefully, paused, and finally said, "Well, Sonny, out here we figure that any man who takes off his hat to milk the cows is a gentleman."

Reporter Hooper, telling the story on himself, then produced a vignette of a farm lad he had found who trekked to the fair to play in a band. The boy was small but he had mastered the trombone by using first a coat hanger, then his feet, to enable him to extend the "slide" of the trombone all the way down where his short arms couldn't yet reach. Unwittingly, Hooper had probably found the quality that New York always wanted in "the farm story."

I was in Chicago too when Hooper drew the Iowa State Fair, and I was a bit miffed that I wasn't sent. I was born and raised in Iowa and the fair, together with the Sidney Rodeo and the Drake Relays, were the glamorous events of my childhood.

My crack at a farm story came late in 1954 when photographer Gordon Parks and I descended upon the Bruene family farm, 240 acres near Gladbrook, Iowa. Our mission was to explore "the farmer and his government," a study of the ways in which federal farm programs had influenced, for good or for bad, the long-range planning and year-to-year operation of a modern, well-run farm. The Bruenes had kept voluminous and accurate records for years, through which one could follow their responses to federal requests to limit or expand production, switch from one crop to another.

Gordon and I spent days with the Bruenes, me going over their books and payment records, Gordon cheerfully tromping through snow-covered corn-stubbled fields, in and out of hog houses, machine sheds, cattle barns, and granaries.

The Bruene kids had never in their entire lives seen a black until Gordon appeared, and they found him so charming that after the first day he had to make most of his photographic rounds with one kid hanging onto each leg. After we left, a sow belonging to one of the children produced seven piglets which were named Gordon, Roger, Alexander, Buchanan, Parks, and Junior, that being the full version of Parks's name. Because there was one left over, it was called Dodie. We were both highly flattered.

Unlike most farm stories, that one actually ran in the magazine, though it took the combined efforts of veteran text writer Ernest Havemann and the expertise of a Cornell University economist to put my laboriously researched farm economics into readable form for publication.

Perhaps the most cherished of all farm story episodes was that of Eliot Elisofon somewhere in Nebraska in the forties with reporter Ray Mackland, who later became picture editor of the magazine. Elisofon, who would have made a great Cecil B. DeMille if we hadn't already had one, looked at "the farm" with the creative eye of an artist. He stood lost in wonder at the cross-hatched pattern of growing grain, at the thrusting silos, the chugging machinery, the graceful gestures of a man throwing out corn for the chickens or hunching his shoulders under the weight of a bucket of cobs.

Each night in his hotel room he would create a scenario for the next day: four tractors here, two silos there, farmers moving from here to there doing exactly this and that. Once he had worked it out, he transmitted it all to Mackland and decreed that all should be in order at 11:00 A.M. next day. Each day Mackland would wheedle, cajole, plead with the farmers to bring themselves and their equipment to the proper place at the proper time. On the rare occasions when Mackland succeeded, Elisofon was invariably late to what could only be called the photo-call. When he finally arrived, clean-shaven, ebullient, beaming, he would announce that "the great Elisofon is here."

This approach produced no applause from the farmers, and finally Mackland attempted to remonstrate with the photographer.

"First you really shouldn't ever be late," he said. "And then, besides, you should never say 'the great Elisofon is here.' "

Eliot thought this over for awhile, and then he agreed.

"You're absolutely right," quoth he. "I shouldn't say that. *You* should say it."

□ □ □

Weather stories, unlike farm stories, ranged farther afield than Chicago. They could happen anywhere and often did. We were forever trying to photograph "spring comes to the . . ."—and each time, of course, spring stubbornly refused to come. Stories like this were scheduled weeks in advance, and despite the best efforts of reporter and photographer to convince spring that it would lose its chance to appear in *Life* if it didn't show up within the allotted time, it often didn't. No amount of breathing on buds or murmuring assurance to pussy willows would hasten the process. We lost as many spring stories as we got.

Other kinds of weather, however, were gifts from on high: chickens and/or kittens adrift on a barn door (floods); bits of straw impaled miraculously into the sides of houses (twisters); upended cars and palm trees aslant of retirement villages (hurricanes); fairy wonderlands of trees and provocative still-lifes of smashed automobiles (ice storms); vast expanses of white on white, and people skiing down Fifth Avenue (blizzards).

EKT, who had seen them all, never could decide which was the bigger cliché—chickens on the roof of a floating henhouse, or the sun-whitened steer or buffalo skull which documentary photographers produced in dust-bowl stories. He threw away "hundreds" of pictures of each and considered the weather story a necessary evil.

One primary defect in this kind of story was that the weather itself, the point of the coverage, created great difficulties of movement for the reporting staff. Even if they managed to get the story, the weather erected barriers to getting the finished product back to New York or out to Chicago for printing.

On one occasion in late 1950 a tremendous gale struck the East Coast. It happened on Saturday morning, less than twenty-four hours before closing time, but Thompson discarded one weather story for an even better one.

Already scheduled for the upcoming magazine was a combination lead about how irrigation had hurt a city in Texas and how floods hurt California and Nevada. Photos, text, layouts, were in Chicago but all were decreed OUT.

The gale was IN.

Photographer George Silk, who lived in New Jersey, wasn't home when the office telephoned him to cover the big wind. His wife explained that he had rushed out of the house, cameras flying, about an hour before when he happened to notice his neighbor's tall television aerial blowing away and taking off in the general direction of Greenland.

Photographer Burt Glinn, at work in Manhattan, was busily focusing on a burst steam pipe when the pipe let go in still another place and a jet of steam tore off his shirt pocket and blew away a package of cigarettes therein. Photographer Tony Linck, assigned to see what was happening on Staten Island, found the ferry out of service. He dashed to his car and by circuitous tunnels and bridges achieved the island, only to be swept into the nearest ditch by wind-blown waters when he got out of his car. Up to his shoulders in water and mud, he made a few pictures, got back to the car, headed for Manhattan—and the car stalled on a flooded road.

Photographer Ed Clark, on another occasion, was sent to cover a hurricane in Fort Myers, Florida, and was blown through a plate glass window when he ventured out to aim his cameras at the wind. That didn't scare him half as much as trying to get back to a functioning airport with his film. The wind was so loud that nobody in the car heard the whistle of an approaching train, and the reporter driving the car managed to miss it by only about ten yards when she spotted its headlights in the gloom.

One team covering an avalanche scored a coup and then had to hire a daredevil skier to carry the precious film down the mountainside—all roads were closed. Flood coverers customarily entrusted their film to helicopter pilots and prayed a lot. Hurricane coverers often found airports closed and highways impassable, had to wirephoto their film and telephone their captions.

As years passed and the staff adjusted itself to the frustrations and bitter truths of weather stories, one word came to stand for the whole horrible experience. The word was "derbis" (pronounced deŕ-biss). It came from reporter Jane Estes, a light-hearted member of the staff who always said that she was hired only because she happened to be in Manhattan on a very rainy day and walked into the *Time-Life* building to get out of the downpour. Somebody handed her a form, and she filled it out . . .

Because of her mental and physical indestructibility, Jane often drew weather assignments, disaster assignments, go-off-without-your-suitcase assignments. She always went; she always bought emergency blouses ("I own more blouses than Lerners',") and she always came back with the story. Once she was pursuing a disaster in California which involved a stalled train and either an avalanche or a landslide. However, as she pressed through whatever physical perils were present, she was suddenly flagged down by a state trooper.

She got out her press pass, patted her hair, rolled down the window, and inquired, "What's up, Doc?"

"You can't go up that pass, lady," the trooper said. "It's choked with derbis."

Thus "derbis" came into office language, as did other gems collected by reporter Estes on her travels. One of our favorites was her account of the southern deputy sheriff confronted with a murder case who swore that he hadn't known a thing about it until "the police cars went by with their sy-ringes wide open."

Years after she brought these words into our lives, Estes moved to the West Coast. Most of us hadn't seen her for ages until one late night in 1964 when the elevator doors parted and there she stood, left arm, shoulder, and chin fully involved in holding an enormous stack of photographs of the disastrous Alaska earthquake, right arm and hand clutching handbag and shoes.

"Jane!" we chorused.

"Hi gang," she caroled. Then, nodding at her pile of pictures, "Say, you talk about *derbis!*"

□ □ □

Weather, for all its maddening unpredictability, remained always an ace in the hole for a bad week in which absolutely nothing interesting seemed to be happening. If all else failed somebody always proposed a "weather lead." Often this suggestion fell on very deaf ears among reporters bored with it all.

One such occasion occurred in the fifties when *Life* news director

Robert Elson heard on the radio that there was a cold front moving in on New York. "Fronts" of all kinds are difficult to photograph, but Elson hopped on this one. He went straight to head researcher Valerie Vondermuhll: "There's a cold front coming to New York. Photograph it."

Barely suppressing her yawn, Vondermuhll went home to her apartment on the Hudson River at Riverside Drive, and went peacefully to bed. Next morning, to her horror, she looked out the window and saw "the most beautiful cold front coming in, with clouds, the wind, the lot. It was the most unmistakable cold front I've ever seen." And she had not assigned a photographer.

Even worse was the staff's failure to produce the blizzard story to end all blizzard stories. This was in Chicago, in the mid-fifties. Ralph Graves was the *Life* bureau chief, and he had on his desk a picture script for blizzard coverage. The script had been written by George Hunt, who preceded Graves both as Chicago bureau chief and as managing editor. Hunt had envisioned the ultimate story on a snowstorm, and he had organized it as carefully as a U.S. Marine assault on an atoll. His script called for the deployment of twelve to eighteen troops to key areas at key times: Midway airport when the first warnings came, the Loop when it began to disrupt traffic, the lake when shipping was in trouble. Snowfall warnings were calculated, the actual fall calibrated, the progression of difficulties foreseen, and staff movements calculated to cover them.

When Hunt handed over the bureau to Graves he also handed over the blizzard script.

"It's all in there," he said. "All you have to do is push the button."

Time passed and every reporter and photographer in the bureau was given a copy. We knew, God knows we knew. But George's blizzard, like spring, kept not coming when we and the button were ready. A year or two passed and then came the spring of 1955. It was March or April and we were lost in dreams of forsythia, crocuses, violets. Correspondent Richard Meryman and his wife Hopie were having a bureau party at their home, with some visiting guest artists from New York.

It started to snow even before we left the office, but we were unconcerned. After all, it was spring. By the time we got to the Merymans' house on the near north side it was a bit tricky. I remember smugly passing stalled cars all along the route, complimenting myself that I still drove a stick shift, with the aid of which one can rock in and out of drifts with little effort.

It was a memorable party. No "civilians," just staff. Great food, great singing, great conviviality. When the snow got about eight inches deep on the window sills we balled it up and threw it at lamp-posts, neighbors, and passers-by in the street who accepted our challenge to an exchange.

As we went out into the night we had some difficulty identifying our cars, which had turned into picturesque free-form snow sculptures. It was something of a record snowfall for its date, and I don't think one person in the entire group ever remembered the blizzard script.

Next morning in the office the telephone rang with what seemed peculiar insistence. Reporter Estes responded and we all heard what she said.

"Yes, the blizzard. Yes, the button. Well, a kind of funny thing happened out here. You know that button? Well, it didn't work."

□ □ □

Then there were the animals. Chuck Champlin's problems trying to organize the prize bulls, Anne Denny's perishable earthworms, the studio's wild beasts, were par for the course.

Reporter Nancy Genet, at work on a special sea issue, tried to push an octopus back into its tank so Fritz Goro could photograph it, and the beast, made frantic by the lights, decided to climb her arm for refuge. "It was a very pleasant little octopus, only about four-feet-four from end to end, and it was so frightened that it kept flushing all kinds of colors, from pink to red to purplish, blue, green, everything. I'm sure it was more terrified than I was, but if you've ever tried to push away one tentacle, or two, and then have all the others come out . . . really you don't forget the experience."

Photographer Ralph Morse, bent on making a study of animal motion, decided that his friend the monkey was bored with the project when the monkey began hurling bananas at the photographer's head. Correspondent Dick Pollard, on the other hand, realized that he was persona grata with a pet chimpanzee named Bobo when the chimp, all dressed up in short pants, a jacket with an eton collar, and a pair of well-polished shoes, stuck out a paw. Pollard shook it and found his palm full of chimpanzee feces—"A sure sign, I was informed, that Bobo liked me."

Bobo didn't, however, like the photographer. Every time N. R. "Nat" Farbman aimed his Rolleiflex, the nattily clad Bobo ambled over with a peeled banana and stuffed it smack into the lens.

Photographer Nina Leen had a passion for snakes, a preference for which nature editor Patricia Hunt was particularly grateful, because other staffers tended to shun serpents. Photographer Leen photographed a twenty-foot-long anaconda in Florida, aided by three handlers in goggles and swim suits. She once carried around for two weeks a small box containing the eggs of corn snakes, so she could take a picture when they hatched. Eventually they did, she got her picture, and then one of the babies escaped from the box and panicked her housekeeper. One of her real coups was a photo of a cobra in the act of discharging its poison. To get this, she rented some cobras from the Bronx Zoo, set herself up with a rapid-fire camera, lights, and snake handlers. When she was ready, the handlers in masks waved white rags at the cobras. Nina went through three spitting cobras and 200 feet of film to achieve one picture—only one frame—which captured the terrifying sight of the spitting snake.

Her enthusiasm for the undulating critters encouraged reporter John Dille to buy a four-foot ball python as an office pet. Dille kept "Butch" in his desk drawer, to the wonder of cautious colleagues who came to peer from a discreet distance, but one night he absentmindedly left the grey and yellow python on a chair in the copy room, where it was sat upon by Berenice Adelson. Adelson commendably kept her cool, but there was so much female shrieking from other sources that "Butch" was banished.

One of the most spectacular sets of animal pictures ever published was taken by John Dominis on a ten-month safari to Africa in 1966. Dominis was neither hunter nor animal expert, but he is a patient man with courage and he was fascinated by the assignment. He decided not to scatter his fire, but to concentrate on one species of great cat at a time—first the leopards, then cheetahs, then lions. He found leopards the most cunning and daring. On one occasion he spotted a female leopard, drove within a few hundred yards to photograph her, and she dashed into the bush. He drove in after her until she charged his truck, bit both tire and fender, scratched the door, and disappeared. Another day, attempting to photograph a leopard pursuing a baboon, Dominis peered through the windshield of his Land Rover to see the baboon headed straight for him, with the leopard in close pursuit.

"I figured the safest place for me was on top of the car," he recalls, so he halted abruptly, got out, scrambled up to his tripod-mounted camera on the roof, and started to focus. Almost before he had time to shoot, the baboon ran straight through his straddled legs, all but upending him. "Then there was that leopard, headed straight for me. Fortunately, it chose to run around me instead of through me . . ."

Dominis's story was a triumph. Most of the rest of us, faced with animals, were defeated. A typical tale of woe is that of trainee-reporter Eileen Lanouette (later Mrs. Emmet Hughes), who in the late forties went with photographer Bernard Hoffman to illustrate an article for the nature department on animal behavior. The nature and religion departments were at that time combined, a rather intriguing bit of match-making, under the direction of John Haverstick. Haverstick dispatched Lanouette knowing that she was allergic to house cats, mad about dogs, and had seldom seen any animal larger than these two.

Trouble began even on the flight from New York to Raleigh, North Carolina, where the story was to be shot on the spacious grounds of an insane asylum. Lanouette, just out of college, had never been on a plane before. When that particular one skidded off the runway at landing, veteran Hoffman turned green and reporter Lanouette kept right on chattering, having no idea that this landing was different from any other.

Next day they went to work. A stringer had had erected, on the insane asylum grounds, a series of wooden structures which looked like tombstones. They were set at different heights and they were supposed to be occupied by dogs and cats. The idea was that cats, being preying animals, could hear higher sounds than dogs, and would react by leaping onto the tombstones. Or something like that. A dog, provided by the stringer, submitted patiently to being transported daily to the experimental grounds, but none of the eighteen cats the *Life* team procured could tolerate the automobile journey nor the firm instructions to leap to the top of the tombstones on signal.

Several days passed, during which the inmates of the asylum took to passing their afternoons on the lawn watching the *real* crazies. Eventually Hoffman decreed that this experiment had failed, and that they should advance to the next one. That one involved bulls. Research studies had shown, according to the script, that bulls do not react to the color red but instead to any old color if the fabric which bears it has a sheen and is flapped provocatively in their faces.

To show this truth, Lanouette and Hoffman moved to a farm which had a lot of bulls. For some inexplicable reason, the "tombstones" were also moved to the new location and set up.

On the day shooting was to begin, Hoffman sent Lanouette into the fields to hang up a white flag and a red one. As she went about her duties, the farmer's herd of Angus cattle ambled onto the turf. Angus cattle are curious and friendly, and they wandered over to have a look at Lanouette. She panicked, dropped flags and photo equipment, and fled the field. Hoffman sternly ordered her back. By this time the Angus had decided to investigate the white-painted tombstones, as well, and in the process had befouled them here and there.

Hoffman told Lanouette to clean up the tombstones. Dutifully she went off to the farmhouse, politely she asked for two pails of warm soapy water. As she staggered back to the scene of action, the Angus cattle appeared again so she put down both buckets and ran. The Angus drank the soapy water, got a terrible attack of diarrhea, and the *Life* team was expelled from still other premises.

Nature reporter Kay Doering, assigned to the same story, had her own problems. She auditioned sharks for Hoffman, to prove that they would go after food they could smell but not see, and she carefully nurtured a pair of pigeons for his eventual use, until they laid eggs in her office. Too tender-hearted to upset the impending birth, she got another pair for photos. She DDT'd endless flies and piled their bodies near a frog which science said would snap only at moving objects, not dead ones. She had a special dark chamber built in the *Life* studio for bats, so that Hoffman could photograph their habits. When it came time to photograph them, they refused to come out and had to be flushed with brooms and probes. Doering was philosophical. "Probably," she said, "they'll turn up next spring, flying around . . ."

Exotic animals like bats, anacondas, octopi, chimps, engaged the attention but the real hazard for all of us lay closer home. We weren't

Reporter Eileen Lanouette Hughes grapples with an elephant while covering filming of The Bible *near Rome in the early sixties.*

CREDIT: VELIO CIONE © TIME INC.

too bad on dogs and cats, but when it came to hogs, cattle, sheep. and chickens we were in constant peril: the specific nomenclature of domesticated animals is very mysterious, to anyone who doesn't raise them or butcher them, and few among us had ever participated in these activities.

Boston-bred Irene Saint, a demon for verity in every story and trainer of a whole generation of checker-reporters, once sent a suggestion about the Chicago stockyards in which she used the terms "calf," "heifer," "cow," and "steer" interchangeably throughout. How she happened to miss "bull" in this mishmash no one knows.

Dakota-bred Ed Thompson used to summon Iowa-bred me, on occasion, to ask challengingly, "What kind of pig is this?" Since Chester White was the only kind I'd ever established clearly in my mind, that's what I always replied. I wasn't much better on cattle. Holsteins I knew on sight, but the rest were a mystery. I also couldn't tell soybeans from winter wheat, in a picture, though I was good at corn.

It turned out to be a lot easier to identify something like a tapir, an orchid, or a praying mantis than plain old homegrown hogs, oats, and sheep. The epitome of our mass discomfiture may have been reached in January 1957, when we identified pigs as calves in a photo caption.

Our devilishly delighted readers flooded the place with letters, and letters correspondent Barbara Beals turned to a bit of doggerel:

When calves turn to pigs
Almost overnight
We can proudly claim:
LIFE is *always* right.
But until that day
(Which has not yet occurred)
We must humbly admit:
LIFE erred.

18

Hits, Runs, and Errors

Most of us were happy most of the time, but there was an occasional revolt.

None that I can recall was provoked by such prosaic matters as working hours, pay, or vacations. Instead they were set off by some editorial stance taken by the magazine, or by what somebody considered the erosion of our *Life*-style. On the latter issue theater editor Tom Prideaux led a rebellion in the new *Time-Life* building against canned music inside the elevators. Like all high-rise buildings this one had several elevator banks for different sets of floors, and like most new buildings in Manhattan it had canned music inside all of them. Prideaux, who loves music but didn't yearn to be a captive audience, thought that he should be allowed to ride thirty floors in silence, or in conversation with his friends, and he rounded up enough like-minded colleagues to persuade the building management to cut off the sound in the elevators which served the *Life* floors.

It was also Prideaux who once quite innocently came close to setting off a strike vote at *Life*. The time was the late forties, the issue was some murky affair about Communism and the Newspaper Guild, and the staff was agog at the mere thought of rebellion. Still, there was strike talk in the air, and Prideaux and friends—Mary Leatherbee, Lincoln Barnett, Lois Feldkamp, and others—decided to write a review about the whole situation. They all had been amused by a news conference conducted by managing editor Dan Longwell at which he asked, with urgency, "What shall we do about spring?" (shades of the weather story). So they set about writing a song with that title.

Prideaux can still sing the first verse, which blithely related spring to the issue of Communism:

> What shall we do about spring?
> Spring, a most subversive fellow,
> Makes the fields explode with yellow
> When the red red, dirty red robin sings.

Hints of a "musical review about *Life*" spread quietly through the staff, and on the night of the strike vote many *Life*rs cherished Walter Mitty dreams of writing skits, songs, dialogue, for a great show about the magazine. If we were on strike, we calculated, we'd have plenty of time to devote to the musical project.

Then, however, sterner unionists from the New York Newspaper Guild said that we would be required to picket the building, carrying militant signs. Picket the place? Carry signs? Not free to help write a great musical? The final strike vote was cast by all Guild members of Time Inc., but a defection of disillusioned *Life*rs helped doom it. There was no strike, and in the end there was no musical. Everybody just went happily back to work as usual. (As a footnote, the only strike in Time Inc.'s fifty-year history occurred in the spring of 1976 and was a bitter, wrenching experience for all hands.)

These were isolated episodes of insurrection, however. The typical protest was ideologically motivated and concerned matters larger than the *Time-Life* building. One night in the early fifties researcher Doris Getsinger became so infuriated by an editorial Mr. Luce himself had written about General Douglas MacArthur—Luce admired him extravagantly—that she balled it all up, strode to the nearest window, and hurled Luce's exalting words into outer darkness.

It was a futile gesture and she knew it. At least eight more copies of the offending words were lying about on desks within reach of her own. But it made her feel a lot better. It made some other people feel a lot better too, and one of them even picked up a pencil, grinning from ear to ear, and proceeded to finish "checking" the editorial, which ran as written.

Another earlier revolt had more effect. This one occurred in the late forties when the then–text editor, Oliver Jensen, commissioned and scheduled a story written by a former German prison-camp official. His was not an extermination camp but a military prison in which, by his account, captured American airmen were cajoled into cooperating with their captors and providing information. The headline was something about "EVERYTHING WAS GEMÜTLICH IN THE PRISON CAMPS."

By sheer chance the checker assigned to this opus was a Jewish woman named June Herman. The more she checked, the madder she got. By still another chance, that night the foreign news department was flying its martini flag and a large segment of the staff gathered there early in the evening. Suddenly into this happy gathering marched the German author himself, in the temporary custody of text department researcher Eileen Lanouette. "Lanny" disapproved of the textpiece, but she felt that if her boss Jensen had invited the author into the building he should be taken to the party. Shortly after their arrival, in came June Herman, fire in her eyes.

Because of complicated closing schedules and fast-shifting assignments, people in domestic or foreign news often had only a vague idea of what the rest of the magazine was up to, and seldom knew the plan of long-range departments like science, specials, text. Gradually word of the "*gemütlich*" story spread through the crowded room, and murmurs of outrage broke out in every quarter. As the evening wore on the umbrage grew and the German author was escorted discreetly from the scene.

That was far from the end, however. By about 10:00 P.M. a large delegation decided to march upon the managing editor's office and kill the story. It was offensive; it was too soon after the war; the staff wouldn't have it. Several tense minutes and impassioned speeches later, the barricades fell. "*Gemütlich*" was *heraus,* but some other article had, obviously, to be substituted in the space. Rather quickly the bosses selected one about John Ringling North, the circus impresario. Herman thought that it had been checked and was ready for publication, but it had not. Thus it had to be checked that night and the next day, and every passionate participant in the protest march felt honor-bound to stay and help check it. Researcher Lanouette, swept into the revolt by sheer physical presence, was commissioned to find John Ringling North and get him to confirm details of the story. Frantic telephone calls later, she learned that he never arose before 3:00 P.M., wouldn't answer his telephone, and wouldn't send wires. She spent all that night trying to find North, all the next afternoon sitting under the umbrellas of Rockefeller Plaza with an emissary from North, checking facts and figures about circus affairs. Being a revolutionary, we all learned that night, is very hard work.

□ □ □

There were always muted border skirmishes on the magazine about politics, but they were not unique to *Life*. Many publications in the forties, fifties, sixties, had staffers whose political convictions lay somewhat to the left of their employers. EKT admits that *Life* had a strong pro-Republican tilt in pre-Eisenhower days despite the fact that a poll of the staff would have shown that the majority was pro-Democratic. The tilt shifted toward even-handed coverage in the Eisenhower and Kennedy elections, and it is ironic that even in earlier campigns *Life* was accused by Republicans of "killing the candidate": e.g., a Robert Capa picture of Robert Taft "catching" what was obviously a dead fish provided for the occasion; and a caption which pointed out that Thomas E. Dewey, photographed from the side, was sitting on a telephone book to make himself look taller.

There was seldom any unpleasantness about these things at *Life*. Some field correspondents complained that their on-the-spot judgments and assessments of events were altered by editing in New York, often political. I tend to believe them, particularly if they were filing from sensitive areas like China, Indochina, the Middle East. But on the scene in New York there was never much muscle applied to mind-changing. There was a delicate selection of writers for stories, and the choice was seldom difficult: each person's view was quite well known, having been bellowed on frequent occasions to anyone who could stand the noise. Head-on collisions were thus usually avoided. There was always somebody on the staff who truly believed whatever point the editors wanted to make, and would write it.

Though I was never a political writer, I recall that the only two times I was removed from stories came from an excess of partisanship on my part. The first instance came when I was assigned to do a short textblock on General de Gaulle's veto of British entry into the Common Market in the sixties. I was so livid with the general that even after my fourth attempt to write the short piece my anger still showed. Somebody, probably George Hunt, told me gently to forget it, and gave it to another writer. The second time was a small caption about Roy Cohn and some legal tangle involving his business affairs. I had had a scunner against Cohn ever since McCarthy days, and after several tries to express my distaste I was again plucked politely from the fray and told to go peddle my private crusades in my own office.

By and large this kind of inner churning was regarded with tolerance and amusement, at least among staffers who didn't become personally committed to the fortunes and eventual retinues of politicians. Personal opinions, however passionately held, were not the stuff of vendetta or even of resentment except in very rare cases.

This general tone of tolerance was set, more than outsiders could believe, by the proprietor himself, Mr. Luce. One example will suffice: In the autumn of 1956 Mrs. Luce was serving as U.S. ambassador to Italy, and Mr. Luce was in Rome with her. On Thanksgiving, *Time* bureau chief Walter Guzzardi had a party. It was one of what we used to call "his and hers" parties—about six Rome employees of Mr. Luce, and several dozen of Mrs. Luce's people from the embassy.

We gathered in an atmosphere more of gloom than of Thanksgiving: the Soviet Union had just crushed the Hungarian uprising; Britain, France, and Israel had just attacked Egypt—the world seemed hurtling to disaster. And there had been far too little reaction from Washington, in my view. At one point in the festivities I heard myself saying, in quite a loud voice, "I miss Harry Truman."

A silence began to grow in my immediate vicinity, but I ignored it. "Britain and France have gone mad," I proclaimed, "and that man in the White House just sits there. Harry Truman would have done something. Maybe the wrong thing, but *something.*"

By now the silence was spreading like oil on water. I could almost hear conversations halting three rooms away. Finally one voice broke in, and it came from right behind me. Unbeknownst to me, Mr. Luce and I had been standing almost bottom to bottom.

"What did you say?" intoned that voice.

"Well, Mr. Luce, I said . . ." and once again I launched into what I had said. The silence vibrated like a tuning fork until I got to the end. And then Mr. Luce asked, "Do you know what I hope happens to you?"

By then I was so paralyzed that I called him "sir."

"No, sir" I quavered.

"I hope," he said, and he got a quizzical look in his intense eyes, the tiniest quirk around his mouth, "I hope that when you grow up [long pause], you will get to be the editor of a great big magazine. And that everybody who works for you is a Republican."

There was a stunned moment, and then a tension-shattering roar of laughter from all over the house. I never appreciated Mr. Luce quite so much as at that moment.

On other days, under other circumstances, he could be less flexible and less amusing. Both his stubborn, persistent backing of Chiang Kai-shek and his running feud with Franklin D. Roosevelt created tensions and incipient revolts at many levels in the company. So did, of all things, his attitude toward modern art. He thought he liked art, and he was a member of the board of the Museum of Modern Art in New York, but it turned out that he absolutely loathed anything which wasn't *conventionally* modern: i.e., modern scenes rendered in a conventional manner. However, as he had forgiven me my stand on Harry Truman, he forgave art editor Dorothy Seiberling her appreciation of abstract expressionism. Having made it clear that he didn't like it, he let her select what she considered the best of it, and run it in the magazine.

He also tolerated, to a degree, criticism of that giant in his pantheon of heroes, MacArthur. Luce's idealization of the general caused little staff unrest until the Korean war, when MacArthur's stated wish to bring Chiang into the conflict with a landing in South China, and his advocation of bombing North China, upset many staffers.

Among them was Hugh Moffett, who was then serving as war correspondent in Korea. Moffett admired MacArthur's exploits in World War II but he thought the general was so wrong in Korea that he ought to go. He reported this honestly, and shortly thereafter got the impression that perhaps he himself would have to go. At a face-to-face lunch with Luce back in New York he waited to be fired, found himself being interviewed about Asia in general and China in particular, and his knowledge of the geography of China so impressed the boss that the subject of MacArthur never even came up. Much later, he learned that Thompson had advised the proprietor, ''You'd better listen, Moffett might be right.''

□ □ □

Vietnam became an agony of conscience for the entire staff. *Life* covered the war assiduously with a procession of dedicated men, most notably photographer Larry Burrows. Many employees thought the magazine's position was altogether too hawkish, and about Christmas time of 1965 some began to participate in the muted protests which led slowly to final rejection. Among the most hawkish men on *Life* was managing editor Hunt. He undoubtedly had heard rumblings in the halls, and he knew he had some peace marchers among the employees, but the first time his attention focused completely on the problem was when he got a long, carefully reasoned memo of protest from Dorothy Seiberling. As art editor she had worked happily and creatively with Painter Hunt; now she must protest to Marine Hunt.

He considered her arguments and called a troubled meeting with twelve or fifteen staffers to explain his, and the magazine's, position. In his opinion the war was valid if not commendable, necessary if not glorious. He felt its primary defect was that it was being fought the wrong way: as a marine he would have fought it from easily defendable and evacuable enclaves, but the army was committed to "search and destroy." Feeling that "eighty percent of the staff was probably against me," he softened his position somewhat and then, as he had announced long before that he would do, he resigned after eight years as managing editor.

Ralph Graves took over, and one of his first acts was to run one of the most effective antiwar stories ever published: a stark, simple gallery of the photographs of every U.S. military man killed in Vietnam in one week. There were no histrionics, there were none of the typical *Life* peripheral pictures—of caskets being loaded on planes in Vietnam and unloaded in California, of a funeral, of a family interview in depth. So determined were Graves and his staff to "keep it simple, keep it direct," that they rejected the week of the Battle of Hamburger Hill because it was "a battle event." They wanted just an ordinary week.

The idea for the story came from writer Loudon Wainwright, who later wrote the text and kept that, too, simple and direct with no hint of strident, shrill protest. What the story intended to say was, "It's not just numbers and body counts. It's real real people, with real faces."

Keeping it simple required a huge operation involving every bureau in the country and almost every stringer. Once the names of the dead had been obtained, somebody had to go to each family and ask for a photograph, check the name and age and hometown of each man. In more cases than anyone likes to remember, the routine military "mug shot" in uniform was the only picture the families had of their sons. They were people unaccustomed to the luxury of photo albums and snapshots of family events. Yet they handed the precious "mug shots" over, trustingly, to be sent to New York.

There Muriel Hall became the true boss of the story. It was her job to make sure that not one picture was lost, not one mistake was made in identification and description. Her first act was to order that every incoming photograph go to the lab to be rephotographed, so that a negative would exist. Each family which had surrendered a precious picture to *Life* was to get it back again, with a new copy, and with the knowledge that a negative lay safely in the magazine files so other prints could be made if the original somehow was lost in the mails. It was endless, meticulous, dogged work but Graves says, "I can't recall a story on which the staff was so completely dedicated to getting it *right*."

The story of the Vietnam dead appeared in the issue of June 27, 1969, page after page of small photos—rigid, formal, often bad quality: innocent faces, scowling faces, smiling faces, young faces. The layout, row upon row like the white crosses of Arlington, was almost unbearably moving.

Response was instant. Telephone calls, letters, poured in by the hundreds. Some families wrote to say that they were in favor of the war and that their sons had been too. They wanted everybody to know that they weren't bitter about their loss. Several readers suggested that *Life* repeat that story every week until the war ended. Others, apparently believing that the magazine could do anything, suggested that they give the same coverage to North Vietnamese war dead in one week.

□ □ □

Similar conviction and dogged determination to make it *right* lay behind some notable *Life* crusades. Many of them, predictably, arose from racial tensions and inequalities in the turbulent fifties and sixties. A series on segregation, begun in 1956, included the story of a black family in Alabama which had begun to make a quiet breakthrough into decent, self-respecting life. The head of the household was a pulp-wood cutter who had managed to acquire his own beaten-up truck. His wife, younger than he, was a schoolteacher. They had hopes for their relative well-being, were pleased with their progress, but still critical of white attitudes which restrained them.

In retrospect their openness to the *Life* team, and *Life*'s treatment of the story, both seem naive. Good intentions abounded, but when that issue of the magazine came out the pulp-wood cutter and his wife were ostracized in their small town. There was no violence, but the man lost his job, the woman was criticized for her comments by the local school board. Grocery store owners refused to sell the housewife food, filling station men refused to put gas in the cutter's old truck. Local white vigilantes even stole the truck, at one point, and chained it to a tree in another man's yard.

When word of all this got to New York, correspondent Dick Stolley was sent from Atlanta to Alabama to see what he could do to straighten things out. Very little, it developed. In one chilling interview after another, Stolley was told that "that piece in your magazine is the awfullest thing I ever read." It became clear that as emotions rose the woman would lose her teaching job. Night after night Stolley sat in an Alabama cabin and listened to terrified people trying to decide where to go. In the end *Life* moved them—lock, stock, barrel, and ancient truck—to other jobs in another city, but some damage was irreparably done. The marriage broke up under the added strain of ostracism and uprooting, the wood cutter drifted back to the familiar scenes of home hoping eventually to be forgiven for talking to those Yankee reporters, and the woman found that her teaching skills were not high enough for more sophisticated teaching standards in larger schools out of Alabama. All the magazine could do was stay in touch and offer aid and sympathy. Eventually it was able to pay for the daughter's college, by surreptitious means of which possibly even the parents are not entirely aware.

On two other occasions, both involving blacks, there were happier endings. A black school had burned in West Memphis, Arkansas, across the river from Memphis, Tennessee, and the town fathers decided instead of replacing it to build a new school for white children. Reporter Helen Fennell, from Atlanta, and photographer Ed Clark, from Nashville, were assigned to the story and greeted with suspicion by citizens who had little regard for "that 'sick' Yankee magazine." Turning on their best southern accents, the team toured West Memphis recording the miserable places the black children had as temporary schools—churches, store fronts, empty houses—and the rainy season misery of trying to live and learn in knee-deep mud. The story ran fairly big in *Life,* four or five pages, and readers all but swamped West Memphis with books, school supplies, money. *Life* went back a year later to do a sequel, which had become a popular feature for stories which attracted enormous reader interest, and Fennell was able to report that the town had passed a bond issue and the black children had a new school.

"The most exciting thing for me about working for *Life* was that you didn't just go out there to skim the surface," she says. "You got right in with the people, and sometimes you got to go back and find out what had happened."

Reader reaction was even more stunning to a W. Eugene Smith story in 1951 about a black nurse-midwife in South Carolina. Photographer Smith took a two-week midwife-training course before going out on that assignment, and he became so involved in the life of the black nurse and her patients that at one point he gave blood to a child, on another occasion delivered a baby when the nurse was too busy to handle it. The midwife, Maude Callen, did a lot of her work in a makeshift hospital room inside a black church, where she put up bedsheets as screens. One caption in the story noted: "She dreams of having a well-supplied clinic, but has small hope of getting the $7,000 it might cost."

Within a year readers had sent more than $18,000 to Maude Callen and Smith returned to take a picture of her with her husband in a new fifty-seven-by-thirty-two-foot clinic which she said looked to her "like the Empire State Building." In two years readers had sent a total of $29,000 and Mrs. Callen's clinic was a thriving concern.

□ □ □

For every error ever made—in our opinion—by management or the world at large, we staffers could produce one of our own. Sports reporter Jack McDermott met his future bride at an office party, brooded three weeks before he got up the courage to ask for a date (he took her to see the Harlem Globetrotters), and finally became engaged at a Saturday lunch. Unfortunately he had to close a story on the Brooklyn Dodgers that same afternoon, and by his count there were seven errors in the story, certainly a record for McDermott and perhaps a record for the magazine. He managed to save himself to a degree on his wedding day in a chapel at St. Patrick's when his colleague David Zeitlin interrupted the ceremony to inquire, "Are you absolutely sure that's Al Kaline sliding home in the picture on page eighty-seven?" McDermott was sure.

On another famous occasion *Life* managed to misidentify half the players on the Notre Dame football team and also to offend virtually every extant Notre Dame alumnus by showing the boys in all their gap-toothed splendor, without the false teeth which they normally wore in public to cover the evidence of real teeth they had lost in gridiron fun and games. The implication was, of course, rough football, and some Notre Dame stalwarts even accused *Life* of having created gaps where there were none by blacking out the players' teeth. That particular charge was easily refuted, and peace was made with an apology and a reprinting of the players' pictures correctly identified this time, and with their falsies in place.

The checker on that story was Clay Felker, who shortly thereafter decided he didn't like putting dots on words and went away to become editor and publisher of *New York* magazine.

Even more clamorous than the great Notre Dame booboo was the case of the automobile wrapped around a slender sapling. The wrecked car, its brand name clearly visible on the radiator, was photographed by an amateur photographer who happened on the scene shortly after the accident. The amateur sent his picture to *Life,* which promptly ran it. The picture alone told an eloquent story, but for layout purposes several "filler lines" were added to the caption space and the caption writer padded it out by writing that postwar cars seemed to be much less sturdy than prewar ones—an opinion rather widely held at the time.

The moment the magazine came out, the automobile company that had manufactured this particular model cancelled its advertising contract with *Life*—and also with *Time* and *Fortune.* The main trouble came from use of the word "sturdy," which to automakers means the tensile strength of steel in the frame and to many drivers means whether or not they can put their fingers through the fender. In the disarray which followed publication, *Life* tried to find the clobbered car to submit it to tests. A dealer from a nearby town had spirited away the wreck, however, and had given the owner a brand-new replacement. After which the owner refused to talk, and nobody ever saw the wreck again.

In desperate defense of itself, *Life* asked a research organization if it could rebuild the car and submit it to "sturdiness tests." Automakers admitted privately that inspection practices had become lax because of the scarcity of steel, but none would go on record to that effect. The research organization pointed out that manufacturers got different tensile strengths from different batches of metal, so there was no way to pin down the truth about any individual car.

Eventually the furor died away, the automobile company returned its advertising to the magazines, and head researcher MacPhail consoled the checker who had dotted the caption. It was MacPhail's conviction that until a checker had collected two or three "errors reports" he or she hadn't yet really learned the trade.

MacPhail's comforting words soothed, but still the appearance of an "errors report," in screaming gaudy color, upon a reporter's desk was enough to strike terror into the most insensitive heart and lead to superhuman efforts to avoid another.

Thus it was that every checker on the magazine laughed with glee the time that MacPhail herself went to the Kentucky Derby as a reporter, dutifully wrote all the captions in her notebook, and then placed the notebook inside photographer Ralph Morse's camera case for safe-keeping. The camera case was shipped straight back to New York after the race, MacPhail and Morse were shipped to Chicago for the closing, and the chief of research didn't have her captions. She did have a good memory, however, and she was able to remember what she had scribbled down on the three Morse pictures which eventually made the magazine.

One of the weirdest of *Life* errors occurred during the ecumenical council in Rome in 1962, and is directly attributable to me. On the second spread of an otherwise commendable color story headlined "THE GREAT COUNCIL SHINES IN ROME" was the photograph of a bald, cherubic cardinal kissing the papal ring of Pope John XXIII. I—and the caption—identified him unequivocally as Francis Cardinal Spellman of New York. Wrong. The man was Thomas Cardinal Tien Ken-sin of China. He looked so much like Spellman in the picture that not a single American reader, including Spellman himself, caught the error. It was pointed out to me eventually by a member of Cardinal Tien Ken-sin's staff, and my informant was correct on a tell-tale technicality: the cardinal's ring was on the wrong hand. The Chinese prelate had injured his right hand in an accident which left it paralyzed, so he wore the ring on his left hand. And there it was, clear as day to the trained eye, in the photograph in *Life*.

Among those who know, one of the favorite clangers of all time involves actor Alan Arkin and the young reporter who wanted to immortalize him in *Life*. The reporter was new, idealistic, not yet quite a pro. He admired Arkin enormously, and he particularly admired a short little film Arkin made in which he played a Puerto Rican who sat about in Central Park playing the guitar and delivering folk aphorisms in a marvelous accent. The reporter went to the entertainment department to suggest that he meet the actor at the fountain by the Plaza Hotel, take him to Central Park to recreate the movie scene, perhaps have a box lunch, and there interview him. The appointment was made for 12:30 and the reporter rushed out at 12:15, excited about his assignment.

At about ten minutes to 1:00 P.M. the entertainment department got a phone call from Arkin asking, "Where is your boy?"

"We don't know," they confessed. "He left here over half an hour ago."

Arkin decided to mosey on over to the *Time-Life* building, where he spent half an hour in amiable conversation with Prideaux, Leatherbee, and Co., and then left.

Around 2:30 the young reporter turned up, ecstatic. "I have two whole notebooks full of stories," he said.

Arkin had used a sort of Puerto Rican accent, he reported, just like in the film, and he was marvelous. The two had sat in the park, had a box lunch, had a wonderful time.

"But Arkin," somebody finally revealed, "was here, looking for you. Here in the office."

Dumbfounded, the reporter gazed from face to face and slowly the whole horrible truth dawned. He had fallen, hook, line, and box lunch, for some antic city slicker who found it fun to play Alan Arkin for the young man from *Life*.

19

Truman Would Have Won Again

Through the years *Life* published a series of special issues devoted to a single subject: the United States at mid-century, Africa, Germany, Christianity, the air age, the American woman, entertainment, the sea, the Bible, the Soviet Union, Picasso. Some were also double issues at year's end, big fat volumes which remained on the newsstands for two weeks instead of one and which had the incidental advantage of providing a week's breathing space for members of the staff eager to fly off for Christmas to wherever they had originally come from.

Special issues were often a year in the making, produced by a small New York staff which was removed from all other duties and, in the new building, isolated into a windowless space which became known to its toilers as "the Bay of Pigs." A stream of orders went out from this nucleus to bureaus and stringers all over the world; to artists, photographers, reporters; and a stream of requests went out to experts in whatever field the special was to cover. U.S. military brass, universities, research centers, scientists, computers—every physical or human aid known to man was pressed into the preparation of a special.

One of the most spectacular was called "Air Age," dated June 18, 1956, with a cover flag which read "Man's New Way of Life in World Reshaped by Conquest of Skies." The issue was in preparation from November 1955 until June 1956, a rather quick production time for such a complicated subject, but its nucleus of planners received an enormous boost because a previous special. "Christianity," closed at Christmas time and almost that entire staff was shifted immediately to "Air Age." People at *Life* became quite accustomed to shifting abruptly from one area of expertise to another, and found it amusing—"angels, airplanes, what's the difference?"

Despite the months of preparation, the lead story in "Air Age" was shot in only twenty-four hours by twenty-eight photographers deployed to the fifteen busiest U.S. airports. Their job was to show exactly what went on in a single twenty-four hours to move thousands of people, tons of freight, millions of pieces of mail, across and within the nation by air.

Many a newsmaker used to complain that *Life* photographers were everywhere, and so it must have seemed during that twenty-four hours to startled air travelers most of whom knew nothing whatever about the upcoming special issue. Two sweet old ladies photographed as they got on a plane in Boston found the cameras turned on them again only a few hours later on a helicopter ferry in Los Angeles. A photogenic young lady who boarded a plane at New York's Idlewild somehow eluded the *Life* cameras there but she turned up on film sent from Washington, D.C., and later in a take from Miami.

Photographer Howard Sochurek produced a twelve-page story on the unearthly images of very high altitude flight, working at 30,000 feet and 40,000 feet while crammed into an Air Force plane flying at sonic speeds and constrained behind a helmet and oxygen mask. Leonard McCombe logged almost 66,000 miles on one single story about the life of an airliner captain on the New York–Teheran run.

But the pièce de résistance of the issue was a single spectacular picture showing every operational airplane of the U.S. Air Force in the air at the same time, on the same negative, on an almost impossible fly-by. It had never been done before and, judging from the reactions of the sweating pilots who did it, it will never be done again.

The overall plan was worked out by photographer J. R. Eyerman, Los Angeles correspondent James Goode, and U.S. Air Force officers at Eglin Field, Florida. Mere assembly of more than three dozen types of aircraft was the least of the problems: the trick was to

Overleaf: *Twenty-two of the airplanes which flew for* Life *from Eglin Air Force Base in 1956 to make a "triple gatefold" which unfolded from the inside out of the magazine to make a picture almost as long as an arm. The arm was provided by U.S. taxpayers—plus maybe a leg.*

CREDIT: J. R. EYERMAN © TIME INC.

get them all in the same picture. The heavier and slower planes had to take off first, get into position, and wait to be overtaken by the smaller, faster ones, which could slip into previously assigned slots in the complex pattern. The carefully calculated fly-by speed was 200 knots (276 mph), the top speed of the slowest transport aircraft. The smaller, faster jets could hardly slow down that much without going out of control in turbulent winds.

Hours of planning, calculation of speeds and altitudes, consultation with pilots, went into the preliminaries. Then, using a set of small model airplanes which could be skewered into a planning board by means of sharpened rods affixed to the models' undersides, the crews worked out more than a dozen possible flight plans.

When all was in order, they settled upon a rendezvous point in the sky. A *Life* photo plane had to be maneuvered into exactly the right position to catch the fly-by in the correct light, and an air force officer joined the *Life* crew in that plane to direct the whole project by radio.

Then, ten times in three days, the largest concentration of different airplanes ever flown in formation flew for Eyerman's cameras. They went by so fast, had such difficulty getting into the perfect formation, that on some passes Eyerman could make only one exposure. He was using a gigantic K-38 camera with a twelve-inch lens which could expose a nine-by-eighteen-inch color transparency. While the pilots sweated out their delicate jockeying with planes in front, beside, behind, below, and above them, an air force crew of 275 men waited on the ground to service the planes before the next fly-by. The picture *Life* ran was finally made on the tenth flight, the third day: forty-two planes eventually were involved and spent a total of 304 hours and 5 minutes in the air without a single mechanical failure or human miscalculation.

The cost of all this—to the U.S. taxpayer, in the final analysis—was impressive: at least $300,000 in jet fuel, one participant estimated, without counting the cost of moving planes and personnel from all over the U.S. to Florida, and tying up Eglin Air Force Base for the better part of a week.

Former *Life* staffers admit ruefully that a similar caper, if attempted today, would provoke a flurry of congressional inquiries or would be nipped in the bud by budget-minded military officials. Those were the days, however, in which the military services and the U.S. government itself were all out to catch the attention of the magazine-reading public and when, as photographer Eyerman has said, "pressing the button for *Life* magazine just made the world stand still."

□ □ □

Another story in the big "Air Age" issue set out, ambitiously, to create an air map of the Atlantic Ocean showing the precise location of each of 110 aircraft crisscrossing the water at the same time on a typical night at 3:00 A.M. Greenwich Mean Time.

So well did that work out that six years later some of the same staffers decided to do an even more ambitious project for the special issue on "The Sea," dated December 21, 1962. That issue provoked all manner of adventure in trying to find and photograph enormous whirlpools, spectacular bores, sea-drenched lighthouses. Probably the most difficult single feature in the issue however was a double-truck drawing which charted the merchant shipping flow of the entire world.

Because ships are slower than airplanes, and merchant shipping has more erratic time schedules than have passenger lines, researchers decided to pinpoint their world map not on a day but on a week along the sea lanes. Then they decided not only to show the position of all the ships but also to indicate where they had sailed from, where they were bound, and what national flags they flew. It was an incredibly complex concept, requiring the cooperation of shipping companies all over the world, the expertise of London's W. G. Weston, Ltd., a kind of holding company for shipping information, the services of a patient and imaginative artist, and several mathematical minds to get it all together. Reporters Alison Kallman and Valerie Vondermuhll master-minded it in New York; researcher Kate Sachs in London worked with Weston; the artist tore out half his hair, but it was done.

When the magazine appeared, shipping people were staggered. They snapped up newsstand copies and telephoned for more, but the great U.S. public was totally unmoved. Few readers had any notion of the hours of work, the endless checking and cross-checking, which had gone into a single world "map." Virtually no letters commented on the chart. The researchers declare stoutly that they didn't care: "You do things because they need doing, because they never have been done . . ." But Vondermuhll added, a bit wistfully, "I like to think that somewhere, in somebody's recreation room, that particular chart is still pinned up, maybe even framed, on display."

One member of the staff who was not surprised by the lack of reaction to this superhuman effort was Ed Thompson. "If we said there were, say, three hundred and ninety-two ships in the chart, then somebody would turn around and write in that there were only three hundred and ninety-one," he says. "Otherwise they didn't bother.

The problem was that we got too good at this kind of thing. We'd pull off some kind of 'Look Ma, no hands!' and the readers would yawn and say, 'Of course.' It got to be a backlash: we were in trouble if we didn't do it, and if we did we didn't get any credit for it.''

The ''Air Age'' and ''The Sea'' were triumphs of a form of journalism at which *Life* was the first and the best practitioner: the translation of complicated, sometimes esoteric, information into words, pictures, and paintings which a wide public could understand. The issues became collectors' items; teachers applauded them; scholars studied them for minor errors or personal credit; school kids pirated them for essays and cut them up for classroom scrapbook assignments. Other people put them carefully away in attics for another read or another generation.

Occasionally *Life* even managed to alter the stance of the nation—just a tiny bit. It can be claimed that *Life*'s crusading coverage on the position of the black in U.S. life, a series on black history, a series on segregation, helped change both public and official attitudes, and its special issue on the Soviet Union helped pave the way for the wary détente of the seventies.

Throughout the fifties the magazine took the traditional hard line and had nary a good word for the Soviets. Early in the sixties photographer Philippe Halsman brought in a fascinating portfolio of ''the Russian elite'' which included politicians, space experts, dancers, puppeteers. *Life* ran them with a minimum of wisecracks, a maximum (for the time) of admiration for their individual achievements. Shortly thereafter photographer Stan Wayman, stationed in Moscow, suggested an entire special issue on the Soviet people and the nation, an issue to examine the situation without necessarily taking sides. Assistant managing editor Moffett, to his surprise and then-consternation, was assigned to fly to Moscow and organize preparations for the special.

When he arrived he found some officials upset about what we all had thought was a friendly *Life* story (Halsman's): There *is,* one high ranking bureaucrat assured him, no ''elite'' in the Soviet Union. Moffett concluded quickly that although there might be no *word* ''elite'' there certainly was such a class. However, looking backward is not his style, and he got on well with Leonid Zamyatin, who was then in charge of dealing with Western journalists. In addition, he and Wayman refused to sit in their hotel rooms making telephone calls and waiting for official appointments. In Moffett's words they ''roamed around, making jokes, slapping legs, looking things over. We just sort of fanned out here and there, and it worked out okay.''

Moffett's relaxed country-boy manner, combined with Wayman's guileless face, helped to convince the Soviets that they truly intended to do an honest special issue on the Russian people and that these two capitalist Yanks, at least, had no burning desire to do them in. Hiring some facilities from the new Novosti press service and some of its men, at generous prices and in Western currency, didn't hurt. There were surprises on every hand: when the special issue came out quoting a Soviet housewife as saying "My God, how much better it is now . . ." several readers wrote in to inquire "How come she said 'My God,' when she's supposed to be an atheist?"

Moffett and Wayman's initial efforts worked out so well that sometime later Moffett was back in Moscow, this time with managing editor Hunt, to do yet more on the Soviet Union. The first time Hunt was introduced to Zamyatin, the latter launched into a tirade about *Time* magazine which had just done a cover story on Brezhnev and had attacked him. It was typical old-fashioned slam-bang American journalism, and Zamyatin was furious. Hunt, however, just happened to have in his pocket a clipping from *Izvestia* which had been particularly nasty about the managing editor of *Life*. When the two men finished giving each other hell, Hunt stalked out of the place. The next thing he knew he had an invitation, from Zamyatin, for what he thought was a small informal luncheon in Moscow's House of Journalists.

"Moffett and I went over there and walked in expecting about ten people around a table," Hunt recalls. "Instead there were at least three hundred people there, a huge table up front, and all of a sudden Zamyatin was proposing a toast—to me. It was one of the most critical things that ever happened to me as a journalist or as a human being. I had to reply. I had to do something. I had done a little homework; I knew something about Russian history. In the end I just thought, 'George, get up on your two dumb feet and say something.' So I stood up and told them I wasn't going to talk to them as a journalist, nor even as an American. I was going to talk as a lieutenant colonel in the United States Marines. I told them a little bit about my war in the Pacific, and then I saluted the Russian people for what they did in Leningrad, in Moscow, for all they did in the demoliton of Hitler and his whole miserable gang.

"Felix, the Moscow bureau interpreter, was translating for me, and while he translated I had a few seconds to collect my thoughts. In about mid-talk I realized I had a bear by the tail. That room was so silent. It went on for about half an hour I guess, including the translating, and when it was over and everybody stood up, and there was just devastating applause. Afterward Zamyatin came to me and said, 'George, you and your people can go anywhere in the Soviet Union that you want to go.' The whole thing was started by Wayman and Moffett, I had my day, and then all the others who followed were willing to approach the Soviets as people.''

There was inevitable pulling and hauling within the company over the flood of Russian stories; there were problems for chief *Life* editorial writer Jack Jessup; there were dissenters from within and without, but the climate was shifting subtly.

□ □ □

As important as the special issues, and often even more time-consuming, were the series which *Life* ran for years. One of the first, underlining the magazine's interest in and commitment to art, was the ''Picture History of Western Man'' which ran in the late forties, followed by ''The World We Live In,'' ''The World's Great Religions,'' ''America's Arts and Skills,'' ''The Epic of Man,'' ''Crisis in U.S. Education,'' ''Picture History of World War II,'' and others.

The great series ran in parts—six, eight, thirteen—each part being researched, photographed, painted, for eight months to a year before publication. Most of them later were gathered together and published as highly successful books. A few inspired impressive spin-offs in entire series of books in later years: *Life*'s ''The World We Live In'' formed the basis of the whole nature series of *Time-Life* Books, and ''The Epic of Man'' was the natural father of another long book series published under the general title of *The Emergence of Man.*

There were other spin-offs, in contacts and ideas for the future, within the staff. When ''The World We Live In'' was published in book form its credits listed not only dozens of staff reporters and photographers but also 240 individual scientists who had contributed their expertise to the production and seventeen separate scholarly or research institutes which had provided information, photographs, or research help. This wide casting of the nets became known in the shop as ''the vacuum cleaner syndrome.'' It paid off not only in high quality editorial productions but also in contacts: almost a decade after the ''World We Live In'' series, the highly important but difficult to understand International Geophysical Year came up, in which the world's scientists agreed to cooperate in a massive effort to coordinate what they had all learned about Planet Earth and to explore the regions still mysterious. *Life,* using the contacts it had made and the trust it had built up, was able to go straight back to the same geologists, oceanographers, geophysical laboratories it had used before. A dramatic four-part series which ran November 7, 14, 21,and 28, 1960, called ''New Portrait of Our Planet,'' virtually picked up where "The World We Live In" had left off, and chronicled the tremendous amount of knowledge the explorers and scientists had acquired in the intervening years.

Artists were crucial to many of these special series, and some became particularly well known—Chesley Bonestell, Antonio Petruccelli, James Lewicki. Among the staff favorites was Alexander Leydenfrost, an extraordinarily skillful and speedy artist whose specialty was aerial views of bits of the world which suddenly popped into the news. He could, armed with maps and any available photographs, plus what the staff called "artist's scrap"—any old piece of information or geographical projection which might help, draw almost anything as if shot from heaven. Not until the Apollo space program began sending down real photos from on high did everyone really know how good Leydenfrost was. One staffer still retains a prized possession that she calls "an early Leydenfrost"—a drawing of New York as viewed from somewhere above Hackensack, New Jersey circa 1864, all recreated by Leydenfrost. This artist was also particularly cooperative with researchers: assigned to do a view of the China mainland as seen from just east of Hong Kong, he was handed an armload of maps, photographs which showed Kowloon, the Hong Kong harbor, shots from Portuguese Macao, but very little of what would have to be the near foreground of his drawing—the eastern side of Hong Kong itself.

"Don't worry too much about this," said Leydenfrost. "Clouds are not only beautiful, they are often very useful."

A similar impasse was solved by a similarly inventive layout man on the staff when *Life* wanted an aerial photograph of the diminutive Republic of San Marino, in Italy, with the boundary line between San Marino and Italy drawn onto the aerial photo. When not even Italian aerial experts and map makers could locate precisely some sections of the boundary, the artist simply made the painted-on line a bit wider. No matter where the true boundary lay, the wide line would cover it.

Science stories, in series or as singles, became for the popular reader almost the sole province of *Life*. Spectaculars like "DNA, the Secret of Life," "How the Computer Gets the Answer," "The Nature of the Atom," explorations of the chemical causes of mental breakdown, analyses of the inner function of the human brain, became simple teaching tools for a nation and were distributed in thousands of full-color educational reprints for use in schools.

Among the most stunning of all these were photographs by Sweden's Lennart Nilsson which *Life* ran in April 1965 under the general heading "LIFE BEFORE BIRTH." Nilsson had worked seven years to make the color photos, highly magnified, of sperm entering the cervix, of the growth of the placental mass, of the human embryo developing from a mere 3½ weeks of life through the cycle to the growth of the fetus itself, the appearance of bone cells, and finally the appearance of the feet at 8 weeks. Most of his epoch-making photographs were taken, by special arrangements with Swedish doctors and hospitals, of embryos which had had to be surgically removed for medical reasons. But one picture, made with a tiny but wide-angled lens and a tiny flash beam at the end of a surgical scope, was actually taken inside the mother's womb only one inch away from the head of a living 15-week-old embryo with the veins in the head and eyelids showing clearly, the eyes still sealed shut.

Nilsson's photos, which possessed not only intimate revelation but also an eerie, other-worldly beauty, were among the major pictorial achievements of the century. They also managed to ricochet into a cherished office joke. At about the same time Lennart Nilsson's photos were going to press, a story on Swedish soprano Birgit Nilsson was in preparation. When Birgit went back to Sweden for the premiere of a role she intended later to sing at the Metropolitan Opera in Manhattan, a picture assignment editor asked Lennart to cover her Stockholm opening. For a day or so there was silence. Then came a cablegram, Wagnerian in its outrage, from that great Wagnerian, Birgit.

"Lennart Nilsson, no kin," it said (Birgit had picked up Time Inc. style during her years in New York), "not only wants to photograph me at the opera house, he also wants me to swallow that little camera to photograph my vocal cords. This I will not do because I know where it has been." Signed Birgit Nilsson.

□ □ □

Rivaling science as a *Life* specialty was art. Readers of the original magazine prospectus had been promised "the best contemporary art" and, whether what they got was the best or not, they got a lot of it. When the travel restrictions of World War II were lifted, there was an explosion of art reproduction on its pages. In 1949 *Life* sent photographer Frank Lerner to Rome to photograph the ceiling of the Sistine Chapel in color (Lerner had to photograph it, painfully and for months, the way Michelangelo had had to paint it, flat on his back on a high scaffolding), and the same year published a three-page story on the "drip paintings" of Jackson Pollock.

The Sistine Chapel had never before been photographed in such accurate color nor so close to the frescoes, and Jackson Pollock had never before received full-color treatment in a popular magazine, but neither story was entirely successful with readers. There were a number of subscription cancellations from Bible Belt readers who objected to the fact that Michelangelo had painted Adam nude, and there were even more outraged citizens who berated both *Life* and Jackson Pollock for showing them "the kind of thing my kid could do, if I gave him a brush and some old paint cans."

Undeterred, though occasionally chided by the proprietor, the art department went right on covering its field from classical to medieval to Renaissance to Andy Warhol, from Byzantine frescoes in Ravenna to De Kooning and Rauschenberg, from stained-glass windows to modern mobiles.

Art also joined hands with history and archaeology to present some specials on Leningrad's Hermitage Museum, on the U.S. Civil War, on American folklore, and notably on ancient Greece, ancient Rome, ancient Egypt. Editor Edward Kern, an archaeology and history buff, was in charge of Greece and Rome and puffed his thoughtful way through at least a barrel of pipe tobacco as he brooded over everything from the concept of the story to the photographs, the art, and the writing.

The chronicle of the Roman empire was particularly aggravating, because both its inner and outer reaches were considerably less well organized in the 1960s than they had been either B.C. or immediately A.D.

Kern and his crew collected the telex messages which poured back and forth from *Life* headquarters in New York to correspondents and photographers in the field. Some of them were published as an editors' note in March 1966:

> EXBRAKE ROME [photographer Brian Brake telexing from the Rome office] Extremely depressed with color results as everything turning green.
>
> EXBAVAGNOLI ROME [photographer Carlo Bavagnoli to New York] Pompeii officials deny permission to shoot at night. Consultant flatly states that Romans dined at three peyem and went to bed at six.
>
> EXESPINOSA ROME [correspondent Robin Espinosa] Possible to build scaffolding for Mili in Trajan's forum but need know exactly where, as bureaucracy takes three to four days.
>
> EXBRAKE MADRID Trying to arrange helicopter for lighthouse. It could be wonderful from air. EXBRAKE Glad you like helicopter idea. Will cost $3,000. EXBRAKE Impossible to get anything for $500. EXBRAKE Good news have found photographic plane for $50. EXBRAKE Not so clever after all. Plane fell apart on test run.

EXESPINOSA ROME Due to customs redtape weekends suggest Mili arrive on weekday never, repeat never, on Sunday.

EXCARTWRIGHT ROME [temporary bureau reporter on Rome Series] Have ruled out Rubicon. Experts say present Rubicon is not Caesar's and there's really no certainty where he crossed what.

EXBRAKE BEIRUT Had terrible trouble with customs in Syria who nearly opened exposed film to see what we'd shot. Saved by office driver.

EXLANIUS ISTANBUL [stringer] Justinian's cistern should not be confused with another cistern called cistern of thousand and one columns but which in reality has only two hundred and twenty-four.

One endless and complicated exchange dealt with Brake's wish to photograph Hadrian's Wall in north Britain—with snow on it. He was working on Roman remains in Egypt but instructed the London office to inform him the moment snow fell in the north. Researchers rang Greenwich almost hourly to inquire about weather conditions. Messages from Brake to New York announced that he would be in Tunis Friday, Algiers Saturday, Cairo Sunday, but "please check snow . . ." Finally an ecstatic cable: "Bacon [London correspondent] advises snowing Hadrian's Wall." Next came Bacon:

EXBACON LONDON Snow will last till Monday but cannot promise this.

EXBRAKE CAIRO To Bacon, London, please meet at Heathrow [airport] Saturday morning with heavy duffel coat.

EXBRAKE VIA LONDON Have arrived Hadrian's Wall but cannot find it as snow drifts nine feet deep.

Virtually every road in Northumberland was closed that weekend, but combined efforts to find a helicopter somewhere in the north paid off, and Brake's picture of the great wall in the snow made a superbly dramatic addition to the Rome series.

The equivalent of the special issue in the word department was the special article. Though conceived and executed always as primarily a picture magazine, *Life* used more and more words as it matured, and it was from the beginning eager to buy and publish long textpieces of exceptional interest.

Among the first were lengthy excerpts from memoirs of the Duke of Windsor. In three consecutive December issues in 1947 *Life* published "The Education of a Prince," and in the spring of 1950 four installments of "A King's Story," covering the period from just after World War I to his abdication and marriage to Wallis Simpson. The duke wrote the material himself, using dozens of No. 2 pencils on legal-size yellow pads which he then tied together with red "India" string in a manner traditional to the British government. As he worked he had *Life* staff writer Charles J. V. Murphy by his side, editing and advising and helping prepare the excerpts for publication. By mid-1948 he also had Murphy's secretary, Edith Sweeney, and *Life* reporter Monica Wyatt.

This trio moved into a villa at Cap d'Antibes, near the duke's villa, and then followed him around the world for over two years—to Paris; Palm Beach; Locust Valley, New York; Calgary, Canada. They traveled always with three metal trunks full of books, manuscripts, notes. But it wasn't all fun: Reporter Wyatt, in order to check the facts, read all of the duke's official diaries, all of his letters from childhood to 1936, and spent a month at Buckingham Palace looking over personal clippings stored away in the palace archives. Secretary Sweeney meanwhile was typing copy. Everybody groaned whenever there were major manuscript changes, because the duke did not believe in paper clips and any big change meant unstringing and then restringing the pages of each segment as the duke had originally organized them.

So fascinated did the duke become by the whole *Life* operation that he asked to watch the final editing process in the *Time-Life* building. Ushered into the office of EKT, he took one look around the room at the shirtsleeved staff and promptly took off his own jacket, remarking, "I can't think in my coat." When later it came time to take him to publisher Andrew Heiskell's office to meet the business types, the duke prepared to stroll off just as he was. EKT stopped him. "Your Royal Highness, if you're going to the business department, you'd better put your coat on."

If the Duke of Windsor was bemused by *Life*'s persistent checking and office informality, Winston Churchill was sometimes appalled. Even though he and Luce were friends, a fact which greatly aided the prolonged negotiations to acquire excerpts from his memoirs, Churchill at first could not believe that anyone on earth would have the temerity to edit or cut his words. The further indignity of being "checked" elicited thunderbolts in ponderous Churchillian prose.

Yet he was checked. In fact the phrase "Luce fellowship" was coined by a New York researcher who was working on an installment of the Churchill memoirs.

She had to bone up on the Indian Mutiny to check that part of the manuscript, and spent two weeks reading everything she could find on the subject. Having enjoyed every minute, she sighed and said, "That was a perfect Luce fellowship."

When such studious attention to detail had revealed enough minor errors to convince Churchill that checkers were useful, he asked the *Life* crew to check all the hundreds of thousands of words of the original manuscript in addition to the few dozen thousands selected for the magazine. Then it was their turn to be appalled, and politely they told him no.

In the midst of all the delicate negotiations, which began in 1946, office jokers made up a lengthy cable in beautiful Churchillese addressed to Dan Longwell, the former managing editor who had taken over nursing the Churchill prose into print. The cable said, after considerable preliminary, that Churchill had changed his mind. He was very sorry, he couldn't do his memoirs after all, but Mr. Clement Atlee would be happy to write his instead. Like most such elaborate office gags, this one read so well, sounded so genuine, that Longwell and his staff nearly had apoplexy before the jesters confessed.

Despite such *lèse majesté,* many of the finest writers of their eras were happy to appear in *Life*. English readers got their first glimpse of the memoirs of their former king Edward VIII in its pages, and all the world's fans of Ernest Hemingway first read *The Old Man and the Sea* complete in one issue of the magazine in 1952 before it appeared in book form. Evelyn Waugh, Graham Greene, Alan Moorehead, Robert Penn Warren, Carl Sandburg, James Michener, Norman Mailer, Arthur Miller, Romain Gary, Theodore White, John Hersey, even Richard Burton (the actor, not the explorer) were published in the magazine.

Editor Graves, survivor of "the historical Jesus" and other epics for the magazine, was always of the firm opinion that no matter what writer wrote which, his text needed cutting. "Every writer comes in at least one thousand words too long," he proclaimed at frequent intervals. Then Ernest Hemingway checked in with 30,000 words of *Dangerous Summer,* an account of the *mano a mano* duel of bullfighters Luis Miguel Dominguin and Antonio Ordóñez in Spain. Graves sat down and cut those precious words to 15,000, at which point Hemingway refused to let *Life* run it at all. Graves had to back down on this one. *Dangerous Summer* finally ran, uncut, in two installments in 1960.

The real comeuppance lay ticking away, however, until Graves became managing editor. He had commissioned Norman Mailer to write a preflight article about the crew, the machinery, the atmosphere surrounding the first mission to the moon, Apollo 11. Mailer produced a tome of 25,000 words and Graves, though he liked the words, was staggered. Once more he sat down to cut—and then discovered that Mailer's contract gave him specific control over all such pruning.

Mailer won that argument as did, on another occasion, Robert Graves (no kin). Distinguished author Graves had carried on a running feud with *Life* for years, ever since the magazine asked him to write an article on "The State of the Roman Dominions in the Eastern Mediterranean During the Ministry of Jesus"—and then turned down his manuscript. No amount of imploration would lure him back until one day in 1965 when, out of the blue, he mailed in from Majorca a piece about love—"Are Women More Romantic Than Men?" Because Robert Graves's knowledge roamed a scholarly spectrum unmastered by many men, and because he also loved to adopt intellectual positions unpopular with his peers, *Life* set two researchers to work checking his more flamboyant statements. Virginia Sadler and Brooks von Ranson interviewed seven consultants, read forty books, and finally sent back to Graves a list of questions ranging from his definition of the origin of the word "knight" ("registered businessman") to his particular assessment of Lawrence of Arabia.

In due course back came another missive from Majorca—this one written by hand—in which Graves made a few concessions to the checkers' carefully collected evidence of other opinions. However, he refused to budge on T. E. Lawrence ("I am the accepted authority") and he refused even to debate the general subject of love.

He was, it was clear, his own accepted authority on that complex subject as well, and further discussion was closed.

Dealings with the great and famous were always exhilarating to the staff, sometimes less so to the moneymen. General Douglas MacArthur, for example, demanded from *Life* "whatever Churchill got" for his memoirs, and then another 10 percent for General Courtney Whitney, his press aide, who presumably did a lot of the writing. The general didn't cause much trouble after that for the magazine, but he proved a bit sticky with the publishers of the full text, McGraw-Hill. Not only did he refuse to write either an index or a table of contents, he first refused permission for the publisher to provide them. His point was that "reviewers look at those two sections and then write reviews. I'm going to make those blank blanks read the whole book." In the end, he yielded.

Generals Eisenhower, Bradley, Van Fleet, and Field Marshal Montgomery, did articles for *Life;* Richard Nixon sold excerpts of his book *Six Crises* to the magazine before the ultimate crisis overtook him; portions of Khrushchev's taped memoirs ran in *Life*. General Charles de Gaulle's written memorial to himself went to the magazine, to everyone's surprise, at bargain rates. When he had finished the final volume it was placed on the market. Primarily to "show the flag," *Life* bid $15,000 for magazine rights and, to the astonishment of editors Thompson and Graves, were the high bidders.

© TIME INC.

EKT and HST take a walk during preparation of the Truman memoirs. Life *people liked writing "Harry S (for nothing) Truman," but most of the staff fell for him.*

Getting former President Harry Truman down on paper and then into the magazine was another matter entirely. Shortly after Eisenhower was elected president in 1952, word went out that retiring President Truman intended to write his memoirs. *Colliers* magazine, the INS, the Hearst newspapers, were all bidding, and *Life* tried to calculate how high it would have to go to win. Though Truman himself never said so directly to anybody on the magazine, it appeared that he would hold out for five thousand dollars more than they paid "Ike" (for 1948's "Crusade in Europe").

Truman, never known for his sagacity in personal financial affairs, left the dealings to fellow-Missourian John W. Snyder, who had served as his secretary of the treasury. EKT and John Snyder hammered out the financial details, and back in Independence, Mo., Truman went to work. Like all writers, including professionals, the expresident kept lagging behind his deadline and batteries of writers, editors, reporters, trekked off to Independence to encourage, suggest, nudge, and gallop around the block behind Truman, panting out questions as he took his daily constitutional.

Occasionally they got a nugget. I remember trailing him one early morning when suddenly he announced, "I want to be buried in a cherry-wood casket."

Pant . . . "Why?" . . . pant . . . "Mr. President?" I inquired.

"Because I intend to go through hell a-poppin'," he replied with a gleeful chuckle.

With the aid of his own staff, the *Life* staff, archives and official documents and family letters, Truman's book finally got written and excerpted.

Truman was embroiled, amazed, bemused like many a man before him by the checking process. Because his best anecdotes and sharpest judgments came when he spoke off the cuff, occasionally lapsing into the language he used for critics of his daughter Margaret's singing ability, he posed a special problem for researchers. They knocked themselves out checking his every word and fact, and Truman almost lost his temper when they bedeviled him about the ownership of a pony in the Truman childhood. He couldn't remember whether it belonged to him or his brother Vivian, and he also couldn't understand just why it was so important.

In the end, however, he asked Ed Thompson if he could have lunch with the people he had never met—the researchers, the copyroom experts, the *Life* typists, all the beaters and bearers and messengers who had nursed his manuscript into print. The near-incredulous luncheon guests, "feeling nine feet tall," assembled expecting to be awed and were instantly reduced to roars of laughter by a beaming Truman who discussed the embarrassment of "a former Democratic president who finds he suddenly owes his livelihood to a Republican like Harry Luce."

He was grateful for that livelihood, he quickly added, but he was even more grateful to the young ladies and gentlemen in that room "who refused to let me make a mistake." He told them he thought his story had been told well and accurately, and then for two hours he went through his repertoire of statesman stories, country-boy anecdotes, and salty evaluations of his peers. Harry Truman could have run for president again that day and carried the luncheon party in a landslide.

20

The End

The end of the magazine came with sickening suddenness to most of the staff. There had of course been rumors, but there had been rumors in 1961, too. There had been rumors in 1969, in 1970. We had all seen, with creeping chill, the end of *Colliers,* of the *New York Herald-Tribune,* of the *Saturday Evening Post,* of *Look.* Few of us ever dreamed that it could really happen to *Life*. The mystique was very powerful, inside the office as well as outside.

When the *Life en Español* and *Life International* editions were both closed, to save money, their staffs were quite painlessly absorbed by the other magazines and by the burgeoning books division. "The bookdiv" as *Life*rs called it, first set up shop in some of the upper floors of the new building and inspired a much-quoted comment from special projects editor John Thorne. Thorne trekked up to the bookdiv one day and came back to report that it was "just like heaven."

"Heaven?" we asked.

"Yes," he said, "First of all you ascend. Then you come out into this great big open space, quiet and airy and calm—and there are all your old friends you never thought you'd see again."

Bookdiv gave everybody's spirits a temporary lift. Then more cuts came: European staffs were all but eliminated, veterans were urged to take contracts or early retirement and fade away. The New York work force was cut almost in half.

With that, most of us thought the worst was over. *Life* was alive and kicking and all was well. Some of us who had taken contracts for considerably less money than our former paychecks, in return for the privilege of living and working in some favorite city around the U.S. or the world, found that we were getting a lot of stories in the magazine. We were happy in our new lives. I was quite giddy with joy when managing editor Ralph Graves offered to pay my way from Rome to the U.S. to cover the final Apollo space launch. I had been in on the beginning of Apollo and I yearned to see and write about the final flight. More than that, it seemed to me that *Life* must be looking up if they'd bring me all the way over for it—even if they did suggest that I might be able to find a cheap charter flight.

Apollo 17 lifted off in the very early morning of December 7, 1972. It was nostalgic at Cape Kennedy. I flew back to New York with my colleagues feeling a bit sad that Apollo was over but exhilarated by having seen all the teams again—ours, NASA's. There was no particular urgency in my writing the story, because it was scheduled to run after the moon landing itself, to close in the December 29 issue of the magazine. There was thus also no urgency in my getting to the office. When I wandered in, at about 11:30 A.M., the next day, the first person I saw was Loudon Wainwright standing in the reception center on the ground floor. I rushed to greet him; he took one look and burst into tears. Fearing for who-knows-what calamity, I mumbled something.

"You don't know, do you?" he said, and then the horrid statement burst out. "It's dead. *Life* is dead."

So then of course I burst into tears, and a receptionist who had been around the place for years looked at the pair of us and *she* burst into tears. It was quite soppy in the reception hall. It was pretty soppy upstairs, too, behind a brave mask of stiff-upper-lip, and there was the occasional sound of voices raised in sharp outrage as a swarm of "other" reporters and photographers moved in to do their own coverage of our demise. Towering Co Rentmeester, probably the biggest photographer on the staff, attempted to flatten a television cameraman who had in some way offended him, and hushed-voice knots of chums stood or sat in every office.

All that day, and during the numb week which followed, I forgot to ask Ralph Graves if he had known this was going to happen when he asked me to come back. I also forgot to ask people precisely what

CREDIT: CO RENTMEESTER © TIME INC.

had happened at the announcement meeting. While I was preparing this book, in 1976, I finally asked Ralph.

"I don't remember whether I knew or not, when I asked you to come back," he said.

"But you could have stopped me."

"Oh, sure. But there were various things I didn't stop, that I didn't want to stop."

There were others he had to stop. *Life*'s special double Christmas issue, bearing on its cover the detail of a 1645 painting by Georges

Life's last weekly managing editor Ralph Graves (arrow) *stood in the background of the last Christmas party and sent copies of the photograph to all former employees.*

de La Tour called simply *The Newborn,* was on the presses at that time, and most of the work had been done for what was to be the last weekly issue, dated December 29, 1972. Beyond that loomed, however, plans and projects for issues which would never be printed.

Graves was determined that nobody should be assigned to do what he called "fake work." But he also had to keep the terrible secret to himself. Suddenly came the problem of closing one single page, in combination form, for the issue of January 25, 1973. Graves's solution was brilliant:

"Chuck Elliott, who was copy editor then, was always bugging me about 'Now, Ralph, you are aware that we have to close so many pages for the issue of something-or-other.' It made me mad because I always did know. I kept track. So I always just said yes, yes, yes. But then came this one page and I picked out one which had already been engraved. It was part of a long story that Elliott loved and wanted to get in the magazine. So by deciding that that page would 'close' for January 25 I accomplished three things at once: I shut up Elliott, I made him happy, and more important not a single person anywhere in the world had to do a bit of work on that one page."

Graves had one more problem: writer Tom Flaherty and the letters from the children. In October 1972 *Life* published a special section on children six-to-twelve and had included a questionnaire for children only, inviting them to write to *Life* and discuss issues that were important to them. To the astonishment of everyone more than 250,000 children completed questionnaires and sent them in. Almost 5,000 also enclosed letters to expand their answers, explain their problems, hopes, frustrations. A summary of their answers, plus excerpts from their letters, had been scheduled for the first issue in January 1973.

"When I knew there wasn't going to be a first issue in January, I couldn't stand the thought of all those 250,000 kids who had answered the questionnaire. If it wasn't ever going to be . . . I was so moved by the response . . . finally I figured out a way to fit the story into the last issue. To do so, I had to force Flaherty to write it earlier than he would have had to do in normal circumstances. I said I had to have it early for layout reasons, for space planning."

Before the end of November 1972, Graves knew the end was near. No doubt one or two other people did too, but the first official word came about 5:00 P.M. on the December afternoon before the announcement to the staff and the world. Hedley Donovan, editor in chief of Time Incorporated, summoned Graves to his office, together with assistant managing editors Philip Kunhardt, Robert Ajemian, Don Moser, and David Maness, staff writer Loudon Wainwright, articles editor Steve Gelman, copy editor Charles Elliott, and director of photography Ronald Bailey. He gave them a drink, and he told them. He had to leave the group once, for about five minutes, to go sign some papers, take care of some formalities.

When Donovan had finished, the group trooped back to Graves's office, sat down to have another drink, and looked at each other. Each felt an aching need to *do* something—anything—they decided to start calling the rest of the staff to tell them about the meeting. Because announcements of this kind affect the stock market, SEC rules demand that the markets be notified on the first order of business in the morning. Then the wire services would know, the *New York Times* would know, and Graves was determined that the staff should get the news from the company, not the Associated Press. Thus the meeting would have to be early. For many offices 10:00 A.M. was considered late; at *Life* it was fairly early. There would be a memo on every desk, of course, but a lot of people would do Christmas shopping, or household errands, before they came in. If they didn't have warning telephone calls, a lot of them would be late.

"You really would have thought, that evening, that none of us had lost our jobs," Graves said. "All we cared about was getting everybody in here on time. We sat there with great enthusiasm taking the list of the entire staff, divvying it up, starting the phone calls. It was as if we were covering a story again, getting organized, feeling the excitement of a project we were doing together."

Hour after hour the calls went out. To his closest colleagues, Graves told the truth. To most, the callers said nothing but "There's a meeting tomorrow morning, you ought to be there. I can't tell you more, I have to make some more calls."

Carefully timed cables and telegrams went to bureaus and stringers, to staffers on exotic assignments in faraway places. George Silk, in the midst of a two-and-one-half month story on wildlife parks in Nepal, had his camera bags in the hotel lobby, ready to vanish into the wilds again, when a bellboy handed him a telegram: "Sorry, George, but they've decided to close the magazine. Details later. Ron Bailey."

Silk, "feeling as if I'd been pole-axed," called for a cable form and quickly printed a game reply: "Your message . . . badly garbled. Please send half-million dollars additional expenses." Then he went out and drank a lot.

Before 10:00 A.M. next day, most of the staff had assembled in the auditorium on the eighth floor of the *Time-Life* building. Outside in a tense little knot were Donovan, chairman of the board Andrew Heiskell, publisher Garry Valk, and managing editor Graves.

Donovan spoke first and at length. He was totally controlled, logical, solemn, measured. He described how hard the company had fought to save *Life,* how much money it had lost in the process. He discussed shrinking advertising, rising production costs, crushing postal rate increases. He said almost all the right things, said them with dignity, and sat down to total silence in the hall.

Next came Heiskell, who had been a reporter at *Life,* a writer, an emergency correspondent—he helped cover the *Andrea Doria* sinking from the decks of the *Ile de France*—and the magazine's publisher.

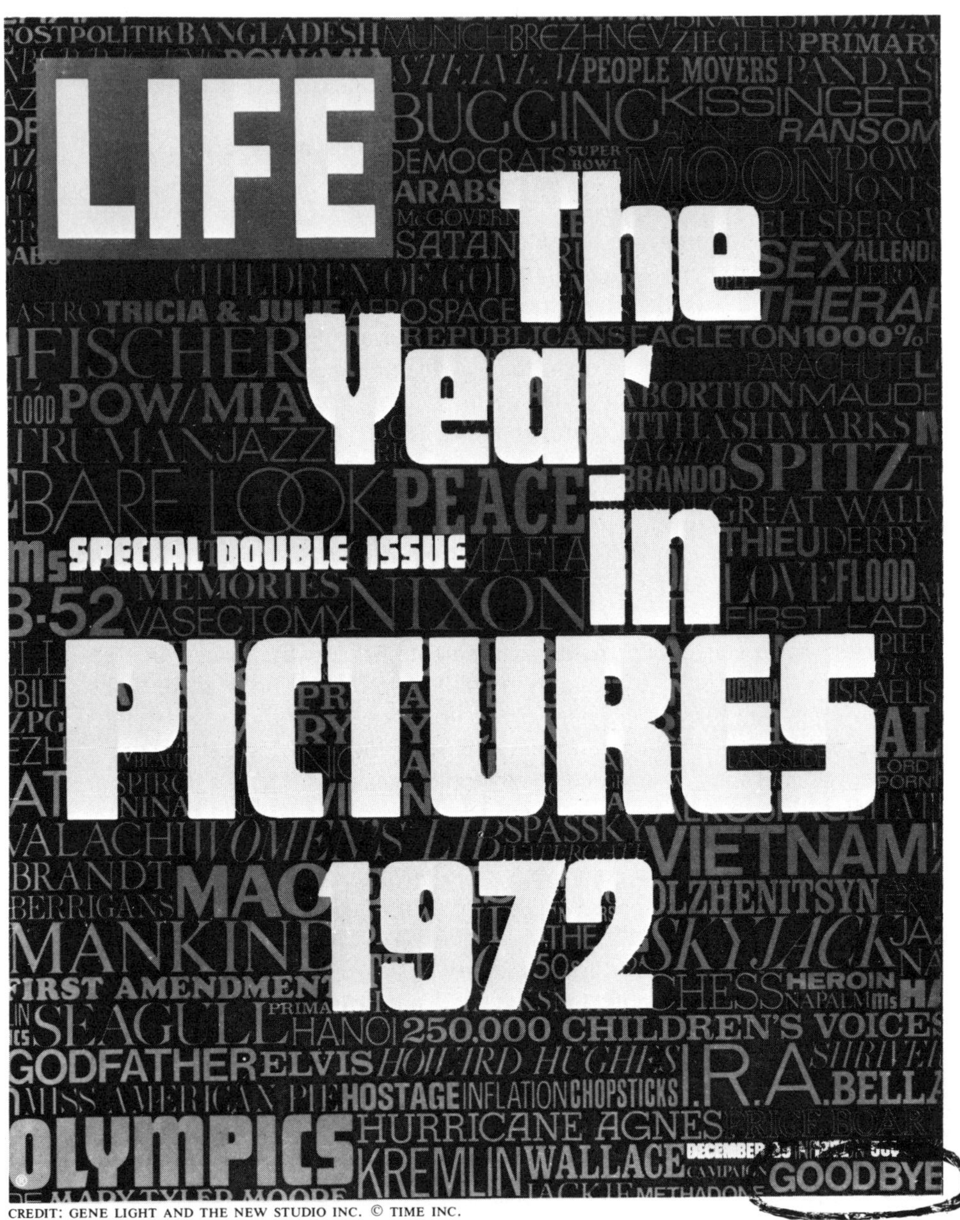

CREDIT: GENE LIGHT AND THE NEW STUDIO INC. © TIME INC.

On the cover of the last issue of the weekly, a compendium of pictures of the year's events, layout men inserted their own salute at the extreme bottom right corner. Some of the staffers didn't notice it at the time; those who did fought tears.

He spoke with emotion, his voice barely under control, of "this painful decision" and of the "great things that *Life* has done . . . things you can be proud of . . . the creation of the photo essay, a new form of art, the coverage of the wars . . . the publication of Churchill memoirs . . . the 'History of Western Civilization,' 'The World We Live In' . . . the contribution *Life* made in bringing art and science understandably and interestingly to the public . . ." At the end he said, tears glittering on his face, "Thank you for all you have done."

Then Ralph Graves walked to the microphone.

> There is nothing I can do to soften this sad blow. But I do want to say how grateful I am to you for the work and the spirit that kept *Life* going as long as possible. I am especially grateful for this past year, under all the adversities of personnel cuts and tight budgets . . . we've continued to put out issues of *Life* that we can all be proud of . . .
>
> I hope the younger, newer people on the staff will forgive me on this occasion if I say a few words to those staff members who, like me, have been here a very long time. Many of us have spent our whole professional lives on this magazine, and we have thoroughly enjoyed doing so. We have seen each other two hundred days or so a year for many years and I, for one, never got tired of it. That didn't keep us from bitching about the magazine, or the hours, or even about each other. But we always kept coming back for more. I think we know each other better than we know anyone outside our own families.
>
> Ed Thompson used to say that at *Life* it was all very well to be a first class journalist, but to really enjoy it you also needed to be a bit of a slob. He always said this about himself, and he meant that no matter how many things went wrong, how many packets got lost or delayed, that he never lost his affection for the staff and for the magazine.
>
> That goes for me, and I trust for you. It is a very rare thing in the American corporate world today, and now we must end it. This is a sad ending but I hope none of you will remember *Life* or each other in terms of this morning. We worked on a great and famous magazine and we published many wonderful stories and we had a remarkable experience together . . .
>
> I'm getting up an employment committee to help all of you find other jobs. That's my only assignment and I will do the best I can with it. But I won't pretend that any place else is going to be like what we shared together at *Life*. And I thank you all for that gift which we gave to each other.

Graves had written the last sentence to read "that gift we so gladly gave to each other," but when he came to the word "gladly" he knew that he just couldn't say "gladly." "I *meant* that word, it was important to me, but I knew I couldn't get to the end if I . . . if I . . ."

In a split second the auditorium rang with applause, with cheers. The staff of *Life* was on its feet rendering a final salute from the heart to "that gift." For five seconds, ten seconds, the applause went on while Graves tried vainly to introduce publisher Valk. Then after sixteen seconds the hall quieted down, Valk spoke, and it was over.

It remained for editor Frank Kappler to deliver a punchline true to the spirit of the magazine.

"That," he said, steadying his voice carefully as the gang trooped from the hall, "is the strongest rumor I've heard yet."

Index

Index

Index